The Smoke Ring

The Smoke Ring

LARRY NIVEN

SF

A Del Rey Book
BALLANTINE BOOKS · NEW YORK

A Del Rey Book
Published by Ballantine Books

Maps by Shelly Shapiro

Library of Congress Cataloging-in-Publication Data

Niven, Larry.
  The smoke ring.

  "A Del Rey book."
  I. Title.
PS3564.I9S6   1987   813'.54   86-26579
ISBN 0-345-30256-7

Manufactured in the United States of America

First Edition: May 1987
10 9 8 7 6 5 4 3 2 1

It is reassuring to know that the human race is still capable of producing big, roomy minds. This book is dedicated to Dan Alderson.

Contents

Prologue: Discipline   1

Section One: CITIZENS TREE
Chapter One: The Pond   7
Chapter Two: Discipline   21
Chapter Three: Refugees   37
Chapter Four: The In Tuft   49
Chapter Five: The Silver Suit   67
Chapter Six: The Appearance of Mutiny   85

Section Two: THE LOGGERS
Chapter Seven: The Honey Hornets   97
Chapter Eight: The Honey Track   111
Chapter Nine: The Rocket   123
Chapter Ten: Secrets   137
Chapter Eleven: Happyfeet   153

Section Three: CIVILIZATION
Chapter Twelve: Customs   171
Chapter Thirteen: The Termite Nest   189

Chapter Fourteen: Docking   197
Chapter Fifteen: Half Hand's   213
Chapter Sixteen: High Finance   229
Chapter Seventeen: Serjent House   241
Chapter Eighteen: Headquarters   251

Section Four: THE DARK AND THE LIGHT
Chapter Nineteen: The Dark   273
Chapter Twenty: The Library   291
Chapter Twenty-One: The Silver Suit   307
Chapter Twenty-Two: Loop   323
Chapter Twenty-Three: Beginnings   337

Dramatis Personae   355
Glossary   359

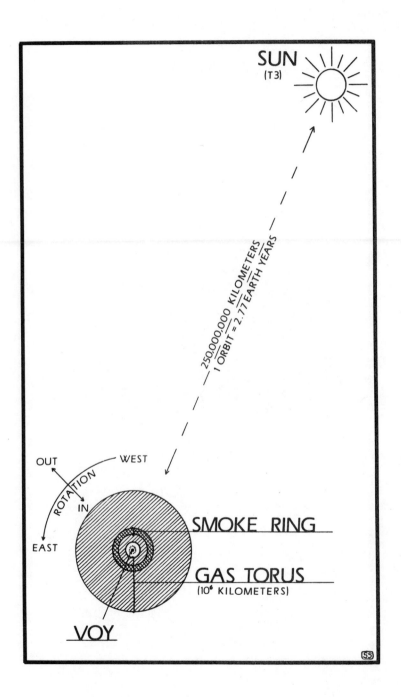

SUN
(T3)

250,000,000 KILOMETERS
1 ORBIT = 2.77 EARTH YEARS

OUT
WEST
ROTATION
IN
EAST

SMOKE RING

GAS TORUS
(10⁶ KILOMETERS)

VOY

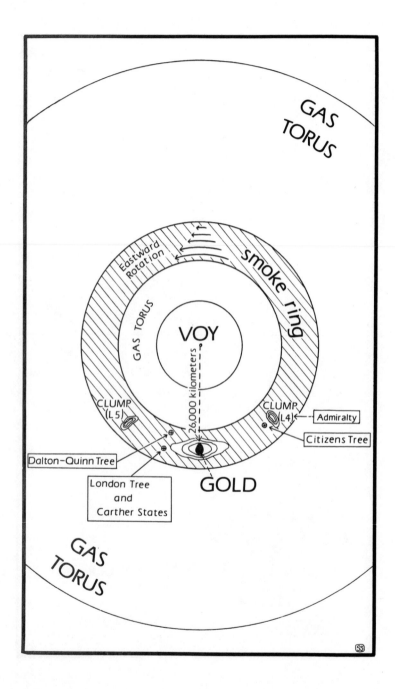

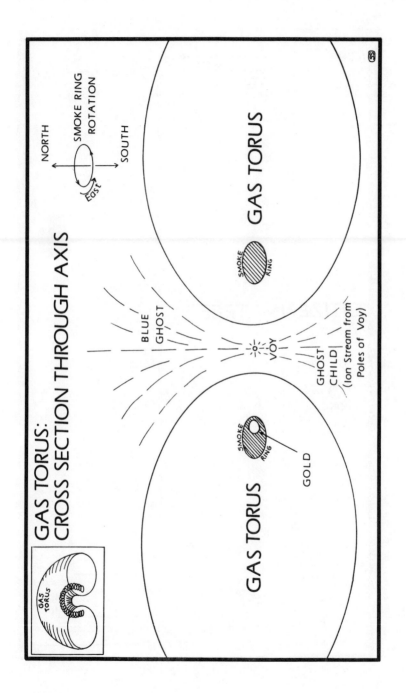

GAS TORUS:
CROSS SECTION THROUGH AXIS

GAS TORUS

NORTH
SMOKE RING
ROTATION
SOUTH
East

BLUE
GHOST

VOY

GHOST
CHILD
(Ion Stream from
Poles of Voy)

SMOKE
RING

GAS TORUS

SMOKE
RING

GOLD

GAS TORUS

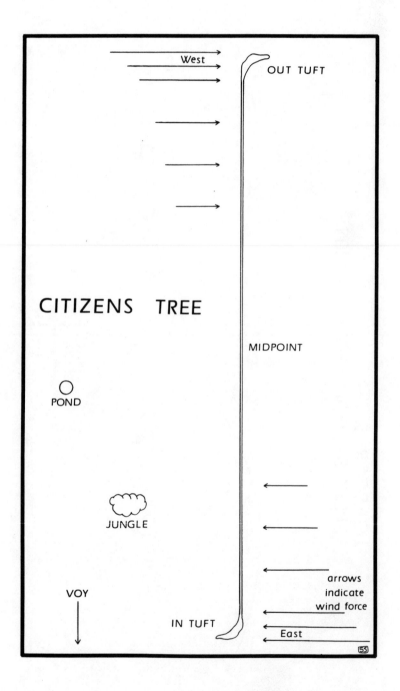

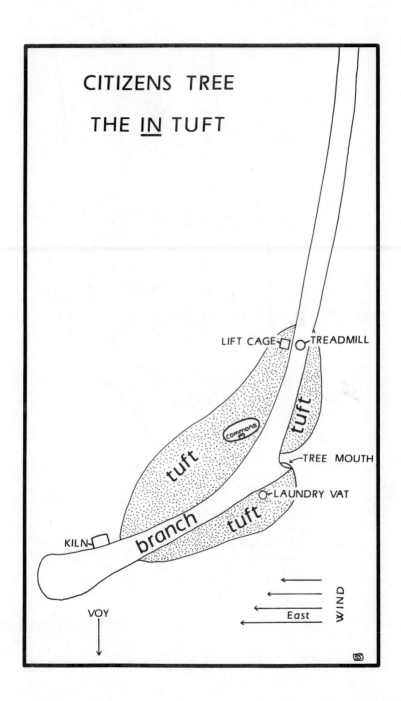

CITIZENS TREE
THE IN TUFT

LIFT CAGE — TREADMILL

tuft

commons

tuft

TREE MOUTH

LAUNDRY VAT

tuft

branch

KILN

VOY

WIND

East

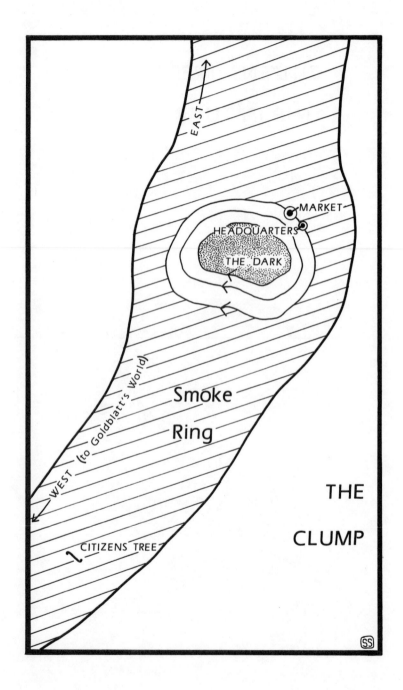

The Smoke Ring

Prologue

Discipline

THE PLANET BELOW HIM WAS HIDDEN TO ALL OF SHARLS'S senses save for the Neutrino Screen, the Neudar. What had been a gas giant planet a billion years ago was still a world two and a half times the size of the Earth: an egg of rock and nickel-iron hidden in world-sized storms. The storms spread out into a cloudy ring occupying the entirety of Goldblatt's World's orbit around the neutron star.

Sharls watched storms spin outward from the gas giant. Streams of fog and cloud and dust ran slow near the Smoke Ring's outer rim, faster at the Smoke Ring median, faster yet as they neared Levoy's Star; and everywhere there were flattened whorls of hurricane. The gravity gradient was savage this near the ancient neutron star. The innermost limits of the Smoke Ring circled Levoy's Star every two hours.

The Smoke Ring was tinged with green—it had its

1

own billion-year-old ecology—and somewhere in that cloud were men.

The temptation to go to them was a constant low-level irritant.

When moving between stars, *Discipline* burned the near-infinite hydrogen of interstellar space; but *Discipline* had been at rest for a long time now, and onboard fuel was limited. Refueling could not have progressed far when the mutiny came. Sharls's supply of deuterium-tritium mix was finite. He had no way of knowing how long he must wait for the children of *Discipline*'s crew to rediscover civilization, to build their own spacecraft, to come to him. He was always short of power. The solar collectors on his two remaining CARMs didn't give him much.

Sharls ignored the stars, most of the time. He watched the Smoke Ring. When the boredom became too much for him, he edited it from his memory. Boredom was a recurring surprise.

Five hundred and thirty-two Earth years was one hundred and ninety-two orbits of Levoy's Star round its companion star. But the natives of the Smoke Ring measured years from the passings of the neutron star (Levoy's Star, "Voy") across the face of the yellow dwarf (T3, "Sun"); so a Smoke Ring "year" was 1.384 Earth years. Sharls had been waiting in the L2 point behind Goldblatt's World for three hundred and eighty-four Smoke Ring years.

Best to sit it out in a stable orbit, and watch, and wait for men to develop civilization. Best to edit the memory of boredom . . .

Discipline's computer/autopilot stored its information as a human brain did, or a hologram, though Sharls could feel differences. Memories from his time aboard *Dis-*

cipline were sharp and vivid. Those he had edited were gone completely. But memories from his time as a man, transferred long ago from a human brain now long dead, were blurred, hard to retrieve.

So: it wasn't like a relay clicking over.

But somewhere in the computer there was a change of state. Five hundred and thirty-two years, and *enough is enough*. Sharls Davis Kendy was done with waiting.

Section One

CITIZENS TREE

Chapter One

The Pond

from the Citizens Tree cassettes, year 19 SM:

PONDS

WATER DROPLETS COME IN ALL SIZES HERE. CLOUDS MAY HOLD EVERYTHING FROM FINE MIST, TO GLOBULES THE SIZE OF A FIST, TO SPHEROIDS THAT HOUSE ALL MANNER OF LIFE. THE BIGGEST "POND" WE'VE SEEN MASSED TEN MILLION METRIC TONS OR SO; BUT THE TIDE FROM LEVOY'S STAR HAD PULLED IT INTO TWO LOBES AND THE DIFFERENTIAL WINDS WERE TEARING IT APART.

THE ECOLOGY OF THE PONDS IS ONE RATHER THAN MANY. LIFE IS QUEER AND WONDERFUL, BUT IN EVERY POND WE HAVE EXAMINED IT IS THE SAME LIFE. PONDS ARE TEMPORARY; POND LIFE MUST OCCASIONALLY MIGRATE. IN THE SMOKE RING EVEN THE FISH CAN FLY.
                              —CAROL BURNES, LIFE SUPPORT

LAWRI AND JEFFER SWAM BENEATH MURKY PONDWATER,
trailing forty square meters of fabric stretched across
the net more commonly used to sieve harebrains from
the sky. They gripped its corners in strong toes and
swam with their arms.

The sheet resisted. The leading edge tried to crumple.
Tethers at the corners of the harebrain net got in their
way. *We could have had some help,* Jeffer thought. *Lawri
wouldn't have it. Lawri's idea, Lawri's project! She'd be
doing this by herself if she possibly could.*

Air! He slapped her thigh. She dropped the sheet
and they swam toward the light.

Air is the sweetest taste, though one must risk drown-
ing to appreciate it.

They were at the arc of the pond nearest Citizens
Tree. The center of the trunk was a mere three klomters
east. Seventy klomters of trunk ran out and in from the
pond, ending in paired curved tufts. The in tuft, *home,*
looked greenish black, with Voy's blue pinpoint shining
almost behind it. A single line ran from the trunk, and
divided.

The sheet was a ghostly shadow deep within the pond.
Lines ran from the corners, up through the water and
out, to join the main cable that ran to the trunk.

"Almost in place," Lawri said doubtfully.

"Close enough."

"All right. You go get the carm ready. I'll draft some
hands to pull it in."

Jeffer nodded. His legs scissored and shot him into
the air. He drifted toward the main cable in a spray of
droplets.

It was easier than arguing. Lawri would not leave Jeffer to organize the final stage. When Lawri the Scientist

got an idea, nobody else got credit. Particularly not Citizens Tree's other Scientist, her husband.

Partway around the curve of the pond, Minya and Gavving floated in the interface between air and water, surrounded by thrashing children.

Lines ran from each child toward the cable from Citizens Tree. The children were taught the backstroke first. It kept their faces in the air. Some preferred the frog-kick that let them look beneath the water. Swimming was a balance of surface tension versus the thrust of arms and legs.

If a child kicked himself entirely out of the water, an adult must go after him. A child who went beneath the surface could panic and must be pulled out before he drowned. There were carnivores among the waterbirds. Minya and Gavving wore harpoons. They had three of their own among the swimmers.

Gavving used lazy strokes to change his attitude, moving his field of view in a clockwise circle.

"Look at Rather," Minya said.

The oldest of the children were swimming together. Daughter of two jungle giants, golden-blond Jill had grown to merely normal height in the tide of Citizens Tree. She was thirty ce'meters shorter than her parents . . . but the contrast between Jill and Rather was startling. At fourteen, Minya's dark-haired firstborn son was less than two meters in height. Jill had more than half a meter on him.

Yet Minya never spoke of Rather's height. Gavving looked again and said, "Right. *Rather!*"

Rather paddled over, reluctantly. Fine green fur, barely visible, grew a mi'meter long on his left cheek. Gavving gripped the boy's arm and lifted him partway out of the water, against surface tension. The green could be traced down Rather's neck, over his shoulder, and partway across his chest.

"Fluff," Gavving said. "Why didn't you tell someone?"

Rather grinned guiltily. "I've never swum before."

Minya snapped, "You go straight—"

"No. Finish your swim. You'll pay for it. You've seen your last of the sun for a while. Have we raised a fool? It's almost reached your eye!"

Rather nodded solemnly and paddled away. Minya watched him go, her mouth pursed in anger. Her husband wriggled and was silently underwater; kicked, and was beneath her; grasped an ankle and dove. Minya doubled back on herself and kicked him across the jaw. Gavving reached through the defense of her waving arms and legs and had her head between his hands; pulled her to him by main strength and kissed her hard. She laughed bubbles.

He kicked toward the surface with Minya in tow. They blew water from their faces before they inhaled, and were back on duty before any child could get into trouble.

Debby was some distance from where the children swam. She stayed just under the surface, motionless, peering, her spear poised. She expelled stale air—which stayed before her as a bubble—raised her head, snatched a breath, ducked again.

Debby had lived her first nineteen years in free-fall. Fourteen years in the tree tide had put muscle on her without shrinking her height. Her children—and Ilsa's, the children they had borne to Anthon—were no taller than ordinary tree dwellers. But Debby was two and a half meters tall. Her fingers were long and fragile; her toes were sturdier if less agile, and the big toes measured six ce'meters. Her rich brown hair was beginning to show gray, but she still wore it a meter long. For swimming she wore it looped in a braid around her throat.

The water was murky. This was a new skill for Debby, but she was learning.

She struck. The ripple of her thrust expanded outward around the great globule, past playing children and the Scientists working their cloth sheet.

A silver shape wriggled on Debby's spearpoint. Debby reached above her head, tugged hard at the tether, and gasped as her head broke the surface. The waterbird, suddenly thrust into air, expanded its small wings and thrashed mightily. A blow to the head end quieted it. Debby pushed it into a net bag to join five others.

Her chest still heaved with the need for air. She rested quietly on her back, her hands fluttering from time to time to keep surface tension from pulling her under.

Eastward, a thousand klomters past Citizens Tree, the cloud patterns thickened into a flattened whirlpool. The Smoke Ring converged beyond and below the whorl in a stream of white touched with blue-green, narrowing as it dropped toward the dazzling point of Voy.

Things tended to collect in that special part of the Smoke Ring, east of Gold by sixty degrees of arc. The citizens had reason to know that the storm-whorl around Gold was dangerous. They assumed that the Clump was too. They had never taken the tree nearer than this.

They had never visited a jungle.

Human beings certainly lived elsewhere in the Smoke Ring, but Citizens Tree had never attempted to contact them.

Citizens Tree was placid, safe. Working within the pond was as much excitement as Debby ever got these days. Life in Carther States had been different. The occasional raids from London Tree forced the citizens to be always prepared for war, until in one magnificent raid they had ended London Tree's power forever.

Debby's connection with the jungle warriors had ended too. A mixed group of copsiks and warriors had stolen London Tree's carm. The vehicle was old science, powerful and unfamiliar. They and their prisoners had been lucky to bring the carm to any kind of safety; but Carther States was lost somewhere in the sky beyond Gold.

From westward came a cheerful cry. "Citizens! We need muscle!" Debby saw Lawri the Scientist floating in the sky with one hand on the main tether.

Debby snatched at the net bag (six was a nice day's catch), kicked herself into the sky, and began reeling her line in. She was first to reach the Scientist. Clave and Minya and Mark the Silver Man were leaving the pond, reeling in lines. Gavving had stayed to gather the children.

Four tethers led to the corners of the sheet-covered net, which was now deep underwater. Lawri stationed them along the main tether as they arrived. "Gather it in," she directed them. "Make loops. Steady pull."

Debby wrapped her toes and her fingers around the cable, and did her savage best to contract her body. No loop formed. She knew she wasn't as strong as a tree dweller, but the others were having trouble too.

Lawri called, "Good! It's coming straight out."

That was not obvious to Debby. She strained . . . and gradually the pond bulged. The sheet and its net backing were rising, carrying tons of water. Debby pulled until her knees and elbows met, then shifted her grip and continued pulling.

The pond stretched, and tore. A baby pond pulled clear, leaving a trail of droplets the size of a man's head. Water flowed over the edges of the cloth but was not lost, for surface tension held it. The main pond pulsed as surface tension tried to form the sphere again.

"Keep pulling!" Lawri shouted. "Steady . . . okay. That should do it."

The citizens relaxed. The bud-pond continued to move east on its own momentum, toward the tree, with the net and sheet now in the middle of a pulsing sphere.

Debby coiled line that was now slack. Glancing toward the trunk, she saw what the curve of the pond had hidden earlier.

Parallel to the trunk and many klomters beyond it floated a slender dark line. A young tree, no more than thirty klomters long, and injured; for the in tuft was missing, chopped away somehow. The view was confusing, for the midtrunk was wreathed in cloud . . . dark, dirty cloud . . . smoke!

Debby tugged abruptly at another line. The motion set her drifting toward the Chairman. Clave caught her ankle as she arrived. "Something?"

Debby pointed with her toes. "That tree. It's on fire!"

" . . . I believe you're right. Treefodder! It'll be coming apart. Two fires to worry about."

Debby had never seen a tree break in half, but Clave spoke from dreadful experience. They might have to move the tree. It would take time to get the carm ready—

Clave had already thought that far. His voice became a whipcrack roar. "Citizens, it's getting toward dinner-time, and we've got all these waterbirds. Let's break up the swim."

His voice dropped. "You go *now*, Debby. Tell Jeffer we may need the carm. We'll get the women and children down into the tuft, if we've got time. Your eyes are better than mine. Do you see anything leaving the tree? Like clouds of insects?"

There were black specks, big enough to show detail. "Not insects. Something bigger . . . three, four . . . birds?"

"Doesn't matter. Get going."

It had taken Jeffer the Scientist a fifth of a day to cross three klomters of line.

Free-fall brought back memories. When Quinn Tribe was lost in the sky after Dalton-Quinn Tree came apart, his crew would have given eyes and limbs to reach a pond. Fourteen years later, the grandmother of all ponds floated three klomters from Citizens Tree; and now their main problem was to get rid of most of it. Jeffer wondered if the children appreciated their wealth.

Perhaps they did. Most of Citizens Tree, thirty naked adults and children, had come to swim in that shimmering sphere of water.

There was no foliage on the high trunk. It was thick rough bark, with fissures deep enough to hide a man. Jeffer found and donned his tunic and pants, then anchored his toes in a crevice and thrust to send himself gliding out along the bark, toward the carm.

The lift cable ended two hundred meters short of the carm's dock. The citizens may have feared that careless use of the carm might spray fire across a rising cage. More likely, they feared the carm itself. They would not lightly come too near that ancient scientific thing.

The carm was old science. It was roughly brick-shaped, four meters by ten by thirty-two, and made of starstuff: metal and glass and plastic, sheathed with darkly luminous stuff that took the energy from sunlight. The bulk of it was tanks for hydrogen and oxygen and water. Nostrils at the aft end—four at each corner, and a larger one in the middle—would spurt blue fire on command.

They had neglected the carm of late, and Jeffer accepted some of the blame. The carm made two "flavors" of fuel out of water and the power in the batteries. The batteries held their full scientific charge—they filled themselves, somehow, as long as sunlight could reach the carm's glassy surface—but the hydrogen and oxygen tanks were almost empty. It was high time they filled the water tank.

The carm's bow was moored in a dock of wooden beams. Double doors led into a hut with cradles for passengers, moorings for cargo, and a broad transparent window. The window looked forth on nothing but bark. Ventral to the window was a gray sheet of glass and a row of colored buttons.

Jeffer went forward. A touch of a blue button lit the gray glass panel. Blue governed what moved the carm: the motors, the two flavors of fuel supply, the water tank, fuel flow. Jeffer read the blue script:

$$H_2: 0,518$$
$$O_2: 0,360$$
$$H_2O: 0,001$$
$$POWER: 8,872$$

The batteries danced with energy. Why not? The carm wasn't using power. Nobody in Citizens Tree had bothered to fill the water tank in seven years; so power wasn't needed to split water into hydrogen and oxygen. The water tank was virtually dry.

And he could get something done while he waited for Lawri's pond. Jeffer touched the blue button (the panel went blank) and the yellow (there appeared a line diagram of the carm's bow, the hut section). He touched a yellow dot in the image, and turned his fingertip. Then he moved aft.

The residual goop in pond water stayed in the tank after the pure water was gone. Jeffer's finger motions had (magically, *scientifically*) caused a spigot in the aft wall to ooze brown mud. He cupped the globule in his hands. He tossed it at the airlock, and most of it got through. Another globule formed, and he sent it after the first. He wiped his hands on his tunic. The mud flow had stopped.

Next he pulled several loops of hose from cargo hooks. He rotated one end onto the spigot, then tossed the coil through the twin doors. Done! When Lawri's blob of pond arrived, she would find the carm ready to be fueled.

Jeffer returned to the controls. He had a surprise for his wife.

Two sleeps ago, while the rest of the tribe was roasting waterbirds from the pond, Lawri had held one of the creatures up for his perusal. "Have you ever really looked at these?"

Jeffer had seen waterbirds before . . . but he'd kept his mouth shut, and looked.

There were no feathers. The modified trilateral symmetry common to Smoke Ring life expressed itself in two wings and a tailfin, all in smooth membrane on collapsible ribs. The wings could be held half collapsed for motion within the denser medium of water. Only one of the three eyes looked like a normal bird's eye. The others were big and bulbous, with large pupils and thick lids. The bodies were slippery-smooth.

"I've eaten them, but . . . you're right. I've seen everything from mobies to triunes to flashers to drillbits, and they don't look like this. Earthlife doesn't either. Do you think it's so they can move through water?"

"I've tried looking them up in the cassettes," Lawri had said. "I tried *bird*. I tried *water* and *pond*. There's nothing."

Jeffer's next sleep had ended with a dream fading in his mind, leaving a single phrase. " . . . even the fish can fly."

He'd had to wait until now to try it.

He tapped yellow (the display vanished), then white (and got a tiny white rectangle at the dorsal-port corner). White read the cassettes; white summoned Voice. "Prikazyvat Voice," he said.

The voice of the carm was a throaty bass, as deep as Mark the dwarf's voice. "Ready, Jeffer the Scientist."

"Prikazyvat Read *Fish*. Read it aloud."

The cassette was one that Jeffer had stolen from London Tree, but it was no different from Quinn Tribe's lost records of Smoke Ring life forms. As Voice spoke, print scrolled down the display screen: words recorded long ago by one of *Discipline*'s abandoned crew.

FISH

IF THE BIRDS WITHIN THE SMOKE RING RESEMBLE
FISH—LEGLESS, DESIGNED TO MOVE THROUGH AIR
WEIGHTLESSLY, AS A FISH MOVES THROUGH WATER—

THEN THE FISH THAT LIVE WITHIN THE PONDS RESEMBLE BIRDS.

EVERY FISH WE HAVE EXAMINED BREATHES AIR. THEY ARE NOT MAMMALS, BUT LUNGFISH. THE SINGLE CLASS OF EXCEPTIONS, *GILLFISH*, ARE DISCUSSED ELSEWHERE.

SOME CAN EXTRUDE A TUBE TO THE POND'S SURFACE. A FEW CAN EXPAND THE SIZE OF THEIR FINS VIA MEM-BRANES, TO MAKE THEM SERVE AS WINGS. ONE FORM, *CORE FISH*, INFLATES ITSELF WITH AIR, DIVES TO THE CEN-TER OF A POND, AND EXPELS A BUBBLE. IT CAN STAY SUB-MERGED FOR UP TO A DAY—SEVERAL SMOKE RING DAYS—REBREATHING ITS AIR BUBBLE, MAKING FORAYS TO HUNT, AND THEN RETURNING.

THE WHALE-SIZED *MOBY* USES ITS POND AS A LAIR FROM WHICH IT BURSTS TO SWEEP THROUGH PASSING CLOUDS OF INSECTS. *MOBY* IS A COMPROMISE FORM, AND THERE ARE OTHERS.

CLEARLY EVEN THE LARGEST PONDS CAN BREAK UP OR EVAPORATE OR BE TORN APART BY STORM. EVERY CREATURE THAT LIVES IN A POND MUST BE PREPARED TO MIGRATE TO ANOTHER: TO BEHAVE LIKE A BIRD. EVEN GILLFISH—

"Prikazyvat Stop," Jeffer said. This memory that had surfaced from his adolescent training under Quinn Tribe's Scientist was going to put him one up on his wife!

Back to work. He tapped white, then green, then each of the five green rectangles now onscreen. Within the great window that faced the bark, five smaller windows appeared, looking starboard, port, dorsal, ventral, and aft. The ventral view had a blur and a flicker to it. The rest were clear, like the window itself.

The aft view looked along the line that led west to
the pond. Citizens were returning to the tree. Behind
them a bud of pond was already drifting toward the tree,
with the harebrain net showing as a shadow within. Lawri's crazy idea was working.

They swarmed back along the cable toward the midpoint of Citizens Tree. Gavving and Minya and Anthon
hung back, counting heads to be sure that all children
were accounted for. A girl lost her grip and drifted; she
was chortling and trying to swim through the air when
Anthon scooped her up.

As children arrived, Clave herded the smaller ones,
with some difficulty, into a rectangular frame with a slat-
ted floor: the lift cage. He stopped when twelve children
were inside. Leave room for a couple of adults.

The rest clung to the rough bark or floated like bal-
loons on their tethers. There were wrestling matches.
Eight-year-old Arth was getting good at using the recoil
of his opponent's line. He was Clave's youngest, and
just beginning the tremendous growth of adolescence.

Debby had arrived first. Clave could see her a
hundred meters out along the bark, climbing toward the
carm.

The bud-pond continued to move. Lawri wore a pro-
prietary smile. Still, Citizens Tree had better have more
line next time they tried this. The pond was too close.
If the tree had brushed it there would have been a flood.

The lift now held a score of children. Whoever was
in the treadmill would have a problem braking that
weight. It couldn't be helped. Clave looked about. Mark
and Anthon looked ludicrous together, Mark short and
wide, Anthon long and narrow, their heads pointing in
opposite directions— He called, "Anthon, Mark. Take

the children down and bring back any adult you can find.
Be prepared to fight a fire."

Anthon stared in astonishment. *"Fire?"*

"Burning tree. It's around the other side of the trunk
now. Go down and get some help. Rather— Where on
Earth is Rather?"

Mark pointed outward. "I didn't know any reason to
stop them," he said defensively. "They won't fit in the
lift this trip—"

Clave cursed silently as he watched Rather and Jill
clawing their way out along the bark. There was no tide
to hurt them here. If they slipped, someone would go
get them. But he could have used their help.

Jeffer couldn't guess how long it took him to realize
that the background had changed. Behind the five camera views superimposed upon it, the window no longer
showed bark a few ce'meters distant. It showed a huge
face, strong, with massive bones: the brutal face of a
dwarf.

Chapter Two

Discipline

from the Citizens Tree cassettes, year 6 SM:

FIRE

MAKING A COOKFIRE IN FREE-FALL IS AN EXCESSIVELY INTERESTING EXPERIENCE IF WHAT YOU REALLY WANTED WAS DINNER. IT'S TAKEN ME EIGHT STATE YEARS TO PERFECT MY TECHNIQUE.

THE FIRST LESSON IS THAT A FLAME DOESN'T RISE IN FREE-FALL. I LEARNED THAT WITH A CANDLE, WHEN I WAS A CADET DREAMING OF STRANGE WORLDS. IF THERE'S NO WIND (TURN OFF THE AIR FEED), THE CANDLE FLAME SEEMS TO GO OUT.

BUT IT ISN'T OUT YET. THERE'S WAX VAPOR, AND THERE'S THE AIR AROUND IT, AND AT THE INTERFACE IS AN ENVELOPE OF PLASMA WHERE GAS AND OXYGEN INTERACT. IT CAN STAY HOT FOR MINUTES. COMBUS-

TION CONTINUES AT THE INTERFACE. WAVE THE CAN-
DLE AND *POP*! THE FLAME IS BACK.

IN THE CASE OF A COOKFIRE, THE WOOD CONTINUES
TO CHAR. WAIT AN HOUR, THEN BLOW ON THE COALS
WITH A BELLOWS. THE FIRE JUMPS TO LIFE AND THERE
WENT YOUR EYEBROWS.

—DENNIS QUINN, CAPTAIN

DISCIPLINE HAD BEEN DETERIORATING.

Cameras outside the hull showed rainbow-hued scars
from matter that had penetrated the electromagnetic
ramscoop while *Discipline* was in flight. They also
showed newer micrometeorite pocks. Sharls could ward
off anything big enough to see coming, by turning on
those magnetic shields for a few seconds, but they ate
power in great gulps.

One day he might regret even the little power he used
to maintain the gardens and the cats.

Within the hull, time had discolored metal and plastic.
The air was dust-free; metal was clean, but not recently
polished. Many of the servomechs had worn out. All
but a few of the crew cubicles were kept cold and dark
and airless. Kitchen machinery was in storage, with
power shut down. Some of the bedding had decayed.
Water mattresses had been drained and stored.

Sharls kept the control room free of water vapor and
almost cold enough to freeze carbon dioxide. He hoped
that the computer and its extensions would survive
longer in the cold. But the gardens and corridors and
even some of the cubicles were kept habitable. Sharls
left the lighting on a day-night cycle, for the birds and
cats and plants.

The gardens were surviving nicely. It was true that

some of the plants had died out completely; but after all, his ecosystem was missing its most important factor. Human crew were supposed to be in that cycle, and they had been gone for half a thousand years.

Scores of cats prowled the ship hunting hundreds of rats and a lesser number of turkeys and pigeons. The turkeys made a formidable enemy. The cats had learned to attack them in pairs.

Sharls trained the cats to respond to his voice. He had released the experimental rats long ago. The birds were already loose; they must have been released during that blank spot in his memory, the mutiny; but by themselves they wouldn't have fed the cats. They were too agile, for one thing. With all of the animal life in the system now, the gardens had a better chance of surviving.

By watching the cats and rats and plants and turkeys and pigeons interact, Sharls hoped to learn how an ecological system would behave in a free-fall environment . . . like the larger ecosystem that flowed beneath *Discipline* in endless rivers of curdled cloud.

Or had he simply become lonely? In his youth Sharls had never been a cat lover. (A sudden memory: his hand swelling with white patches rimmed in red, itching horribly. A kitten had scratched him playfully while he was stroking it.) And now? They didn't obey orders worth a damn . . . but neither had his crew.

A computer program would hardly have retained allergies; but who would expect a computer program to become lonely?

Discipline skimmed above the curdled whorl of the fourth Lagrange point. A fraction of Sharls Davis Kendy's attention watched on various wavelengths. This close, he could confirm an earlier sighting: minor amounts of carbon were being burned at sites around the edges of that endless storm. This was no forest fire: too small, and it had gone on for years. It might indicate human industry at a primitive level.

Now, where was CARM #6?

. . . Funny that the cats hadn't gone with the mutineers. The crew had loved cats. Somewhere in the lost part of his memory, there must be a reason. Perhaps Sharls had pulled free of the Smoke Ring without warning. He might have done that if the mutineers planned something really foul, like cutting the computer out and trying to run *Discipline* manually.

The mutiny was a blank to Sharls.

He had edited those memories. He even remembered why. The descendants of the mutineers would need Sharls Davis Kendy someday. It was not good that he hold grudges against specific ancestors, against old names. But had he been *too* thorough?

—There! CARM #6's communications system had come alive.

It was a thousand kilometers behind him and something less than six thousand kilometers in toward Voy. Kendy did several things at once. Before his new orbit could carry him away, he restarted the drive. He beamed, "Kendy for the State. Kendy for the State."

The CARM autopilot responded.

"Link to me. Beam records."

He'd made mistakes enough during that unexpected contact twenty Earth years ago! At least he'd accomplished something: he'd broken the program that denied him access to the Cargo and Repair Module. The drive systems were beyond his reach. The original mutineers must have physically cut the fiber-optic cable. But the CARM would talk to him!

He'd instructed the autopilot to take photographs at ten-minute intervals. Reentry was in progress when he sent that message. Static might well have fuzzed him out. But pictures were streaming in:

Time passed at a furious rate. CARM #6 flamed as it plowed through thickening air, veering from plants and ponds and creatures. It dipped into a pond to refuel, then bedded itself in the Voy-ward tuft of the largest of a cluster (grove?) of integral trees. It stayed there, with not much of a view at all, for most of a Smoke Ring year. Flickering shapes carved cavities through the foliage and wove small branches into wasp's-nest structures. Abruptly the CARM backed into the sky, skittered outward under inexpert handling, and docked at the midpoint of the tree.

With another part of his mind, Kendy fiddled with *Discipline*'s fusion motor. He could not match his orbit to that of the CARM. He must stay well outside the Smoke Ring to protect *Discipline* from corrosion. The best he could do was twice the CARM's orbital period, to dip low above the CARM's position once every ten hours and eight minutes. But he'd be in range for half an hour while his motor was firing.

More of his attention went to watching the CARM's lone occupant in real time.

Jeffer the "Scientist" was stored in memory. He had aged twenty Earth years: hair and beard going gray, wrinkles across his forehead (broken by a white line of scar that was a healing pink wound in Kendy's records), and knuckles turning knobby. Height: 2.3 meters. Mass: 86 kilograms. Long arms and legs, toes like stubby fingers, fingers like a spider's legs: long, fragile, the hands of a field surgeon.

The Smoke Ring had altered *Discipline*'s descendants.

The tribes of London Tree and Dalton-Quinn Tree had all looked like that. The jungle giants who had grown up without tidal gravity were hardly human: freakishly tall, with long, fragile, agile fingers and toes; and one of the twelve was a cripple, and others had legs of different length. Only Mark the Silver Man had looked like a normal State citizen. They had called him "dwarf."

They were savages; but they had learned to use State technology in the form of the CARM. Still human. Perhaps they could be made citizens again.

To Kendy, who thought with the speed of a computer, the "Scientist" moved much too slowly. Now he was at the controls, auditing a cassette; now checking the camera views in present time . . .

The incoming CARM records showed clouds and ponds and trees and trilaterally symmetric fishlike birds swirling across the sky. Natives flickered through the CARM cabin: the same savages, growing older; a growing handful of children.

At fifteen years minus-time the CARM backed out of its timber dock for a journey of exploration. It visited a green puffball several kilometers across, and when it emerged there was vegetation like a houseful of green spaghetti bound to its dorsal surface. It hovered in the open sky while men darted among a flock of birds— real birds with real wings: turkeys—and returned to its dock with prisoners.

At thirteen years minus-time it left the trunk to return with a dubious prize: several tons of black mud.

There were no more such forays. The Cargo and Repair Module had become a motor for the tree.

It was docked when the main drive fired for several hours. Kendy watched side views as the integral tree drifted across the sky. It had been circling too far from the neutron star. Air grew thin away from the Smoke Ring median.

The tree was lower now; the air would be as thick as mountain air on Earth. And now the CARM was not being used at all; but there was plenty to watch. The Smoke Ring environment was fascinating. Huge spheres of water, storms, jungles like tremendous puffs of green cotton candy.

In present time, the aft CARM camera showed nearly thirty natives maneuvering between the tree and a tremendous globule of water. They were using the free-fall environment better than any State astronaut. The State had need of these people!

Discipline's own telescope had found the foreshortened tree, with the pond to mark it. And what was that on the opposite side of the tree? Infrared light glowed near its center . . .

Half a thousand years of sensory deprivation were being compensated in a few minutes. After more than five hundred years, Sharls Kendy had left the stable point behind Goldblatt's World. He had burned irreplaceable fuel, and it was worth it! Sharls tried to absorb it all, integrate it all . . . but that could wait. The "Scientist" might leave at any minute!

He beamed: "Interrupt records." It was twenty Earth years of nothing happening, and the tiny CARM autopilot couldn't handle too many tasks at once. "Activate voice."

"Voice on." The .04 second delay was almost too short to notice.

"Send—" He displayed a picture of himself as a human being, with minor improvements. At age forty-two Kendy had been handsome, healthy, mature, firm

of jaw, authoritative: a recruitment-poster version of a
State checker.

These were not obedient State citizens. They hadn't
trusted him twenty years ago. What words might give
him a handle on Jeffer the "Scientist"?

He sent, "Kendy for the State. Jeffer the Scientist,
your citizens have been idle too long."

Jeffer jumped like a thief caught in the act. Two long
seconds passed before he found his voice. "Checker?"

"Speaking. How stands your tribe?"

Out beyond the terrible whorl of storm that surrounded Gold, out where water boiled and froze at the
same time and the legendary stars were a visible truth,
lived Kendy the Checker. He had claimed to be something like an elaborate cassette: the recording of a man.
He had claimed authority over every human being in
the Smoke Ring. He had offered knowledge and power,
while they were still near enough to hear his ravings.

Perhaps he was only a madman trapped somehow
aboard the spacecraft that had brought men from the
stars. But he had knowledge. He had coached them
through that terrible fall back into the Smoke Ring,
fourteen years ago.

The face in the carm's window had not been seen
since. It was the face of a dwarf, a brutal throwback. The
jaw and orbital ridges were more massive even than
Mark's, the musculature more prominent.

"We lived through the reentry," Jeffer told him. "Ilsa
and Merril are dead now. There are children."

"Jeffer, your tribe has possessed the CARM for fourteen of your years. In that time you have moved the
tree twice and thenceforth done nothing at all. What

have you learned of the people of the fourth Lagrange point?"

The what? "I don't understand the question."

"Sixty degrees ahead of Goldblatt's World on the arc of the Smoke Ring and sixty degrees behind are regions where matter grows dense. They are points of stability in Goldblatt's World's orbit. Material tends to collect there." The dwarf's brutal features registered impatience. "East of you by twelve hundred kilometers, a vast, sluggish, permanent storm."

"The Clump? You're saying there are *people* in the Clump?"

"I sense activity there. A civilization is growing twelve hundred kilometers from where your tree has floated for fifteen Earth years. Jeffer, where is your curiosity? Has it been bred out of you?"

"What do you want from me, Checker?"

Kendy said, "I can be in range to advise you every ten hours and eight minutes, once every two of your days. I want to know more of the people of the Smoke Ring. In particular, I want to know about you and about the Clump civilization. I think you should link with them, perhaps rule them."

Jeffer's one previous experience indicated that Kendy was harmless. For good or ill, he could only talk. Jeffer gathered his courage and said, "Kendy, the tales say that you abandoned us here, long ago. Now I expect you're bored and—"

"I am."

"And you want to talk to someone. You also claim authority I won't grant you. Why should I listen?"

"Are you aware that you are being invaded?"

"What?"

The face of Kendy was suddenly replaced by a dizzying view. Jeffer looked into a river of storm, streaming faster as the eye moved inward toward a tiny, brilliant violet pinpoint. Jeffer had seen this once before: the Smoke Ring seen from outside.

Before he could remember to breathe, the view jumped. He was looking at what had been the center of the picture, vastly enlarged.

"Look." Scarlet arrowheads appeared, pointing— "Here, your tree."

"Citizens Tree, from the out tuft? Yeah, and that must be the pond." Both were tiny. Opposite the pond was . . . another tree? And dark cloud clinging to the trunk?

The view jumped again. Through the blur and flicker in the illusion of a window, Jeffer watched a tree on fire. Moving between the two trees were creatures he had never seen before.

"Treefodder! Everybody's on the other side of the trunk. Those bird-things will be on the tree before any-one knows it."

"Look in infrared." The picture changed again, to red blobs on black. Jeffer couldn't tell what he was looking at. The scarlet arrowhead pointed again. "You are seeing heat. This is fire in the intruder tree. Here, these five points are just the temperature of a man."

Jeffer shook his head. "It doesn't mean anything."

The enlarged picture returned . . . and suddenly those tiny "creatures" jumped into perspective. "Winged men!"

"I would have called those enlarged swimming fins rather than wings. Never mind. Have you ever heard tales of winged men?"

"No. There's nothing in the cassettes either. I've got to do something about this. Prikazyvat Voice off." Jeffer made for the airlock without waiting to see the face fade. His citizens wouldn't have a chance against winged warriors!

The sun was at three o'clock: dead east, just above where the Smoke Ring began to take definite shape. *Kendy can only talk, sure, but he talks with pictures, and he tells things nobody can know. He'll be in range every other day at this time. Do I want to know that?* But Jeffer had other concerns, and the rest of that thought lay curled unfinished in the bottom of his mind.

Jill was leaving Rather behind. She glanced back once and moved on, and there was laughter in the sound of her panting.

Jill was his elder by half a year. When he wanted company it was generally Jill he wanted; but they did compete. There had been a year during which she could beat him at wrestling, when she suddenly grew tall and he'd lagged behind. She'd taught him the riblock the hard way: she'd held his floating ribs shut with her knees so that he couldn't breathe. He could wrestle her now— he was a boy *and* a dwarf—but her longer arms and legs gave her an unbeatable advantage at racing. He'd never catch her.

So he moved outward at his own pace, giving due care to his handholds and footholds in the rough bark, following the blond girl in the scarlet tunic. Her long-limbed mother had already reached the carm ahead of them.

At fourteen-plus, Rather was considered an adult. He was built wide and muscular, with heavy cheek, jaw, and orbital bones. His fingers were short and stubby, and his toes, though strong, were too short to be much use. His hair was black and curly like his mother's. His beard was sparse, without much curl to it yet. His eyes were

green (and green tinged his cheek, with a growth of fluff
that would be many days healing). He stood a meter and
three-quarters tall.

Dwarf. Arms too short, legs too short. He should
have gone around the trunk. Jill could have told the
Scientist about the burning tree; Debby might already
know. He could have been getting a closer look!

The carm loomed ahead of him. It was as big . . . no,
bigger than the Citizens Tree commons.

Debby shouted into the airlock. Someone emerged:
Jeffer. They talked, heads bobbing. Debby moved to
the front of the carm; Jeffer was about to go back
inside—

Rather heard Jill calling. "Scientist! There's a burning
tree coming toward us!" She paused to catch her breath.
"We saw it, me and Rather, we—while we were swimming—"

Jeffer called back. "Debby told me. Did you see anything like winged men?"

" . . . No."

"Okay. Help Debby with the moorings, there at the
bow." He noticed Rather struggling in Jill's wake. "Get
Rather to help you."

Debby and Jill were both fighting knots, and Jill was
muttering "Treefodder, treefodder, treefodder," when
Rather caught up. "I bent my finger," she said.

Debby said, "I hate to cut lines. See what you can
do."

The carm's tethers hadn't been moved in years, and
the knots were tight. Rather's stubby fingers worked
them loose. *Dwarf. Clumsy but strong.* Presently the
carm was held by nothing but its own inertia. Jill did
not look pleased. Debby and Rather grinned at each

other. It was something, to do a thing an adult warrior could not!

Jeffer called from the airlock, twelve meters beyond the bark. "Come aboard!"

Debby jumped and Jill followed. Rather hesitated until he saw them bump against the airlock door. The jump looked dangerous. Tide was gentle, but one *could* fall into the sky. Rather had never been inside the carm, and he wasn't sure he wanted to be. The starstuff box was like nothing else in or on the tree.

But he had to follow. He caught the edge of the outer door as it passed, pivoted on the strength of his arms, and entered feet first. *Can't jump right, can't reach far. What if I'd missed?*

It was weird inside the carm. There were openings in the back wall, and hard round loops sticking out of the dorsal and side walls. Farther toward the front were rows of cradles almost the size of an adult, ten in all, made of nothing like wood or cloth.

Rather made his way forward. The others were in the first row of cradles. "Take a seat and strap yourself in," Jeffer ordered. "Here, like this." He fastened two elastic tethers across Jill's torso. "Lawri showed me how to work these, years ago."

The cradle had a headrest that fitted nicely behind his ears. Jill's and Debby's dug into their shoulders. *It's true,* Rather thought suddenly. *The carm was built for dwarves!* He liked the thought.

"The winged men weren't very close," the Scientist said. "We've got time." His fingers drummed against the flat panel below the window.

There was tide pulling Rather forward, and a whisper-roar like a steady wind. The bark receded; the tree backed into the sky. Jill gripped the armrests of her cradle. Her mouth was wide. Debby said, "Clave didn't say take off, Scientist. He said get ready."

"No time. They're headed for the trunk. Also the carm is *mine*, Debby. We settled that once."

"Tell it to Clave."

"Clave knows."

The invaders kicked themselves through the air, slowly, in the last stages of exhaustion. Five, it looked like, until Rather realized that the older woman carried a half-grown girl in her arms.

Jeffer nudged the carm toward them, in along the trunk.

Smoke Ring people came long, longer, or dwarf. These invaders were of the longer persuasion, like jungle giants, born and raised in free-fall. They were quite human: an older man and woman and four girls. The wings were artificial, bound to their shins, made of cloth over splayed ribs. One girl trailed behind, struggling along with only one wing.

They were in sorry shape. Closer now, and Rather could see details. The man's hair was burned, and the loose sheet that covered him was charred. The wingless girl was coughing; she didn't even have the strength to cling to the woman who carried her.

Their legs stopped pumping as, one by one, they saw the carm.

Debby said, "I don't see anything like bows or harpoons. Can we take them aboard?"

"I thought of that, but *look* at them. The carm scares them worse than being lost in the sky. Anyway, the man's almost there."

The burned man hadn't seen them. Kicking steadily, far ahead of the others, he reached the bark and clung.

Without a pause he pounded a stake into the bark, moored a coil of line, and hurled the coil at the older woman. She freed a hand and caught it, pulled herself toward the tree, then snapped the line to send a sine wave rolling toward the trunk. The nearer girl caught the line in her toes as it bowed toward her.

Clave came around the bulge of the bark. He slowed when he saw the strangers. Gavving and Minya joined him. They moved toward the strangers.

There were four on the trunk now: a girl, the man, and the older woman with her coughing burden. Rather watched Clave take the burned man's line, hurl a sine wave across the one-winged girl's torso, and pull her in.

"Looks okay," the Scientist murmured.

Clave looked up and waved. Jeffer nodded and set the carm moving. "It's all right," he said. "They sure don't look dangerous. I wonder what happened to them? Where are they *from?*"

"I never saw strangers before," Jill said. "I don't know what to think."

"That burning tree is still coming at us," Rather said.

Jeffer nodded. The carm surged, turning.

Black smoke wreathed the middle section of the tree. Flame glowed sluggishly from within, illuminating blurred curves and oblongs. Debby said, "There's stuff in the fire. Made stuff, machinery. It'll burn up."

That was knowledge burning in the core of the fire. Jeffer hated what he had to say. "We can't save it. If we had Mark and the silver suit . . . no. That might burn even him."

"You're not taking us into the fire?"

"We can push anywhere. The tide will hold the tree straight." Jeffer had already taken them below the inward limit of the firecloud, where a black plume drifted east. The carm was passing north of the trunk. Jeffer tapped: the carm turned. "It's still dangerous. The tree could come apart while we're on it."

He moved in on the trunk. The bow grated against bark; Jeffer's crew surged forward against their elastic bands. "I think the carm was *built* for pushing," he said. He tapped a blue dash in the center of the panel, and the whisper of power became a whistling roar. Tide surged against his back.

This was what it was to be a Scientist. Knowledge, power, mastery of a universe. This was what Kendy the Checker had to offer. At what price? Who but a Scientist would have the strength to resist?

The sun passed zenith and started down its arc. Jeffer had changed the display; he watched sets of letters and numbers. The roar of the main motor strummed his bones.

Chapter Three

Refugees

from the Citizens Tree cassettes, year 4 SM:

TIME

WE'VE BEEN TRYING TO KEEP TO EARTH TIME, BUT THAT WORD "DAY" IS ABOUT AS USEFUL AS BALLS ON A CHECKER. THE CLOSER YOU GET TO VOY, THE SHORTER THE DAYS GET, DOWN TO ABOUT TWO HOURS. CLOSER THAN THAT, THE AIR'S TOO THIN AND THERE'S NO WATER TO SPEAK OF. AT A TEN-HOUR ORBIT, SAME THING, THERE'S NOTHING TO BREATHE. WE'VE BEEN KEEPING TO SHIP-TIME. TWENTY-FOUR HOURS CONSTITUTE A "SLEEP." A "DAY" IS ONE ORBIT AROUND VOY, WHEREVER YOU HAPPEN TO BE. GOLD'S ORBIT IS A "STANDARD DAY."

THE STATE TAKES ITS DATES FROM THE YEAR OF ITS FOUNDING. WE'VE DONE THE SAME, DATING SMOKE RING YEARS FROM FOUR YEARS AGO. OUR YEARS ARE

HALF A ROTATION OF VOY AND ITS COMPANION SUN
. . . HALF BECAUSE IT'S MORE CONVENIENT.

IF *DISCIPLINE* EVER DOES COME BACK FOR US,
KENDY WILL HAVE TO LEARN A WHOLE NEW LANGUAGE.

—MICHELLE MICHAELS, COMMUNICATIONS

THE HUTS OF CITIZENS TREE WERE ENCLOSURES MADE BY
weaving living spine branches into a kind of wickerwork. The Scientists' hut was larger than most, and more
cluttered too.

The Scientists were the tribe's teachers and doctors.
Any hut would have harpoons protruding from the walls
and high ceiling; but here the wicker sprouted starstuff
knives, pots of herbs and pastes, and tools for writing.

The hut was crowded. Lawri stepped carefully among
five sleeping jungle giants.

She'd covered their wounds in undyed cloth. The
strangers moaned and twisted in their sleep. The youngest girl, with her hair burned down to the scalp on one
side, of her head, was holding herself half in the air.

The noise from outside wasn't helping. Lawri bent to
get through the doorway. "Could you hold it down!"
she whisper-snarled. "These citizens *don't* need . . . oh.
Clave . . . Chairman, I'm trying to give them some quiet.
Can you take the talk to the commons?"

Clave and Anthon were intimidated into silence. Jeffer asked, "Can any of them answer questions?"

"They're asleep. They haven't said anything sensible."

Her husband merely nodded. Lawri went back in.
Rustling sounds receded. For a moment she felt re-
morse. Jeffer would want to see the strangers as much
as anyone.

When the burns healed, the strangers would be handsome, but in weird fashion. Only birds wore the gaudy colors of their scorched clothing. Their skin was dark; their lips and noses were broad; their hair was like black pillows.

The youngest girl stirred, thrashed, and opened her eyes. "Tide," she said wonderingly. The dark eyes focused. "Who're you?"

"I'm Lawri the Scientist. You're in Citizens Tree. You're safe now."

The girl twisted to see the others. "Wend?"

"One of you died."

The girl moaned.

"Can you tell me who you are and how you came here?"

"I'm Carlot," the girl said. Two tears were growing. "We're Serjent House. Loggers. There was a fire . . . the whole tree caught fire. Wend got caught when the water tank let go." She shook her head; teardrop globules flew wide.

"All right, Carlot. Have some water, then go to sleep."

Carlot's drinking technique was surprising. She took the pottery vessel, set two fingers to nearly block the opening, then jerked the pottery vessel toward her face. The jet of water struck her lower lip. She tried again and reached her mouth.

"Would you like something to eat? Foliage?"

"What's that?"

Lawri went out to strip some branchlets of their foliage. Carlot looked dubiously at the fluffy green stuff. "Oh, it's *greens*."

"You know it?"

"I've been in a tree tuft." She tasted it. "This is sweet. Older tree?" She continued eating.

Lawri said, "Later I'll get you some stew. You should
sleep now."

Carlot patted the wicker floor. "How can I sleep with
this pushing up against me? All my blood wants to settle
on one side."

London Tree, Lawri's home, had been bigger, with a
stronger tide. In Citizens Tree you could drop a stone
from eye level and draw a slow breath and let it out
before the stone struck. But this Carlot must be used
to no tide at all.

She turned over, gingerly. Her eyes closed and she
was asleep.

They moved through the green gloom of the corridor,
back toward the commons. Anthon said, "I always wondered. Lawri doesn't take orders from you either, does
she?"

Jeffer laughed. "Treefodder, no!"

Clave said, "I really wanted to ask them some questions before we tackle the firetree."

"We can't wait," Jeffer said. "Let's go see what we can
scavenge. This is the most interesting thing that has happened to us in fourteen years."

"It's bound to bring changes."

"Like what?"

Clave grinned at Jeffer. "They've already changed
your home life. You can't sleep in the Scientists' hut
and Lawri won't leave."

"I've got the children too. I'm living in the bachelors'
longhut with my three kids and Rather. Look, I want to
go *now*, before that burned tree drifts too far. Anthon?"

"Ready," said the jungle giant.

Clave nodded, reluctantly. "Just us three? Stet. We'll

round up some kids to run the treadmill. And let's take those wings along. I want to try them."

The tree still burned. Fire had eaten six or seven klomters in from the midpoint along the lee side, progressing alongside the waterfall channel, where there was partial protection from the wind. The flames streamed east like the mane of a skyhorse. At the midpoint there were only red patches glowing in black char. In the center of the burn was a prominent uneven lump. Jeffer eased the carm toward that.

Clave said, "I don't understand why it hasn't come apart."

Anthon nodded uneasily. Jeffer said, "It's a short tree. With a tuft missing it's even shorter. Tide would pull harder on a grown tree, but that thing could still come apart while we're on it. I don't *ever* want to go through that again."

Anthon asked, "Why do trees come apart?"

"They do it when they're dying," Clave said.

Jeffer said, "When a tree drifts too far away from the Smoke Ring median, it starves. It saves itself by coming apart. The tide takes half of it out, half in. One half falls back to where the water and fertilizer are. The other half . . . dies, I guess."

"I still don't see any bugs," Clave said. "It's the bugs that eat a tree apart, isn't it? The tree isn't getting fed, so the bark lets the bugs get inside—"

"I don't know everything, Clave."

"Pity."

They were close enough now to make out black lumps at the center of the charred region. There: a shape like a huge seed pod split open from inside. There: a thin shell of char, a bell shape not unlike the fire-spitting

nostrils at the carm's aft end. A ridge of white ash joined
the bell to the split pod. Beyond: several fragile sheets
of charred wood, the remains of an oblong hut with
interior walls.

Clave reached for the wings he'd bound to cargo
hooks. "Scientist, can you hold the carm here? We'll go
see what there is to see. If the tree breaks in half, you'll
still have us tethered."

Jeffer stifled a protest. He ached to explore that ruined structure, but— "I can handle it. Take lines too."

The sun would be dead east in a few tens of breaths.

A stick protruded from the butt end of each fan-
shaped wing. After some experimentation they settled
for lining the stick along their shins and binding them
with the straps. The wings tended to hang up on things
even when folded. Clave and Anthon wriggled through
the airlock and flapped into the sky.

Jeffer tapped the white button. "Prikazyvat Voice,"
he said.

The carm said, "Ready, Jeffer the Scientist."

Clave and Anthon fluttered erratically through the
air. Suddenly Anthon moved purposefully toward the
blister of charred machinery, moving easily, as if he had
always been a bird. Clave moved after him, fighting a
tendency to veer left.

They swept away the white ash that lay between the
bell and the tank. The ash enclosed them in cloud. When
the cloud dispersed, they had exposed a length of tube
and a loose webbing of metal strands around it.

"Kendy for the State. Hello, Jeffer."

Jeffer didn't jump. "Hello, Kendy. What do you make
of all this?"

"You'd know more about the injured plant than I.
I've been studying the machinery." Within the bow win-

dow the metal strands and the enclosed pipe began
blinking, an outline of red light. "These, the pipe and
the chicken wire, are metal. The ruptured tank—"
another blinking outline "—appears to have been a large
seed pod. The cone is half of a similar seed pod. The
ash around the pipe appears to be wood ash.

"We're looking at a steam rocket, Jeffer. Your invaders used a wood fire to heat the pipe. They ran water
through the pipe and into the nozzle. Very inefficient,
but in your peculiar environment they could move a tree
with that. Slowly, of course."

"Why would they pick an injured tree?"

"Ask them. Did any survive?"

"One's dead. Five more are in bad shape. My wife
won't let me near them. Wait a few days and see."

Clave and Anthon flew along the split in the great
tank. They reached the cluster of black oblongs at the
other end.

The Checker said, "Their wounds won't become in-
fected. We didn't bring disease bacteria."

"What?"

"I was thinking aloud. I want to talk to your invaders.
Take them on a tour, Jeffer, when they're ready. Show
them the CARM."

"Kendy, I'm not sure I want them to know about
you."

"I will observe only."

Clave and Anthon were flapping back to the carm.
They carried blackened cargo, and they no longer wore
tethers. "Company coming," Jeffer said.

"Jeffer, you've concealed your contact with me from
the rest of your tribe, haven't you?"

"I haven't mentioned it to them yet."

"I'll keep my silence while others are aboard. Play the game any way you like."

Clave and Anthon returned black with soot. They untied the now-clumsy wings, then wiggled in, pushing armfuls of blackened salvage ahead of them. Clave crowed, "I love it! It's really flying!"

"You never did like tide, did you, Clave? How's the leg?"

"It never gets any better." Clave flexed his right leg. The misshapen lump on his thighbone bulged beneath the skin and muscle. The compound fracture he'd suffered in Carther States had healed, but in the jungle there had been no tide to tell the bone to stop growing. "It feels like I strained it. If I have to fly any distance I'll use just one wing."

They set to mooring their loot along the walls. Two tremendous hooks, wood stiffened with metal. A meter's length of metal band with tiny teeth along one edge. A hardwood tube had kept its shape if not its strength; the remnants of charred plastic hose clung to one end.

"Weapons and tools," Clave said. "There was wire twisted together like a harebrain net, but it was burned through in too many places. Nothing else worth taking except the pipe. We've got to have that pipe. We moored the lines to it, Jeffer. Let's pull it loose."

"It must be important, given that you've moored the carm to a tree that's about to come apart. Why? Just because it's metal?"

"I've got a vague idea what this setup is for," Clave said. "We could duplicate everything except the pipe, in theory anyway. The pipe isn't just metal, it's starstuff, something out of the old science."

"Why do you say that?"

"We couldn't find a seam," Anthon said. "It gleams when you rub away the soot. Clave, I'm not sure I like any of this. Jeffer's right, that tree could come apart and throw us spinning across the sky, and for what? Wings, sure, those are wonderful, but the rest of this is just weird!"

Clave the Chairman said, "Pull that pipe out, Scientist."

Anthon fumed and was silent. Jeffer said, "Strap down. Let's hope the tethers hold."

Under attitude jets the carm shuddered and lurched. Then six meters of metal pipe two hundred ce'meters across pulled loose in a cloud of ash.

When Anthon and Clave went out to retrieve it, Jeffer went too. They watched, grinning, while he thrashed and spun; and suddenly he was flying, kicking stiff-legged across the sky like any swordbird.

They bound the pipe up against the hull and took the carm back to Citizens Tree. The burning tree continued to drift west and in.

Lawri kept the citizens away from her hut for five days, a full waking-sleeping cycle. That became impossible when she sent Rather for food. Rather came back with waterbird stew, and Clave, Jeffer, Gavving, Minya, Debby, Jayan, Jinny, Mark, Jill, and a host of children. She kept them outside while the strangers ate. Then she and Jeffer pulled the hut's entrance apart. It could be rebuilt later.

The man named himself: Booce Serjent. He shaped his words strangely. He named the others: his wife Ryllin, and their daughters Mishael, Karilly, and Carlot.

"We've delayed the funeral until you're strong

enough," Clave said. "Can you make yourself discuss funeral practices?"

Booce shrugged painfully. "We cremate. The ashes go into the earthlife tanks. What do you do here?"

"The dead go to feed the tree."

"All right. Chairman Clave, what has happened to *Logbearer*?"

"I don't understand."

"*Logbearer* is our ship. You saw a burning tree? The fire started around *Logbearer*, in the middle."

"We went there. We brought back a metal pipe and some other stuff."

"You saved the main feed pipe! How?"

"We used the carm. It's an old starstuff relic, still working. We use it to move the tree."

Booce smiled and sighed and seemed about to drift off to sleep.

Lawri asked, "What are you? Carlot said *loggers*."

"Let him alone. I'm awake." The older woman sounded tired. "I'm Ryllin. Yes, we're loggers. We take lumber back to the Clump and sell it there."

Chairman Clave asked, "You mean there are men in there?"

Ryllin's laugh chopped off as if it had hurt her. "More than a thousand. With children, near two thousand."

"Thousands. Huh. And you move trees. Don't you have trees in the Clump?"

"No. The tide's wrong."

"How do you move a tree?"

"You cut off one tuft. Then the wind only blows on the other tuft. Booce generally takes us west, so of course we want the log to go east. So we cut the in tuft. The wind pushes just on the out tuft, so it pushes the tree west, and that slows it down. The tree drops closer to Voy and speeds up—"

The children and some adults were looking confused. *We taught them this!* Lawri thought angrily. *West takes you in.* Pushing a tree against the Smoke Ring's rotation—west—would drop it closer to Voy. Lower orbits were faster orbits. The tree would move east toward the Clump.

"—But of course we need the rocket too," Ryllin was saying. "A rocket is a tank of water, and a nozzle, and a metal pipe with a fire around it. You run water through the pipe. The steam sprays away from where you want to go. Without the pipe there's no *Logbearer*. You understand reaction effects?"

The citizens looked at each other. Children understood the law of reaction before they could speak!

Ryllin said, "Well, when you get to the Clump you sever the other tuft and work the log to a mooring with the steam rocket. Then you have to sell it. We've done it all our lives. But the pipefire got away from us . . . Lawri? I'm tired."

Gavving said, "Sell?"

"Forget it, Ryllin. Everybody out," Lawri ordered. "Chairman, can you move them?"

The citizens drifted away in clumps of heated discussion.

Four sleeps after reaching Citizens Tree, all of the Serjents were on their feet. Various citizens volunteered to lead them about. They moved tentatively, slowed by healing burns and unaccustomed to tide. They listened intently, and spoke in vowel-twisting accents and strange words . . . but for Karilly, who huddled close in the circle of her family, silent.

Booce and his family came back tired. Their new home was primitive, and roomy, and oddly beautiful. The citizens had managed well with so little.

Lawri the Scientist looked them over and judged them well enough to attend a funeral.

Chapter Four

The In Tuft

from the Citizens Tree cassettes, year 7 SM:

INTEGRAL TREES

. . . THESE INTEGRAL TREES GROW TO TREMENDOUS SIZE. WHEN SUCH A PLANT REACHES ITS FULL GROWTH, IT STABILIZES BY TIDAL EFFECT. IT FORMS A LONG, SLENDER TRUNK TUFTED WITH GREEN AT BOTH ENDS: TENS OF THOUSANDS OF RADIAL SPOKES CIRCLING LEVOY'S STAR, EACH SCORES OF KILOMETERS LONG.

LIKE MANY PLANTS OF THE SMOKE RING, THE INTEGRAL TREE IS A SOIL COLLECTOR. THE ENDPOINTS ARE SUBJECT TO TIDAL GRAVITY. AND WIND! THE TUFTS ARE IN A PERPETUAL WIND, BLOWING FROM THE WEST AT THE INNER TUFT AND FROM THE EAST AT THE OUTER TUFT. THE TIDE-ORIENTED TRUNK BOWS TO THE WINDS, CURVING INTO A SINGLE, NEARLY HORIZONTAL BRANCH AT EACH END, GIVING IT THE APPEARANCE OF

AN INTEGRATION SIGN. THE TUFTS SIFT FERTILIZER
FROM THE WIND: SOIL, WATER, EVEN ANIMALS AND
PLANTS SMASHED BY IMPACT.

FREE-FALL CONDITIONS PREVAIL EVERYWHERE EX-
CEPT IN THE INTEGRAL TREES. THE MEDICAL DANGERS
OF LIFE IN FREE-FALL ARE WELL KNOWN. IF *DISCIPLINE*
HAS INDEED ABANDONED US, IF WE ARE INDEED MA-
ROONED WITHIN THIS WEIRD ENVIRONMENT, WE
COULD DO WORSE THAN TO SETTLE THE TUFTS OF THE
INTEGRAL TREES . . .

—CLAIRE DALTON, SOCIOLOGY/MEDICINE

FOLIAGE FRAMED HALF A WORLD OF SKY.

The treemouth faced west, at the junction between
branch and trunk. Spine branches migrated west along
the branch, carrying whatever their foliage had picked
up from the wind, to be swallowed by the conical pit.
Citizens came too, to feed the tree. The treemouth was
their toilet, their garbage disposal, and their cemetery.

Lawri the Scientist had described all of this in advance.
Booce tried to tell himself that it made sense; it was
reasonable in context; it only took getting used to.

Wend had been placed at the lip of the pit. She'd had
time to ride the spine branches halfway into the cone
of the treemouth. Booce was glad that he could not see
her better.

Burning was cleaner. Reducing the body to ashes
burned away memories too . . .

How was Karilly taking it?

Karilly was the quiet one. She obeyed orders, but
rarely showed initiative. She almost never spoke to
strangers. A good child, but Booce had never really
understood her.

She hadn't been burned. All of them had watched Wend die; how could it be worse for Karilly? But she hadn't spoken a word since the fire.

Chairman Clave spoke, welcoming Wend into the tribe. Lawri spoke of a citizen's last duty, to feed the tree. Ryllin spoke her memories of her lost daughter. Karilly cried silently; the tears sheathed her eyes in crystal.

Older citizens ate first. Booce saw his daughters hanging back—they had learned that much already—while a Citizens Tree girl-child filled his bowl with waterbird stew from a large, crude ceramic pot. He lurched away across the woven-spine-branch floor of the commons, following his wife, trying to keep his bowl upright.

"You think of the tide as something to fight," his wife said softly. "Think of it as a convenience."

"Hah."

"Tide gives you a preferred direction. Something to push against. Look." With the bowl held in one hand, Ryllin leapt one-legged into the air and spun in a slow circle before her feet touched the floor again. She hadn't spilled a drop.

"Moving isn't unpleasant in a tide, it's just different. These, ah, *citizens* make us look clumsy, but we can adjust, love. We *will* adjust."

"Stet. I've climbed trees all my life. . . . Company."

They were surrounded by children. A pudgy half-grown girl said, "How do you move a tree without a carm?"

Booce said, "Let's sit down and I'll tell you."

A dozen children waited patiently while Booce and Ryllin nested themselves in foliage. Then they all settled at once.

Booce thought while he ate. He said, "You need a rocket. My rocket was *Logbearer*, and it was my father's rocket before me. To make a rocket you need a rocket."

One asked, "How did anyone build the first rocket?"

Booce smiled at the dwarf boy. "The first rocket was given by *Discipline*. It had a mind—the Library—and the Admiralty still has that, with more knowledge in it than you'll find in your little cassettes. Anyway, you've got to have a rocket so you can get to the pod groves."

A woman of Booce's own size settled within earshot. Booce pretended not to notice. "The biggest pod you can find in the pod grove becomes your water tank. You cut another pod in half and it's your rocket nozzle. You run the pipe into the stem end. You wrap sikenwire around the pipe to hold the firebark. You light the firebark. You pump water through the hot pipe and it turns to steam and goes racing out the nozzle, and that pushes you the other way."

The pudgy girl (though all the children looked a bit pudgy, well fed and compressed by tide) asked, "Where does pipe come from?"

"I don't know. *Discipline*, maybe, if there ever was a *Discipline*." The children snickered. Booce didn't know why, so he ignored it. "There's a hundred and twenty meters of pipe in the Empire, so they tell me, and forty-eight of that makes up the pipes in eleven logging ships. *Woodsman* carried a spare pipe, but they're richer than we are.

"So. A rocket is one and a half pods, and a pipe, and some sikenwire, and the hut complex at the other end of the tank. You need big hooks for towing, saws to carve up wood, and crossbows, because you've got to find your own food. A trip takes a year or two. Most of us travel in families.

"Now you find a sting jungle. The honey hornets live in the sting jungles, and there's nothing so big they can't kill it. You need to cover yourself all over to get at the nest. Honey is sticky red stuff, sweeter than foliage.

"Now you pick a tree. If it's more than forty klomters long, the wood'll be too coarse and you'll be forever coming home. Thirty's about right. You moor your rocket at the midpoint, but you don't use it yet. You paint a line of honey down the trunk to one of the tufts. Then you gash the bark in a circle above the tuft, and paint honey along that. You know the bugs that eat a tree apart if it starts to die?"

Heads nodded. The Serjents had been told of the death of Dalton-Quinn Tree. Children must hear that tale early.

Booce said, "The bugs follow the honey down. They eat the honey above the tuft. Then they're stuck, because they've eaten all the honey. There's nothing left to eat but wood. After a few sleeps the tuft drops off."

There were sounds of dismay. "We don't use occupied trees, you know," Booce said gently. "The tree would die anyway when it gets near the Clump. Integral trees want a straightforward tidal pull, straight through Voy."

The pudgy girl asked a little coldly, "How many trees have you killed?" Booce saw that she was almost an adult. Her height had fooled him: the tide had stunted her growth.

"Ten."

The dwarf (an adult too, with beard beginning to sprout) asked, "Why do you cut off the tuft?"

"To move. You know the rule? West takes you in, in takes you east. I want the tree to move east, back to the Clump. So I cut the in tuft. Now I've got a west wind blowing on the out tuft, and nothing at the in stump to catch the wind. The tree accelerates west. It drops toward Voy. Things move faster when their orbits are closer to Voy, so the tree moves east. After a while I'm in from the Clump and still moving. That's when I need the rocket. I have to cut off the other tuft, then fire the rocket to move the tree into the Clump."

The dwarf boy asked, "What then?"

"Then I sell the log for what I can get, and hope nobody else brought a log in at the same time. If there are two of us competing, we might not get enough to pay us for the work."

Most of the children looked puzzled. The dwarf asked, "What went wrong this time?"

Booce's throat closed up. *His* decision! With some relief he heard Ryllin say, "We were in a hurry. We thought we could get more water for the rocket. So we set the rocket going before the tuft dropped off. That started a fire. Wend was trying to get out of the huts when the water tank—well, it got too hot and—"

Booce jumped in, hastily. "The water tank split open. Wend got caught. Carlot and I were burned pulling her out of the steam. We were steering the log for that pond out there, and your tree moved in front of it, so it was the closest. So we made for it. And you found six of us clinging to the trunk like tocs in hair, and—and Wend was dead, and the rest of us were ready to die, I think."

The adults had all been served. The children drifted toward the cookpot. Booce ate. He'd let his stew get cold.

Likely he would never see the Clump again. It was as well. He and his family would be paupers there. He had never owned anything but *Logbearer* itself, and even that

was gone. But was it really beyond belief that these people could build another *Logbearer?*

When all the adults were eating, the children drifted
into line at the cookpot. Rather was just ahead of three
tall and dark young women, and just behind his brother
Harry.

"Take Jill's place," Rather told Harry.

"Why should I?"

"Beats me. Will you do it?"

"All right."

The favor would be repaid. Rather would take Harry's
place at the cookpot or in the treadmill, or show him a
wrestling trick; something. These things didn't need discussion. Harry stepped out of line and talked to Jill
where she was serving stew. Jill served herself and Harry
took her place.

The blond girl joined Rather. "What's that for?" she
asked; but she seemed pleased.

"I've been listening to the old ones. Now I want to
talk to the girls. Come along?" If they wouldn't talk to
a dwarf boy, maybe they'd talk to a girl.

They followed the Serjent girls as they made their
exaggeratedly careful way across the commons' wicker
floor. The refugees settled slowly into the foliage, keeping their eyes fixed on their bowls. Stew still slopped
over the edge of Carlot's bowl. "The hole's too big,"
she said.

"You just need practice. —I'm Jill, he's Rather."

"How do you eat when you're at the midpoint?"

Jill and Rather settled across from them. Rather
stripped four branchlets for chopsticks. Jill said, "I'd
take a smoked turkey along. What do you use? Bowls
with smaller holes?"

"Yes, and we carry these." Carlot produced a pair of bone sticks, ornately carved. "You're lucky. You've always got . . . spine branches?"

"These are branchlets. The spine branches are the big ones."

The third girl, Karilly, had not spoken. She was concentrating fully on her bowl.

Mishael said, "You seem to be happy."

Rather found the comment disconcerting. "What do you mean?"

"You, all of you. You've got your tree and it's all you need. Lumber from the bare end of the branch. The clothes you wear, the cloth comes from branchlet fibers, doesn't it?"

"It's foliage with the sugar washed out."

"And the dye is from berries. Water comes running down the trunk into that basin, and you eat foliage and catch meat from the sky. And there's the carm. Without the carm you'd have to build a rocket to move the tree."

"Right." Rather thought, *We don't know how to do that. The carm is all that keeps us from being savages. Is that how they see us?* "We had to leave the tree to get our lines. And the adults keep talking about earthlife crops. They couldn't bring seeds and eggs with them."

"You could buy them in the Market if you were rich enough."

Jill said, "We don't know those words. Rich? Buy?"

Carlot said, "Rich means you can have whatever you want."

"Like being Chairman?"

"No—"

Mishael took over. "Look, suppose you want earthlife seeds or pigeons or turkeys. Stet, you go to the Market

and you find what you want. Then you've got to buy it.
You need something to give the owner. Metal, maybe."
    "We don't have much metal," Rather said. "What are
the people like? Like you?"
    "Sometimes," Carlot said. "What do you mean? Tall?
Dark? We get dark and light, short and . . . well, mostly
we're about as tall as me, and the men are taller."
    "No dwarves?"
    "Oh, of course there are dwarves. In the Navy."
    "What do you think of dwarves?" He hadn't meant
to ask so directly; he hadn't realized how important the
question was to him.
    Carlot asked, "What do you think of my legs?"
    Rather blushed. "They're fine." They were hidden
anyway; Carlot was wearing the scarlet tunic and pan-
taloons of Citizens Tree.
    "One's longer than the other. My teacher's got one
leg longer than mine and one leg like yours, and it never
bothers *him*. And the Admiral's got an arm like a turkey
wishbone. I've seen him. We're all kinds, Rather."

    It was Mark's habit to eat near the cauldron, where
others might find him. Rarely did he get company. This
day he was mildly surprised when Clave and Minya settled themselves across from him. They plucked branchlets and ate. Presently Clave asked, "What do you think
of the Serjents?"
    "They're doing all right."
    "That wasn't what I meant," Clave said, while Minya
was saying, "What will they do to Citizens Tree?"
    "Oh." Mark thought it over. "Half of you came from
the in tuft of a broken tree. You were from the out tuft,
Minya. Three from Carther States. Lawri and me from
London Tree. London Tree used to raid Carther States

for copsiks. Fourteen years we've been living here, and nobody's killed anyone yet. We can live with the Serjents too."

Clave said, "Oh, we can live with them—" while Minya wondered, "What do they think of us?"

Clave snorted. "They think we're a little backward, and they'd like to talk us into going to the Clump."

Where was this leading? Mark asked, "Are you thinking they want the carm?"

"No, not that. Not impossible either . . . Have you talked to Gavving or Debby lately?"

"They don't like my company. Neither do you, Minya."

Minya ignored that. "They're trying to figure out how to build a steam rocket, starting with just the metal tube they brought back!"

"Uh-*huh.*" Mark saw the point now. "They can build us a machine that moves trees around. They can tell us why we should all go to the Clump. So you're a little nervous, Chairman? We could lose half the tribe. Lawri keeps saying there aren't enough of us *now.*"

"And what do you want, Mark?"

Mark would have wished for a wife or three, but he saw no point in telling Clave or Minya that. "I want nothing from the Clump. We're here. Twelve adults, twenty children, happy as dumbos in Citizens Tree. We shouldn't be announcing that all over the sky. Even if the Clump doesn't keep copsiks, maybe somebody out there does. Things aren't perfect here, but they're good. I wouldn't want to wind up as somebody's copsik."

Clave nodded. "That's what I'm afraid of."

Minya said, "We worked so hard to make this our home. Gavving knows how close we came to dying. How can he risk what we've got?"

"We seem to be agreed," Clave said briskly. "Well? What do we do about it?"

Lawri and Jeffer were missing dinner. Lawri had led her husband east along the branch, beyond the region of the huts. In a dark womb of foliage and branchlets, they were making babies.

Resting, relaxed for the first time in many days, Lawri plucked foliage and put it in Jeffer's mouth. He talked around it, indistinctly. "Does this remind you of being young?"

She lost her smile. "No."

He leered. "Little London Tree boys and girls never snuck off into the foliage—?"

She shook her head violently. "It isn't like that for a girl in London Tree. When boys get old enough, they don't need us. They go to the in tuft. Copsik women belong to any male citizen. Jeffer, you know that much!"

"I should. That's how Mark got Minya pregnant, before we got loose."

She changed position to lie along his length. "If he did. Any man can father a dwarf."

"Even Rather doesn't believe that."

"Bother him?"

"Yeah . . . But women had children in London Tree, didn't they? And married?"

"Yes, if we were willing to act like copsiks ourselves. How else could we compete? I would've been some man's copsik if I wanted to make babies. So I never made babies."

Jeffer looked into her eyes as if seeing her for the first time. "Are you glad I came?"

She nodded. Perhaps he couldn't see her blushing in the near-darkness.

"Why didn't you ever tell me?"

That was a stupid question. Knowing how she needed him, he'd use his advantage to win arguments! "This wasn't what we came to talk about."

"Did we come to talk?"

"What did you find on the burned tree?"

"We didn't keep any secrets. —That's right, you weren't there when Booce was telling us what we had. Well, we got a pot full of charred stuff—honey, he said—and a metal thing for cutting wood, and hooks . . . miscellaneous stuff. And the metal pipe. Everything else that burned—I've forgotten what he called it all, but it can all be replaced, except the—what did Booce call it? The sikenwire."

"I want to go to the Clump," Lawri said.

"Me too. Clave would never let both Scientists go." Jeffer kissed her cheek. "Let's wait till the last minute and then fight about it."

"What about the sikenwire?"

"We'll think of something. Do you think Clave will let us take the carm?"

" . . . No."

She felt him shrug. "Okay. We go as loggers?" She nodded (their foreheads brushed) and he said, "I'd guess Clump citizens will all look like jungle giants. We should have a few. Anthon and Debby'll come. A couple of the Serjents for guides. Defenses . . . we wouldn't want to risk the carm in the Clump, but we could take the silver suit."

"Wrong. A lot of citizens don't want anything changed. Clave thinks we're too close to the Clump already. He wants to take us farther west. Mark agrees with him."

"Yeah, I've talked to Mark. Treefodder. Without him

we can't use the silver suit . . . Lawri? Clave wants to move us west?"

"What are you thinking?"

"We don't know enough yet. Forget it. Look what you missed when you were a little girl . . . "

Whatever the disagreements now roiling through Citizens Tree, there was at least this bone of consensus: they all wanted to fly.

The Serjent girls were willing. From branchwood sticks and from cloth that was made on the looms below the branch, they made wings. Karilly worked quietly and skillfully and without words. Mishael and Carlot explained as they went, and corrected the mistakes of the children who emulated them. The work went fast. Citizens would wear their old tunics and pants for half a year longer, for cloth was not made quickly; but twenty-four wings were ready within twelve days.

Jeffer took Mishael, Minya, Gavving, and eight of the older children to the midpoint via the lift. Other children ran with zeal in the treadmill, knowing that theirs would be the next flight.

Jeffer had chosen with some care. These were the children who had not shied back from crossing to the pond on the day of the firetree. Yet there had been lines to cling to then. Today there was only bark, and some of them clung to that.

Rather flew, and was instantly in love with wings. Jill looked like she was facing death, but when wings were bound to her ankles and Rather was already in the sky, she flew. Mishael served as instructor. Jeffer learned how to kick, how to turn. When the sky was filled with winged adults and children, the rest gulped hard and loosed their hold on the bark and flew.

They were in the sky for one full circle of the sun.
The adults had their hands full herding them back to
the lift. Arth made a game of it, fleeing across the sky
until Jeffer and Gavving closed in on him and pulled his
wings off. The sun was rising up the east before they
had the children rounded up.

Then Jeffer sent the others down without him. He
told Minya, "I want to do some maintenance. Start the
lift again after you're down."

"Kendy for the State. Hello, Scientist."

"Hello, Kendy."

"How are your refugees?"

"Four of the Serjents recovered. One of the girls,
Karilly, looks okay but she doesn't talk."

"Shock. She may recover. When may I see them?"

"Kendy, I wanted to give Mishael a tour of the carm.
The Chairman vetoed that. He's afraid they'll try to steal
the carm."

"Nonsense. What do the rest of your tribe think?"

"We're split down the middle. Half of us want to go
see what's in the Clump. They've got a place . . . the
Market? . . . where we could get anything we want. The
Serjents told us about it."

"And?"

"The Chairman is scared spitless of the Clump. He
thinks we're too close now. Some of the others feel the
same way. Jayan and Jinny, of course, but Mark and
Minya too. Even the Serjents don't all want to leave.
Mark's asked Ryllin for permission to marry Karilly, and
she gave it."

"Good. How do you feel about this, Jeffer?"

"I want to see the Clump. Booce told me they've got
something they call the Library, but it sounds like a carm

autopilot. I want to scan their cassettes. Kendy, I'm doing what I can. I just took some of them flying. They like that. Maybe they'll start wondering what else they're missing."

"I remember Clave. He leads his citizens where they want to go. Call a council. Force your citizens to make a decision."

"What good does that do us?"

"If you lose the vote, you'll know where you stand. Then make Clave set a date for moving the tree. Decide what you need and who you need. Is there any chance you can talk Mark around?"

"None."

"The Serjents told you how to go about setting up a logging enterprise. Tell me."

The children slept on, exhausted by their flying. Gavving was making an early breakfast on a slice of smoked dumbo meat. He said, "The Admiralty has earthlife plants."

"We've lived without them for fourteen years," Minya said sleepily.

"We lived without lifts and the carm for longer than that. It was because we didn't *know*."

"The Admiralty has never touched us. We wouldn't know it exists, except that Booce tells us so. But you want to know more. Aren't these matters more properly discussed in council?"

Gavving looked closely at his wife. "You looked like this fourteen years ago, when you were trying to kill me. The whole tuft is like that. There hasn't been fighting like this since the War of London Tree!"

"I haven't forgotten London Tree. We made a home here. Any change is for the worse."

"Dear, are you sorry they came?"

"No!" Minya said with some force. She was fully awake now. "There aren't enough of us. We all feel that."

"Lawri the Scientist talks about the gene pool being too small—"

"We don't need that gibberish. We can *feel* we're too few. Now we have three more women, even if Ryllin is too old to host a guest, and they're *different* from us—"

"They are indeed!"

"Well, that's good!"

"Suppose they want to go home?"

"They can't," Minya said flatly.

A child stirred: Qwen. Gavving lowered his voice. "Suppose we built them another rocket. Suppose some of us wanted to go with them."

Minya stopped to sort words through her head. Gavving waited patiently. Presently she said, "They'd have to be crazy. We'd have to be crazy to let them go. Gav, have you forgotten London Tree?"

"No. I haven't forgotten Quinn Tuft, either, or Carther States. *They* didn't make citizens into copsiks, and neither did your people."

" . . . No. But we attacked you the instant we saw you."

"True."

"Do you remember being lost in the sky, clinging to a sheet of bark and dying of thirst? We faced dangers we can't even describe to our children, because they were too strange! We fought hard for Citizens Tree! And now *both* Scientists want to cross a thousand klomters to the Clump shouting 'Here we are!' Why do you want to risk what we've got?"

"They've got things to trade. They've got wings—"

"We've got wings."

"We picked jet pods, when we could find them. All this time. And it's so *simple*! Minya, what would you have given for a pair of wings, when we were stranded in the sky? Everything in the Smoke Ring can fly except men, and all it takes is spine branches and cloth! They've got a rocket that moves a tree, and it isn't stolen starstuff, it's made mostly from things they find in the Smoke Ring. What have they got in the Clump? What haven't we seen yet?"

She put bitterness in her laughter. "A thousand people and a drastic need for copsiks, maybe."

Gavving sighed. "Stet, you don't want anything changed. What should we do? They're *here*."

"Make them welcome," said Minya. "Teach them how to live in a tree. Get the girls married. Make them part of us. Gavving, Mark intends to marry Karilly."

"Karilly's sick in the mind. She isn't getting over it."

"Sure, and Mark's a dwarf. He's needed a wife, and none of us would touch him. I never did feel *sorry* for the copsik runner, but . . . but he's willing to take care of her. And I think you ought to marry one of the other girls."

Bang! Gavving stared. *This* was a woman afraid of changes? "I am married."

"Clave has two wives. Anthon did, until Ilsa died. I'm getting too old to make babies, dear."

"You don't mean—"

"No!" She hugged him. "But it won't give me a guest to carry."

"You're serious? Okay, who?"

She hesitated. Then, bravely (he thought): "I would

have thought Mishael. She's the oldest. Gavving, she showed me how to fly. I like her."

"Have you mentioned any of—"

"No, you fool! A woman doesn't ask a woman to be her wife!" And when he laughed she smiled, weakly. Gavving saw how difficult this was for her. Minya must have thought long and hard about this.

"There's room to extend the hut," she said. "We'd have another pair of hands, adult hands. The children are growing up, they're not as much fun any more—"

And if some of us marry Serjent women, we'll have their loyalty when the Admiralty comes to us! Logbearer *can't be the only ship in the sky.* Gavving wondered if his brain was working in the service of his seeds. Minya had not referred to Mishael's alien beauty.

And if we do visit the Clump, his brain ran on, *we'll need guides. Booce or Ryllin would have to go. With their daughters among us, we'd have their loyalty—*

Chapter Five

The Silver Suit

from the Admiralty cassettes, year 3 SM:

WE WERE CHOSEN FOR THIS. NO CITIZEN LEAVES
EARTH ORBIT UNTIL THE STATE HAS LEARNED HIS TOL-
ERANCE FOR FREE-FALL. ONE IN TEN THOUSAND HAVE
THE GENETIC QUIRKS TO SURVIVE MONTHS OR YEARS
OF FREE-FALL WITHOUT SOFTENING OF THE BONES,
WITHOUT FAILURE OF THE DIGESTIVE SYSTEM, WITHOUT
THE TERROR OF FALLING.

WE SERVED THE STATE BY FLYING TO THE STARS.
WHEN THE DRIVE WAS OFF WE PLAYED AT FLYING,
WHILE CRAMPED IN A SEEDER RAMSHIP WITH BARELY
ROOM TO FLAP OUR ARMS. HERE IS REAL FLIGHT.
OF *COURSE* THE SMOKE RING SEEMS AN INCREDIBLE
DREAM COME TRUE—TO *US*.

— SHARON LEVOY, ASTROGATION

"KENDY FOR THE STATE. HELLO, JEFFER. IT'S BEEN MORE than thirty days."

"I was busy. We got our council. It's over."

"How did it go?"

"We lost."

"Who sided against you?"

"Clave. Jayan and Jinny. Minya. Mark."

"Five out of ten. If you count the Serjents, twelve."

"Thirteen. Mishael's old enough, and married too, but she acts like a junior wife. She won't make Minya *or* Gavving angry. Gavving doesn't want to fight with Minya. The Serjents don't think like citizens yet. Anthon won't get into the arguments. I'm not really sure where he stands. The rest of us want to see what's out there, but we don't all want it enough. Debby loves arguing, but she's not very good at it. We didn't give Clave any trouble at all."

"You're disappointed. Don't be. Did you think that flying would bring them around? People tend to side with authority, and authority tends to protect its own power. Clave is the key. Clave has everything he wants in Citizens Tree."

"Kendy, do you see us as savages?"

"Yes. Don't take that too seriously, Scientist. I would probably see the Admiralty as savages too. I want to educate you all."

"Then educate me, Kendy. I can't just take Booce and Ryllin and go off into the sky. We—"

"You must go, Jeffer. The wealth of the L4 point is almost irrelevant. It takes many people to hold a civilization together. There are too few of you here to be more than savages!"

Jeffer didn't react to the insult, barring an increase in infrared radiation from his cheeks, neck, and ears.

"We'd need things Citizens Tree can't spare. Lawri's on my side, but we can't both go. The tree needs a Scientist. We'd have to take the carm too. We—"

"Take it."

"You're not serious. Dalton-Quinn Tree died because we couldn't move it. I won't see it happen to Citizens Tree."

"Bring the carm back when you're through with it."

Jeffer paused to think. (Kendy never did that. It was another reason to distrust Kendy: he seemed to *leap* at his answers, without forethought.) "We might lose the carm."

"You can build a steam rocket. Jeffer, I'm drifting out of range."

"We've got *one* pipe, and we need that to be loggers. Without the pipe, Citizens Tree couldn't build a steam rocket. I wouldn't have *believed* that so much could change in twenty sleeps. Kendy?" The signal dissolved in noise.

Kendy returned to his records.

For twenty State years CARM #6 had been taking pictures, not just through the CARM cameras but through the fisheye lens on the pressure suit too.

Here: the squirrel cage that ran a muscle-powered lift, and the lines leading up. Far too much footage of that.

Here: fire burned in a great bowl of soft clay. The silver suit moved around the edges of the fire, poking it, or adjusting sheets of bark that had been set as vanes to channel the wind into the burning wood. The look of the clay began to change.

Here: less fire than smoke. What looked like enough spaghetti to feed Sol system's entire State government had been spread leeward of smoldering wood. The pressure suit moved around and within the mass, turning it

and loosening the strands—vines—with the handle of
a harpoon so that the smoke would cure them. These
were the lines that now served Citizens Tree.

Ingenious. A poor way to treat State property; but
they were making use of local resources too.

The platform around the cookpot was of boards tied
with line. It had always been flimsy, and that didn't matter much in Citizens Tree's low tide; but over the years
the lines had loosened. Jayan and Jinny complained
about the way the platform lurched while they tried to
make dinner. So Rather and Carlot had been sent to
repair the platform.

Rather enjoyed the work. It called for muscle rather
than dexterity. He lifted one end of a new branchwood
plant into place. He called, "Hold this," and waited until
Carlot was set. Then he bounded down to the other end
and hoisted that.

Carlot giggled.

Rather began to tie the planks. One loop of line to
hold it, then he could work on a more elaborate mooring. He asked, "What's funny?"

"Never mind," Carlot said. "Are you going to tie this
for me?"

"I thought I'd just leave you there. You make a good
mooring, and decorative too."

"Oh." She held the planks in place with one arm while
she reached out. Her right leg was twenty ce'meters
longer than the left, and she usually reached with that.
Her long toes grasped a coil of line and pulled it to her
hands. She tied a temporary binding.

In the twenty-two sleeps since their arrival, all of the
Serjent family had become dextrous in Citizens Tree
tide.

Rather wrapped a dozen loops of line around the plank ends, then began tightening them. Heave on a loop, pull the slack around; again. From the opening beyond the treemouth the wind blew steadily, drying sweat as fast as it formed.

Carlot called from her corner. "That's as tight as I can get it."

Rather was finished at his end. He jogged down to Carlot's end (ripe copter plants buzzed up around his feet) and began pulling in slack. She'd left a good deal, of course. Carlot was agile, but not strong. He asked, "What got you giggling?"

"Just the way you scurry."

Rather's hands paused for less than a second, then continued.

"You did ask," she said defensively. "You have to go running back and forth because you can't reach as far as—"

"I know that."

"Did you make this cauldron yourselves? I wouldn't have thought you could do that here. It's big enough to boil two people at once."

"Hey, Carlot, you don't really *eat* people in the Empire, do you?"

She laughed at him. "No! There's a happyfeet tribe that's supposed to do that. But how did you make it?"

"The grownups found a glob of gray mud west of the tree. Maybe it was the middle of a pond that came apart. They brought some back. We took all the rocks in Citizens Tree and piled them in a bowl-shape, out on the branch where we couldn't do any damage. I was just a kid, but they let me help with the rocks. We plastered the mud over the rocks. We got firebark from another tree and piled it in the bowl-shape and fired it. It took

a dozen days to cool off, and then it was like that. We
did it twice—"

"You're cute," she said solemnly.

Carlot was a year older than Rather. An exotic beauty
was growing in her. Half her hair had been burned off,
and she had cut the rest to match. Now it was like a
skullcap of black wire. She was two and a half meters
tall, with long fingers and long, agile toes, and arms and
legs that could reach out forever.

Carlot affected Rather in ways he wasn't quite ready
to accept. He said, "Put it in the treemouth. When do
I get to be overwhelmingly handsome?"

"Cute is good. If I weren't your aunt—"

"Treefodder."

"Are you not my nephew?"

Rather studied his work. "I think we're done. —It's
an Empire thing, is it? You don't make babies even with
relatives of relatives? Fine, but you've got a thousand
people in the Empire! At least that's what your parents
say. We had ten adults and twenty children when you
came. I won't get much choice about who I marry."

"Who, then?"

He shrugged. "Jill's a half year older than me. All the
other girls are younger. I'd have to wait." The subject
made him uncomfortable. He looked up past the treadmill and along the trunk, to where a handful of citizens
were trying their wings. "I wish I was up there. You've
been flying all your life, haven't you?"

"I *should* be there, showing you people how to fly.
This damn fluff," Carlot said. Long sleeves were sewn
loosely to her tuftberry-scarlet tunic. She pulled one
away. The green fur along her arm had turned brown;
the patch had shrunk. "How's yours?" She touched his
cheek. The patch felt half numb and raspy; it ran from

his face down his neck and across part of his chest. "It's drying up. Ten days, it'll be cleared up."

"Too treefeeding slow."

"We just have to stay in the shade for a while. Fluff needs sunlight."

"Yeah."

From eastward, his first mother's voice called above the wind-roar. "Rather!"

Rather bounded toward Minya across the floor of braided, live-spine branches. Carlot gave him a good head start, then bounded after him. Her asymmetric legs gave her an odd run, a pleasure to watch: bound-BOUND, boundBOUND, low-flying flight. Soon she'd be faster than Jill. She reached Minya a good six meters ahead of Rather, turned and flashed a grin at him. She lost it immediately.

"—Crawled too far toward the treemouth, and now he can't—" Minya stopped and began again. "Rather! It's the children. Harry and Qwen and Gorey went crawling around in the old west rooms. Gorey went too far, and Harry and Qwen can't reach him, and he can't get out."

"You can't get to him?"

"I didn't try. Rather, we don't know how long it was before Harry came to get us."

"Oh." Harry would have tried to rescue Gorey himself, then spent more time working up the nerve to tell his mother. And Gorey was only five! "I'll need some kind of knife," he said.

"What?"

"I'm no narrower than you are, First Mother. I'm just shorter. I may have to cut through some spine branches."

———

The wind didn't reach Mark's long hair and beard. They held the sweat like two sponges. The slab of hard branchwood strapped to his back massed as much as he did. He scrambled up the slope of the treadmill, panting, trying to stay higher than Karilly and seven children. With a weight on his back, Mark was the equal of any two adults.

The treadmill was six meters across and four wide, a fragile wheel of branchwood sticks. Water running down the trunk helped to spin it, but runners were still needed.

It was getting easier; the treadmill was spinning faster. The cages must be almost passing each other. "Out!" Mark panted. "Runners, out!" Seven laughing children jumped from both sides of the treadmill, until only Mark and Karilly were left.

Above was a sudden glare as the sun passed into view.

Karilly's dark skin shone with sweat; she breathed deeply as she bounded uphill alongside him. He knew she could understand him. "Karilly. When the up cage is at the top it . . . doesn't weight anything. It takes all of us . . . to lift the down cage. Right now . . . the cages are next to each other. I can run by myself. In a little while . . . the down cage will be falling. I'll have to get out. Use the brake. Slow it down." She watched him as if she were listening. "So you jump out now."

Then he saw that she was afraid.

"Okay." He let the cage carry him around. Inverted, he scrambled down the other side. "I'm slowing it. Can you get out now?"

Karilly scrambled out.

Twenty klomters over his head, Lawri and her student flyers must be wondering what had gone wrong. Mark started the cage spinning again, letting his body do its accustomed work while his mind drifted.

Long ago and far away, there had been civilization.

London Tree had had stationary bicycles to run the elevators to the tree midpoint. and copsiks to run the bicycles. Citizens Tree was primitive. They had London Tree's carm, of course: a thing of science dating from the day men came from the stars. Otherwise they must build everything.

Mark had shown the refugees how to build a lift. Mark had wanted to make bicycles, but the Scientists had built the treadmill instead. They kept the silver suit next to the treadmill with its helmet open. Citizens at the carm could call for the lift through the radio in the suit.

Below him he could see the hollow space of the commons, and two children bounding east. The tall, dark girl was far ahead of the smaller boy, who moved in slower, shorter steps, as if tide were heavier for him.

His son. His size proved it. Mark would not have wished that on him; yet Rather would be the next Silver Man. Mark wondered if the citizens would appreciate their fortune. In the short lifetime of Citizens Tree there had been no need for an invulnerable fighter, and the silver suit had become a mere communications device.

Had it not been for one stupid, stubborn act, Mark would still be a citizen of London Tree. But he would never have seen the stars, and he would never have seen his son.

The treadmill was spinning by itself. Mark jumped out. He set the branchwood slab down. He looked up along the trunk, but he couldn't see the down cage yet. "We'll let it run for a bit."

If Karilly could talk, would she still smile at him like this? He took her hand. "Lawri wanted you with them.

You were afraid to go up, weren't you?" He had known a London Tree citizen who was afraid of falling. It was instinct gone wrong. If such a woman were born in a place like Carther States, would she be afraid all the time? Until the added terror of a fire pushed her over the edge.

"Lawri wanted me up there too. I wonder what it's like. Flying."

But the silver suit caught his eye. *No.*

His business in London Tree had been war. Were there copsik runners in the Clump? Karilly would know. "I wish you could talk. The Scientists can't marry us till you can say the words. The key word is *yes.* Will you try? *Yes.*"

"Mark!"

He jumped. "Debby?"

She called from below. "Yeah. Shall we relieve you?"

Mark swallowed his irritation. "The empty's coming down. You want to brake when the sun's at about eleven."

"We'll do it." Debby and Jeffer climbed up to join them. "Hello, Karilly."

Jeffer said, "You didn't go flying? You should try it."

"Not me. I'm the Silver Man. I fly with the silver suit. Come on, Karilly." Maybe somebody would need muscle at the cookpot platform.

The tunnels ran through the tuft like wormholes in an apple. Unused tunnels tended to close up; but passersby ate from the foliage as they passed, so the tunnels in normal use stayed open. One such tunnel ran past Rather's home.

At its west end Rather could have circled the hut with his legs. This was the oldest section. As the spine branches migrated west along the branch, eventually to be swallowed by the treemouth, enclosures tended to shrink. The newest sections were the largest.

This disappearing section had been small when new. It had housed only Gavving and Minya and the baby Rather. Other children had come, and Gavving wove new rooms eastward, faster than the treemouth could swallow them. By now there were seven children, and a new wife for Gavving, and a far bigger common room; for the Citizens Tree populace was growing too. The original rooms had disappeared into the treemouth. These that he was passing now, wicker cages alongside the tunnel, were still less than Rather's height. The children tended to claim these for their own.

Rather found a deformed door. As he crawled inside he heard Minya saying "Keep going, Carlot. Go to the common room and get my old matchet off the wall and bring it back. Hurry."

Harry, eight years old and Rather's height, was crying into Mishael's chest. Rather nodded to Mishael. "Second Mother. Which way did he go? Straight west?"

Mishael, seven years older than Carlot, had Carlot's dark, exotic beauty in fully developed form, and legs that caused even Rather to stare: long and slender and perfectly matched. She'd cut her trousers into loose shorts, odd-looking in Citizens Tree. The low roof cost her some dignity. She had to crouch. She looked uncomfortable and annoyed. "Straight on in. And he's stopped talking. I think he's mad at us."

Rather said, "You know this is no big deal, don't you? It happens all the time."

"I *don't* know. Rather, I still get the shivers in your crawling huts! Your parents just don't understand that. And poor Gorey, he is frightened."

"Sure. Carlot's coming with Mother's matchet. Send her after me. I need it to cut my way through." It didn't feel odd to be speaking thus peremptorily to his second mother. Mishael wasn't that much older than Rather; she was new to all this, and it showed.

Rather crawled west.

Memories tried to surface around him. His parents' bedroom: he'd lived in a basket, in a corner too small for a baby now. The private dining area, and ghosts of wonderful smells: were they in his nose, or in his mind? The common room, and too many strangers: he'd cried and had to be taken away. The spaces were distorted and tiny, a green-black womb. The spine branches were still growing. He tore them away with his fists; tore through an old partition.

He didn't like this. His past was too small to hold him. "Gorey!"

From west by north, Gorey yelled piercingly. He sounded more angry than frightened. How had he gotten *there*? What had been a kitchen wall had crumpled and grown half a meter thick! He must have found some way around—

"Rather?"

Carlot, behind him. He reached far back and took what was pushed into his hand. "Thanks." He pulled it to the level of his face, turned it with some difficulty and pushed the blade further.

"Can you get to him?"

"One way or another."

For years the matchet had been no more than a part of the wall. He'd never really looked at it. The handle was long and a bit too wide for his short fingers. The blade was sixty ce'meters of black metal, tinged red by time. Time and use had serrated the edge. It had once belonged to a Navy man of London Tree.

In this restricted space he must use it as a saw. He didn't try to cut the wall. He cut branchlets west of him. He turned starboard, still sawing through miscellaneous branchlets. "Gorey?"

Cautiously, doubtfully: "Rath?"

"Here. Give me your hand. Can you reach me?"

"I can't move!"

Rather saw a thrashing foot. He pulled on it experimentally. Gorey was pinned between a spine branch and a smooth dark wall: the main branch itself. He must have tried to crawl between them. Rather wriggled forward. He sawed the spine branch half through, reached farther and broke it with his hands. Gorey wriggled out and wrapped himself around his brother and clung. Presently he asked, "Are they mad?"

"Sure they're mad. How did you get here? Hide and seek?"

"Yeah. Harry said he was gonna catch me and feed me to the triunes, so I kept going. Then I was afraid the treemouth would get me and I got *really* scared."

"Harry wouldn't get that close to a triune family. You know that."

"Yeah, but I was mad."

"You'd starve to death before you reach the treemouth. Here, grab my foot and follow me."

The boy's fingers were long enough to overlap Rather's ankle. He was already taller than Rather. They crawled out, with easier going at every meter.

In the common room Rather's mothers greeted him as a hero, while Gorey was scolded and petted. Rather took it with what grace he could. He wondered if Carlot was laughing at him; but in fact she seemed to think he had done something actively dangerous.

It made him uncomfortable. He was vastly relieved when Gavving poked his head through the door. "Treadmill runners!" he called. "Rather?" And Rather was rescued.

Harry and Carlot came with them. As they neared the treemouth Gavving said, "Harry, Carlot, why don't you see if they need help with the laundry pot?"

They split off, Harry grumbling.

Rather followed his father up through the tunnels toward the treadmill. His nerves were prickling. Something odd was going on. "Father? Do they really need treadmill runners?"

"No," Gavving said without looking down.

The treadmill was at rest. Debby and Jeffer lay in the foliage nearby, eating and talking. They sat up when Gavving appeared. "Got him," Gavving said.

This must have something to do with the Serjent family; and the conference before the last sleep, from which children were barred; and the arguments that divided half the families in the tree. *Do my mothers know about this? Would they approve?* Rather asked instead, "Should we have brought Carlot?"

"No need. Rather, we have to find out something." Gavving pointed at a short, faceless fat man made of silvery metal. "Try that on."

"The silver suit?"

"Yeah. See if you can get into it."

Rather looked it over. This thing had a fearsome, quasi-scientific reputation. It was a flying fighting machine, stronger than crossbow bolts, stronger than the airlessness beyond all that was known. Rather had never before seen it with its head closed.

Jeffer instructed him. "Lift this latch. Take the head and turn it. Pull up. Turn it the other way."

The head came up on a hinge.

"This latch too. Now pull this down . . . now pull it apart . . . good."

The suit was open down the front, and empty.

"Can you get in?"

"Where's Mark?"

"Debby?"

"No problem. We relieved him and he took Karilly to the kitchen."

"Father . . . wait. Listen. I'm the only boy in the tree with two mothers and two fathers." Rather plunged on despite the sudden hurt in Gavving's face. "We've never talked about this, but I always knew . . . sooner or later I'd . . . does Mark know what you're doing with the silver suit?"

"No."

"What's it all about?" Four big adults could make him do whatever they wanted; and it didn't matter. They needed his cooperation, and he didn't know enough to give it.

Jeffer the Scientist said, "It's about seeing what's outside Citizens Tree. It's learning about the Smoke Ring, what we can use, what we need to be afraid of. Or else it's about staying savages until someone comes out of the sky to teach us the hard way."

"We're going to the Clump," Gavving said. "We'll be safer if we can take the Silver Man."

"Uh-huh. Mark doesn't want to go?"

"Right."

They watched as Rather tried to get into the suit. He

had to get his legs in first, then duck under the neck ring. He closed the sliding catches, the headpiece, the latches. The suit was loose around his belly, snug everywhere else. "It fits."

Jeffer closed the helmet on him. He rotated it left until it dropped two mi'meters, then right.

Rather was locked in a box his own size and shape. The suit smelled faintly of former occupants, of exertion and fear. He moved his arms, then his legs, against faint resistance. He turned and reached and plucked a handful of foliage . . . good. He could move. He could move like a normal man.

The air was getting stale . . . but Jeffer was already turning the helmet, lifting it. The adults were smiling at each other. Gavving said, "Okay. Get out of it."

Getting out of the silver suit was as difficult as getting in. Rather said, "Now tell me."

"Some of us are going to visit the Clump. Do you want to come with us?"

"Who's going? How long will it take?"

"Me," said Jeffer. "Gavving. Booce and Ryllin. Anthon and Debby. The Clump is all jungle giants. We need people that size."

"How does the Chairman—"

"He'll try to stop us."

"Father, I don't really like the thought of not ever coming home."

Gavving shook his head. "They'll want the carm back. They'll want us back too. Citizens Tree isn't so crowded that they can afford to lose anyone who breathes. They'll want to know what we learned. They'll want what we bring back. Half the citizens are on our side anyway; they just don't want to buck the Chairman."

"You're taking the *carm*?"

"We are." Gavving clapped him on the shoulder. "Think about it. We've got two sleeps to get ready. Whatever you decide, don't mention this to anyone, particularly your mothers."

"Father, you'd better tell it all." Rather didn't consider whether he had the right to ask. Clave wouldn't like this; Minya wouldn't like it; and if he agreed to this—it was only just coming to him—if Rather agreed, then *he* was the Silver Man.

Jeffer said, "It isn't just the wealth of the Clump Admiralty. It's—"

"Tell me *what* you're going to do."

They told him.

Chapter Six

The Appearance of Mutiny

from Discipline*'s log, year 1893 State* = *370 SM:*

MEDICAL READOUTS SHOWED THAT THE INHABIT-
ANTS OF CARM # 6 LIED TO ME. THEY REACTED
STRONGLY TO ACCUSATION OF MUTINY. I LOST MY
CHANCE TO QUESTION THEM IN DETAIL. THEY MAY
HAVE MUTINIED AGAINST LEGITIMATE HOLDERS OF THE
CARM. HEREDITY WILL TELL.

IT'S A BAD HABIT. I WILL BREAK THEM OF IT.

— SHARLS DAVIS KENDY, CHECKER

CLAVE PULLED HIMSELF OUT OF THE ELEVATOR FIRST. WINGS
were tethered next to the cage, and he pulled one free
and tied it in place along his left shin. "This was a good
idea, Gavving. Wings aren't much use in the tuft."

"Oh, we'll keep some there too. Hunters used to carry
jet pods. Wings are better. But there's no point porting

them up and down every time someone wants to fly. What are you doing?"

"Fixing this." He chopped with his matchet at his other wing. When ten ce'meters were gone, he tied the wing to his right shin. He felt distinctly lopsided.

Jeffer and Gavving were also winged now. The three flapped out toward the carm, spurning the convenient handholds the bark afforded. Clave's flight wavered, then steadied. He'd been right. This was easier on the warped muscles in his thigh.

Jeffer was first through the airlock. "Prikazyvat Voice."

The carm's deep voice said, "Ready, Jeffer the Scientist—"

A woman's voice broke in. "Jeffer, it's Lawri. I think I want to join you."

"Come on up. Bring something to eat. We'll be running the main motor for maybe two days."

"Will do. Lawri out."

"What was that about?" Clave asked.

"Lawri doesn't trust me with the carm." Jeffer laughed. "Now we refuel the beast."

Clave sighed. "Pump?"

"Right. You pump while I do a checklist. Otherwise we'll lose the pondlet when we go under thrust."

Some pumping had been done, but megatons of water still nestled against the trunk. Clave ran the hose from the carm to the pondlet. The pump was a wheel and a tube and piston, all carved from hard branchwood. Clave braced his back and arms against the bark and kicked the wheel around with his feet on the spokes. "Help would be appreciated," he grunted.

Gavving joined him.

The pump leaked. The pond didn't dwindle fast, but

it dwindled. They broke to drink thirstily, then resumed pumping. The sun had dropped from zenith to nadir—which at the midyear was not behind Voy, but north by three full degrees—when Jeffer poked his head through the airlock. "Stop! The tank's full!"

Clave tossed his head to shake some of the sweat out of his hair.

"Come inside." Jeffer ushered them forward to the front row of seats. "Strap down."

He tapped, and vertical blue dashes appeared in the panel below the window. Four clusters of four each at the corners of a square, and a larger dash in the center. He tapped the central dash.

The sound within the cabin was like the roaring of wind at the treemouth. Clave felt a featherweight of tide and knew the tree was in motion.

Jeffer told them, "We're already placed right, with the motor aimed west. We thrust eastward. That puts Citizens Tree in a wider orbit, so we slow down and drift west, away from the Clump."

Clave wondered if he wanted to watch from outside. "Is it dangerous out there?"

"Could be. You don't want to fall into the flame. Anyway, the view's better in here." Jeffer's fingers danced, and the carm window sprouted five smaller windows. "The ventral view got ruined when we fell back into the Smoke Ring—"

"Jeffer, you don't lecture this much unless you're nervous. What's wrong? We've moved the tree before."

Gavving laughed. It appeared that he had a touch of nerves too. "Remember how twitchy we were then? Merril was sure we'd break the tree apart and kill ourselves."

Clave shrugged. He went aft and braced himself in the airlock.

What remained of the pondlet stretched itself out from the trunk, then broke into one big drop and a line of little ones. The mother pond they'd robbed twenty-two sleeps ago drifted west. The sun passed Voy and began to climb. A fat triple-finned bird, dead west by a klomter or three, suddenly went into an epileptic seizure, split into three slender birds, and scattered. Clave was late in understanding what he'd seen: a triune family suddenly washed by the invisible heat of the carm's exhaust.

Clave went in and strapped down again.

He had been anticipating Lawri's arrival for some time, but the carm's roar covered her entry. He turned to see her halfway up the aisle . . . and Debby behind her. And Ryllin. And Booce and Carlot. Clave fumbled to release the buckle that bound him to the chair.

It took too long. He was between Jeffer and Gavving, with Lawri behind him. He sighed. "What's it all about?"

Jeffer's fingers danced. The board went blank. He said, "We can fight or we can talk. Or we can talk and then fight, but there's only one of you, Clave. Cripple me and Lawri flies the carm."

Call for help? If he could get past Jeffer to use Voice, the elevator would still take a day to get up . . . forget it. Voice connected to the silver suit, which Rather was now pulling headfirst through the airlock.

It would have felt good to hit somebody. Clave said, "I'll be good. Now what's it all about?"

"We're going to visit the Admiralty," Jeffer said.

Rather and Booce were moving things inside: two smoked turkeys, a huge amount of foliage, water pods.

"All of us?"

"Not you, Clave. Lawri's staying too. Citizens Tree needs a Chairman *and* a Scientist."

"How did you decide—"

There was a bit of an edge in Lawri's voice. "We knew one of us would have to stay. Now I've missed my time of blood. I'm hosting a guest. I wondered why the copsik was being so affectionate."

"You should all be staying. You're taking the carm?"

"The carm, the silver suit, and the pipe from *Logbearer*."

They all looked very serious. The background roar prompted Clave to ask, "Are you planning to set the tree moving first? Or was that a lie too?"

"We'll give you a day's thrust," Jeffer said. "No more. I won't be here to decelerate you, and I want to be able to find you again."

"With what? Would London Tree have let you keep the carm? The Admiralty won't either!"

Patiently Gavving said, "We've talked that over. We won't take the carm into the Clump. They'll never know it exists. Jeffer will hide the carm somewhere. The rest of us will go in as loggers, with Booce and Ryllin to show us how."

Clave's mind was racing. "Now listen to me. Will you listen?"

"Yes, Chairman."

"First, are you all volunteers? Rather, how did they suck you into this?"

"They can't go without the silver suit," the boy said.

"Oh, they'd go. Wouldn't you, Jeffer?"

"Yes."

"I'm going anyway," Rather said.

He didn't look like he'd change his mind. Rather didn't even bother to argue, though the boy was good at that. Clave knew how *he* would enlist a fourteen-year-old boy. Put him in the silver suit, call him the Silver Man, offer him status and adventure . . . "Carlot?"

"I'm going home," the girl said defiantly.

"Debby?" But a glance told Clave he'd lost that battle. Debby was fiercely happy. He hadn't seen her like this since the War of London Tree. "What about Anthon?"

Debby said, "I never told him. Jeffer, I did get him talking. He likes Citizens Tree just fine and he doesn't want any changes. Have you noticed how fat he's getting?"

"Too bad," Jeffer said.

Clave said, "Stet. I accept that you're going to do this. I've heard your speeches, and you've heard mine, and the treemouth can have them both. But don't you see that this will tear Citizens Tree apart? It's mutiny. Hold it! I mean it's mutiny the way you've planned it. If we don't fix that, Citizens Tree will never recover. It's got to look better than it does."

The mutineers looked at each other.

"Here's how it's got to be," said Clave. "First, I'm going. Gavving isn't. You said it and you're right. The tree needs a Chairman and it's Gavving."

Gavving said, "That's silly. You're—"

"I'm the treefeeding Chairman, and if I go the expedition is official. Besides that, I've got to see to it that you return the carm and the silver suit. The citizens would be crazy to settle for less. I hereby appoint you my Chairman Pro Tem until I return."

Coolly Gavving asked, "Anything else?"

"Yes. You don't get both Booce and Ryllin. One of them stays. There has to be some reason for the Serjents to bring us home."

"We can't do that," Ryllin said. "Booce takes care of

Logbearer. I take care of business. I do all the buying and selling. Anyone who sees one of us in the Clump will expect to see us both."

Clave was massaging the lump on his thigh. Sometimes that helped him think. *Think!* "The citizens you deal with, the . . . merchants? If they deal with Booce, what will happen?"

Ryllin said, "My husband is very good with machinery, not so good at trading. He did much better after he had the good sense to marry me. But *Logbearer* understands him, he—"

"Without you they'll get a better trade?"

"Damn right they will," Booce said bitterly. Then: "Yes, they will."

"They'll like that? They won't be too curious about where their luck comes from?"

It was Ryllin who nodded. "It's all right, love. Think of a story. They'll want to believe it."

"But we're missing three daughters too!"

"The house. They must have finished building our house by now. The girls and I are with *Logbearer* or we're at the house, wherever you're not. Maybe I'm somewhere in the Market buying furniture. That was the whole point of this last trip, we were going to—we were—" She turned away suddenly.

Emotional displays weren't needed here! Clave said, "We're not hiding anything but the silver suit and the carm. Otherwise we can tell any story we want. What's next? Gavving, Lawri, Ryllin, you back each other up when you go back to the tuft. Whoever's asking, the Chairman had to be talked into this, but I did agree, and I put the fine details in."

Rather called from aft. "Jeffer, the pipe's moored to

the hull. We've got everything else, but it all has to be moored."

"Go ahead. I'll check you later. Gavving, are you willing?"

"Treefodder. Well, it'll probably keep Minya from killing me . . . Clave, will this work? Is it enough?"

"Only if we come back. We come back with the carm and something else too. It almost doesn't matter what."

"Stet. I'm the Chairman Pro Tem."

Jeffer killed the main motor. "Somebody go out and get our lines untied."

Rather went. Debby joined Booce aft. They began mooring what remained of the cargo: two big hooks, spare clothing, sacks of undyed cloth, harpoons, crossbows.

Lawri said, "Jeffer, let me show you something." She eased up next to him and tapped at the controls, whispering. Her shoulder blocked Clave's view. Clave's mind still raced, seeking flaws . . . he was looking for holes in a harebrain net! There was no way to make mutiny smell sweet.

"Are we bringing the spitgun? No, of course not." The weapon Mark had been carrying when he was captured was now in custody of the Chairman. "Gavving, it's in the older part of my hut, what used to be the common room. If you don't have the spitgun, you're not the Chairman. Get it before anyone notices."

Rather scrambled back through the airlock. Gavving, Ryllin, and Lawri left. Jeffer let them get well clear before he pulled away on the little jets.

The tree receded. Three tiny citizens fluttered toward the elevator dock. A cage had nearly reached the dock. One of the occupants was shrieking and waving its fists.

"Somebody must have found Mark," Debby said. "Relax, Clave, we only tied him up."

"Yeah. But if I'd known a rescue party was coming . . . skip it. You'd have closed the airlock in their faces. I hope you treefeeders can find something worthwhile in the Clump. It's *my* reputation on the line now."

Section Two

THE LOGGERS

Chapter Seven

The Honey Hornets

from the Citizens Tree cassettes:

YEAR 384, DAY 1590. JEFFER, SCIENTIST. WE HAVE
DEPARTED CITIZENS TREE TO EXPLORE THE FOURTH LA-
GRANGE POINT, WITH ATTENTION TO RESOURCES AND
POPULATION. THE MISSION AS OUTLINED IS REVISED AS
FOLLOWS: CHAIRMAN CLAVE NOW LEADS. THIS EXPE-
DITION HAS BECOME AN APPROVED ACTIVITY OF CITI-
ZENS TREE. I NOW TURN THE LOG OVER TO CHAIRMAN
CLAVE.

CLAVE, CHAIRMAN. CREW CONSISTS OF JEFFER AS
SCIENTIST AND CAPTAIN, CITIZENS DEBBY AND
RATHER, BOOCE AND CARLOT SERJENT AS GUIDES,
AND MYSELF. PRIORITY AT ALL TIMES WILL GO TO PRO-
TECTING THE CARM AND OTHER VITAL PROPERTY OF
CITIZENS TREE. NO KNOWLEDGE IS WORTH GAINING
UNLESS IT CAN BE REPORTED TO CITIZENS TREE.

CARLOT WAS WATCHING OVER THEIR SHOULDERS. "YOU use—"

"Prikazyvat End log," said Jeffer.

"—the same dates we do?"

"Why not?"

"Well, how do you know?" Carlot demanded. "Years, you just watch for the sun to go behind Voy, but what about days? We sleep a couple of days out of five, right? But maybe you lose count—"

"Who cares?" Clave said. "Who knows how many days there are in a year? It depends on where you are."

Jeffer summoned up numbers on the panel. "The carm logs a standard day, about four and a half per sleep. We used to keep marks on sticks in the Scientist's hut. How do you keep time?"

Carlot said, "The Admiralty posts the time."

Booce laughed. "They must get it the same way! The Library looks a lot like this panel, Jeffer. Like somebody ripped out this part of the carm."

"Keys like this too?"

"I wasn't close enough to see. They don't let ordinary crew near it. Let's see . . . in the crossyear ceremony Radyo Mattson did the talking, but there was a Navy officer standing in front of the Library, and his hands moved . . . "

And Kendy watched them all.

The carm autopilot heard everything. Every ten hours and a little, it squirted its records at *Discipline*. Kendy sorted the conversations for what he could use.

Two CARM autopilots separated for five hundred and thirty-two years and eleven months were both keeping Smoke Ring time, with *Discipline*'s arrival set at zero. Interesting. The mutineers must have adjusted them after it was certain that they would never return. They had severed relations with the past, with Kendy, with Earth, with the State itself.

Yet they used *mutiny* as an obscenity. Puzzling.

The carm flew east, airspeed seventy-one kph, partially fueled, carrying water that would become fuel. Solar collector efficiency was running at fifty-two percent, the collectors partially shadowed by the old pipe moored to the hull.

It was a liquid oxygen pipe ripped from a CARM. Many CARMs must have been dismantled when they stopped working. The Admiralty "Library" was certainly the control panel from a ruined CARM; but was it still functional?

The cabin interior was offensively dirty. Kendy detected traces of old meals eaten aboard; feathers and bird shit from the turkey roundup ten years back; the black clay that had returned the same trip; and mud repeatedly expelled from the water tank. Dirt was not dangerous, only aesthetically distressing. Kendy foresaw no problems other than those of microsociology.

He was on course.

Humankind was scattered. No telling how far they had spread through the Smoke Ring. They had settled cotton-candy jungles and the tufts of integral trees; he knew of four tiny civilizations outside the L4 point. But the Admiralty seemed to be the densest gathering, the most numerous, the best organized: the political entity most suited to become the heart of an expanding empire.

It would not resemble the State at first. Conditions were fantastically different. Never mind. Give them communications, gather them into one political group. Then shape it.

He must know more. Hearsay from a family of wandering loggers wasn't good enough. The Admiralty "Library," *that* would tell him how to proceed next . . . but he already knew that he must eventually contact the officers themselves.

Somehow the CARM must be moved into the Clump.

Jeffer had seemed to have matters well in hand. The effects of mutiny on Citizens Tree did not concern Kendy . . . but Clave had ended a mutiny by joining it! Now he must persuade Jeffer and Clave both. But Kendy couldn't talk to Clave. Exposing Jeffer's secret would lose Jeffer's trust.

It was precisely the kind of problem a Checker enjoyed most.

For now Kendy watched six savages in a recording made over the past ten hours. They had much to teach him.

Booce speaking: "We own—owned our own ship. I suppose that made us richer than most. I inherited *Logbearer* from my father, and I made my first trips with him. Ryllin was another logger's daughter, and she was used to the life. We had four daughters and a few lost ones out of maybe twenty pregnancies, all while hauling logs. I've become a good maternity doctor . . . " The cassette ended.

Men had changed in the Smoke Ring.

Pregnancy was easy in low gravity. Women became pregnant many times during their lifetimes.

Infant mortality ("lost ones") was high, perhaps around sixty percent; the natives seemed to take it for granted. *Discipline* had carried no diseases. Yet the growth of bones and organs was altered by altered gravity. Some children could not digest food. Some grew strangely, until their kidneys or livers or hearts or intestines would no longer work because of their shape.

The environment was user-friendly for those who survived childhood. Kendy's citizens came in odd shapes. Kendy caught a reference to Merril Quinn and learned that she had died six years ago, in early middle age. Merril had had *no* legs. She had fought against London Tree, and not as a cripple.

Distorted children had wandered through the CARM to be photographed. Ryllin Serjent had an awesomely long neck, quite lovely and graceful and fragile looking. Carlot's legs . . . Kendy wished he could see her walk or run.

They matured more slowly. Carlot claimed fourteen and a half years; she would be twenty by Earth's reckoning. But she looked no more than fifteen.

Men had not evolved for the Smoke Ring. Infant mortality must have been ghastly among the original crew. Five hundred years of natural selection was taking care of that. As with the cats a few generations back: the near future should see an impressive population explosion.

Kendy would guide the civilization that resulted. He had been right to move *now*.

The CARM was coming back into range. Kendy's telescope array picked it up falling east and out, slowing.

In present time, Booce and Carlot and Rather were on watch while the others slept. The CARM moved through a patch of thin fog. Fog didn't block the CARM's senses. Kendy noticed the anomoly some time before the crew did.

He saw birds of unfamiliar type. They had lungs (the CARM's sonar could see the triple cavity), but they had retained part of what must once have been an exoskeleton: an oval of hard sky-blue shell covered one side. Fourteen of these birds, each about the mass of a boar pig, were strung in a line across the sky. They were folded into themselves, fins and wings and heads folded against that oval of shell. Sky-blue blobs, cool in infrared, comatose or dead.

Booce had noticed now. He shook Jeffer awake. "A whole flock of dead birds. What killed them?"

"Nothing that can touch us with the airlock closed." Jeffer's fingers danced. "Outside air's okay, nothing poisonous. Well, *treefodder!*"

"What?"

"The temperature. It's *cold* out there."

Kendy had already found the source of the cold.

The present-time transmission showed Jeffer easing the CARM alongside one of the big birds. The other crew were in and around the airlock. Debby sent a tethered crossbow bolt into the bird. It twitched. She loosed another . . .

. . . while Kendy set a blinking light around the image of the pond.

Only Jeffer was there to see it. He said softly, "Stet."

They had pulled the bird aboard. Clave said, "Well, it's dead now."

"I've got something," Jeffer said. "Clave, there's a pond in that dense cloud. Do you see anything odd about it?"

"No life around it. That cloud's awfully thick for being so small. What does it mean?"

"I don't know."

Ice. The pond was a core of foamy ice within a shell of meltwater. Ice was rare within the Smoke Ring. The pond was huge now, several hundred thousand tons, but Kendy guessed that it had been bigger yet. A tremendous pond must have been flung out of the Smoke Ring by a gravity-assist from Gold. In the near-vacuum of the gas torus it would have boiled and frozen at the same

time, and later fallen back, reduced by evaporation, reduced further by reentry heat. Now it cooled the sky
around it as it melted. Kendy could hear the *pings* as
bubbles of near-vacuum crumpled within the ice core.

"I don't like it here," Booce said. "It's too strange."

"Your wish is granted. Strap the bird down and take
your seats." Jeffer waited while they did that, then fired
the aft attitude jets. The carm surged away.

Carlot pointed into the aft view. "Look!"

The shieldbirds tumbled in the carm's hot wake. One
by one they fluttered, then spread a rainbow of wings
and tails and fluffy feathers. They basked in the heat,
catching as much of it as they could. Now their shells
were no bigger in proportion than a warrior's shield. As
Discipline moved out of range, the birds were lining up
and flying west, putting distance between themselves
and the melting glacier.

"There's no point picking out a tree till you've got
honey," Booce said. "You can find a tree a hundred
klomters from the Clump and still go half a thousand
klomters to find your sting jungle."

Their catch was moored by cargo hooks, divested of
skin and guts and some of the scarlet meat. Booce was
holding raw bird flesh sliced thin and rolled around a
stalk of lemon fern. He used it to point into the dorsal
view. "And *that* is a sting jungle. The green dot, straight
out."

"Stet." Jeffer tapped attitude jets to life. The carm
turned. Carlot squeaked and grabbed Rather, startling
him awake. Booce dropped his meal to snatch at a seat
back.

Jeffer hid a grin. These sophisticated Admiralty folk
found the carm as unsettling as Jeffer's own citizens did.

He aimed the carm east of Booce's green dot. East takes you out . . . "Half a day and we'll have honey. What else do we need?"

"Some way to collect it," Booce answered.

"We'll put Rather in the silver suit. No treefeeding insect will sting him through that!"

"Right. Better than armor."

"Tell us about the Admiralty," Clave said.

Booce closed his eyes to think. Then: "You're lonely out here. There's too much space. Everything is dense in the Clump. Think of a seed pod, and think of the Admiralty as the shell. There are more people in the Market alone, any time of day or night, than you've ever seen.

"We pull the logs back to the Clump over the course of a year or two, and we arrange an auction in the Market. Twice we've been attacked by happyfeet bandits. Once we got back just as another log was being docked, and we got half what we expected for the wood. But over the years we put enough money together to buy my retailer's license. This was going to be our last trip. We were going to settle in the Clump, and I'd work the wood myself and sell finished planks and burl, while Ryllin set about finding good husbands for our daughters. That was the point: they're reaching that age . . . "

Clave asked, "Can we really make the Admiralty believe we're loggers?"

"We'll *be* loggers," Booce said. "Rebuilding *Logbearer*'s no problem. We should have more weapons in case happyfeet come by, and it all has to look like Admiralty gear . . . and we still won't look like a typical logging family. But we don't have to, because I've got my retailer's license."

"What does that mean?"

"It means we don't have to sell the log straight off. The Navy ships will escort us in and give us a berth. I can set up shop in the Market and sell wood, and hire anyone I like; which means that the rest of you can be workers hired off a happyfeet jungle, or bought as copsiks. Some of the happyfeet keep copsiks. The Admiralty doesn't, so you'd be free if I bought you."

"Free, but not citizens."

"Right."

"Why can't you have hired us off a tree?"

Booce thought about it, and smiled. "You have a gift, Clave. Tell as much of the truth as possible. Debby, you're from Carther States, directly. You were stranded in the sky, you made your way to a tree, and now you want to live in a jungle again. Okay, Debby?"

Debby's lips were moving as she silently repeated the details. "Stet."

"We'll have to say Citizens Tree is close to the Clump. Otherwise we got home too fast, and we'd have to explain about the carm."

Clave nodded. "So then we sell the log. How?"

"Set up in the Market and announce an auction. Buy your earthlife seeds with the money and go home. The Admiralty'll take half in taxes—"

Clave exclaimed, "Half?"

Jeffer said, "Taxes?"

"Taxes," Booce said, "is the money the Admiralty takes to run itself. Everybody pays, but the rich pay more. A good log is wealth. For the price of the carm you could be very rich indeed."

"The carm is what makes us what we are. We won't risk that," Clave said.

"Then don't take it into the Clump. The Navy won't

want something that powerful floating around. They'll pay well, but they'll buy it whether or not you're selling."

Jeffer tapped the forward jets awake. They were pulling near the sting jungle.

Certain mooring loops fit the silver suit too perfectly, as if it were their specific purpose. Four sets. For four suits?

Jeffer pulled it loose. "The silver suit is yours, Rather. I'm going to teach you everything about it."

Rather had seen the silver suit as a mark of rank. He hadn't thought of it as an obligation. "Did Mark show you how to work it?"

"I've watched him. Lift this latch. Take the head and turn it till it stops. Pull up. Turn it the other way. Lift. Now this latch. Now pull this down . . . pull it apart . . . good."

The suit looked like the flayed skin of a dwarf.

Legs first, then arms. Duck under the neck ring. Rather closed the sliding catches, the latches. "Do I have to close the head?"

"Cover yourself. You don't want to be stung," Booce said. "Those little mutineers can sting a moby to death."

Rather closed the headpiece. He said, "The air's getting stale."

They couldn't hear him. He couldn't really suffocate this fast, could he?

Jeffer lifted the headpiece. "*Listen* first. Put your hand here." He guided Rather's fingers to a row of square buttons on the outside of the neck ring. He pushed one (colored lights lit below Rather's chin), and another (air jetted inward from all around the neck ring). He used Rather's fingertip to roll a small wheel back and forth (the air jets grew weaker, then stronger). "Close the helmet."

Rather did as Jeffer had shown him. Air from the neck ring hissed around his head.

Clave was saying something inaudible. Jeffer guided Rather's fingertip to another tiny wheel, and suddenly Clave's voice was a roar. "—use up the air? Does that thing have to be closed? We're not going back out of the Smoke Ring again, are we?"

"Let's hope not. Rather, you're leaking. Close that flap at your chest. The way Booce talks about honey hornets, you don't want anything open."

Rather felt it out, then used finger pressure to close a snap he'd missed.

Now he was being shown little wheels on his chest. He moved the left one experimentally. His left foot kicked upward and he was wheeling in the air, banging his head and elbow, snatching for a mooring loop while his other hand rolled the wheel back to zero. He banged both knees before he could stop his spin.

Clave and Debbie were helpless with laughter. Jeffer had jumped clear. "Leave those alone while you're inside! You fly with those. Now I'm going to walk you out the airlock. Play around with the jets. If you get in trouble we'll come after you."

Rather braced himself in the airlock, feeling imprisoned. The sting jungle was a fat, fluffy ring half a klomter across, dark green around the outside, slowly rotating. The inner rim flamed in orange and scarlet. Rather, looking out through the airlock, saw motion there like jittery fog.

Clave and Booce eased him into the sky.

They couldn't have any idea what the boy was going

through, Kendy thought. How would they? None could fly the ancient pressure suit. Rather would have to be an agoraphile and an acrophile both.

Kendy had explained the pressure suit with diagrams and pointers; but had he shown Jeffer how to replenish the suit's oxygen and fuel? Replay that memory . . . no. Do that soon, if it wasn't already too late. What Kendy was watching was already two hours past.

But the CARM was in range again, and in present time the boy was aboard, and out of the suit, and still alive. Kendy kept the tape running:

Debby and Clave hovered a safe distance away. The boy floundered. He was all over the sky, spinning, faster . . . slower, tilting himself back and sideways to slow the spin . . . learning to move arms and legs to change his attitude. He found the throttle dials and turned both jets to minimum. He circled the CARM, then arced off toward the green doughnut that Booce had made his target.

Jeffer spoke through the suit radio. "Not yet, Rather. Come back. You don't have anything to carry the, the, Booce?"

"Honey."

"The honey. Booce, what does he need?"

"That's what the sacks are for."

Rather oriented toward the carm, increased the thrust, doubled on himself for two seconds, then arched backward as he fell toward the airlock. Fir sprayed from his ankles, arcing forward. Nice, Kendy thought. Of course he wasn't a complete novice. He'd flown with those giant swim-fin fans.

The boy left his helmet open (but didn't turn off the air jets!). Debby began strapping twelve coarse sacks to his back, got yelled at, and strapped them to his chest instead, where he could reach them. She used several loops of line. The savages were never without line, Kendy recalled. Good practice in a free-fall environment.

In present time Rather was leaving the airlock again, and the signal was fading. Kendy waited.

The great green torus became landscape as Rather came near. It was darker than integral tree foliage, and fluffy, finely divided to catch as much sunlight as possible. Scarlet and orange peeked over the curve, becoming clearer. Orange horn shapes, rocket-nostril shapes, quite pretty. Thousands of them.

The jittering mist cleared too: not steam roiled by wind, but myriads of particles swirling round the blossoms, dipping in and out. Now the motes abandoned the horn shapes and streamed toward Rather.

They were all around him, a humming black cloud of rage.

"Scientist? I'm in the center. I can hardly see. The honey hornets are—"

"Look for red," said Booce's voice.

Orange and scarlet. Orange horns the size of drinking gourds, and scarlet of another shape. Rather jetted closer.

The honey hornets came with him. Thousands of thumb-sized birds: tiny harpoon for a nose, invisible blur of wing behind. He could hear the angry buzz through his helmet. "I've got a red thing . . . Booce, it's a kind of a sloppy polyhedron half a meter through, covered with lots of little triangle holes. It's growing between these horn shapes."

"Those are flowers. It didn't grow there, it's attached. Did you take a knife?"

"No. Wait a breath, there's a matchet on my leg. It must be Mark's."

"Cut the honeypod loose and put the sack around it. Tie the neck shut."

Rather swung the matchet behind the scarlet polyhedron. The silver suit made all movements stiff. Presently the honeypod was floating loose. Rather pulled a sack free, opened the mouth, and swept it around the honeypod.

"Got it? Tie the bag *shut*. Done?"

"Done. There's sticky red stuff all over my gloves."

"Stet. Now keep doing that till you run out of sacks. Don't lick the honey."

"With my helmet closed?"

"Don't *ever* lick honey. It's suicide."

Chapter Eight

The Honey Track

from the Citizens Tree cassettes, year 1426 State:

GOLDBLATT'S WORLD

GOLDBLATT'S WORLD MAY HAVE BEGUN LIFE AS A
NEPTUNE-LIKE BODY IN THE COMET CLOUD AROUND
THE PAIRED STARS. IN GOLDBLATT'S SCENARIO, THE
BODY WAS CAPTURED SOME MILLIONS OF YEARS AFTER
THE SUPERNOVA EVENT. THE COLLAPSING CORE OF THE
SUPERNOVA, SPEWING ITS OUTER ENVELOPE ASYM-
METRICALLY DUE TO A TRAPPED MAGNETIC FIELD, MAY
HAVE PICKED UP A SKEW VELOCITY THAT NEARLY
MATCHED THE VELOCITY OF THE PROTO-NEPTUNE.
ROBBED OF ITS ORBITAL VELOCITY, GOLDBLATT'S
WORLD WOULD FALL ALONG A DRASTICALLY ECCENTRIC
ORBIT, PASSING VERY NEAR LEVOY'S STAR. EXTREME
ROCHE TIDES WOULD WARP THE ORBIT INTO A CIRCLE
WITHIN A FEW SCORES OF PASSES.

IT SEEMS LIKELY THAT GOLDBLATT'S WORLD'S ORBIT AND THE ASSOCIATED GAS TORUS HAVE BEEN CONTRACTING FOR ALL OF THEIR BILLION YEARS. MEANWHILE LEVOY'S STAR HAS BEEN COOLING—SINCE NEUTRON STARS NO LONGER UNDERGO FUSION—MAINTAINING A RELATIVELY STABLE BALANCE OF TEMPERATURE IN THE SMOKE RING.

NOTE THAT THE ROCHE LIMIT IS NEVER AN ABSOLUTE. IT VARIES AS THE DENSITY OF THE ORBITING BODY. A GASBALL WORLD MAY BE WITHIN ITS ROCHE LIMIT, AND THIS ONE PROBABLY WAS. BUT THE ROCK-AND-METAL CORE IS DENSE. GOLDBLATT'S WORLD WOULD HAVE BEEN WELL OUTSIDE ITS ROCHE LIMIT AFTER THE GASBALL LOST SOME OF ITS GAS AND THE ECCENTRIC ORBIT BECAME MORE CIRCULAR.

THE PLANET IS NOW NO MORE THAN TWO AND A HALF TIMES THE MASS OF EARTH . . .

—SAM GOLDBLATT, PLANETOLOGIST

"YOU SEE THE PROBLEM? TOO MUCH OF IT IS GIBBERISH," Jeffer told the children. Rather and Carlot were nodding, but their eyes were glassy. "You can look up some of the words. You can guess a little. Goldblatt's World is Gold. There's a file on Earth and Neptune and the rest of the solar system, but it's hard going. Roche tides, Roche Limit—that seems to be a balance point between tide and some other force, maybe the same force that changes your orbit if you pass too close to Gold. Fusion is power: it makes the Sun burn, and *Discipline* ran on fusion. Oort cloud, magnetic field, supernova—Lawri and I never figured those out."

He turned to Booce. "The kids need this, but I hate to make you sit through it again at your age—"

Booce's eyes were glassy too. "No, no, no. This is all new to me."

"Didn't you have classes? There's the Library—"

"For officer's kids only," Booce said brusquely. "Go on with this. What's eccentric?"

"That's a round path that isn't a circle. It goes out and in. Booce, am I committing a crime if I teach you and Carlot these things?"

"But I want to learn!"

"Shush, Carlot. It's never come up before," Booce said. "You're not showing us the Library, after all."

Carlot demanded, "Scientist, what's the point in stopping *now*?"

Jeffer laughed. He tapped, and the window was restored. The Clump was nearer now, and a score of parallel dashes lay across the carm's path. "You're right, Carlot, but the lesson's over anyway. We're getting too close."

Debby answered with a raspberry.

"Booce?" Jeffer said. "Any special favorites?"

"The smallest, I'd think, but let's have a better look." Booce disengaged his seat tethers and moved aft. "Jeffer, would you open those doors?"

"Will do." He did. "Booce, don't you trust the windows?"

"I prefer my eyes. Swing us around, will you?" He braced himself in the airlock. Others of the crew had followed him.

Jeffer began the maneuver. In the forward view, now moving into the port view, one of the trees had begun blinking: a green halo going on, off, on, off.

Nobody was near. Jeffer whispered, "Why?"

Now a point far in along the trunk was doing the blinking. Then that stopped—

An arm stabbed past Jeffer's ear, and he had to repress a shriek. "There," Booce said, pointing at one of the trees. "Thirty klomters, and it seems healthy."

"What about this one, Booce?" Jeffer tapped the tree that had blinked at him.

"Nothing wrong with it. It's bigger, twice the mass. Take us longer to get it to the Market, but of course there'd be more wood too, and there's the carm . . . Why that one?"

"A hunch. You've got no objection?"

Now Clave was behind him too. "Jeffer, are you playing dominance games?"

"I—"

"I'm the Chairman, you captain the carm, Booce is the logger. Booce chooses the tree."

Jeffer repressed a sigh. "Yes, Chairman. Booce?"

Booce pointed to Jeffer's selection. "That one."

Ten klomters above the tuft, the wood of the trunk had grown to enclose a node of foreign matter. Jeffer saw Booce catch his daughter's eye as Carlot was about to speak. She held her silence.

At the tree midpoint Jeffer nosed the carm against the trunk. He ran the attitude jets while his crew pounded spikes into the bark to mark a rectangle the size of the carm's bow. The carm drifted while they chopped out a dock with matchets.

Even on this younger tree, the bark was a meter thick. They made life easier for themselves by chopping along cracks. The five of them lifting together could rip great mattresses of bark away from the wood beneath, then saw off sections. Booce and Carlot used the saw, then let others take over until they got the hang of it.

Booce and Carlot rejoined Jeffer in the carm. Booce said, "They seem to be doing all right."

"But it's *scarred*," Carlot objected.

"And how much wood will that cost us?"

She shrugged. "Five percent? And weren't we in a hurry to get home?"

Booce was smiling. "Exactly. Jeffer, why this tree?"

"You'll be painting a line of honey down the trunk, stet? Have a look at that scar."

"Can you tell me what I'm supposed to find?"

"No, I can't."

"Jeffer the Scientist, Citizens Tree gave us shelter and a place among you. We're grateful. I will not quarrel with any decision you make. You won't need to test it again."

Jeffer could feel his ears and cheeks burning. "If that scar isn't more interesting than you expect, you can count on it that I won't make a fool of myself twice. Stet?"

"Stet. I won't raise this subject with the Chairman, ever."

"You are kind. What's next?"

"The honey line."

In the cabin the roar of the main drive was like a great beast heard far away; but outside the airlock the roar was deafening. A translucent blue flame reached out from the carm's main rocket nostril. Warmth backwashed against the bark.

Carlot's eyes were big with fear. Rather pulled at her arm to set her kicking toward the in tuft, and followed, with Booce following him.

They stopped where the noise had decreased somewhat. The rough bark itself absorbed sound. Booce screamed, "That noise is beyond belief! What is that damn carm, a ship from the stars?"

"Jeffer says it rode here on the starship. My father never saw *Discipline*." What Rather said would be true whoever his father was. "But he's seen the stars. They're real."

"I'm afraid of it. I admit it. Look, the noise is scaring the bugs out of the bark! Let's get to work."

Booce used a branchwood matchet to open a hole in one of the honeypots. The interior was partitioned; the cells held red, sticky honey. Booce used the blade to paint it on the bark.

"You'll find a few hornets still in there," he told Rather. "They try to sting through the sack if you give them a few days to get restless, and then they die. But don't count on it. Don't let one get at you. Now you paint dabs a couple of meters apart. Closer, you waste honey. Farther apart, the bugs lose their way."

Rather had thought he was a climber, but this was different. He had problems keeping up. He was almost lost among the sacks he was carrying. Booce and Carlot climbed head down; they would have left him behind if Booce had not been stopping to paint the trunk.

They took a breather when the sun was at nadir and the shadows had become confusing. The sun was passing closer to Voy as the year waned.

A day later they took a longer rest. "This is the part I like best," Booce said. "We're usually in too much of a hurry. This time your carm is already pushing us home. We can take our time, do what we like!"

"Like what?"

"I'll show you as we go." Booce began tearing up sheets of bark greater than a man, mooring them edgewise against the bare wood. When he had them arrayed he set them alight.

The smoke tended to stay where it formed. Booce moored a four-kigram slab of shellbird meat in the cloud. They broiled smaller steaks on their matchets, closer to the fire, and ate them still hot.

"The smoked meat will keep till we're down," Booce said. "But there are other things on the trunk. You've never climbed?"

"When we were children we did a little climbing, but just on the lower trunk. We weren't supposed to go more than a klomter up. If you fell, the foliage would catch you. Any higher, we rode the elevator."

They slept carefully tethered in cracks in the bark. Sometimes, for moments, the roar of the carm could be heard above the wind. A dark cloud had formed above them and was gradually drifting down.

The bugs of the tree had found the honey.

They breakfasted on smoked bird. Then Carlot did the painting while Booce carried the food.

The sun circled them, once and again. Always they stopped when the shadows were pointing straight out. Water was beginning to flow sluggishly in alongside their path. "Bugs like it damp," Booce said. "The bark's wet enough for them around the midpoint, but not lower down. You have to paint down the east side, alongside the waterfall, or they won't come. Also the trunk blocks the wind. You don't want the bugs blown away."

There was fan fungus like so many pallid hands reaching from the bark. Carlot showed Rather how to tear the red fringe off before eating the white interior. It was bland, almost tasteless, but went well enough with the strongly flavored smoked meat.

With lunch came entertainment: a gust of roses on
the wind. The stems were four meters long. Dark-red
blossoms fragile as tissue paper pointed straight toward
Voy, soaking up blue Voy-light. Rather had never seen
the like. He and Carlot watched the roses blowing east
until they were out of sight.

Rather took his turn painting. Booce kept a close
watch, but it seemed simple enough. A dab the size of
a baby's hand; the next dab two meters lower.

A dark cloud flowed after them down the trunk.

The wind grew stronger, though the trunk blocked
most of it. The growing tide made climbing easier for
Rather. The water flowed more strongly. It was cleaner
than pond water, cleaner than the water that reached
the basin in the commons. It tasted wonderful, and
painting was hard, thirsty work.

In two days, Rather's arm was one long cramp.

He was too tired to help with dinner. Booce managed
alone. He found shelled things hiding in the bark and
pulled them loose. Roasted, their white flesh made a
fine meal.

Again they wedged themselves along a wide crack in
the bark, with Carlot between the men. There were dangers on the trunk.

Rather's aches kept him awake. He presently noticed
Carlot's feet stirring restlessly. "Carlot?"

He would not have spoken twice, but she answered
at once. "Can't sleep?"

"No. My father told me about climbing *up* a tree.
When they got to the top the tree came apart."

"That's one reason we don't just chop off the tuft or
burn it loose. This is easier, but it also gets the bugs
away from the midpoint. When the tree dies, they're
not there to eat it apart."

"How do you get rid of the out tuft?"

"Oh, some of the bugs won't follow the honey. They'll be breeding while we travel. When we get close to the Clump we'll paint another trail out."

"Why are you awake?"

"Tide. I have trouble sleeping in tide." But her voice trailed off raggedly. He stopped talking, and presently slept.

After breakfast Booce said, "There's something I want to see on the west side of the trunk. Leave the gear here."

Climbing was easy if you didn't have to paint too. In less than a day they had half circled the trunk. Above them by a quarter klomter, the bark bulged like a wave surging across a pond. They climbed toward that.

"Jeffer wanted us to look at this," Booce told them. "Something must have hit the trunk while it was younger. The wood's grown around it."

The wood bulged to hide it like some secret treasure. Rather was almost inside the crater before he could see anything. Carlot, ahead of him, had stopped. Booce was at his shoulder. Rather heard him gasp.

Carlot said, "Metal!"

"I must apologize to Jeffer," Booce said. "Metal indeed! The tree may consider it poisonous; see how reluctant the wood is to touch it! But the Admiralty won't think so."

Rather asked, "We want this?"

"We do. Secret auction, I think." Booce was deep into the crater, running his hands over the reddish-black surface of the metal. "Six or eight thousand kilos. No point in trying to move it. We'll have to show it to the Navy anyway, unless . . . hmm."

Carlot looked at her father. "We don't want to attract attention."

"Exactly. I have to think about this. Well, my merry crew, I think we've earned a holiday."

They climbed back around the trunk, taking their time. Booce knew just where to find the shelled burrowers. After lunch they spent a day tethered in the now strongly running waterfall, first washing each other and squeezing honey out of their clothing, then wrestling. They still got some painting in before sleeptime.

In twenty days they had reached the wild tuft.

Rather had never appreciated foliage before. It had surrounded him all his life. He gorged, savoring the taste and texture. "You love it too," he observed. "Carlot, Booce, why don't you live in a tree?"

"Oh, there's foliage in the Clump too," Carlot said. "All kinds. Rather, I can't wait to show you!"

They slept in foliage. Rather slept like a dead man, from exhaustion and the familiar sensation of sleeping under tide, in a womb of soft foliage. He woke early, feeling wonderful.

Carlot lay not far from her father. Her face was grief-stricken. She thrashed in slow motion, unconsciously trying to hold herself against the tide.

Rather took her hand, gently. "Hey. Nightmare?"

Her eyes opened. "Oh. Rather. I was trying to get to Wend. She was screaming and trying to fly with just her bare feet—" She shook her head violently and sat up. "Something I have to tell you."

"Okay."

"When we were swimming. Father noticed you were up."

"Up? Oh, *up*. You're very pretty," Rather said a little awkwardly.

"We can't make babies."

"We can't? Hey, the jungle giants and the London Tree citizens didn't have any trouble. I'm a dwarf, but—"

Carlot laughed. "*Father* says we can't. He wants me to marry another logger. I think he wants it to be Raff Belmy, from *Woodsman*, but definitely another logger. I thought I'd better say something before . . . well, before you got to thinking."

"Thinking. Well, it's too late, then."

"It's all right, then?"

"Sure. Go back to sleep." The truth was that Rather was almost relieved. Carlot with her clothes off made his head swim and his blood boil: an uncomfortable feeling.

And Booce didn't want his daughter to love a dwarf savage. Should he resent that? Somehow he didn't.

Breakfast was more foliage. Then Booce gave Rather the matchet. "Pry the bark off. We want a complete ring of bare wood half a meter across. We'll paint along behind you."

Three and a half days later he was halfway around. The bark was soft, easy to pry loose, but the trunk must have been a good two klomters in circumference. They returned to the wild tuft to sleep and eat. Rather was one vast ache, but it still felt good to be sleeping in tide, in foliage.

After breakfast Rather was still on the matchet. The Serjents seemed to share Citizens Tree's faith in a dwarf's superior strength. He finished the job before they slept again. They were ahead of schedule. Jeffer would not bring the carm down for them for another six or seven days.

From the base of the trunk they watched a moby attack the bugs descending along the honey track. Mobies normally skimmed clouds of bugs from the sky for their food. This was a tremendous creature, mostly mouth and fins, riding the wind toward the trunk and the bugswarm at a hundred meters per breath. It realized its mistake just in time. It thrashed madly, gaping, irresistibly comical, as the wind hurled it toward the tree. Its flank smashed loose a shower of bark as it passed.

The bugs descended like a cloud of charcoal dust. They reached the ring of painted bare wood and spread to north and south. The cloud condensed, growing darker, swarming a few ce'meters out from the bark.

"Carlot. Do you like it on the tree?"

She nodded, watching the bugs.

"Booce? I've watched you. You like it here."

"I love it."

"Then how can you kill trees?"

Booce shrugged. "There are plenty of trees."

Chapter Nine

The Rocket

from Logbearer's *log, Captain Booce Serjent speaking:*

YEAR 384, DAY 1280. TEN DEGREES WEST OF THE CLUMP. WE'VE FOUND A GROVE AND CHOSEN A SHORT ONE, 30 KLOMTERS.

DAY 1300. REFUELED IN A RAINCLOUD. EVERYTHING'S WET.

DAY 1310. ANCHORED AT MIDPOINT OF TREE.

DAY 1330. RYLLIN AND KARILLY MUST HAVE LAID THE HONEY TRACK BY NOW. BUGS ARE FOLLOWING THEM DOWN TO THE TUFT. I'LL TAKE *LOGBEARER* IN TO PICK THEM UP. WE'RE ALL EAGER TO RETURN TO THE ADMIRALTY, BUT THERE'S NO WAY TO HURRY THE BUGS.

DAY 1335. RYLLIN AND KARILLY ARE ABOARD. FROM THE IN TUFT THEY SPOTTED A POND 50 KLOMTERS WEST AND A LITTLE IN. THE WOMEN ARGUE THAT WE CAN FIRE UP THE ROCKET AND START OUR RETURN

WITHOUT WAITING FOR THE BUGS. THE POND WILL LET US REFILL THE WATER TANK. IT WOULD GAIN US TWENTY TO THIRTY DAYS.

NOW IT'S MY CHOICE. THERE'S A RISK, BUT I'VE NEVER YET HELD OUT AGAINST THE WOMEN. I'LL GIVE UP EARLY, SAVE TIME.

DAY 1360. THE BUGS HAVE REACHED THE HONEY BAND AROUND THE IN TUFT. ORDINARILY I WOULD BE DOWN THERE SUPERVISING, BUT I CAN'T DO THAT WHILE WE'RE UNDER ACCELERATION.

WE MAINTAIN STAGGERED WATCHES AGAINST HAPPYFEET. IF THEY FIND US WE CAN READY *LOGBEARER* FOR INDEPENDENT FLIGHT IN HALF A DAY. THE ROCKET IS HOT AND RUNNING.

DAY 1370. I'LL STOP FEEDING THE PIPEFIRE SOON. LET IT BURN OUT BEFORE THE BUGS CUT THE TUFT LOOSE. I CAN GUIDE US INTO THE POND ON THE LAST OF OUR STEAM.

IF THE ROCKET RUNS DRY IT'LL TEACH THE GIRLS CAUTION. WE'LL STILL FILL THE TANK BEFORE WE REACH THE CLUMP. YOU ALWAYS BUMP A POND OR TWO WHEN YOU'RE MOVING.

DAY 1380. A MATURE TREE IS DRIFTING TO BLOCK OUR PATH. DAMMIT. MAYBE IT'LL MOVE PAST.

NO FURTHER ENTRIES.

THE CARM PICKED THEM UP ON THE BRANCH AND RETURNED to its dock with the cabin half filled with foliage. Rather suspected that they would not eat foliage again, nor sleep in decent tide, for a long time.

He heard the argument when Clave wanted to restart the motor. "There's no point," Jeffer told him. "We'd be using fuel to fight wind. We're doing fine."

Booce added his voice to Jeffer's. "We'll sail even further in after the tuft severs. Leave us something to breathe!"

Had anyone else seen Clave glance aft? Clave had taken less than a breath to read the faces of his crew, but Rather had caught it.

Not so long ago, far away in Citizens Tree, Gavving had spoken thus to his eldest son: "You're a citizen now. Watch Clave during a meeting. He leads where we'll go. He always has. You don't have to go Clave's way just because Clave says so . . . "

The motor stayed off.

The tree moved ponderously west and in. Its westward motion slowed over several days. The days were shorter, and Voy had come nearer. The smallest children learned never to look directly at Voy; but Rather could tell. In the corner of his eye the violet-white pinpoint was more intense, closer and *smaller*, with less sky to blur and distort it.

It took six days to make a sleep; then seven. Time whirled around them until they stopped caring. The journey had become more important than their destination.

The crew lived on the bark, all but Jeffer. They found the carm too strange. Even Rather left the carm after a few sleeps. He had learned that he liked strangeness; but he sensed that Jeffer saw him as an intruder. *The Scientist captains the carm.*

Debby and Booce disappeared down the trunk to monitor the progress of the bugs. They returned with smoked dumbo meat and two cured skins, which Booce shaped into armor that looked remarkably like the silver suit. "We won't use it this trip, but it's standard gear. The Navy will expect us to have it."

A grove of integral tree sproutlings passed Voy-ward of the tree, the first the citizens had ever seen. They were a few scores of meters long, tufted only at the out end. "The seeds drop away, out and in," Booce told them. "After they sprout, they have to sail back to the median. They'll grow the other tuft when there's enough to feed them."

The day came when Carlot called her father and pointed outward. "Isn't that a pod grove?"

Backlit by the sun, the cluster might almost have been a miniature tree grove hundreds of klomters out. "Small . . . yes. Too far, though."

"Why?" Debby asked.

"Well, it'd take too long to . . . I'd forgotten the carm. Let's ask Jeffer."

Jeffer summoned up his windows-within-windows. "Sure, we can get there. Clave, want to take a trip?"

"Can we find our way back? The tree looks big when you're tied to it, but from six hundred klomters away—"

"Trust me."

Forty plants grew in a loose cluster, all much alike. From a fibrous cup that faced west, a long, limp leaf trailed eastward, waving sluggishly in the wind. A thick vine reached a hundred meters out from the boll, ending in a kind of collar. Each collar held a brown egg-shape.

"Those are jet pods," Debby realized suddenly. "We used to ride them in Carther States."

Booce directed Rather to one of the largest plants. Carlot and Debby hung back. Rather the Silver Man circled the pod, cautious in the face of a new thing: a fibrous brown egg as big as the common room in his father's hut. There was tide enough to pull the vine taut.

Smaller pods grew in a spiral around the stem end, ranging from fist-sized to man-sized. Replacements, he surmised, that would grow after the ripe one dropped away.

Satisfied, Rather wrapped his legs around the stem for leverage and swung his matchet.

The sound blasted his whole body. The sky spun round him. Tide was pulling him apart. His fingers and toes felt like they were inflating as spin pulled blood into them.

Against the tide that was pulling him rigid, Rather forced his legs vertical to his torso, pulled an arm against his chest, and fired the ankle jets. The spinning sky slowed. He aimed his feet against the spin and brought it to a stop.

Battered and deafened, he pulled his helmet open to hear what Booce was shouting at him.

"That one was ripe! Try another plant!"

Rather jetted toward the grove. Booce guided him from a distance. "No, that one's stunted. We want a big one."

"Aren't the big ones likely to be riper?"

"That's why we use armor! Try there—"

The pod exploded, blowing him west and away, while seeds *spanged* off the silver suit. The spin was less this time; the blow had been more direct. Rather opened his helmet. "I think I had more fun on the tree!"

"It's too wet here. The pods like to spread their seeds when there's water around. Try that one. *Close your helmet!*"

Rather seriously considered telling the alien merchant to go feed himself to the tree. But he was already moving toward a third vine. *There isn't any other Silver Man,* he thought. He swung viciously at the base of the pod. *And what am I, if I'm not the Silver Man?*

The pod dropped out and away. Carlot and Debby flapped after it.

The next one didn't explode either. Rather chased the seed pod down, with Booce chasing him. They braced their shoulders against the pod and started back. They were near the carm when Rather's jets died.

He fiddled with the throttle wheels. Nothing.

"Booce! Don't leave me!"

"What's wrong?"

"The suit won't move!"

Booce laughed. "Are we going to have to put wings on that thing?"

"Can you push me—"

"Can and will. Here comes Debby. I'll push you and the ladies can have the pods." Booce seemed indecently cheerful, and Rather was a long time understanding why.

Booce had found a flaw in Citizens Tree's intimidating science.

"You ran out of fuel, that's all," Jeffer told him. "See that little red light below your chin?"

"It was on when I started out. I don't know what it means."

"Means you're out of hydrogen. There must be a way to refuel the suit. I'll search the cassettes. If I can't find anything we'll have to ask Mark, after this is all over. Calm, now! We've got pods and we've got honey. Maybe we won't need the silver suit again."

A forty-klomter-long tree is hard to lose from six hundred klomters away. Jeffer had no trouble bringing them home.

Booce attacked the first pod gingerly, hacking at the stem with the matchet, flinching back at each blow. At the sixth blow the pod suddenly spewed foggy air under terrific pressure. Booce threw himself into the sky. He flapped back, staying well clear.

He opened the other pod in the same cautious fashion. Then he and Carlot sawed it in half. The inside was lined with fist-sized puffballs, each with a dangling tendril. Booce scraped these away.

He sawed the stem off the first pod, leaving a small hole. He shaved the edges until the hole was just smaller than the metal pipe, and quit for dinner.

They resumed work after breakfast. It took four of them to shove the ends of the pipe into the holes in both pods.

Clave asked, "Now how do you get water in there?"

"Punch a little hole in the other end of the tank. Put the pipe in a pond and suck. You need good lungs to be a logger."

"We're too far in to find many ponds."

"I know. Usually we fuel *Logbearer* before we go to work on the tree. But, dammit, we've got the carm, and there'll be a pond somewhere, and *Logbearer* is whole again! Except for the lines. And cabins. We'll need wood to build cabins."

"We'll go for wood after the next sleep," Jeffer said. "The out branch, I think. The in branch may be about to fall off."

"No. Another thirty days at least."

Carlot said, "Father—"

"Don't trust that," Booce said instantly. "We'll use the out branch."

"You're the logger. What changed your mind?"

Booce sighed. "I was guessing. I don't *really* know when the in branch will fall off. Jeffer, there's likely to be a shock when the branch tears loose. Stay aboard the carm. Stay strapped in when you sleep. Leave the motor off."

"Stet. Will the rest of you be okay on the trunk?"

"As long as we keep our wings handy. Always have your wings in reach . . . always. But you should be in the carm in case we need rescue."

The steam rocket still required attention. Booce and Carlot festooned the water tank with lines and wove a braid of lines around the bow end. "We'll moor the cabins here. Other than that . . . I still don't know what we're going to use for sikenwire. There has to be some way to hold the coals in place."

Clave had a suggestion. "We could arrive crippled. Get a push from the carm to drift the log into range, then signal for help somehow. Tell the Navy we lost our sikenwire, got home by luck."

"Mmm . . . maybe. I'd look like a fool, but maybe. I just don't want to be in too much of a hurry." He stopped abruptly. Then he said, "Ryllin and the girls, they—*we* were in a hurry to get back to the Admiralty. We started the rocket running before the tuft dropped off."

"What's—?"

"Did I tell you you're rich?"

"I don't know what it means," Clave said.

"That wart on the trunk is thousands of kilos of metal. With metal you can buy anything that's for sale in the Market. It also makes us a target. Someone might try to steal it."

"Good news and bad news."

"Right. We'll set up shop to sell the wood, and take our time selling the metal. No hurry."

Food had grown short again. Debby and Clave flew in along the trunk until they found a covey of flashers.

With the trunk as a backstop they fired their full complement of arrows and shot half a dozen of the small birds. It took them six days.

They built a fire on the trunk to cook the birds. *Logbearer*'s crew was ready for a feast.

Booce was the exception. He ate little. He was uncharacteristically silent, his eyes on the fire, until Carlot said, "Dad? Twenty, twenty-five days?"

"About that," Booce said. Then: "I guessed last time. I should be in the tuft watching the bugs."

"Dad, you couldn't warn us from down there anyway."

"I could start climbing ten or fifteen days early . . . "

"Dad—"

"I'm glad we don't have the rocket running. We were running the rocket when it happened."

The silence stretched. Debby asked, "What happened?"

Booce told it.

Booce was fast asleep when the cabin's yielding wooden wall slammed into his face and chest. His grunt of surprise was lost among feminine shrieks. He was reaching for his wings before his eyes were fully open.

The women were a flurry of action around him, snatching for their wings, moving out. Ryllin reached the door, looked about her, then immediately turned toward a violet-white glare that hadn't been there when they'd gone to sleep. Carlot and Karilly followed. Wend hadn't found her wings. She was near tears as she searched.

Booce left her. Nothing terrible could happen to Wend aboard *Logbearer*, and this would teach her *always* to know where her wings were.

He saw it all at a glance:

Logbearer was moored against a vast wall of bark, the east side of the trunk. Coals in their retaining net burned bright orange along the middle length of the pipe. The nozzle cone pointed east toward the Clump. Some meters from the cone, live steam condensed into a white stream klomters long.

The Clump was a distant whorl of white-and-gray storm, with the misty white tube of the Smoke Ring converging beyond and below it. The eye might follow that white line down the sky . . . and where the tree converged to a point, there was Voy.

The glare-white pinpoint had been masked by the in tuft when Booce went to sleep. The in tuft was gone. It had torn loose days before Booce expected it. Freed from its weight, the tree had lurched outward. Booce had guessed as much; now he could see it.

In toward Voy, a fluttering black silhouette was haloed in blue light.

Mishael had been outside on watch. The lurch had torn her loose. She was far in along the trunk, flapping out-and-east to bring her out, just as she'd been taught. But he'd never taught her to lose one of her wings!

Ryllin and the girls flew toward her: foreshortened black silhouettes. They made slow progress. In-and-west would have taken them straight in, but the west was a wall of black bark.

Booce followed slowly. Mishael seemed to have it under control.

With the in tuft gone the center of mass was higher on the tree. Tide was pulling Booce away from the tree, and in. A new breeze announced that the tree was under sail, accelerated by the wind on the out tuft. He kick-flapped to adjust. Ryllin and the girls had nearly reached

Mishael. Karilly looked up and flapped to turn. She was shouting at him. The wind tore her voice away. He tried to hear. She kicked toward him, screaming—

Booce turned toward *Logbearer*, too late.

The lurch and the breeze and Booce's inattention, these had caused the disaster. A flurry of coals had been jarred loose from the sikenwire cage. Irradiated by the pipefire, the bark had been drying and warming for tens of days. It had been ready to ignite.

Under normal circumstances an integral tree is in equilibrium with the wind. A steady gale blows at each tuft, and no wind blows at its center. Air must move past a fire to keep it burning. But a tree under sail is moving, and there is wind. Coals reached the bark and blazed up.

Booce flapped hard toward a *Logbearer* already embedded in flame.

He hadn't panicked then. There was a hose, and pressure in the water tank, for the fire would be heating it. He would use the hose to spray water and steam on the fire. Booce breathed deeply as he flew, hyperoxygenating. He'd hold his breath while he worked. The danger was that he might breathe flame.

Wend crawled gingerly through the cabin door. Her feet were wingless, her eyes and mouth wide in terror. She saw Booce, gathered herself, and leapt toward him, into the sky.

The water tank ruptured.

Booce saw Wend blown outward in a wind of live steam laced with boiling water. He flapped to catch her, hearing his own howl. She was flying past him. He stretched impossibly and caught her bare ankle, and felt the scalded skin slide loose beneath his hand.

———

There were comforting hands on Booce, on his shoulders and arm and ankle, for touching was the way of Citizens Tree. Rather hung back, uncertain, reluctant to take such liberties. Booce was a mature adult.

Where was Carlot?

Booce was hoarse, for he had been shouting, howling; but he sounded almost calm now. "Everything's blurred after that . . . Lawri the Scientist was feeding me foliage and I couldn't remember anything. It all came back a bit at a time."

Rather eased away from the cookfire and flew toward Voy. Behind him Booce was speaking mostly to Debby, who was rubbing his temples.

"It never happened before . . . not to us. Sometimes a logging concern just disappears. We wonder why. We never find out. For Ryllin, for the girls, I should give it up. But logging's all I know . . . "

The memories must have been too much for Carlot. If she wanted to hide . . . a crack in the bark? Bark walls would muffle the agony in her father's voice. She might have gone in any direction . . . but the cracks ran out and in. Try *in*.

Rather coasted above the bark. He didn't mind being seen. She'd have kept going until she couldn't hear the words.

"Go away."

He somersaulted and kicked air to stop himself. "Carlot?"

No answer. It had come from his left, from the north. There: scarlet showed in a crack. He said, "I wouldn't have found you if you'd kept your mouth shut."

She was pulled into herself, like the shellbirds around the ice pond. Her wings were on her back. He fluttered into the crack beside her but didn't touch her. "It must have been bad."

"It was bad."

He tried again. "Want a hug?"

"I want Wend back."

"You have to learn to think of her as a lost one."

"She was fifteen!"

("She wasn't even two!" Jill had wailed after a sister sickened and died. Ilsa had hugged her daughter frequently. When Ilsa died at thirty-one, it had been no better for Jill.

(Age didn't matter. Touching helped.) Rather worked his fingers into her hair and began a scalp massage. She didn't move. He said, "I've had brothers and sisters die. We all have. You forget."

She'd removed her sleeves after the fluff died. The skin of her arms was smooth and richly dark, and she suddenly wriggled about and had him in a deathgrip.

Rotating, they drifted in the sky. Rather still wore his wings; his instincts told him to return to the tree. He held her.

She wasn't sobbing. Presently she pulled her chin off his shoulder and kissed him.

He asked, "Better?"

"Yes. I don't want to go back."

"Will you be all right here? Shall I stay?" Half a dozen finger cactus drifted east, less than a klomter distant. A windborne finger cactus could be lethal. These were only drifting, and drifting away at that . . . but you never stopped *looking* for danger.

Carlot hadn't answered. He said, "Your father might get upset if we stay here too long—"

"Father's made mistakes before."

"He tells you who to make babies with, though. Mishael had to ask, and she's older than you."

"Do you want to go?"

" . . . No."

"I thought hard before I took my clothes off in front of you."

He remembered swimming in the waterfall, and laughed. "I noticed. But Booce was there."

She freed him, and all the muscles in his body jumped. *Loose in the sky!* But he had wings. Carlot drifted, rotating away from him . . . donning her wings? No: she pulled her tunic over her head, then rolled her pants off and balled them up together.

He looked. *Now* she was tying her wings to her ankles. Her clothes too. Nudity was not strange to him, but this was different. Carlot was long, one and a half times his own height. Her breasts were perfect cones, an abrupt break in the long smooth stretch of her torso. Rather resisted the urge to touch her. He spoke hurriedly, before he could lose that fight. "Now, what would happen if we really did make a baby? Could you still marry anyone you want to?"

She said, "It's all right. We just have to watch what time we do this."

"Yeah?" Rather had never heard anything about how *not* to make a baby. "When can you do it?"

"Now."

"I've never done this before." He swam toward her.

"I'll show you. Take these off."

Chapter Ten

Secrets

from the Citizens Tree cassettes, year 31 SM:

FISHER PLANT IS BOLL-SHAPED, 100–300 ME-
TERS IN DIAMETER. IT CAN EXTEND A LONG WATER-IN-
FLATED ROOT INTO A PASSING POND, FOR FERTILIZER AS
WELL AS WATER.

FISHER JUNGLE MAY BE CONSIDERED A LARGE
(400–700 METERS) FISHER PLANT WITH A STING. MAY
ATTACK BIG BIRDS AS WELL AS PONDS. PREY ARE
BROUGHT INTO THE JUNGLE TO ROT.

FINGER CACTUS—THE NEWLY BUDDED FORM
LOOKS A LITTLE LIKE A GREEN POTATO, WITH EYES. FIN-
GERS SPROUT FROM THE EYES, AND BRANCH AND RE-
BRANCH, UNTIL AN ADULT IN FLOWER MAY BEAR 20–
30 FINGERS. EACH FINGER IS TIPPED WITH A SPINE.
ANY CREATURE THAT COMES TOO NEAR MAY BE
SPEARED; AND THEN ROOTS GROW INTO THE VICTIM.

LATER IN LIFE, FINGERS BUD NEW FINGER CACTUS.
DANGEROUS.

RATHER WOKE BECAUSE HIS EYES BURNED.

They were filled with tears. Blinking did no good.
The tears were under his eyelids, filling them. The pain
had him whimpering. He tried lifting his eyelids with
his fingertips to let the water out. That hurt. Mopping
his eyes with his tunic brought agony. He couldn't see!

"Carlot?" He remembered that she wasn't with him.
They had not returned to the cookfire until all were
asleep except Debby, on watch. She had winked at them
. . . they had separated . . .

Sleep, then daggers in the eyes. He would not have
wanted Carlot to see him like this. But he was alone,
and blind!

"Clave? Debby? Anyone?"

Rather could feel bark surrounding him. Yell again?
He'd yelled when the silver suit's jets gave out. The
memory embarrassed him. He'd had gritty eyes before,
when he was tired . . . but not like this! "Someone help
me! I can't see!"

"Rather?"

"Debby? My eyes are on fire and I don't know why!"

Her hands were cool and rough on his cheeks. "Open
them."

"I can't . . . " He got them open, just a slit for just a
moment. The light was agony.

"They're bright red. I'll get Clave. Don't loose your
tether."

"No way!"

The pain grew no worse and no better. It was a long
time before he heard voices.

"Rather?"

"Clave! What's wrong with me?"

Long fingers held his head still; thumbs lifted his eyelids. "You're not blind. You're not dying either. It's an allergy attack. Your father used to get this way when Dalton-Quinn Tree was dying of the drought. We were too far in toward Voy. Dry, thin air and not enough sleep."

"What do I do?"

"Gavving mostly suffered. In half a day he'd be over it. Don't rub your eyes. Let me think."

It seemed to hurt less now that he knew it would go away. It hadn't killed Gavving. And if they both had the same allergy, then— *He's really my father! I should tell him! Mother too . . . and Mark?* But the pain was more urgent. "Clave, if this happens when I don't sleep, and I can't sleep because it hurts too much . . . Clave?"

His line went slack. "I've thought of something. Just relax. I'll tow you."

"Kendy for the State—"

"Kendy? Treefodder! It's been a long time."

"That's not my fault, Jeffer. Every time our orbits have matched, there has been someone else in the carm. Where are they now? I don't find them outside either."

"They're asleep. I was too. Everyone but me sleeps on the bark. Kendy, how do I refuel the silver suit?"

Diagrams appeared: carm and silver suit, side by side. Parts of the schematics blinked blue as Kendy talked. Jeffer saw that tanks along the calves of the silver suit were what made the legs so bulky. "Hydrogen here, oxygen here. There's hose under these little panels. The spigots are recessed, here and here, under these covers on the hull. You open them from the control panel.

Bring up the schematic, then twist above these dots, this way." An arrowhead circled.

"Good."

"Remember. Oxygen line from here to here. Hydrogen from here to here. Getting it wrong may cause an explosion."

"What keeps the gases cold?"

"In a pressure suit? No, the gases are just under pressure. That's why the tanks go dry so fast." Kendy's face was back in the bow window. "Did you find six metric tons of metal ore?"

"Yes. Thanks. Booce says it makes us rich."

"Good. I see you've been building a steam rocket. Is it finished?"

"Booce still has to build cabins. We'll go to the out branch for the wood. He still doesn't know how to hold the pipefire—"

"Here's the carm," a voice said. "Feel the airlock walls? *Treefodder!*"

Clave was in the airlock with Rather behind him. The display went blank, a breath too late.

Clave got his mouth closed. "First things first. Scientist, Rather's having an allergy attack. You remember how Gavving was during the drought? Rather, you need thick wet air. So, we'll close the airlock and turn up the pressure and humi . . . um, wetness. Do it, Jeffer."

Jeffer let his fingers dance. Close both doors, humidity up, pressure up. Pressure in his ears. He worked his jaw. He untethered himself and moved aft.

Rather's eyelids were puffy; the eyes were scarlet. Jeffer said, "It goes away after a while no matter what you do. This might help. Or not. Work your jaw to pop your ears." He turned to Clave. "Well?"

"How long has the Checker been back?"

"Since the Serjents reached the trunk."

"Why didn't you tell someone? *Me!*"

"Let's go outside."

He opened the inner airlock door and gestured Clave in. From the look of him Clave might explode any minute; but he came. They were nose to nose while the inner door closed and the outer opened.

"Keeps the pressure in," Jeffer said. "That's why it's called airlock." He kicked out into the sky.

Clave followed on mismatched wings. "You're stalling."

"No. Kendy can't reach us except when the sun is dead east, but anything that goes on in the carm, Kendy hears it later. He can't hear us now."

"He wouldn't have heard us in the Citizens Tree commons!"

"Yeah. Clave, the truth is that I didn't trust anyone else to talk to Kendy. I don't trust Kendy, and he's very persuasive."

"Am I too fluff-brained to say no?"

"Clave . . . all right, so I was arrogant and wrongheaded. Now let's go tell the Serjents."

"Uh—"

"Hey, citizumf!" It wasn't really a shout, but Clave's long fingers closed over Jeffer's face. After a moment the palm lifted to expose an evil grin.

Clave said, "You still should have told *me*. Rather didn't see anything. Did you tell Lawri?"

"No."

"What does Kendy want?"

"He wants the Clump. He wants to know *everything* about the Clump."

"This trip was his idea, wasn't it?"

"I told you he's persuasive. Clave, we have to tell

Rather about this before he talks to anyone. He already knows too much. Nobody else, right?"

"Right. Then I want to talk to Kendy."

"He comes in range every four days lately. Four days from now, when the sun is dead east."

Jeffer found Rather in the Scientist's seat, hands poised above the controls. "Freeze," he said. "Now move away."

Rather obeyed. "I was trying to open the airlock."

"Use the little lights on the doors. Rather, any citizen knows better than to fiddle with the controls. Once I nearly killed us all with one ill-considered tap of one finger. But I don't have to explain that to you. I only have to say, Jeffer captains the carm, keep your tree-feeding hands off the controls. Stet?"

"Stet. Sorry, Jeffer. I've seen you open the doors, and I was feeling shut in."

"How are your eyes?"

"Okay."

He held still while Jeffer looked. Rather's eyes were pink and the lids were puffy, but he didn't blink. "From now on you sleep in the carm with me. I should have someone here anyway in case we get shaken up when the tuft tears loose."

Rather had already summoned the blue diagram of the carm's cabin. Jeffer opened his fingers over the lines that represented the airlock. The doors opened behind him. He said, "Help me get the hose linked up. Then take it outside."

Booce met them at the door. "I'll take that, Rather. We're filling the rocket. How are you doing?"

"Better."

Debby, Clave, and Carlot waited at the rocket. Booce and Rather crawled along the bark, dragging the hose after them. Booce spoke quietly. "Did you know that Carlot was a crossyear child?"

"No. What's it mean? The crossyear is when Voy crosses the sun—"

"Children born at the crossyear are unpredictable. They can go any way at all. Rather, I'm trying to tell you that you and Carlot are not to marry. She'll marry a logger."

Rather didn't answer. Carlot's expression was unreadable until the moment Booce's back was turned. Then she winked. Rather felt his face glowing.

To work. Booce forced the hose into the rocket nozzle. "Jeffer says he can fill it without anyone sucking on the end. Clave, give us a hand here. Now push. *Jeffer! Ready!*"

The three were braced to hold the hose in place. Clave said, "There's a signal Jeffer uses that tells the carm to push what's in the water tank back out. It gets rid of mud—"

The hose writhed. Water sprayed out around the join. Rather could feel the power of the water trying to tear the hose out of his hands.

They held it, held it . . . and suddenly the hose bucked loose and thrashed like a live thing. Rather dodged and was flailing in the sky. Booce bellowed, "Enough! Jeffer, it's full!"

They were soaked before the hose went limp. Jeffer called cheerily from the airlock. "When do we see a test?"

Booce looked embarrassed. "I still don't know how to substitute for the sikenwire. We've got time—"

"Yeah. Well, we've used up too much water, one way

and another. I want to refuel the carm. Clave, Rather, come along. We won't be long, Booce. The rest of you can start dinner."

The three of them returned to the carm. Clave asked, "What do we do for a pump?"

Jeffer was smiling. "I've thought of something. There's a pond thirty klomters out and a little east . . . "

The sun wasn't much past zenith. A pinpoint diamond blazed next to it, out and a bit west: sunlight focused through a pond. Jeffer set the carm moving straight out.

The out tuft ran at them and past them. The pond wasn't far beyond, and not much bigger than the carm. Jeffer set the forward jets firing when they were close. They came to a stop just in from the water globule.

Jeffer opened the airlock. He told Rather, "Get into your wings and follow us. Bring the silver suit. We'll refuel the jets."

Jeffer led them outside and around to the carm's dorsal surface. Rather followed, tugging the silver suit by its limp wrist. There Jeffer took the suit from him. He watched as Jeffer produced narrow hoses from under a hatch . . .

Clave said, "Forget the suit for a while. Let Jeffer do it. Rather, you missed something during the allergy attack. What do you think happened then?"

"All I know is, you caught Jeffer at something."

Jeffer grunted. He had the hoses hooked to holes in the suit's legs.

Clave said, "You missed your chance to see Sharls Davis Kendy. You'll get it again in, what, half a day?"

Jeffer looked at the sun: past two o'clock, a few degrees out from west. "A little more than that. The thing is, this is a secret, Rather."

"Everybody's got secrets. . . . Kendy? The Checker?"

"Tell him, Jeffer."

Jeffer said, "Kendy's back. He pointed out the Wart for us. He talked to me the day we rescued the Serjents. We've talked since. I gather it costs him something, maybe shortens his life, and he still can't reach us more than once every two days."

Rather said, "The tales Mark and Gavving tell, Kendy would have killed you all if he'd known you stole the carm."

"I don't think he could have done that," Jeffer said, "but he might have wanted to. We stole the carm to get away from London Tree. We had Lawri tied to her seat, and Mark the Silver Man too. Kendy might have called it mutiny. You know some of this."

Rather said, "You were copsiks. They owned you. I never understood how you could live with Lawri and Mark after that."

Clave said, "What were we supposed to do, throw them into the sky? They earned their citizenship, Rather. When the air was leaking out of the carm, Lawri found the way to plug the leak. When Kendy was asking questions, Mark covered for us. We could have told Kendy we were escaped copsiks, but I'm not sure how he would have felt about that. Maybe Kendy's people kept copsiks."

"Kendy."

"Yeah. He—Scientist, you understand this better than I do."

Jeffer said, "Give me a minute." He was moving the hoses. "Need to refuel the legs one at a time . . ."

"Stet. Now, Sharls Davis Kendy claims to be the recording of a man. I don't understand that. Neither does Lawri. We don't even know how cassettes work, really.

I wondered if he was just some madman who reached the old starship, like we almost did, and was living aboard. But it's been fourteen years, and he doesn't sound any older. He wanted to know all about us. Whether we were mutineers. Well, treefodder, we *did* steal the carm, we *were* mutineers, much as I hate the word."

"That's all in the past," Clave said.

"Yeah. Now he wants to see the Clump. Clave, remember how he talked fourteen years ago? I think he still wants everyone in the Smoke Ring to be one big happy tribe taking orders from Sharls Davis Kendy."

The dark pond blazed at its eastern edge. Rather wondered if there would be time for a swim. He was not comfortable in this maze of secrets. "Kendy isn't the Chairman. We don't have to do what he says."

"No."

"Well, we want to see the Clump too. And if he can't touch us— Why not tell the Serjents?"

"Boy's got a point," Clave said.

"You didn't tell them either."

"Maybe that was just reflex."

"Just talk to Kendy, Chairman, and then I'll point out something."

Clave merely nodded. To Rather, he said, "One more thing. Kendy hears everything anyone says aboard the carm."

Rather laughed.

Jeffer asked, "Anything else to discuss? I think I'm finished here. Now let's refuel the carm. Go back in and strap down."

"We still don't have a pump."

The Scientist's answering grin was a little mad. Clave sighed.

———

Jets grumbled, then died. Rather watched a wind-rif-
fled wall of water move toward the bow window.

Clave asked, "Shouldn't you close the doors?"

Jeffer grinned and shook his head.

Clave said, "I wish to point out, *Captain*, that we're
going to hit that pond."

"Yeah."

The pondlet struck. Rather sagged in his straps. Clave
grunted. He asked, "Do you honestly know what you're
doing?"

"I honestly do."

Through the great window the interior of the pondlet
was open to view. A flock of tiny silver torpedoes sped
away through the murk and disappeared through the
shivering silver surface.

"The carm's hundreds of years old and nothing's hurt
it yet. Now I reduce the interior pressure." Jeffer's fingers moved; the air system hissed; water entered the
airlock in an expanding silver bubble.

The doors closed. Water remained inside, flowing
over the aft walls, the curve of it becoming more and
more concave. Waves curled and sloshed as Jeffer
turned the carm away from the pond.

He grinned at them. "Now I set the pressure back to
normal and turn down the humidity. That tells the carm
to make the air dry by taking water out of it. The water
goes to the tank. See? We can't run out of fuel now. It's
something Lawri never thought of."

"It's treefeeding *wet* in here, Scientist!"

"But you don't have to pump. Next on the agenda is
Kendy. Checker, when you hear this, please introduce
yourself."

Clave asked, "What if he's not there?"

"He'll hear it when he runs the record—"

There was a face in the bow window.

Kendy was a dwarf. Rather had expected that, but he was still taken aback. Deepset eyes examined him, judged him, within a face like carved rock. A giant's gravelly voice said, "Kendy for the State. Hello, Chairman Clave. Hello, Rather the Silver Man. Scientist, your manner of refueling the CARM is likely to destroy it. If the impact had torn away the solar cell arrays, how would you break up water? A CARM doesn't fly on water."

Jeffer looked nettled. Clave said, "Welcome back, Kendy."

"Thank you, Chairman."

"Why did you hide from me?"

"I felt that Jeffer was better equipped to judge his political situation than I."

Clave bridled. "And I'm not?"

"If Jeffer had told you, he would surely have had to tell his wife. Do you trust Lawri's judgment?"

"I give up. Between you, you . . . stet."

"I watched your nonmutiny with some interest. You're a natural leader, Clave. You should be ruling many more than your thirteen citizens."

"Thank you, Checker. Where do you propose I find another thousand citizens, all of whom are inclined to trust a tree-living outsider?"

The language was cold and stiff. Jeffer and Clave did not trust Kendy, and Kendy clearly knew it. He said, "You need not turn a compliment into a policy statement, Clave. I can't force you to obey my orders. You can't stop me from observing through the CARM's instruments. You know that I know things you do not. Can't we work together?"

"Maybe. Thanks for showing us the Wart."

"You're welcome. Has Booce found a way to confine the pipefire?"

"Not yet."

"Even with sikenwire, the pipefire is dangerous. You do have a source of metal. You can make a firebox from the Wart."

Clave grinned. "What a good idea."

"You probably don't have the facilities to make a smelter—"

"What?"

"A smelter refines metal. It melts metal ore and burns away impurities. You shape the metal by pouring the liquid into forms. Gravity is needed, or tide, or spin. The Admiralty may have such technology, but I gather you do not."

"We do not. You'd set the tree on fire for sure!"

"But you do have a saw. It was moored in the cargo section. Use it to cut slices from the Wart."

"Kendy, you'd ruin the teeth."

"No. That saw was taken from *Discipline*. Most of the tools aboard *Discipline* were made to last. Even with trivial items, the major cost was transportation. The chicken wire must have been made in the Admiralty, but your hose is reinforced with hullmetal alloy. The pipe is hullmetal. So is the saw. You won't damage it by sawing slices from a mass of soft iron. Here—"

Kendy's angular visage was replaced by a line drawing of the steam rocket, then another line drawing: a rectangle with tabs at its edges. "Cut three of these. Use the first as a template—"

"How do we hold the parts together? Tethers would burn."

"Set the plates in place and pound on the tabs until

they bend down. They'll fold over each other." Three
rectangular plates formed a triangular prism. The tabs
along the edges blinked green, then bent themselves
over to interlock. *Logbearer* reappeared, and the three-
sided box now enclosed the pipe and pipefire.

Clave said, "I'll ask Booce. You won't get much air
flow to the coals."

"Mount the rocket two or three kilometers in or out
from the center of mass. The wind will keep the coals
alight. You couldn't make a completely closed box anyway. It will leak."

"Mmm . . . yeah. You've been thinking hard about
this."

"I can solve simple mechanical problems. What will
you do with the CARM when you reach the Clump?"

Clave was still studying the diagram. "We'll hide it
before we get there. Take the log in with the steam
rocket. Take our time selling it."

"You'll want to keep the CARM safe, but near
enough for rescue if something goes wrong. Now, the
Clump is more crowded than the Smoke Ring in general,
but one may still think of it as mostly empty space. Two
thousand people won't crowd a region the volume of
the Earth's Moon! You'll find plenty of hiding space."

"Kendy, we can't steer the carm into the Clump and
just look around! We'd be seen!"

"I have a better view of the Clump than you do, even
if it's not a good view. If you approached from north or
south of the Clump—"

"What we'll do is take the log in, then look around
while we're selling the wood. If we find a safe way in,
we'll take it."

"Another thing you might consider," Kendy said.
"The CARM is power. There may come a time when

we'll want to use that power . . . " Kendy's voice and picture faded.

"Well, that's that." Jeffer left his seat. He stretched elaborately. "Let's go out. Take some spears. We'll get us some waterbirds before we turn back."

They moved out. Clave said, "Well?"

"*Now* do you see what I mean? He wants the carm inside the Clump. He wants it bad. If he can get some Admiralty citizens into the carm, he could look them over and question them."

"He didn't say anything unreasonable," Clave said.

"Persuasive, isn't he? All right, think about this. There occurred an accident that allowed Chairman Clave to see the Checker talking to the Scientist. That happened *after* Kendy was sure he couldn't talk *me* into this."

Clave smiled. "An interesting coincidence. The carm has outside cameras, doesn't it?"

"Yeah. And Booce would like to be *rich* so that he can give up logging. Do you think Kendy could persuade Booce to trade the carm to the Navy for metal?"

The smile slipped. "We'll do it your way. Rather, this stops with us. All of it. Now shall we get us some waterbirds?"

"I said that to get us outside," Jeffer said.

"Let's do it anyway."

Chapter Eleven

Happyfeet

from the Admiralty Library, year 131 SM, day 160:

VOICE HAS SET US THE TASK OF INTEGRATING THE
DESERTERS—EXCUSE ME, *WANDERERS*—INTO THE AD-
MIRALTY. IT WILL CERTAINLY TAKE GENERATIONS.
EXEC WILLOUGHBY ADMITS THAT IT MAY BE IMPOSSI-
BLE, AND I'VE COME TO AGREE.

HALF A DOZEN COTTON-CANDY JUNGLES NOW
TRADE REGULARLY IN THE CLUMP, MEETING AT THE
CROSSYEAR. THEY OBEY ADMIRALTY LAW, WHERE AD-
MIRALTY NAVY IS PRESENT TO ENFORCE IT. OUTSIDE
THE CLUMP THERE IS PIRACY AND SLAVE-TAKING. WE
BELIEVE THAT THE SEEKERS AND THE LUPOFF FAMILY
WERE INVOLVED IN SUCH INCIDENTS, THOUGH THEY
WERE THE FIRST TO TRADE IN THE MARKET.

WE CANNOT BRING LAW TO THIRTY EARTH-

VOLUMES OF INHABITABLE TERRITORY. THE SMOKE
RING IS TOO HUGE, AND WE ARE TOO FEW AND TOO
SLOW.

—LIEUTENANT RAND CARSTER

BRILLIANT AS IT WAS, THE NEUTRON STAR WAS TOO SMALL
to give much illumination. Yet the sky was never dark,
even at crossyear, when the sun at nadir had to shine
through the full thickness of the Smoke Ring's farther
arc. One must seek darkness in a cloud or a jungle or
a tree tuft, or in the unoccupied depths of the Clump.

Now the sun was dead east, somewhere behind the
slowly roiling blotch that was their destination. It was
gloomy in the shadow of the Clump. Masses near the
white-fringed black mass seemed to blaze in contrast.

"We're better than halfway home," Booce said.
"Debby, I've been looking for more pod plants. The last
thing I ever wanted was to come home with a pod for
my cabin, but we don't have time to build real cabins."

"The rocket's finished otherwise?"

"Yes."

"Good." Debby had been working hard. Her tunic
was off and her pale skin glistened with sweat. "Now,
how do we make it work?"

"Trade secret."

Debby regarded Booce angrily. "We built the treefeeding thing. You won't tell us how to make it go?"

"Classified, Debby."

"Will you tell us how to make it stop? In an emergency, if you and Carlot aren't in reach, how do I stop
it from just burning up?"

"We'll get an extra pod and fill it with water to pour
on the pipefire—"

"Very *good!* Now, suppose you and Carlot both fall

off the tree and lose your wings and we've got to come
after you. Suppose you left the rocket going. What do
I want to do?"

Booce found her persistence disturbing. "Use the
carm, I suppose—"

"The carm is gone."

"They're only refueling it."

"It could be gone again!"

"Then use your wings. *Don't* try to use the rocket.
That's dangerous."

Debby glared and was silent. She was Booce's height
and almost Booce's age, marked by a dangerous and
exotic beauty. Pale-brown skin, pale straight hair, fiery
blue eyes; a face all planes and angles, with a nose like
an axe head. She was the type of woman who would
remake a man, who would run his life for him. As Ryllin
was. And Ryllin was far away . . . and if Booce carried
that thought further, Ryllin would know somehow, and
Booce would regret it greatly. Booce looked at the sky
to escape Debby's eyes.

He'd been watching the sky for days now. They were
closing on the Clump. Matter would be thicker here,
even this far in: more ponds, plant life, animals, pred-
ators, perhaps Navy craft or wandering happyfeet.

West of out, almost behind the log's remaining tuft,
he found paired bright and dark dots: the pond and the
carm. No sign of pod plants. Would they have to cut
wood from the out branch after all? Branchwood was
better . . . but it was hard work, and the cabins would
be crude.

Debby was still fuming. "You know, arguing isn't the
thing I do best. But Clave is going to have this out of
you, because it's *stupid* not to tell us how to use the

basic logger's tool. Won't the Admiralty expect us to know—?"

"No. You're hired labor."

"Right. I forgot."

The days went fast this close to Voy: nine days between waking and waking. North and west, the reddish fringe of the Clump's shadow was sliding rapidly down a tremendous wall of cloud. Storm and lightning inside, and ponds forming . . . The line of sunlight picked out a green dot, a drifting jungle emerging from the fringes of the storm.

Carlot suddenly asked, "Debby, should we know how to use the carm?"

"Yes. *Yes*, we should know how to run the carm! Treefeeding fools they are, Lawri and Jeffer both."

Booce was jolted. "Debby? You can't fly the carm?"

"Nobody knows but the Scientists. *Classified*. Lawri I can understand. But Jeffer, he stole the thing himself, and now he acts just like her! Fifteen years, almost!"

"Dad? She's right. We should all of us know all of that, and we have to start somewhere."

Booce sighed. Crossyear child! Playing around with a dwarf tree dweller . . . but the women always won the arguments. "Debby, as far as any Admiralty citizen is concerned, you know *nothing* about how a rocket works. Understand?"

"Yes, Logger Booce. Now, what is it you loggers have been concealing from us laborers?"

"Go ahead, Carlot."

Carlot considered before she spoke. "All right. Just the way you taught me. Debby, you'll have to imagine the sikenwire in a tube around the pipe. I stuff firebark inside and light it."

Debby nodded.

"The coals are just along the middle of the pipe, not too close to the ends. I wait. I want the metal to get hot. It should glow red. Hotter than that, the nozzle starts to char. That's bad. So I run water through the pipe. The metal stays dark red, and steam comes out the nozzle. You can't see it where it comes out, but it can flay the flesh from your bones, so stay clear."

Her father smiled, nodding approval. He'd taught her well.

"Now, how do I move the water into the pipe?"

Debby mulled it. "No tide—"

"How do I keep outsiders from watching me do it?"

Debby brightened. She kicked herself to the fore end of the water tank. "I'm here, right? There's a cabin, and I'm in it. And here's the plug . . . "

"Just so!" Carlot joined her. "You pull the plug. You blow in it. When the water spurts back at you, you slam the plug in quick."

"I could get a lungful of water that way."

"Sure you could. We've all done our share of choking. Father taught us this so he wouldn't have to do it himself."

"Why does it blow back?"

"I . . . Dad?"

Booce said, "The steam pushes both ways. Out the nozzle, and backward too. That churns the water so more water comes down the pipe. After the rocket settles down, it's thrust that pulls the water through. The back-pressure holds it from going in too fast. You can let the rocket run till the water's almost gone."

Carlot said, "You've got to let the pipefire die before the tank's empty. Otherwise you'll char the nozzle and the tank both. It's a mess if you have to throw water on a pipefire."

The storm was definitely reaching out to enfold the tree . . . and the jungle was closer too. Booce pointed. "Carlot—"

Carlot looked. "Happyfeet?"

"Maybe. Debby, what have we got for weapons?"

"Harpoons. The rocket, I guess."

"Not enough. All right, ladies. Maybe it's just a loose jungle, and even if it's happyfeet they may not have noticed anything, but I think we should hide."

"*Hide?*" Debby was outraged. "Booce, that's not much of a jungle. Carther States was twenty times that size."

The jungle was closer now, a fuzzy green ellipsoid with a shadowy slit in it, as if foliage had been shorn away to form a window into the interior. Booce said, "A jungle that size can hold a family of twenty or thirty. Debby, a tree is big. We can vanish into cracks in the bark and never be seen. I . . . think we've got time. Help me take the rocket apart."

"Booce, it was tough enough putting it together!"

"You think I like this?" But Booce and Carlot were already tugging at pipe and nozzle, and Debby perforce joined them.

"The pipe is . . . priceless. We . . . can't let happyfeet . . . get it." Booce gasped in the thin air. The nozzle jerked loose and tumbled along the bark with Booce wrapped around it. His voice drifted back. "The rest they can have. We'll hide the pipe in some crack and guard it. Now we *really* won't have time to make cabins."

They pulled loose the pipe and water tank. The green puffball was closer yet, and a line of vapor trailed behind it. The vapor trail became a curve . . .

Debby said, "It's dropped five men. Winged. Now it's going away."

Nozzle and tank floated, slowly rotating. Now Booce was free to look. "They're making for the Wart."

"We can't let them have it!" Debby cried.

"Well, the truth is, we can," Booce said. He was pushing the pipe ahead of him, kicking hard. Carlot and Debby flew to help. "Maybe the carm can take it back for us. If not . . . we don't need the Wart to reach the Clump. Those five that were dropped are after *us*."

The log was far east, drifting in the fringe of a storm complex. Rather found it before Jeffer did: shadow backlit by the sun.

Jeffer chased it down. The carm arced over the top of the out tuft, moved in along the east side of the trunk. The dock came into view: a rectangle of bare wood, ragged around the edges. Rather felt the pull of the forward jets and heard pondwater slosh toward him. Water had spread along the carm's walls and was creeping forward.

He wasn't actually getting used to this, was he?

"Where's the rocket?" Clave sounded merely puzzled.

Where they had built the rocket, there was nothing. Wait . . . there, drifting loose, a pale-brown bell shape: the nozzle. There, some distance away, a brown ellipsoid trailing lines. Where was Carlot? Where was anyone?

"What happened here?" Clave demanded. "An explosion?"

Had there been a fire? Rather found only the small black scar of the cookfire. The arrangements around it were undisturbed.

Jeffer said, "We can't search the whole tree. Where's the sun?" Straight east. "We won't get Kendy for another day."

"Take us in," Rather said.

Jeffer looked at him. "Why?"

"Just a guess." Carlot had gone in, last sleep.

Jeffer swung the carm toward Voy and fired the jets. They skimmed above the bark. The fog was around them now.

Jeffer played with the controls. "There," he said suddenly. "Five men." But what showed in the window was an abstraction, orange blobs on red-and-black.

"We're seeing by heat," Jeffer said. For an instant the normal view returned: fog sliding along black bark. Then the red-and-black was back. "Didn't Booce say something about happyfeet?"

"Find our people," said Clave.

"Mmm . . . there." Three orange blobs in a line. By normal light they became three human shapes lined along a crack. "And the rocket pipe, I think. Rather?"

Rather quickly disengaged his seat belt and moved aft. He pulled the silver suit out of the water and slid his legs inside. Clave said, "Good. Get the rest of it on and go join the others. Take some harpoons. They won't have weapons. Jeffer, how did they get here?"

"Good question. I don't see anything that could have brought them. Something could be around the other side of the bark."

Rather waited while Clave bound six harpoons against the silver suit's chest. Air on; voice on. "Can you hear me?"

His voice blurted from the control panel, and Jeffer jumped. "I hear you fine."

"Let me out."

The bark was half a klomter distant. Rather used his jets. He thrilled to the pull of thrust along his body: blood leaving his head, abdomen settling toward his feet.

Not quite a comfortable sensation, but one few others could share.

Behind him, the carm accelerated south around the curve of the trunk and was gone.

Carlot and the others had seen the carm; they waved.

Two klomters toward the blue blur of Voy, a hundred meters out from the tree, green-clad men emerged from the fog. They flew along the bark, peering into cracks as they passed. At this distance Rather could see only that they were five jungle giants, and armed.

They saw him. Their legs stopped moving, though their motion continued. Closer now. One was a woman . . .

Then they were kicking again, turning back toward the storm that was reaching to engulf the tree.

He could catch them. They couldn't know about the silver suit. His tanks were full. Rather fired his boot jets; his course became an arc.

He could catch them. Then what? Kill them? Rather's parents had both killed. They didn't like talking about it. When they did, old anger distorted their faces. Yet this was the Silver Man's duty: from time to time, he killed.

One of the intruders looked back, and then all five were kicking madly, doubling their speed.

His arms were full of harpoons, hampered, while Debby and Carlot and Booce had no weapons at all. Rather swung back toward his crew.

He thumped into the bark not far from Booce. Carlot was looking at him oddly. He opened his helmet and said, "It's me. Five of them almost found you. What happened?"

"Happyfeet," Booce said. "A small jungle, steam-powered. Lupoff family, from the look of them. They want the Wart."

Rather thumbed his personal Voice on. "Silver Man calling the Scientist. Jeffer, they want the Wart. Go for that."

Nothing.

"They can't hear me. Booce, I'll guard you on the surface, but I don't think they'll be back. They looked like they were running."

Booce grinned. "They thought you were Navy."

"What?"

"Skip it."

Rather settled himself on the bark above their heads. Helmet closed. The invulnerable warrior (and Carlot had looked at him as at some alien bird). But the happyfeet warriors were gone from sight.

The storm enclosed the tree. The fringe of it was a fine mist, just beginning to obscure vision. *I wish I could use those other kinds of light Kendy sees by. And the ventral camera's almost blind . . . hydrogen low, oxygen low, water volume low but increasing. We should have built a pump by now. Hey—* "What's that?"

Clave looked. "Jungle. Small. Just opposite the Wart."

Now Jeffer spotted green dots around the puckered bark. Men, and one was pointing toward the carm.

The voice of Kendy startled him. "I'm scanning in infrared. I can't see anything human outside of the Wart area. Take the CARM closer. Give me a view."

Jeffer accelerated in. He asked, "Did you just come into range?"

"Yes. I'm running the record of your approach. You

should have killed the invaders on the east side. They could attack your people."

As the carm approached, the jungle jetted away on a trail of steam: north into the storm, then around the trunk, steam spraying in a wide curve. It was hidden before the carm arrived.

Jeffer brought the carm to rest a quarter klomter from the wooden crater. The happyfeet had been digging around one side of the Wart. Elongated men hovered around the block of black metal.

"Ten," said Kendy. Rings of red light blinked scientifically on the bark, haloing men Jeffer had already spotted, pointing out others. Three interlocked rings circled bare wood. "Four in the open, three between the bark and the Wart, three more in a crack outside the crater."

"We'd better follow the jungle," Clave said. "They could find the rest of us while we're busy here."

Jeffer turned in his seat, but Kendy spoke first. "There's time."

"They're too many to fight anyway," Clave said.

"Nonsense. Spray them with rocket exhaust. Jeffer, have you been shown the throttle for the main drive?"

"Yes." Jeffer didn't know the word *throttle*, but Lawri had shown him how to control the push of the rockets. His fingers danced.

The carm moved toward the Wart. The happyfeet waited, blurred by fog, spears ready. "Brace yourself, Clave." The carm swung around, still approaching the puckered bark, but stern foremost.

Men left the Wart, swimming hard. Others appeared from the bark beyond. Spears flew. The dorsal camera watched a bulbous-headed spear strike the hull and explode in a puff of smoky flame. Authoritative thumps could be heard through the hull.

Jeffer tapped the main drive on.

It felt like suicide. He'd nearly died the last time he did that. The carm surged forward. Jeffer felt his chest sag, his cheeks pull backward in a dead man's grin. But his arm was rigid above his face, fingers almost touching the control panel.

It worked! Moving his fingertip down along the green bar reduced the main drive's thrust to something he could handle. *Throttle.*

A nearly invisible blue washed across ten happyfeet warriors. The invaders burst into vivid yellow flame. They were comets, the flame streaming back from them. Explosions sent bits of men flying—

Clave cried, "Treefodder, Jeffer! Stop!"

Jeffer tapped the drive off. (Hydrogen, oxygen: both quite low. The Wart receded.) "Clave, they attacked us. They've got exploding harpoons."

"They couldn't have *moved* the Wart with us on their tails! We only had to take it away from them!"

"All right, Chairman." Jeffer turned to look at Clave. "Now tell me what they're doing to Booce and Debby and Carlot."

"It's time to learn that," Kendy said. "Time to move, Jeffer. I've lost sight of the jungle from *Discipline*'s position. It circled half around the trunk and was approaching the point where you dropped Rather. We'll have to get there fast, before I'm out of range. The invaders here are harmless enough now."

They were. Some were still writhing, some were motionless, but all were burned black. Jeffer set the carm moving. It was too early to feel guilt.

They were in the cloud now: a thick, swirling fog, growing thicker. Jeffer could see the tree only as a wall of shadow. Kendy said, "Turn starboard. You need not steer so wide of the trunk, Jeffer. I have infrared."

The carm moved around the trunk in a great curve. Lightning flared suddenly aft.

"I have the jungle in view, straight out by five point six kilometers. Straight out, Jeffer."

"I can't see."

"Ventral. Two degrees more. Good. Accelerate. Cut! Rather has the jungle in view. Silver Man, come in."

Rather's tinny voice spoke from the control voard. "I see a big shadow, but no detail. They can't see us either."

"They've found you somehow," Jeffer said.

"You're near," said Kendy. "Swing one-eighty degrees."

"I won't—"

"Citizen, I don't know where the men are! What else can we do but attack the jungle itself? Swing around." There was something strange in Kendy's voice.

Jeffer turned the carm. He half hoped Clave would countermand the order, but Clave said nothing.

"Main drive." Kendy should have sounded excited. He only sounded *loud*.

Jeffer tapped the button. The carm surged. His face tried to crawl around to the back of his head. A yellow light bloomed in the mist behind him, and he heard Rather's gasp. He killed the drive, but the yellow light remained.

The harsh bass said, "Done. I'm losing range—"

Clave said, "You kill too easily, Kendy."

Kendy's voice was becoming blurry. "Citizens, you're missing the point. This was a mobile jungle. These happyfeet may have contacts in the Admiralty. They've seen the carm and the silver suit."

"Men aren't honey hornets, Kendy!"

There was no answer.

Rain drifted across the carm's main window in drops the size of fists, carried by eddies in the wind. The wood outside was black with water. Inside the cabin it was soggy enough. Jeffer's segment of pond had spread a film of water across all the walls and the cradles.

Warm, dry air blew from vents fore and aft, thrusting the water away from it. The citizens clustered around the aft jet.

Next time I'll pump the water, Jeffer thought. *Got to build a pump.*

Carlot said, "We saw that huge shadow come out of the fog. It was scary enough. Then five . . . well, they could have been birds for all I could *see*, except that they were flying toward the jungle and thrashing at both ends. Waving their arms, I guess. It was the bandits who ran away from Rather. The jungle stopped to pick them up."

"They were Lupoffs," Booce said. "I know their clothing. I've met them in the Market. A big family, three jungles, and they'd colonize if they could buy another firepipe. They're crowded."

Clave said, "So?"

"If the Lupoffs find out what happened here, you'll have two jungles hunting you."

"They won't find out." There was no triumph in Clave's voice. Jeffer shuddered.

They were warm enough, dry enough, if they stayed in the air jet. But the storm splashed rain across the bow window, and through the rain came the yellow glow of the burning jungle.

"I wouldn't mind killing a bandit or two," Booce said. "I've been robbed once or twice. It's the scale of the thing that bothers me. There must have been forty citizens in that jungle, not counting children."

Clave jumped toward the fore end of the cabin. After a moment, Jeffer followed. The fore air jet was as dry as the aft.

Clave said, "I'd had enough of that."

"Forty people," Jeffer said. "There just isn't any way to make them stop talking about it."

Clave's voice was a hoarse whisper. "Persuasive, is he? Nobody but you can be trusted to talk to Kendy, right? You burned them while they were trying to rescue their citizens!"

"They attacked us."

"With spears. So?"

"What was I supposed to do? They were threatening *our* citizens!"

Clave sighed. "I'm not blaming you. And if I am, I shouldn't be. But Kendy—" By the flick of his eyes, Clave had remembered that Kendy would hear this. He began pronouncing his words with more care. "Tree-feeding Kendy killed them like a hive of honey hornets, because they were in his way. Because they might talk to the wrong people!"

Silence and discomfort. Debby came to join them. "Wet," she said. "What did you do to get it so wet?"

Jeffer didn't answer. To Clave he said, "I felt much worse when I killed Klance the Scientist to steal the carm. He wasn't expecting it. These citizens were. They were making war."

"Right!" Debby said enthusiastically. "When London Tree raided us, I used to wish we could capture this thing and set their whole tree burning. The bandits aren't the same, but by the State, we finally did it!"

"Don't do it again," Clave said. Jeffer nodded.

CIVILIZATION

Chapter Twelve

Customs

Year 384, day 1992, by heliograph:

STATION TWO TO *GYRFALCON*. *SWALLOW* REPORTS LARGE INCOMING LOG EAST OF ADMIRALTY. MASTER UNIDENTIFIED. YOU WILL RENDEZVOUS FOR CUSTOMS DUTY IF CONVENIENT. LOCATION OF LOG AT DAY 1990 WAS TWO-NINE-OH DEGREES FLAT, FIVE DEGREES NORTH, TWO-EIGHT-OH KLOMTERS RADIAL. ACKNOWLEDGE.

"RICE, DID THIS JUST COME IN?"

"Yes, sir. I was scraping the hull when I saw the light blinking near the Market. Took the message and came straight in, but I don't know how long the helio was blinking."

Petty Mart Wheeler thought it through. *Gyrfalcon* carried six crew; *Swallow*, two. The Navy preferred that

171

civilians notice the big armed ships. In the act of paying customs they should remember what they were buying. So.

"Where are we?"

"I'll find out, sir." Spacer Rice turned toward the instrument closet.

"No, not you. Bosun Murphy, take our position." This was not an urgent mission. He'd use it as a training exercise.

The dwarf nodded cheerfully; her flame-red hair swirled around her. Her short but powerful legs shot her across the cabin to the instrument closet. She chose what she needed and went out.

The long hair would have to go when she reached higher rank. Pity. But dwarves were rare, and Bosun Sectry Murphy must be trained quickly . . .

Through the hatch Wheeler could see a blue light, tiny and intense: a Navy heliograph, reflected Voy-light blinking near the east limb of the whorl. Red hair and a squarish feminine face suddenly blocked the view. "Petty, we're at two-sixty-five flat, six south, two-forty klomters."

"And we've got better than half a tank, right?" Murphy nodded. "Get on the heliograph. We'll rendezvous with the log. Jimson, Rice, get us ready for a burn."

The thick, disordered sky made Rather dizzy. If he fell into that he would be more than ordinarily lost. He climbed with care. Clave and Debby trailed him.

There had been hard work followed by a long climb. They were all tired. Rather's fingers and toes were starting to cramp. But the rocket was in sight, a hundred meters out . . . if that direction was still *out*.

The log was rising through the Clump's eastern

fringes. Wind slapped at Rather from ambush, here, there, everywhere, as if he were embedded in a flock of terrified turkeys. Clouds ran in peculiar directions, not east-west, not flattened spirals, but shallow in-out curves. A line of small green puff jungles flowed in an arc that was not tidelike at all. Confronted by such strangeness, Rather's bewildered eyes sought the one unchanging reference point.

Voy burned blue-white and steady . . . twenty-five degrees east of the stump of the in tuft! Choppy clouds blurred the sun. Shadows pulsed, blurring and sharpening. Overlaid on those, Voy's faint, sharp blue shadows lay in skew directions. Children learned not to see Voy-shadows. Voy-shadows told nothing, for they never moved, never changed, never distracted the eye.

The tree had turned; the trunk was pointing *wrong*.

Booce and Carlot waited at the rocket. Debby called, "Booce! How can you stand it?"

"The tide? I grew up in it. You'll get used to it. The happyfeet do."

"The shadows are making me sick to my stomach," Debby said.

Rather's own stomach was queasy. "Carlot—"

"We're almost home." There was no mistaking her joy. She *liked* it here. "Look, we've got the pipefire going."

"I'll start the water." A smaller pod had been carved into *Logbearer*'s new cabin. Booce crawled inside. "Tether yourselves."

The rocket cone pointed east. Rather poked his nose into the small hatch. "Booce, are you slowing us again?"

Booce's voice echoed. "What? No, tide's different in the Clump. We'll push west, straight toward the Dark."

He pulled a wooden plug from the water tank. He inhaled, put his lips to the hole, and blew.

Rather withdrew his head to watch the completed rocket in action. Yellow-white coals glowed within the iron firebox that had given them so much trouble. The iron glowed dull red. A fourth pod nearby was filled with water in case the plates didn't hold together.

At the nozzle end of the rocket— "Nothing's happening."

His answer was the sound of Booce inflating his lungs. Then the rocket went *Chuff!* and sprayed steam.

"It's going, Booce," Rather said, and looked in.

Booce's face dripped with water. He was coughing and choking while he pounded the plug in with the heel of his hand. His glare was murderous.

CHUFF, CHUFF, Chuff chuffchuffchuff . . . The rocket settled down. A row of cloud-puffs became a steady stream jogged by the play of capricious wind. Rather felt no acceleration. It would be gentle, with so great a mass to be moved.

Carlot came up behind him; her long fingers found his hand and enclosed it. "Father? Shouldn't we—"

Booce sounded like his throat was still full of water. "Yes, go play lookout on the west face, you two. Watch for Navy and anything we might hit."

The maelstrom revealed itself to them as they circled the trunk. Flying was a continuing wonder to Rather, but Carlot did it better. She kept darting ahead, then circled to urge him on. At a vantage point on the west face they doffed their wings and rested.

The Clump was a whorl like a tremendous fingerprint. Inward, matter thickened. There were puzzle trees, distorted cotton-candy jungles, the much smaller puffballs that Carlot had pointed out for him ("fisher jungles"), and greenery that was totally unfamiliar. Ponds took odd shapes in the distorted tide. The sky was thick with birds: skyhorses, triunes, and a thousand tiny red and yellow darts converging on a puff jungle. Everything moved in arcs, tighter near the center of the whorl, and darker. The center itself was almost black, but motion could still be seen there.

The triune families were hard to spot, but two had turned to observe the passing log. They were fat sky-blue cigar-shapes with wide triple fins: male and female and child, linked along their bellies. Three slender blue shapes flashed violent-orange bellies as they converged on the red-and-yellow bird-swarm: another triune fam-ily, separated to hunt.

A thin stream of cloud cut across other patterns of cloud-flow. Rather spotted it in the moment before Car-lot pointed. "There. Navy."

"How do you know?" Rather saw only a dark point at the end of the line of cloud.

"It's coming toward us. Customs. They'll make a burn and intercept us in a day. Oh, *treefodder*."

Rather laughed. She'd borrowed his curse. "What?" She showed him.

Far in toward the Clump's dark center, in the thick of moving matter, was a broad, flat ring-shape with a pebbly inner surface . . . angular structures in pastel colors . . . blatantly artificial. Could it really be as big as it looked?

He judged its size by an even larger natural object nearby: a tree with one tuft missing. The log was smaller than their own, Rather thought. At its midpoint he could make out a rocket-shape, cone and tank and angular cabin.

Carlot said, "I know that rocket. *Woodsman.* Dad
won't like this. They could just as easily have been out
another damn year." She looked into his eyes. "We
won't have much time together. The Belmy family owns
Woodsman. Dad wants to marry me to Raff Belmy."

"Will you do it?"

"Shut up." She pulled him against her by the slack of
his tunic. "I don't want to think about it. Just don't talk,"
she breathed into his ear, and he obeyed. It crossed his
mind that Booce should be told of these things. But
there would be time . . .

Gyrfalcon found the log easily: bigger than average,
with both tufts severed. It was making its burn: a wavery
line of cloud behind it was beginning to arc over. The
rocket would be behind the trunk.

"Instruments," Wheeler instructed. "Rice, get us a
rendezvous track. Murphy, the neudar. That dark blemish in the wood—"

"I see it, sir."

He waited and watched. His crew moved well, Bosun
Murphy in particular. She hadn't yet used the neudar
under field circumstances. She moved slowly, but without mistakes. That would reflect well on Wheeler.

"The blemish is dense. Metal," she said. "Kilotons."

"Now the rocket."

"I can't see anything—"

"Behind the midpoint."

"Oh! I can look *through* the wood!" She tried it.
"Mmm . . . something . . . metal, not much. Our own
iron rocket nozzle would show a mark like that."

"Rice?"

"We need a burn, Petty. Fifty degrees planar, zero
axial, a hundred breaths of burn and we'll go just past."

"Give us the burn, then all hands suit up. Spacer Rice, you're in the cabin, on instruments. Murphy, on the pump."

Gyrfalcon carried a glass alcohol tank and a pair of water tanks. Its valve system had been rifled from the hulk of an ancient Cargo and Repair Module. On long voyages, standard practice was to spray water into the alcohol flame as working mass. Water could be replaced in domains beyond the Admiralty's reach. Alcohol generally could not, though some of the happyfeet tribes carried alcohol distilleries for trade with the Admiralty.

Wheeler and Jimson tethered themselves carefully at the steering platform above the motor. Murphy began to pedal. Pedals could be extended, but a dwarf on the bicycle always delivered more power. Wheeler put his hand in the airflow to test it, then started the alcohol flame. He checked his crew's handholds before he increased the flow.

Thrust pulled at his skin and his bones. He ran water into the flame. Thrust rose again, and heat bathed the inner surfaces of his straining legs.

Rice called down from the cabin. "Cut it!"

Petty Wheeler reached below his feet for the alcohol valve. The roar died to a hiss: water on a hot surface. Next, the water valve. *Gyrfalcon* fell free.

The log was nearer; the plume of acceleration was gone. Using the binoculars, Wheeler found a pair of human shapes on the near side.

"They're not giving us much attention," he said.

Murphy took the binoculars. Presently she said, "They'll have time." She looked until he took them away.

The Navy ship was bigger and more elaborate then

Logbearer. It arrived in a wave of warm steam and paused a hundred meters from the center of the midtrunk. Four men emerged and flew toward them.

Logbearer's crew waited outside the cabin.

"They're fast," Debby said.

Booce chuckled. "Never try to outfly the Navy. Navy wings are different, and the men are picked for their legs."

They were closer now. Rather suddenly gripped Booce's arm. "Booce, they're wearing silver suits!"

"*Ah!* Rather—"

Rather eased his grip. "Sorry."

"Well, *watch* that. It's only Navy armor."

"But it looks—"

"Just armor. There are three vac suits in the Admiralty, and we aren't important enough to see one. Incidentally, they'd love to make it four."

Closer yet. The armor didn't cover them. All wore helmets: head-and-shoulder pieces with an opening for the face. Some wore additional plates. And one was a dwarf.

Their wings! They pointed a little forward, as the foot did; they folded on the forward kick and snapped open on the back-kick. *The Scientist should see this,* Rather thought.

They left their wings on even after they touched bark.

The dwarf was a woman. Red hair showed around the helmet before she lifted it. Pale skin, pointed nose, and pointed chin; hair like flame streaming from a tree afire. Her chest plate stood several ce'meters out from her chest. She was five or six years older than Rather, quite lovely, and Rather's height.

She caught him looking and smiled at him. He forgot

that he could move. Her eyes were blue, and they danced.

He was blushing, and Carlot had caught it, and Rather looked away in haste. And watched a long, long man kicking toward them.

The globe helmet was much larger than his head, with an opening for his face . . . like the silver suit's helmet with the faceplate missing. Separate curved pieces protected his thighs, back, upper arms, and hips. Those were wood painted in silver; but the head-and-shoulder piece was of hammered metal. Wide nose, dark skin, black cushion of hair: he might have been part of Booce's family.

He recognized Booce (and ignored his crew). "Booce Serjent? You may remember me: Petty Wheeler. Welcome home."

"Good to see you again, Petty. You'll remember Carlot—"

She smiled brilliantly. "Good day, Petty Wheeler."

"Oh, yes. You've grown, Carlot."

Booce said, "These others are Clave and Rather Citizen, from Citizens Tree, a few hundred klomters west of us. Debby Carther we hired before we left."

Meeting strangers was outside Rather's experience. Booce had told him what to do. He said, "A pleasure to meet you, sir," and held out his hand.

"Pleased." The Navy man's handshake was strong for a jungle giant. "I'll speak to you later, Rather. Clave, Debby, a pleasure. Booce, do you have anything to declare?"

"Yes. One log, forty klomters or therabouts. If you want to measure it yourselves—"

"No, we'll just take half the manifests as you sell it off."

"And the Wart," Booce said complacently. "Our one bit of luck, and a happyfeet tribe almost made off with it."

"That mucking great chunk of metal halfway in?"

"Heh. You've found it already? We haven't measured that either, but it's thousands of tons. Petty, we'd like the Wart classified. We won't get so many thieves that way."

"All right, but if happyfeet attacked you—"

"I don't want to file charges. They got away, but we hurt them, and I don't want them to know who. They might want to come after us with friends."

"That attitude makes life difficult for the Navy, Booce. We'd rather chase them down. You're sure? . . . All right. We'll want our taxes in metal."

"Fine. I want to keep that makeshift firebox until I can buy more sikenwire. It's not pretty, but it works. Barring that, I'll sell the entire lode to the Navy right now, if you can tear it out and tow it home. Take it off my hands," Booce said.

Rather couldn't help himself: he stared. *But what if he takes you up on it?*

Petty Wheeler laughed. "I don't have alcohol to tow it and I can't authorize that kind of expenditure. But we'll inspect it now, and I'll send a team to cut our share loose after you're moored."

Petty Wheeler's crew began searching *Logbearer* inside and out. Rather's momentary impulse was to stop them. But Booce showed no surprise . . . and of course there was nothing aboard *Logbearer* to be found. Meanwhile the Navy officer turned to Rather and said, "Rather, wasn't it? You should consider joining the Navy."

"Why?"

The man smiled. "The pay is good, particularly for a

tree dweller, if you can get in. We'll shape you up and
teach you things you should know, like how to win a
fight. You'll be holding civilization together. The personal advantage is, you're the right shape. You noticed
Bosun Sectry Murphy? Short, with red hair—"

"Yes?"

"She'll be wearing a vac suit within six years. Guardian
is the highest rank there is, unless you were born an
officer. You could do the same."

"I'll have to think about it."

"Talk to her yourself. Ask Booce, for that matter.
Booce, we'll fly down and inspect your Wart. Would
you like to ride with us?"

"I'd be delighted." Booce looked around at his crew
and added, "We'd *all* be delighted."

Gyrfalcon's hull sported handholds everywhere. The
Navy men spaced *Logbearer's* people high along one
flank. There were shelves for feet and straps to circle a
waist (or just under the armpits on Rather). "Fighting
vessel," Clave whispered to Debby. "They can cover the
hull with archers."

Three Navy worked aft, around the motor. They ignored the civilians.

Something green was trying to grow on the wooden
hull. Fluff, maybe. The wood had been scraped recently.
Rather noticed that much before the rocket fired.

If Wheeler was trying to impress a barbarian dwarf,
he succeeded. The rocket roared and spat flame. Rather
felt his blood settling into his legs. The log's rough bark
surged past, accelerating. Aft, Wheeler and Murphy
used toothed gears to point the nozzle. In a way it was
more impressive than the carm. You could *see* how it all
worked.

The roar of the motor would cover his voice (and the fear in it). Rather asked, "Why don't they let us inside?"

"Classified. Nobody knows what's in a Navy ship," Carlot said. "We haven't seen the whole crew, I'm sure of that. Rather, I noticed you staring at the, um, red-haired woman?"

Rather told a half-truth. "She looks short. I mean, it's surprising, because she's the same size I am. Mark never looked short."

Carlot seemed to relax. "Well, no. He was bigger than you when you were growing up."

Wheeler moved the nozzle ten degrees to port. The ship slewed around, spraying flame. He swiveled the nozzle starboard; the rotation slowed and stopped, and *Gyrfalcon* decelerated. It eased to a stop less than a hundred meters from the blister in the trunk.

"The bandits almost had it torn loose," Wheeler observed.

Booce nodded.

The same four Navy personnel accompanied them to the Wart. Three set to examining the blister that had grown up around the metal and the matchet-chewed wood that extended far back behind it. The fourth sought out Rather. "Petty Wheeler said you might have questions to ask me," said Bosun Murphy.

Rather was not really thinking of joining the Navy. He didn't say so. "I don't know enough to ask good questions."

She smiled enchantingly. "Ask bad ones. I don't mind."

"What are the vac suits? Why are they important?"

"They're old science, as old as the Library. They're invulnerable," she said. "The highest fighting rank is Guardian, and that's the rank that wears the vac suits.

There are supposed to be nine Guardians. We've got eight. This—" She rapped her helmet, then the plates on her thighs. "—It looks like this, but all over. You'll get as high as Petty just because you're the right shape, and then you find out if you actually fit into a vac suit."

"Do you?"

"I don't know. I haven't got that far yet." She looked down at her protruding chestplate unhappily. "Maybe I won't fit. I'd still keep my rank as Petty. Understand, you have to be qualified, you have to be trained. It's just easier if you're the right size."

"Training. What's it like?"

"They'll put you through exercises. You may think you're strong—you're a tree dweller? I can see the muscles. But Petty Wheeler could tie you in knots. After you've been through training you could tie *him* in knots. I could, I think, and you're stronger. Your people, do they use polar coordinates to find themselves?"

"No."

"They'll teach you how to find yourself in the sky. You'll learn how to count, if you don't know—"

"I can count."

"You'll learn how to work a rocket, not a steam rocket but a Navy rocket. They teach you how to obey too. You want to go in braced for that, Rather. A superior officer tells you to fly, you fly, wings or no."

It sounded unpleasant. "Where do the Navy ships go?"

"Mmm . . . Where do you come from?"

"Citizens Tree. A little west of the Clump."

"You're not likely to visit your family. We don't see many tree dwellers. We send ships outside the Clump, but not often, and never more than a few thousand klomters. Mostly we cruise the Clump itself. We collect taxes, of course—"

"Yeah."

"We fight the wildlife. Dark sharks and other things. Citizens find a drillbit nest, or honey hornets, they call us and we burn it out."

"Triunes too?"

"Oh, no, the triunes got the idea fast. They never attack us. Some of them like us. There's a guy, Exec Martin, he hunts swordbirds with triunes. Nobody knows how bright they really are, but they can be trained."

"Why do you burn honey hornets? Booce says they're valuable."

Her expression soured. "Honey is contraband. Put just a tip of a fingernail's worth on your tongue, you dream wonderful dreams. Then you can't stop. Use a little more and you die in ecstacy. Some people will pay a lot for that."

Honey is suicide. Rather hadn't realized that Booce meant it literally. He thought it over, then said, "But it's their choice—"

She shook her head. "Not my decision. Then there's detective work, and riot control, and rescue work. We don't specialize much. You learn to do all of that, but first you learn how to fly a ship."

"What happens to cadets who fail? Murphy, what happens to *dwarves* who fail?"

"Nothing. I mean, they're out of the Navy, of course. They hire out or they build a business, maybe they go diving in the Dark for mushrooms and fan fungus, or they go logging. Hell, what does a logger do if he fails at something?" She looked closely at him. "What's the matter?"

"I'm having trouble with this. There're more people here, so there's more places for people, right? If you can't hunt or do earthlife farming, you just try something else?"

Murphy nodded brightly. "Next question?"

Would we see each other if I joined up? May I call you Sectry? "Thank you, Bosun."

"Any time," she said, and sprang away. She coasted parallel to the bark, toward Wheeler as he emerged from behind the Wart.

"It's big," Wheeler called. "Booce Serjent, you've made your fortune."

"Recouped it, anyway. The first thing I'll do is rebuild *Logbearer*."

"Yes. . . . Well, I've seen enough. Eight thousand tons or so. Those scars on the metal—"

"We used the saw to get the slabs that make up the firebox. It worked better than I'd hoped. It's a good substitute for sikenwire, and the saw's not damaged."

Wheeler nodded, satisfied. "Can we lift you back to your ship?"

"No, we need to cover this somehow before we reach the Market."

"I think you're worrying over nothing. How could anyone steal anything this *big*?"

"With saws. . . . Well, you may be right."

They watched *Gyrfalcon* steam toward the Clump interior. Something bright twinkled at the bow. "He's calling home," Booce said. "They use mirrors to bounce Voy-light where they want it."

"What happens now?" Clave asked.

"Wheeler thinks I sawed off more metal than just those plates for the firebox. He'll watch to see if I sell it on the black market. He could have bought the Wart on the spot, but he thinks I'll give him a better price if he waits. A few days after we dock I'll get an offer. It'll be too little, and I'll boost them a bit and then take it so I can stop guarding the metal—"

"What do we do *now*, Booce? Jeffer must be going crazy waiting for us to call in."

"We're still being watched."

Gyrfalcon was tiny now. Its steam trail was dissipating. Clave asked, "Can they still see? Have they got something like the carm windows?"

"A box they hold to their eyes. Clave, we'd like some way to disguise this mucking great chunk of metal."

So *Logbearer*'s five crew swarmed over the Wart, taking their time, just looking at it from all angles, as if there were some way to hide a conspicuous pucker in the honest wood of a tree. The sun crept from zenith to pass north of Voy. And presently Debby said, "Booce, you've seen more trees than any of us. What kind of a thing causes this kind of scar?"

"Something hits the tree . . . could be stony, it doesn't have to be metal. I've seen this kind of gap with nothing in it at all, just chewed wood healing over. I never did figure it out."

Debby wondered, "Ice?"

Booce's face went . . . stupid? Mouth agape, eyes drifting. He said, "Heh. Yes! A chunk of ice could smash a tree, then melt."

"Still doesn't do anything for us. What else? Disease? Is there something that builds nests? Or the tree bugs could chew just in one place—"

"Sure, a honey pod could hit a tree, and the bugs would chew a huge hole . . . give me a breath, Debby." Stupid again: thinking. "We can do it. Twenty days to reach the Market. Okay. We need a fisher jungle that's got termites, and we need to look like we've been through a disaster, but we've got that already. I *never* thought I'd come home with a pod for *Logbearer*'s cabin!"

"What do you need from us?" Clave asked.

"Stay here, talk to Jeffer. The rest of us will fly up the trunk. This is *nice*. If Wheeler wonders why we're still hovering around the Wart, he'll see us hiding it!"

Rather swallowed his protest, because Clave was saying "You don't need Rather. I want him."

"Stet." Booce had his wings on. "Come, children."

Chapter Thirteen

The Termite Nest

from the Citizens Tree cassettes, year 5 SM:

THE LAGRANGE POINTS

MATTER TENDS TO COLLECT IN THE FOURTH AND FIFTH LAGRANGE POINTS (L4 AND L5) OF GOLDBLATT'S WORLD. THESE REGIONS APPEAR LESS TURBULENT THAN THE STORMS AROUND GOLDBLATT'S WORLD ITSELF, BUT WE HAVE POSTPONED EXPLORING THEM IN DEPTH.

WE INSPECTED ONLY L4. THE MORE OR LESS STABLE REGION IS 600 KM ACROSS. MAPPING THE EQUIPOTENTIAL TIDE CURVES GETS US NESTED CRESCENTS. WHAT SHOWS TO THE EYE IS A MISSHAPEN WHORL DWINDLING EAST AND WEST INTO THE ARC OF THE SMOKE RING PROPER.

THE WHORL IS GREEN AROUND THE PERIPHERY, DARKER AND BROWNER NEAR THE CENTER, WHERE AC-

CUMULATED MATTER BECOMES THICK ENOUGH TO
BLOCK SUNLIGHT. TIDE-STABILIZED PLANTS DON'T
THRIVE HERE. WE'VE FOUND FAMILIAR LIFE FORMS—
TRIUNES AND COTTON-CANDY JUNGLES—BUT ALSO
SOME SPECIALIZED LIFE FORMS NOT SEEN ELSEWHERE.

DEEP RADAR INDICATES SOLID MASSES WITHIN THE
DARK INNER REGION. NONE ARE LARGE.

WE HAVE WONDERED WHY THE CLUMPS NEVER CON-
DENSED INTO ONE LARGE BODY. PERHAPS LIFE ITSELF
ACTS TO REMOVE MATTER FROM THE INNER REGIONS.
THE FISHER JUNGLES' ROOTS DISRUPT LARGE PONDS.
SAPROPHYTES FEED IN THE DENSE CORE, THEN FIRE
SPORE PACKAGES AWAY INTO THE SMOKE RING. BIRDS
ARE FORCED OUT BY FAMINE OR POPULATION
PRESSURE . . .

IT MADE HIS HEAD HURT.

Jeffer ate as he read. When he reached the end he
doggedly scrolled back to the beginning. His students
had found it bewildering. So did Jeffer, but he had an
advantage over his students. He had Kendy.

If Kendy would call!

Today he had hunted the sky. He'd returned to the
dead fisher jungle trailing a sizable shieldbird. A small
fire near the carm had cooked his catch. He was getting
good at it. Sandwiching the meat between two of the
shieldbirds' bone plates cooked it tender without
scorching it.

He almost choked when the carm suddenly spoke.
"Jeffer? This is Clave. Jeffer, can you hear me?"

Jeffer swallowed hard and said, "Prikazyvat Send to
pressure suit. And about treefeeding time too! Are you
alive?"

"Jeffer, we couldn't get to the helmet. The Navy searched *Logbearer*. Even after they left they were watching us. Where are you? Are you hidden?"

"Clave, I found something good. Do you remember Booce's description of a fisher jungle? A green puffball a klomter across, with a long coiled root. It reaches out to put the root in a pond, but there's poison on it and it can attack life forms and kill them and draw them in to rot—"

"Right. They're not supposed to live outside the Clump."

"Maybe so. This one's fifty klomters from the Clump fringes, and it's dead. The axis trunk is hollow. There's a Navy ship coming this way. It's not likely they'll want to sniff around a fisher jungle, but I've got the carm moored inside the hollow anyway. When it goes away I'll tether it above the root so the carm can get some sunlight. Where are you? I can't see anything."

"I'm in the dark. I'm in that channel we chopped past the Wart. We haven't moved the silver suit yet."

Jeffer remembered extending the work done by the happyfeet. His back and shoulders still ached. "We should have let the happyfeet do more of the carving."

"It was worth it. Booce was right. The Navy knows if you're carrying metal. This Petty Wheeler citizen knew about the Wart, but he didn't look for anything behind it."

"What's the Clump like?"

"Crowded. We'll have the log moored in twenty days. Booce has a way to hide the Wart. He's afraid of thieves, and we can't use the silver suit to win a fight, because—"

"No, of course not."

"—Because they'd recognize it. Jeffer, they've got

three silver suits. It's a mark of high rank. Dwarves are in good shape if they join the Navy, and Rather's had an offer."

An offer? "Rather, you there?"

Jeffer heard Clave's distant yell. Presently Rather said, "Here."

"You had an offer to join the Navy? What was said? What did you tell them?"

"I didn't take the Petty seriously. The idea is to learn something about the Admiralty, buy some earthlife seeds, and get back to Citizens Tree!"

"We want to know about the Navy too."

"I learned a little—"

Clave interrupted. "How serious are we? Booce, what has the Navy got that we want to see? I'm not so eager to see the inside of a Navy rocket that I'd feed one of my—"

"The Library! The cassettes! What's on the Admiralty cassettes?"

"All *right*, Jeffer. What makes you think Rather could get to any of that? Booce might know, but he isn't here to ask."

Jeffer finished the shieldbird meat while he thought. "Ask him when you get the chance. Now, I'm getting terminally bored here. Are you free to move the silver suit into the rocket?"

"No. It's too easily recognized," Clave said.

"How about just the helmet?"

"We'll have to ask Booce, but . . . I think not. Let's get Kendy in on this. Are you in contact?"

"He said he was changing orbit. He'll be back in another day. Clave, I wish you could give me some kind of a view."

"I'll think of something. Jeffer, Rather's waving at me."

"Scientist out."

"Clave? You'd better see this," Rather said.

"What? I was talking to Jeffer." Clave crawled out of the cavity behind the Wart. "Oh."

From out of the crowded sky came a shapeless thing colored a dead yellowish brown. Its outline was fuzzed with a jittering motion that caused the optic nerves to twitch. It was coming straight at them, and *Logbearer* was behind it.

"Get out of its way, Rather, it's going to hit! Got your wings?"

They fled. The thing fell toward the Wart with a faint, frightening buzzing sound. Myriads of black flecks swarmed around it, insects much smaller than honey hornets.

It struck the crater around the Wart and deformed like soft mud.

Logbearer bumped the trunk more softly. Debby emerged from the hatch in the forward pod. She stared hard at the intrusionary mass. She called, "It's going to stick."

Booce answered from inside. "Stet. Spread the honey."

Debby waved at Booce and Rather, but that was all the attention she gave them. She began spreading red sticky honey around the rim of the crater.

The swarm of insects followed her. When she closed the circle, most of the insects had migrated to the honey.

"Done!"

"Good. Get aboard. Clave, Rather, I've got to moor this thing. Want a ride?"

Clave bellowed, "Booce, you get out here and answer some questions!"

Booce's head popped out. He thought it over, then flapped to join them. He looked indecently self-satisfied.

"It's a termite nest," he said before Clave could ask. "We'll say we didn't have any choice, it was the only tree around and we had to get back to the Clump because . . . I'll think of something."

"Uh-huh. The honey?"

"Encouragement. When the termites run out of honey they'll eat wood. They'll bond the nest to the Wart."

"What about the silver suit? Were you just going to leave it?"

"Where would it be safer?"

"Jeffer's all alone in the sky. He'd go crazy!"

Booce's grimace told it all. Clave said, "He's the Citizens Tree Scientist, and he is *not* a crazy murderer. He was in a fight with our lives at stake, Booce, and he used what he had. It was more powerful than he thought it was—"

"He used it twice."

"Booce, if you've ever been a happyfeet bandit yourself, tell me now."

Booce was astonished, then amused. "Oh, really! No, I'm *not* protecting my own kind. I'm *not* defending bandits that prey on loggers. Granted they'd generally rather attack some tribe of helpless savages. Your suspicions are right there, Clave, but it doesn't mean I *like* bandits. I wouldn't have burned a whole damn tribe either!"

"Uh-huh. You would have sent them away without

hurting them so much. How? Describe the procedure in detail."

"I can't do that. Jeffer hasn't told any of us how to fly the carm! Clave, the Scientist is not to burn any tribe, ever again. I'm telling you, not him. *You* are to stop him."

"I'll tell him. Now what?"

"Oh . . . we'll leave everything but the helmet where it is. Jeffer's scientific eyes are in the helmet, right? Those little windows in the forehead? We'll moor it in the nest. He'll have a view. We'll be spending enough time around the Wart; we'll talk to him then."

The CARM with its cameras was hidden in a dark place, the pressure suit was in another, the incoming recordings were days old, and in present time Jeffer wasn't present. Kendy skimmed the recordings. He was learning more through *Discipline*'s own senses.

Logbearer was easy to follow: forty kilometers of tree with tufts missing and a metal mass off-center, now rounding the starward limb of the L4 whorl. Maintaining contact wasn't going to be easy here. *Discipline*'s new orbit had twice the period of Goldblatt's World, with periVoy falling north of the L4 point. Tilting his orbit out of the Smoke Ring allowed his instruments to penetrate less of the garbage in the Clump; but the log and the CARM and all of Kendy's citizens would be circling that center on long kidney-shaped paths.

At least he wouldn't have to burn more fuel. If he could establish relations with the Admiralty, his present orbit might suffice for hundreds of years.

Savages in a thriving civilization would find trouble sooner or later. Patience. Some emergency would force

Jeffer to bring the CARM into the L4 point. Then he must open the airlock to the Navy . . .

One problem at a time. Wait. Learn.

Jeffer entered the cabin before Kendy passed out of range. There was fresh pink blood on his tunic and more on his hands.

"Kendy for the State—"

"Hello, Kendy. How can we—"

"Jeffer, if Rather has an offer from the Navy, I want him to accept."

"You would. Rather didn't sound too enthusiastic. Neither am I. How can we get away with not hiding the silver suit?"

"An excellent question." Kendy was using light amplification, but it only showed him iron ore and chewed wood. Clave and Rather had departed the hiding place. "If the Navy has pressure suits, they'll recognize yours. I thought of disassembling it, but they'd know the helmet too. We would ruin the camera if we tried to dismount it, and the electrical source is in the helmet."

"So?"

"Patience."

"Feed your patience to the tree, Kendy. I've got a cryptic entry under 'Lagrange Points'—"

"I've had three hundred and eighty-four years to learn patience. You are almost out of range. Can you feed yourself there?"

"Sure. There's hand fungus, and flashers living on the bugs, and some other things. In a way it's like learning to hunt all over again . . . " The link was lost.

A chance to examine the Admiralty's military arm from inside! But Rather wasn't *enthusiastic*. And Kendy would have to talk Jeffer around before his arguments could even reach the boy.

Patience . . .

Chapter Fourteen

Docking

from Logbearer's *log, Captain Booce Serjent speaking:*

YEAR 384, DAY 1700 THIS TRIP WE NEED NOT FEAR HAPPYFEET.

I FEAR JEFFER THE SCIENTIST. I FEAR THE SECRETS WE HIDE FROM THE ADMIRALTY AND THE SECRETS THE SCIENTIST KEEPS FROM ME. BUT I OWE A MAJOR DEBT TO CITIZENS TREE.

DAY 1710 WE'VE FOUND A SIMPLE WAY TO HIDE OUR EMPTY CREWMEMBER. MAY I NEVER HAVE THE CHANCE TO THANK THE HAPPYFEET FOR MAKING IT POSSIBLE.

DAY 1780 WE'VE GONE FOR MORE PODS. ONE HAS BECOME OUR CABIN, ONE STORES EXTRA WATER IN CASE A FIRE SPREADS. RETURNING WITH A POD FOR *LOGBEARER*'S CABIN GRATES IN MY SOUL, BUT IT WILL SURELY HIDE THE WEALTH WE CARRY.

DAY 1810 MAKING PAINTS GAVE MORE TROU-

BLE THAN I EXPECTED. THE COLORS ARE STILL POOR,
BUT WILL SUFFICE. WE'VE PAINTED THE HONEY HORNET
LOGO ACROSS *LOGBEARER*'S CABIN. NOW WE'LL SEE
WHAT CAN BE DONE ABOUT MY CREW'S WINGS.

DAY 1996   ENTERED ADMIRALTY SPACE.
GYRFALCON HAS REGISTERED LOG AND METAL FOR CUS-
TOMS. ASSESSMENT TO FOLLOW.

DAY 2000   LOG NEARING MARKET. METAL
CONCEALED FROM ALL BUT NAVY. CONDITIONS
OPTIMAL.

DAY 2015   DOCKED. SENT THE CREW OFF
WITH CARLOT. WOULD HAVE GONE WITH THEM IF I
COULD. I NEVER DEALT WITH TREE DWELLERS BEFORE.
I CAN'T GUESS HOW THEY'LL REACT.

I MISS RYLLIN. I NEVER IN MY LIFE HAD TO WEAVE
SO MANY THREADS AT ONCE.

A FAT, BABY-BLUE TORPEDO CRUISED SLOWLY ALONG THE
Serjent log, moving closer to where Rather and Carlot
stood watch. Suddenly it split along its length, and four
slender blue-and-orange triunes dived on some tree-
dwelling life form.

Rather pointed. "Four?"

"Sometimes triunes have twins."

"I've never heard of that."

"You never saw one of those either." She pointed out
a triangular shadow. "That's a Dark shark. They don't
usually come this far skyward. They're dangerous. All
teeth, no brain."

"Skyward?"

"Dark, skyward, spin, and antispin. We use all the
normal directions too."

"How do you keep it all straight?" Rather reached to

wrap his legs lightly around her waist. She did not respond.

A ball of green fluff stretched a quarter klomter of curly tail toward a passing sphere of water.

Booce, Debby, and Clave were around the log's horizon, ready to use the rocket if anything came near. Carlot and Rather kept watch from the east. "We can still keep our eyes on the sky," Rather pointed out.

Carlot pounded his kneecaps with her fists, briskly. "Who's watching *us*?"

"I don't mind triunes watching. Maybe I even like it."

"What about the houses?"

"Houses?"

"You'd say *huts*. Look—"

Beyond the Market, beyond Carlot's pointing chin, six cubes were strung along a spire of wood with a rocket tank and nozzle at one end. "That's Captain-Guardian Wayne Mickl's household," Carlot said. "He's one of the richest officers."

"It isn't close."

"That one is."

A structure floated against the Dark, a cube festooned with platforms, extrusions for tethers, water pods, and other things for which he had no name.

"That's the Hillards, I think. And that puff jungle is the Kerians."

The sky was full of puffballs. The one Carlot pointed out bore a big *K* with other letters within, too small to read. Carlot said, "Crew live in those if they're too poor to buy wood. Usually they clip a logo in the foliage."

Rather laughed. "Okay, I'm convinced." Another puff jungle was marked with a slender figure-eight. "If you're rich, you build with wood?"

"Yes."

"Your family has a house."

"We find our own wood! I'll show you if it comes around. It wasn't finished when we left, but I know the design."

"We're poor, aren't we? Citizens Tree is poor."

"You live poor. The carm makes you rich, except that you can't use it . . . and there's your share of the Wart, once Father sells it. Rather?"

"Speaking."

"I think I'm going to marry Raff."

Rather turned to look at her. The sudden black emptiness in his belly was entirely new to him, yet he couldn't feel any surprise. He got his lips working. "Would you be better off if I went somewhere else?"

She was having trouble meeting his eyes. "I haven't seen Raff in three years. Rather, I think he'd be happier if he didn't know we've been . . ."

"Making babies. I won't announce it."

"All right. But I wouldn't push you into the Navy just to get rid of you! Don't ever think that! I don't know if it's a good idea or not. I don't think for Citizens Tree, and I don't do your thinking either. Don't give up the idea just to stay near me."

"I have no intention of joining the Navy." Rather turned back to the sky. He was still on watch.

Now that he knew what to look for, the sky danced with structures. Puff jungles were everywhere, more of them toward the Dark, and some were marked. There were wooden cubes and clusters of cubes, elaborately colored in bright primaries. He could pick out wind-curdled lines of steam crossing the Dark.

He said, "People change in three years."

Carlot said, "Sure. Maybe we won't like each other. We'll see. I'm telling you, Rather, if we get along I'll marry him. Belmy was the first of the logging concerns, and it's the most powerful."

The helmet had been in place in the termite nest for some twenty hours. Kendy ran the record through his mind, classifying, deducing, making notes. When he reached present time he went back to the beginning.

His mental model of the Admiralty was shaping up nicely.

There were more new plants than new animals. Animals showed the same modified trilateral symmetry here as they did in the Smoke Ring proper. There was a clear absence of tide-stabilized plants: hardly surprising.

The buildings were interesting. Everything less primitive than a carved-out cotton-candy plant was built in rectangular solids. It was as if they still built to resist gravity . . . but not quite, for addenda sprouted at any angle, and openings might appear in any of the six walls. They looked like Escher had designed them.

Some houses had a big square fin sticking out from one corner. The Clump was turbulent. In infrared Kendy could see little whirlwinds, "dust devils" with no dust in them. A house would tumble and keep tumbling without that fin.

Unless it was attached to some larger structure.

Why was there only one Market? It didn't look difficult to construct. Houses were scattered through the outer Clump. Most would have no neighbors at all most of the time. There was no need for such isolation. It was inefficient and lonely.

The tree's attitude changed continually. The view through the helmet camera wavered with it. Kendy was getting only glimpses of the Market, but he could integrate them.

Many of the structures were moored by concrete to the Market frame. Too bad. Kendy would have liked to offer them concrete. If he ever got their attention he'd have to have something to offer, some bit of knowledge to make their lives better. He knew the pattern that would make them a thriving, Smoke Ring–girdling State in a hundred years; but there had to be something quicker.

Electricity? The Clump never had true night either. How did they light their houses?

He recognized a glass tank from one of *Discipline*'s seeding missiles, emitting a sharp spike in the light spectrum: chlorophyll. They'd made it into a hydroponics tank. The faceted hemisphere nearby was an old survival tent sheathed with wood, with transparent facets left open. Other structures on the ring were made from Smoke Ring materials: mostly wood, but one was a cotton-candy jungle tethered to a mast.

A building beyond the Market sported a broad picture window: the windscreen from a CARM. Otherwise, no glass anywhere. No sand?

Crew drifted among the buildings like leaves in an autumn wind. Half-grown children flew in groups tended by one or two adults . . .

I've got to know more. Can I find a way to move the helmet into the Market?

Booce was in position at the rocket, with hot coals ready, and Debby and Clave to watch and to steer. The sky was thick with debris. One might hope that Carlot and Rather would keep to their watching . . . but at least they'd have their chance to talk.

A Navy ship had them in clear view. Supervising, to make sure that the log came to rest a safe distance from the Market. A larger rocket pulled free of Belmy's log and steamed toward *Logbearer*.

Booce and his damaged tree would arrive in a blaze of publicity.

He was returning like a beggar.

But of course there was the Wart . . . and the silver suit behind it. He would have liked to lose that. The worst the Admiralty could charge him with was "concealment of vital resources," but that was a heavy charge. Was it worth the risk, to be able to talk to Jeffer the Scientist?

Not that he had a choice.

He was almost home. The Belmy log was ahead of them, eclipsing the Market. The tuftless end looked chewed. Belmy had sold some of his wood.

Woodsman was prominent in the sky, arriving nozzle-foremost. There was no mistaking that elaborate superstructure, four cubes surrounding the water pod, each painted a different color, each bearing the small black *B* logo. Handholds everywhere, and a steering platform around the nozzle, with a carved rail. The nozzle was mounted a little out from the rest so that replacement water pods could be inserted easily. Hilar Belmy was coming to greet him.

"Almost time," he said, and saw Clave and Debby nod acknowledgment. Booce pushed his coals into the firebox. The fire would need time to catch. "Belmy docked his log behind the Market, of course. We're going to have to dock behind him. Then it gets unpleasant."

Debby asked, "Why not dock just ahead of the Market?"

"Because that's where the Admiralty docks its ships."

"Booce, if you're expecting a fight, you'd better tell us now. Also, what weapons—"

"Bloodthirsty woman. No weapons, no fight. It's just . . . I'm coming in behind Hilar Belmy with a fuel pod for my cabin and a log damaged in two places. Checker only knows what Hilar will think. He'll change his mind when he finds out about the Wart, but . . . That log still has one tuft."

"So?"

"Why on Earth would Hilar Belmy leave one tuft on a log?"

Clave asked, "Why didn't we?"

"Wind. You can bring a log to its mooring with one tuft on, but it's tricky. It usually means you ran out of honey or bugs . . . hmm?"

"What?"

"Just a passing thought. *Hello, Hilar!*" His crew stared. They had never heard so cheerful a sound from Booce Serjent.

Woodsman vented steam, decelerating. Two men rode the platform above the nozzle. They were tall: taller than Booce. Their necks were long, like Ryllin's; there was a great-grandmother in common. Black hair, gray hair, otherwise nearly identical.

The black-haired man waved joyfully. Booce couldn't tell Belmy's sons apart, but that must be Raff, and Carlot would be waving back.

Gray hair was Hilar. He looked good: sturdy, prosperous, a few kilos more massive than his son. "Booce! I thought I'd offer you a tug. How . . . Did you have some trouble?"

"That we did!" Booce's shout became less effortful

as Belmy's rocket drew closer. "Hilar, thanks for the offer, but I'll bring her in myself."

"Stet," Hilar Belmy shouted back. *Woodsman* slowed and stopped fifty meters from the trunk. "Join us after! I want to talk business."

"Stet." Booce dropped his voice. "Now let's do this *right*. Debby, stand by the water pod. Clave, I'll need you to help me turn the rocket." *Logbearer* looked ready. The firebox was dull red; white light glowed through the cracks. The plates had never fit exactly, but they didn't seem to be coming apart. *Logbearer* was tilted nearly parallel to the bark.

Booce entered the cabin. He blew into the flow port (**CHUFF CHUFF** chuff chuffchuff . . .) and emerged panting. "Clave, not quite yet . . . now."

They heaved against *Logbearer*'s fuel pod, tilting the rocket in its bark nest to keep it pointed straight toward the Market. Condensing live steam drew a line across the sky. *Woodsman* stood well clear. The log turned as it approached Belmy's log; and the rocket turned in counterposition, and the log's sluggish motion slowed, slowed, stopped.

Booce dove into the cabin. He knocked the plug loose from the flow port and jumped away. Warm water globules followed him out. "I've spilled the water. Debby, hose down the firebox. We're in place."

The firebox hissed. Globed in invisible water vapor, the coals went out immediately. The gap between the two logs remained constant.

"And *that* was a nominal docking," Booce said in satisfaction.

Carlot and Rather came around the curve of bark. Booce called to them. "Well done, my crew! I'm cross-

ing to *Woodsman* to see what Hilar wants. Carlot, why
don't you show these people the market?"

Carlot reached him well ahead of Rather. "Speak to
you in private?"

They flew clear of the others. Booce asked, "Have
you been making decisions?"

She nodded, jerkily. "Raff probably expects to see
me."

"Then you decide whether to take him along. Will
Rather behave himself?"

She hesitated. "It's not a good idea."

"I'll make your excuses to Raff. Blame everything on
me."

Clave and Debby followed Carlot. Rather hung back
a little. Flying too close to Carlot would be uncomfortable now.

They passed close to *Woodsman*. It was Rather's first
good look at Raff Belmy. He was dark-haired and tall,
three meters or close to it, with long arms, long symmetrical legs, stiff black hair, and a short beard. His neck
was like his father's: long and graceful, but the lines of
muscle showed strongly. If you liked tall, Raff was a
good-looking man. He waved energetically as they flew
past, then ducked into a cabin. There must have been
hasty conversation in there. When Raff Belmy emerged
he did not follow them.

"I'd have liked to talk to Jeffer first," Clave said softly.

"Let him wonder," Debby answered. "We'll have
plenty to tell him when we get the chance."

They passed the Belmy log, and the Market was huge
in their sight.

The wheel was ten to twelve klomters in diameter,
and a hundred meters broad. The inner surface was

partly covered with . . . houses? They surely weren't proper huts. They glowed with color. Most were cubes and oblongs, but there were other, stranger shapes: a faceted hemisphere, a wooden cylinder, a larger cylinder as transparent as the carm's bow window.

Carlot shouted back at them as they flew. "We learn all about the Market in school. It started out as a beam carved along the entire length of a log, three hundred years ago. The Admiralty ran it through a pond to soak it. Then they used tethers to bend it in a circle. Before that, the Market was only shops tethered together."

This tremendous made thing . . . this was wealth. Rather felt the fear and the awe of any savage approaching a civilized city.

People were flying to meet them.

"The older shops are funny shapes. Balls and geodesics. That glass cylinder is the Vivarium. Vance Limited grows earthlife there." Carlot noticed that all three of her charges were dropping behind. She turned in a half circle and rejoined them. "Are you all right? Tired?"

Rather answered for the others. "It's a little frightening. Who are those people?"

"Friends. Traders. I'll introduce you. Raym! Crew, this is Raym Wilby—"

He was an older man, a jungle giant with pale skin and dark, curly hair and beard. He shouted at the sight of Carlot, bounced into her a little too hard, and wrapped her in his arms. As he examined her companions the wide, goofy smile was lost to a look of comical amazement. "Carlot? Shorts?"

She rebuked him. "Raym, these are some of the citizens who saved our lives when our tree caught fire. Hey, John, hey, Nurse!" Others were arriving. Carlot squirmed loose; clasped hands or toes; chattered intro-

ductions. John and Nurse Lockheed were brother and
sister, and looked it, with angular faces (shaved, in John's
case) and white-blond hair. Long-headed Grag Maglicco
was in the Navy as a Spacer First. Adjeness Swart was
small for a jungle giant. Her hair was black and straight,
her nose curved and sharp. She worked in the Vivarium,
Carlot said.

Half a dozen others reached them and Rather started
to lose track. Raym would be thirty to forty years old;
Grag would be a little younger. The rest were around
Carlot's age. Jungle giants all, and expert flyers.

Carlot told her tale as they flew toward the Market.
Other strangers joined them and she had to start over.
Now there were a dozen jungle giants among them, and
all were strangers to all but Carlot. She stuck to her
father's story, and made no mention of Wart or carm or
silver suit.

The citizens were uncharacteristically quiet. There
was too much to see, and they were surrounded by as
many strangers as there were adults in Citizens Tree.

Debby was finally ready to admit that it had been a
mistake. She wanted to go home.

She hadn't been with Anthon in hundreds of days.
Booce was afraid of his wife, Jeffer seemed to be married
to the carm, and Clave . . . the best she could tell, Clave
was vastly enjoying his vacation from his wives. She was
in a sexual desert.

She had other reasons for being on edge. The Market
covered a quarter of the sky. No bigger than a small
tree, it was obtrusively a *made* thing, made by the ancestors of this crew.

They didn't look that powerful. They flew a little
closer together than Debby found comfortable. Easy to

guess why: they'd been flying all their lives. Raym Wilby was chattering to Rather. "The bugeyes, they get whistling drunk when the fringe blooms. You just reach out and pop 'em in a bag—" Debby tried to follow it, but she couldn't. The Lockheeds stayed together, off to one side. Maybe they were shy?

Adjeness Swart flew alongside Debby. Cheerfully she called, "How do you like the Market?"

"Impressive."

"Your first visit to civilization?"

"We like to think we've got a civilization too," Debby said. *We must be gawking like fools.*

Adjeness laughed and waved around her. They had passed the rim of the Market and were crossing the central gap. "If you've got anything like this, the Admiralty would like to know it." And as Debby was throttling the urge to tell this smug Clump dweller about the carm, Adjeness asked, "How much can you see of the Admiralty from your tree? Why haven't any of you come here before?"

"Some didn't want us to come at all. We didn't know what we'd find. Maybe things we wouldn't like. Excuse me." Debby kicked hard to reach Carlot.

Chattering companions surrounded Carlot. Debby tried to ease inconspicuously among them, just to listen . . . but she hadn't counted on Admiralty manners. The locals drifted away from Debby and Carlot and left them to talk.

Carlot look at her questioningly. Debby said, "I'm afraid I'll say too much."

"Adjeness?"

"Yeah. It isn't just the questions, it's her treefeeding superior attitude. Carlot, I feel so *small*."

"Can't help you there, but . . . go fly next to Raym.

He won't let you talk at all." Carlot held her voice low. "Raym Wilby is an old Dark diver. It's gotten to his brain."

"What's he doing with us?"

"He's an old friend of Mother's. I'd hate to have her see him now! I could get rid of him, but it's more trouble than it's worth. Either I'd hurt his feelings or it'd take forever."

"Stet. What's a Dark diver?"

"Ask him. Or just listen."

Debby dropped back. Raym was telling Rather, "It isn't the dark that bothers you, it's the thick. Your eyes get used to the light in there. It's kind of gray, and the colors bleach out. I never heard of a diver getting wrecked unless he was a damn fool, because things don't move fast in there. But you can't move fast either. You drift. Sometimes you get lost, you forget which way is out. You come out never knowing how many days you were in."

Rather asked, "Why do you—?"

"Credit. On a bad trip you only come out with mud, but Zakry pays high for mud. A good trip, you can come out with your hull covered with blackbrain or walnut-cushion or fringe." Raym grinned, and Debby realized what it was that bothered her about Adjeness's toothy smile.

Rather said, "This makes you—"

"No. You never hold onto it."

"—Rich?"

Teeth. Raym was an older man, yet he still had half his teeth. Adjeness must be Debby's age, but her smile was all teeth, with only three or four gaps. The rest were youths: no teeth missing at all.

Angular huts surrounded her. Debby fought vertigo.

Down in all directions; no tide. The Admiralty crew were forming a line as Carlot led them toward a huge transparent cylinder. They had flown all their lives. Their grace made Debby feel clumsy.

Debby eased into line behind Rather. The starstuff cylinder had an opening at one end. Debby brushed it with her wings as she went through. None of the others did.

Chapter Fifteen

Half Hand's

from the Citizens Tree cassettes, year 80 SM:

WE'VE FOUND A FUNGUS WITH IMPORTANT MEDIC-
INAL PROPERTIES . . .

WOODSMAN'S DOOR HAD BEEN BRACED HOSPITABLY OPEN.
A guest need only grip the rounded edge as he flew
past, set his wings in the racks, and swing himself in.
Booce entered an atmosphere rich with blackbrain tea.

Jonveev Belmy was a small woman, not much more
than Clave's height. Booce had watched her auburn hair
turn gray over the years, but it was still long and thick.
She was busy at a turning cookglobe. She stretched a
foot to meet Booce's hand.

Her grip was strong. "Booce, I'm so sorry about
Wend. Is Ryllin all right?"

"She's fine, Jonveev. We're doing business with Cit-

izens Tree, and that's where she is now." He wondered
what Jonveev was thinking. Her concern was real, of
course; but she had never dealt with Booce himself. In
business matters Ryllin and Jonveev did the talking.

Jonveev swung the big globular teapot round her head
to settle the water, then quickly opened the spigot.
Steam puffed. Hilar wrapped the teapot in cloth and
passed it to Booce. "I never saw a log come home like
that. Do you want to talk about it?"

Booce sipped and swallowed. He liked his tea hot,
and this was just off the boil. He savored old memories
as much as the powerful, bitter taste. He said, "Not a
lot—"

Hilar waved it off. "Oh, then we'll—"

"I have no wish to drive you crazy at this time."

"Tell us a story," Jonveev said.

He told it long. Carelessness and bad luck; the fire;
Wend dead, Karilly mute with shock. "There was a tuft
tribe waiting to rescue us. They helped rebuild *Logbearer*.
We found a tree." Booce hesitated. "We were only half
a thousand klomters from the Clump, Hilar, and we
might've had to go halfway to Gold to find a better
choice. It was big and it was close and we wanted to go
home."

"I never saw termites on a tree before."

"A new breed, maybe. They're dying now. They
haven't done that much damage, and it's a lot of wood."

"That it is. We have a problem," Jonveev said.

The tea had come round again. Booce sipped and
passed it on. "I notice you managed to sell some of your
wood."

"Some. Then the whole Market saw you coming and
the orders dried up. I could have sold at a loss, but
Jonveev thought—"

"I thought we might reach an agreement," she said. "The merchants can't whiplash us if one of us announces that his wood isn't for sale."

Booce smiled. Such things had been done. "We'd have to give them time to believe we mean it. Thirty sleeps or so. That'll cost one of us."

"We're willing," Jonveev said. "We'll want something in return, of course."

"Speak further." He sipped. The bitter taste of blackbrain fungus was the taste of civilization and hospitality and homecoming. He wished with all his heart that Ryllin were here. If Hilar was tiptoeing round the edges of a risky venture, Ryllin would have known at once.

Jonveev said, "Booce, we'll agree not to sell our tree until the next midyear. What I want is a loan at reasonable interest. Or I'll offer you the same deal."

Booce was silent.

"The loan would be, say, ten-to-fourth chits. Enough to keep one of us going for nearly a year." She affected not to notice Booce's sudden mirthless smile.

"I don't have that much on hand. And you, I suspect, don't need that much—"

"We'd need it if we don't want to short-change some of our other concerns. But we can float such a loan and recoup it by selling our wood. On the other hand, whatever you're doing with . . . what was it, Citizens Tree? It's bound to bring you money, but not soon, stet? But you have a house that's never been lived in."

The tea caught in his throat. Booce swallowed carefully, managed not to sputter. He said, "Ryllin would wring my neck."

"Well, then, you can't do it," Jonveev said instantly.

On second thought . . . he could put the house up for sale, to buy time. If he set the price high, buyers would hang back and wait, because the Serjents were supposed to be broke. If the Navy bought the Wart metal soon enough . . . he'd have to take a lower price, but he'd be able to keep the house.

But what did the Belmys have in mind? What would a loan do for them? It would be eating interest— "What interest?"

"We'd pay fifteen percent until the next midyear, or take the same."

That was high but not out of line. His first niggling suspicion began to look like the truth. "I'll sleep on it," he said.

Wickerwork ran around the inside of the glass bottle and across the center; wickerwork everywhere, but you had to look twice to see it beneath the plants and mud. The mud was at the interstices, held in place by nets. Plants grew from the mud, bearing red and yellow spheres and cylinders. Leafy vines strangled the wickerwork, the mud, and everything else in sight.

It was a jungle with curving corridors through it. Debby felt a sudden terrible homesickness for Carther States . . . but the jungle of her childhood was drab compared to the Vivarium.

The old man who watched from within one of the openings was an elderly, undersized jungle giant. In the humid warmth he wore only a loose pair of short pants. His knees and elbows were knobby; his skin was yellow-brown, and there was something funny about his eyes. He watched the growing crowd in some surprise. He said, "Late, Adjeness."

"Zakry, these are customers," Adjeness Swart said firmly. "They've been living without earthlife since Checker knows when."

"*Have* they." The yellow man brightened. "Well, we can't have that. Carlot Serjent, how good to see you! Adjeness, why don't you show the crew what they've been missing?"

Carlot and the yellow man disappeared into the greenery. Adjeness Swart said, "Clave told me that. No earthlife crops. Is it true?"

"Almost," Debby said. "We've got turkeys."

Raym Wilby guffawed. Adjeness was suppressing a laugh. "Turkeys, stet. Try this." She reached into a jungle of vines and plucked forth a red sphere. She sliced it apart with her knife and offered wedges around.

It was juicy. Its taste was strong. Debby chewed and swallowed, trying to decide if she liked it.

Rather plucked a slender yellow spike from the muck. Adjeness intervened. "Not that, Rather. You have to cook that. Try this. Don't eat the skin." The sphere Adjeness sliced up for him was orange outside and in. Rather bit into a wedge, and his eyes got big.

Being back on Earth would be like this, Debby thought. Alien. She recognized almost nothing.

There were people darting among the plants. They glanced incuriously at the intruders, then went back to what they were doing. Some sprayed water at the mud globules or the plants themselves. One was pushing a plant ahead of him; muddy pale appendages waved naked at one end. An older man floated slowly along an aisle, turning as he flew, to see in all directions.

Debby tried a slice of the orange sphere. The sweetness, the wonder of it almost paralyzed her. "Treefodder!"

"That's an orange. This—"

"I can see that." Debby reached at random. "What's this, a yellow?"

"Plum. Not quite ripe."

It was bitter, sour. Adjeness gave her a dark-red spheroid from another part of the plant cluster. "This should be better."

It was.

"You wouldn't want to spend all your funds on fruit," Adjeness said. "You'll want legumes too, but they have to be cooked. Let Carlot take you to Half Hand's Steak House before you make any final decisions. Unless you're really rich? Then you can buy everything."

Clave said, "I'm not sure what we can afford. I haven't heard any prices."

Adjeness nodded. "Here. Eat everything but the center, and you can eat that if you want to. Apple."

Rather asked, "Clave, did you eat like this in Quinn Tuft?"

"No. Hey, corn! We had corn before the drought. Here. Strip off the leaves. Now the silk too." He smiled, watching Rather bite into it. "Just the outside, and it's supposed to be cooked."

"It's okay this way. Leave the white stuff?"

"Stet."

Raym's hand sneaked into a bush as if without Raym's knowledge. Three red objects each the size of his thumb went into his mouth all at once. Debby was nearly sure Adjeness had caught it. She only smiled.

Carlot and the slant-eyed man emerged from a leafy wall. Carlot's voice was just slightly ragged. "Crew, Zakry Bowles is our host here. We'll go look at the prices after we know some of what we want. How are you doing?"

"Carlot, it's wonderful!" Rather burst out. "Oranges, plums, I think we want everything in sight. Zakry, can you eat everything here?"

"Almost. Every plant has something you can eat growing on it some of the time. These potatoes, you can't eat what you see. The root's down there in the mud. You don't eat the inside of an ear of corn—"

"Clave told me."

"Or the pit of a plum."

"Oop."

"What did you do, swallow it? It'll come out all right in the end. Let me show you what else we've got—"

Bean vines grew mixed with the corn. They seemed to want to take over everything. "We stopped growing tobacco long ago," Adjeness said. "Only the officers had fire handy, and they weren't buying enough. This is lettuce." Lettuce was leaves. It wasn't as sweet as foliage. Strawberries were as startlingly good as oranges. Squash looked like jet pods. Zakry was enjoying himself.

They went back to the entrance to examine a list of prices. Clave memorized the numbers he was interested in. "Why so much for strawberries and bananas?"

"Strawberries keep dying. I don't have bananas. Can't grow them here at all. They need tide. The Navy buys them off some tree dwellers east of here, when they get the chance. Clave, you haven't established credit yet—"

"Credit?"

Zakry Bowles spoke slowly, enunciating. "You haven't shown that you can pay. But you can pick out what you want now, then come back later, pay me and collect it."

"What we want is stuff we can grow in a tree."

They discussed that at length. Rather joined in; there were things he would not go home without. Debby eased over to Carlot. "What's got you upset?"

"He won't give me credit. We came in with a pod for

our cabin and the Belmy log already in dock. Well, Dave
Kon owes me money. I'll go see him. Excuse me."

Zakry was urging something else on them: a greenish-
yellow fruit with an obscene shape. He showed Debby
how to remove the peel. Clave laughed when Debby bit
into it, but it was good. Carlot was talking to the Lockheeds, and they were nodding.

She came back. "I have to talk to Dave Kon. You'd
be bored—"

"You're leaving us?"

"Stet. Stay with the Lockheeds. I'll meet you at Half
Hand's Steak House."

Half Hand's was across the Market.

They flew through rain. Droplets flew from the edges
of their wings. Rather breathed through his nose; from
time to time he snorted out water. Debby and Clave
were doing the same. The locals had donned masks of
gauzy fabric, except for Raym, who breathed in the rain
as if he cared not at all.

Half Hand's was a faceted dome adjoining a smaller,
less symmetrical structure. You could see through some
of the facets on the big dome: they were starstuff fabric.
The rest was gray concrete. One six-sided facet had been
cut away, and a wooden door hinged into the opening.

Grag Maglicco, the Navy man, suddenly asked, "Have
we all got sticks?" He assessed the blank looks correctly.
"Go on in. I'll join you, couple of breaths." He swerved
aside, headed for an angular hut twenty meters along
the wheel.

The inside was concrete too: concrete troweled over
a structure of starstuff, outside and in. The concrete
bore paintings of intriguing complexity and a variety of

styles, but Rather caught only glimpses of these through a wall of citizens.

Half Hand's was full. Men, women, and children made a hemispherical shell around the newcomers, their toes clinging to two-meter poles protruding from the concrete. There were no foothold poles in the windows, so those stayed clear.

From an open hexagon on the far side drifted smoke and cooking odors. Nurse Lockheed led them that way. She called through the opening. "Half Hand?"

A man came out of the crowd behind her. "Hi, Nurse. You got money?"

"No. Put it on the Serjents' tab. I have a party of eight."

There was nothing wrong with Half Hand's hands. He was a jungle giant, mostly bald, and his arms and legs were corded with muscle. He said, "Serjents? I heard—" Full stop. "Sure, I'll give the Serjents credit. What do you want?"

"Let's see the kitchen."

"Nobody sees the kitchen." Half Hand was peering past Nurse Lockheed. "Shorts?"

"Tree dwellers. They've never seen anything like your kitchen."

"Nobody sees the kitchen."

"I did," Nurse said.

Debby pushed her way forward. "Half Hand? I'm Debby Citizen—"

"Pleasure," he said gravely.

"I wonder if you'd be interested in a description of a kitchen in a tuft."

Half Hand studied her; nodded. "Just you. Nurse, the special's moby."

"How old?"

"Eight days ago, shipful of Dark divers took a moby. Special is moby till we run out. Sausage cost you three times as much. No turkey today."

"We want vegetables, lots, all kinds. Couple of kigrams of moby too, not too rare."

"Moby's ready now. Vegetables soon. You, Debby, you cooked in that tree?"

"Some."

Half Hand beckoned her in.

Rather could feel the eyes. With a conscious effort he *looked*. Of the forty or so diners, only a dozen or so were watching what was happening at the kitchen entrance. Even those concentrated more on eating: their right hands kept pale wooden sticks in constant motion. The eye-pressure still made him flinch.

Grag Maglicco rejoined them. He passed out pairs of sticks of pale wood, no bigger than the branchlets a tree dweller was used to.

A woman brought them a two-kigram slab of meat, black on one side, pink on the other. John Lockheed took it on his knife. He flapped toward the wall, pushing the meat ahead of him. Diners edged aside to give him room or to avoid getting grease on their clothing.

Nurse had to urge them. "Come on."

There were too many people.

But Clave followed Nurse, and Rather followed him.

There was room. Nurse talked to some of the locals around them. John carved chunks from the meat and passed them, knife to sticks. Moby meat was *good*. Tenderer than swordbird, richer than turkey.

Grag's own sticks—like every Clump citizen's—were ornately carved. Some were wood, more were bone. Grag caught Rather looking. He showed Rather his own bone sticks. "You carve them yourself. Circle would mean I'm married. Spiral means I'm looking. A bird would say who I work for. Outline around the bird would mean I own the company. What I've got is the rocket, 'cause I'm Navy. You'd want a honey hornet, for Serjent Logging. Change life style, start new sticks."

John Lockheed pointed out a clump of customers to Clave. Tall men and women, a dozen or so, and a few infants; isolated, clustered close as if for protection. Peculiar footgear, thick-heeled sandals with toes protruding. "They're happyfeet. Half Hand should make them check those shoes at the door," John said. "They're for fighting, for kicking."

"Lupoffs?"

"Yes. Why?"

"No reason," Clave said.

Gourds of red liquid passed among the diners. One came within reach, and John took it. He drank, then passed it to Clave. "Fringe tea. Don't take too much."

It went from Clave to Rather. Its taste was bitter and sweet, not unpleasant. John stopped Rather from passing the gourd to Raym. "Too much in his blood already." Raym grinned and nodded.

Debby and Half Hand joined them; they made room. Debby said, "He's got four citizens doing the cooking, all women. There's a major fire against the back wall, held in by sikenwire. The kitchen's got maybe twenty windows in it, and Half Hand closes some of them to get the breeze he wants, keep the fire going and the smoke out. He's roasting a slab of moby the size of two men. It's black on one side and raw on the other, and he slices off the charred side.

"There's also . . ." She waved a hand and a foot as if trying to describe without words. "I thought it was a ball of hard stuff like the Vivarium. Inside, a froth of water and live steam, and cut-up plants."

"It's a bag," Half Hand said. "Keep it turning, the vegetables cook even. Draining the water is the tricky part."

"I saw them do that. They open the bag and throw the whole glob of cookwater at the lee windows and catch the vegetables in a net."

"Ho! Vegetables are ready then." In fact three jungle-giant women were already flying around the dome's curvature, passing out what they carried.

"We use an open pot," Debby told Half Hand. "Tide keeps it in, whatever you're cooking. We cook meat and vegetables together. If you don't keep stirring it, it all bubbles out."

"M'shell!" Half Hand waved one long-toed foot in a half circle, and the nearest of the kitchen women came toward them. She served red and yellow and green vegetables into small-mouthed bowls. Half Hand said, "We only serve earthlife plants. A man wants foliage, he gets it at home. Meat's different. We take what we get. Nothing turns up, Sanchiss has a turkey farm Darkward."

The vegetables: some were good and some were not, and some you couldn't decide right away. Clave was making notes as he ate. Food that wasn't eaten went into a wooden barrel. From time to time one of the woman replaced the barrel.

Grag Maglicco was asking Debby, "Has Booce been wondering where his house is?"

"He hasn't done anything about it yet."

"Well, we saw Serjent House a few days ago. It was twenty degrees spinward of the Market and maybe fifteen klomters skyward. Doesn't look like anyone's disturbed it. Can you remember to tell him?"

"Stet. Tell me something else?"

"Sure."

Debby waved around her. "I'm surrounded by teeth. How can so many of you keep most of your teeth?"

Grag fished in his tunic and produced a stick like a third eating stick, carved in the same way, with a tuft of bristly vegetable matter at the end. "Scrape your teeth after you eat," he said, and grinned at the tree dwellers' dubious looks.

Another gourd of fringe tea came past. Rather was thirsty; but nobody was taking more than a mouthful, and he didn't either. He passed it to Grag, who drank deeply and sent it on.

"Why do they call you Half Hand?" Debby asked.

"My great-square grandfather was Half Hand. Stuff that moved the old carm sprang a leak, froze his hand. Grandfather was Half Hand too. Got bit while he was Dark hunting. Now me. Soon or late, I lose it." The idea didn't seem to bother him. "Raym, sell me some walnut-cushion?"

"Not this trip. Next time."

"I need it. Goes good with potatoes. Green beans too."

"Next time for sure," Raym promised.

Nurse Lockheed laughed and said, "He can't. He doesn't have a ship."

Carlot was shocked. "Raym? You lost your *ship*?"

Raym nodded without looking at her.

Half Hand quietly moved off toward the kitchen. Nurse reached out and lifted Raym's chin. "Tell them the story, Raym!"

It was the last thing Raym Wilby wanted. Some of the locals were looking embarrassed. Clave was quick enough to catch it. "If it's story time, I'll tell you about the breakup of Dalton-Quinn Tree."

Raym's ship was forgotten as Clave talked.

Rather knew the tale too well. What he noticed was the rise in the noise level. Half Hand's was turning boisterous. Clave's words were just perceptibly slurred, as if he were sleepy; yet he was animated, frenetic, as he relived what had been the end of the world for him and for Rather's parents. Rather himself was feeling strange.

Half Hand was back. "Look out the window or go outside," he said. "See something."

"Water," Rather said clearly.

"What?"

"Water, not fringe tea. Does something to my head."

"Oh. Get you water, stet. *M'shell!* I'll fix it. Tree dwellers shouldn't drink too much fringe. Get to a window, boy. Thank me later."

The nearest window was crowded, but Rather managed to get his head into the grouping. He watched three kitchen women carry garbage barrels outside and fling their contents across the sky. Nothing happened for a time. Rather continued to watch. He felt as if he were dreaming. Fringe?

He dreamed that triunes abruptly converged from all directions, splitting into individuals as they came. Rather shouted: not a warning, just an incoherent yell.

The women heard. They looked at him in the window and laughed. Slender blue-and-orange torpedos dove among them. The wind of their passage sent them tumbling. In twenty breaths it was over. The triunes moved away, regathering their families. The garbage had vanished. The women kicked to stop their spinning—and not one had been touched by the predator birds.

All the strangers around Rather were laughing at him.

The only good thing about it (he decided as he returned to his pole) was that nobody else had gone to a window. Grag and Debby seemed mostly interested in each other, but the rest were held spellbound by Clave's storytelling. He spoke of the foray into the Carther States jungle—

He was on the verge of describing the London Tree carm! "Clave?"

"Me, I didn't notice most of this, what with my broken leg. Yeah?"

"Drink some water. This fringe is strong."

John Lockheed said, "Yes, you're not used to it," and passed Clave the water gourd. Clave drank, and drank again. Rather was given a gourd, and he couldn't understand how he had become so thirsty.

Then Carlot was there and it was all right, and Rather was free to go to sleep.

Kendy saw them streaming toward the log like a covey of brightly colored birds: young men and women stretched like taffy. Wings patterned in primary colors flapped behind, making them seem even longer. Each pattern was different. Birds must find each other in the sky.

The helmet microphone picked up giggling and snatches of talk. Some flew with skewed clumsiness, drunk on alcohol or other recreational chemicals. Kendy ran the record again, but the noise factor was too great; the words wouldn't come clear.

They passed out of the helmet's view and were gone.

Chapter Sixteen

High Finance

from the Citizens Tree cassettes, year 926 State

CHECKER

OFFICER RESPONSIBLE FOR THE ATTITUDES AND EMO-
TIONAL WELL-BEING OF THE CITIZENRY, AND FOR THEIR
BENIGN RELATIONSHIP TO THE STATE.

BOOCE STARTED TEA WHEN HE SAW THEM COMING. HE
looked them over as they entered. Nurse Lockheed had
the giggles. Her brother was furious.

Booce smiled at them. "Half Hand's?"

"Right. Fringe tea." Carlot wasn't happy.

"It was strange," Debby said. "We ate . . . well, we
tried everything. Clave made a list—"

"I hope we can afford it all," Clave said. "Where'll we

229

grow it? We'll have to plant the out tuft and make the lift cables twice as long."

The teapot went among the half-dozen Clumpers who had returned with *Logbearer*'s crew. In a dozen breaths it was empty.

"Jonveev was kind enough to lend me some stuff," Booce said. "The teapot, some blackbrain, some cookware. Carlot . . ." He frowned. She should have brought supplies from the Vivarium and the Market shops.

She handed him a translucent blanket-leaf folded lengthwise. There was food within: vegetables, a slab of cold moby meat, and a baked sweet potato. "Half Hand gave us credit."

"That'll be breakfast. Jonveev fed me."

John Lockheed sensed what was happening. "Many thanks, Booce, and we'd best be going."

Raym showed his astonishment. "We just got here!"

"Raym, *now*. Come on, Nurse. Booce, we're sorry about your trouble, but it didn't ruin a good evening. It's good to see you back safe. Carlot—" He stretched his toes to clasp hers. Then the whole covey of Clumpers moved out into the rain, shooing Raym and Nurse ahead of them.

"Now why did they do that?" Clave asked.

"They know we have to talk about money. You don't do that in front of strangers," Booce said. "All right, Carlot."

"Zakry won't give me credit. We'll have to forage the trunk for food. I went to Dave Kon. He still owes for a klomter of wood from our last trip. He wouldn't pay me. He offered full payment if we'd sell him a klomter off the new log at two times ten-square. I turned him down."

"Right. That mutineer thinks we can't afford to hire

a judgment! See, Clave, the Admiralty won't convene a civil court unless both sides can prove that they can pay court costs. Loser pays. But the Navy knows we have the Wart! One way or another, we'll get money or credit. Carlot, I think I know what Hilar has in mind. Burl."

Carlot thought it over. The tree dwellers watched with no sign of comprehension. She said, "Risky. Nobody knows how."

"Hilar can afford to take the chance. He brought his tree in with the tuft still on. He asked for a loan and offered decent terms. Usually the tree dies, but sometimes—"

Debby suddenly said, "I remember. The idea is to let a tree grow without tide. The wood's supposed to twist into knots?"

"Right. But trees aren't really built for that. I wonder if Hilar knows something? If he can get money to live on, he can grow his burl while we sell our wood. He'd like to get the money from us, if we had it."

"We should be asking Jeffer about this."

Booce grimaced. Then: "Sorry. Debby, you're tree dwellers, you *should* know a lot about them, but you've never seen a tree growing outside of tide."

"You wouldn't grow burl yourself, stet? Belmy's not a fool or he wouldn't be richer than you, stet?" Booce bridled, but Debby went on. "He knows something you don't, something about burl. Jeffer the Scientist knows a *lot* we don't. Let's ask."

"Burl," Jeffer said musingly, watching the faces in the bow window. Debby was hiding anxiety. Booce had asked his question with some belligerence. This had been her idea, not his. *Are you any good at all? Prove yourself, Scientist!*

Blue lines of print scrolled across the faces.

INTEGRAL TREES GROW WELL IN A WIDE RANGE OF TIDES. LOW ATMOSPHERIC PRESSURE KILLS THEM FASTER THAN LOW OR HIGH TIDE. IN DENSE AIR AND VERY LOW TIDE THEY MIGHT SURVIVE. IN FREE-FALL THEY DIE. OTHERWISE WE WOULD FIND TREES GROWING NATURALLY IN THE CLUMP.

Booce was talking. "Hilar thinks he's got me by the seeds. He offered me a loan if I withdraw my tree from sale, but he's not serious. It'd break me. I'd be paying interest, and no way to get it back. Of course he doesn't know about the Wart metal."

"Do you really need to know if he can grow burl?" Jeffer said. "Booce, you're satisfied that he's *trying* it. You only need a short-term loan till you can sell your metal. The Belmys aren't your enemies, are they?"

"No, they're friends. Who would I talk to if I couldn't talk to other loggers? But Hilar would *love* to have me carving the dumbo on my sticks, and all the loggers want to be richer than, say, the architects. Jonveev won't loan me money unless she thinks I can pay it back. Or if I've got some kind of collateral . . . hell."

A TREE SHOULD CONTINUE TO GROW IF THERE IS SUFFICIENT TIDE TO PULL WATER AND NUTRIMENT INTO THE TREEMOUTH AND TO WORK THE INTERNAL VEINS WITHIN THE TRUNK. SPIN THE LOG, JEFFER.

"Tell them about the Wart," Carlot was saying.

"I didn't want to. I guess . . . I've got to. It'd be better if I knew *exactly* what Hilar's planning."

"He'll spin the log," Jeffer said.

"What? What for?"

"Spin tide, Clave. It's a scientific thing. Here, pick up that pot or whatever and throw it round and round your head. Arm's length . . . like that, stet. Feel the pull? Like tide, isn't it? Belmy'll use his steam rocket to start the log spinning, not enough to tear it apart, just enough to keep some pull inside the tuft. The tree needs tide to move its food around—"

"By the State, I believe you're right."

"But the, uh, growth patterns would still be screwed up, with Voy going round and round and weird Clump tides going every which way. I've never seen burl, but isn't that what you want, Booce? Grain that doesn't grow in straight lines? He'll spin it just enough to keep water and fertilizer in the treemouth."

"Yes. Okay."

LOSING CONTACT.

Hilar and Jonveev waited, wearing polite smiles, until Booce had finished talking. "Burl," Hilar said. "It sounds interesting but risky."

"Hardly cost-effective," Jonveev said.

Booce said, "There are other values. It would be indecently lucrative if it worked. You'd have done something nobody else could." They did not comment, and he went on. "Let's assume, just for talking purposes, that you've been considering a burl tree. Who else would you let in on the secret?"

The Belmys looked at each other.

"You'd need masses of tree food. Mud, say, from deep in the Dark. Would you buy it from Zakry? Or haul it yourselves, with *Woodsman*?"

Jonveev sighed. "All right, Booce. What have you got in mind?"

"*Logbearer* could haul the mud to feed the tree. The whole Market knows that my last trip failed. They won't be surprised when *Logbearer* becomes a Dark diver. Let them think I'm looking for fringe and blackbrain while I haul mud for Zakry."

"Mmm," said Jonveev.

"One thing more. I've got eight kiltons of metal buried under the termites."

Their faces were quite blank. After a moment Jonveev said, "That's not portable money. You still can't offer us a loan, not until you sell it."

"An excellent point. Hilar, Jonveev, what I want is this. First, you do your damndest to turn that half tree into burl. Second, I need a loan—"

Hilar was laughing.

"A short-term loan to let me spend money like an old Dark diver while I wait for the Navy to buy my metal. I'll pay twenty percent to the crossyear, and I need ten-to-third chits. I'll pay part of it back in mud at the same price Zakry pays. The rest at the crossyear, and I'll hand you another five times ten-to-third. That'll save any project you had to shortchange. It's not a loan, though. It buys me half the burl."

"*Half!*" Jonveev exclaimed.

"So."

Caught! Jonveev Belmy laughed and said, "We hadn't thought of spinning the tree. But can you really afford to risk that many chits? You're moderately rich now. Why not stay that way?"

"I like the odds. I've got some crew who think it might work, and they're tree dwellers. I think *you* think it'll work, and that helps."

"Two-fifths of any burl, and we want five times ten-to-third chits. We'll get you your loan, but at forty percent to the crossyear. Mmm . . . I'll hand you our cash on hand and give you the rest in ten days."

Booce said, "I'll pay thirty percent to . . . to ten sleeps past the crossyear. The Navy might just hold me up for that long. And classify this. If the Navy knows I took a loan, they'll know I'm still under pressure. I want them to *move*."

Hilar laughed. "Where else could it have come from?"

"I'll visit the house before I start throwing money around. They'll think I had it in the house."

And all of this was reported in garbled form, through Clave and then Jeffer, who had never dealt with finance, to Kendy, who never had either. But Kendy had sketchy records of the capitalistic societies that had died with the formation of the State, hundreds of years ago.

It was a hell of a way to run a civilization. These people *needed* him.

Jeffer, seated before the CARM camera, asked, "Do you understand any of this?"

"Yes, but it would be difficult to explain. What matters is that your citizens will have their earthlife seeds."

"Yeah." Jeffer stretched unself-consciously. "That's good. We'll have to talk fast when we get back to Citizens Tree. The seeds'll help, and we'll carry fresh food too, something they can eat right then. Are you getting what you wanted?"

What Kendy wanted was still beyond his reach. He said, "I've learned some things."

"Tell me."

"The Admiralty is self-sufficient. They're a successful culture, but the crime rate must be high. Otherwise they would need fewer Navy ships, and the houses would have more openings." Kendy displayed the picture the pressure-suit camera was sending from the Clump. Small green outlines flickered as Kendy pointed out ships, then the few but massive doors on nearby houses. "They've settled the outer shell of the Clump, but they only venture gingerly into the dark center. Their infant mortality rate must be as bad as yours. When they add up their population they don't count children, any more than you do."

"I never noticed that. Hmm . . . London Tree didn't either. Is it because so many children die?"

"Yes. Wait a thousand years and the death rate will have diminished. There's nothing else to be done."

"I never thought there was. While I've got your attention, Kendy, I found a listing on the Clump. Lagrange points, it's called. What do these words mean? Equipotential, saprophyte— Something's happening."

A steam rocket emerged from the fog and rain. It came to a halt fifty meters from the helmet camera. "Navy," Jeffer said unnecessarily. "I wonder . . . that's Booce. And a silver suit!"

"I see them. An equipotential is the curve on which some force or energy level is everywhere equal. It might be gravity or tidal force or magnetic force. A saprophyte is a family of plants that don't use light. We'll see some if Clave can take the helmet into the Dark."

Four men flew toward the camera: two in Navy armor, one standard-issue pressure suit, and Booce Serjent. The pressure suit was better kept, cleaner and shinier, than the Citizens Tree suit. There were big Navy-style fins at the ankles. The design painted on the back was repeated on one shoulder and on the fins: a broad green ring with a blue dot at the center.

Kendy tried to make contact with the suit radio. He found nothing. Either it wasn't on, or the frequency had wandered over the centuries.

The helmet was thrown back on its hinge despite the rain. The face inside was a rounded anglo face, without the soft elfin look of most Smoke Ring citizens: a "dwarf" face, shaved, sprouting an Earth day's worth of dark shadow.

The "'dwarf" looked around him. "'This was clever, Booce. Do you have torches?"

"I'm sorry, Captain-Guardian. We can make some up."

"No need. How do I get through this muck?" The dwarf had no accent.

Kendy gloated. No accent! He spoke exactly as a State citizen would have. The officers must learn their speech from the Admiralty Library!

They were drifting out of view. Kendy switched to the fisheye lens. He and Jeffer watched the Captain-Guardian take his wings off and tether them to lines on his chest, shin-sticks uppermost. The two lower-rank Navy men pulled up an edge of the termite nest. The "dwarf" squirmed in. Sudden yellow light flashed through the hole.

Jeffer asked, "Does that light come from the pressure suit?"

"I'll show you how to work the helmet light. Later."

The "dwarf" popped out of the hole. "There's a respectable store of metal here. We'll have to wait for the Council to convene before we make an offer per kilton delivered. Unless you're prepared to accept an immediate offer of, say, two times ten-to-fifth chits for the whole chunk?"

"I can get two or three times that on the Market."

"Perhaps. If we come to an agreement I can give you payment within ten days."

"No, thank you, Captain-Guardian. I'll wait. Maybe I can earn some money Dark diving. Can I offer you tea?"

"You wouldn't want to have to sell your new house. Two and a half."

"No. I should point out that you've been seen coming here. There's a happyfeet jungle in dock, and they might guess what that means. Also I'll be expected to hire an exterminator. I can't hide the metal much longer."

The Captain-Guardian snorted and waved to his escort. They departed.

Booce waited until they were well away. Then he moved face-on to the camera. "Jeffer?"

"Here."

"That was Captain-Guardian Wayne Mickl. Officer by birth, but his effective rank is Guardian. Keeping him happy is a good idea."

"He didn't look happy."

"If he's too happy, we got robbed. Jeffer, how sure are you that spinning a tree will make burl?"

Jeffer laughed. "I never tried it myself."

"Yeah. Are you all right?"

"It isn't too bad. Something like being young again, just old enough to hunt alone. I've got the cassettes when I get bored. I miss Lawri."

"Well, I'm going to move the silver suit. We can't leave it here."

"Where, then?"

"My house. I'll set it up so you can see the commons room. We can talk any time, and when I have guests you'll see them too."

"That's good," said Jeffer.

VERY GOOD. LOSING CONTACT.

Chapter Seventeen

Serjent House

from the Citizens Tree cassettes, year 6 SM:

SHARON LEVOY SPEAKS OF THE ARCHETYPAL REBEL-
LIOUS COMPUTER, HAL 9000, FROM GILLESPIE'S
OPERA *2001.* CAROL BURNES CLAIMS *FRANKENSTEIN*
AND *FAUST* TO BE OLDER AND MORE APPROPRIATE IM-
AGES. ONE-UPMANSHIP IS ALIVE AND WELL IN THE
SMOKE RING. ONE AND ALL, THEY EXPECT ME TO TELL
THEM *HOW IT HAPPENED.*

FOR THE RECORD: I DON'T KNOW WHAT'S WRONG
WITH KENDY.

—CAPABILITY JASPER GRAY
CYBERNETICIST, *DISCIPLINE*

DEBBY WAS IN A HURRY THE NEXT MORNING. IT SEEMED
she'd arranged something at Half Hand's: she was to
meet Grag Maglicco for flying lessons. Booce drilled her

to make sure she wouldn't get lost in the sky, then sent her on her way.

The rest shared out the meal from Half Hand's for their breakfast, then got to work. They fueled and fired *Logbearer* and set it steaming along the trunk. A half turn brought the rocket to a halt opposite the Wart.

Clave, Carlot, and Rather swarmed out and attacked the termite nest with matchets. When *Logbearer* blocked the Market, and floating chaff and chips of bark and wood blocked most of the sky, Clave and Rather ducked into the nest. Clave retrieved the body of the silver suit, Rather the helmet. Booce had kept the rocket hot. He jetted water into it, and away they went.

Secrets. Rather was starting to get the knack of it.

Half the termite nest had been scraped away, not by a hired team but by amateurs. What would the Market think? *Booce must be hurting for money. His crew has exposed damage to the log: a gaping, ugly hole behind the termite nest. They've quit in disgust.* Unlikely that anyone else would pry into that bug-infested darkness.

The house had drifted about the sky since its completion a year and a half since. Debby had relayed Grag's message: it was fifteen klomters skyward and some degrees to spin from the Market. The house was closer than it had been when Grag spotted it, but it was still a three-day trip.

The house was five cubes arrayed around a concrete core. A small puff jungle grew on the roof. The main door was a huge slab of wood five meters long by four wide, half a meter thick. Booce set massive triangular braces to lock it vertical to the doorway. Mountings covered the inner surface: tethers for wings and cloaks, and coils of line, and big knobs to serve as moorings for winches and pulleys.

They tethered *Logbearer* to the door. In its shadow they moved the silver suit and helmet inside.

Secrets. What has been seen? Logbearer *flies to Serjent House. The crew stays for some hours while Booce inspects his new home and shows it off to visitors. Presently Booce will be spending money.*

Navy: *Booce has retrieved funds from some hiding place. He can outwait the Navy to sell his metal.*

Belmy House: *Booce came as misdirection.*

The Market: *Any hiding place in Booce's house must be empty now.*

"Where do we put it?" Rather held the helmet like a severed head.

"Look around," Booce said. "Something will occur to you."

The citizens smiled at each other. They began to tour the house.

Doorways led from one section to another through the star-shaped concrete core. There were only two ways to move. Rather had to squeeze past Clave circling the other way.

The house was roomy: as big as a Citizens Tree hut, though much harder to build. The public room was lined with handholds and with hooks for outer garments and weapons, and a rack for a teapot.

The outer wall of the kitchen had long slots in it for ventilation, a concrete fireplace with a bellows attached, and racks for wood and cookware. Rather found Carlot making tea. He asked, "You already know?"

She nodded brightly.

The sleeproom: tethers and some wiry foliage padding four of the walls.

What was this next room? Curtains fixed across both interior doors, handholds and tethers mounted next to small windows with hatches over them . . .

Ah. This was the treemouth. And the fifth was a storage room, with another oversized door and moorings for tethers, but nothing stored yet.

Rather returned to the public room.

Debby was moving slowly around the perimeter. She seemed more cheerful than she had been lately. "Hi, Rather. Grag brought me back. I gather we're looking for some secret hiding place. Any luck?"

"Not yet. Booce, how do you get rid of the treefodder after you feed the tree?"

Booce stared. "*What?* —Oh. The wind floats it away and fisher jungles gather it in. Now you know why everyone doesn't just tether his house to the Market. Find anything?"

"I didn't see any hiding places. I've never seen a house before."

"You were all somewhere else, so I searched here," Debby said. "Nothing. Booce, are there holes in the concrete?"

Booce laughed. "I could have done that. Access through the walls? Well, any burglar could tear the core apart and all he'd find is concrete and two chunks of sporing fringe buried along the hub. Meanwhile, what do you think of my door?"

"Thick. Like you're afraid someone might kick his way through."

"We tend to make them massive. Not just for burglars. It has to stand up to rough treatment when you're moving heavy stuff."

Clave shook his head in disgust. "We'd know who our

thief is. We'd kick him into the sky. Booce, your trouble is, you've got too many people in the Clump."

Booce was taken aback. "I never thought of it that way. Anyway, let me show you what I did—"

When the door was fully open, one could slide aside a panel in the edge that faced the hinges. The half-meter thickness of the wood had been hollowed out. The silver suit went in easily. The helmet was barely small enough.

"Now we need a hole," Booce said.

"Kendy for the State. Jeffer, would you rather sleep?"

"Mpf? No. Hello, Kendy." Jeffer stretched. "If I didn't want you waking me up I'd sleep outside." He looked at the view in the bow window. "Oho!"

It was dark, but Jeffer could make out Clave's anxious face. His voice sounded faint, distant. "Jeffer? Talk to me, Jeffer."

"Prikazyvat Relay to pressure suit. Scientist here."

"What do you see?"

"You. And a ragged border. What did you do?"

"You're looking through a hole in a door. Booce ripped a hook out. From here it looks like he just put too much tension on it."

"Good enough. I take it we can talk. Rather, you there?"

Rather floated into view, smiled, and waved. Others joined, until five citizens floated in a star with their heads inward.

Booce said, "I've made a deal with the Belmys. Jeffer, would you like to learn something about the Dark?"

"You mean the Clump interior? Sure."

"That's good, because I've agreed to bring back some mud for Belmy's burl tree."

"You're going? All of you? *Logbearer?*"

"Ah . . . no. I think I'd better stay here. I've been weaving financial threads into one very complicated net. Carlot, you can handle *Logbearer* alone, stet? And I gather Raym Wilby is at liberty. He can guide you." Carlot was nodding eagerly. "Oh, and Hilar hadn't thought of spinning the burl log, but he's going to try it."

"Sounds good. Carlot, will you take the helmet so I can see these marvels?"

Carlot looked to her father, who said, "Why not?"

"Good. Rather, tell me about the Navy. Take your time."

Rather talked. Kendy guessed that the boy wasn't hiding anything, but he kept jumping back and forth. Kendy printed questions across the bow window; Jeffer solicited descriptions of Petty Wheeler, Bosun Murphy, Navy armor, the Navy ship, Murphy's description of Navy life, Wheeler's offer . . .

"Is this standard, Booce? Anyone can join the Navy?"

"Not just anyone. They wouldn't have Carlot because of her legs. Otherwise . . . well, any savage could join, but he might not get beyond Spacer First until they've watched him for years. The Navy wants loyalty. They take more men than women, and they won't take you if you're too old to be trained."

"Loyalty?"

"If you're loyal to your tribe, you're not loyal to the Navy. Navy above all, even family."

"The question is, if Rather goes in, can he get out? Booce?"

Booce mulled it. "Up to a point. It would be . . . convenient if Rather let Petty Wheeler make his pitch. Rather, the Navy could put certain kinds of pressure on me until I talk you into doing that. They want the Wart, but they can slow things down for me, and we don't want the Navy taking a *hard* look at us."

"No," Clave said.

"But when Wheeler interviews you, he might learn that you're simply not suited to Navy life. I can help you to help him reach that conclusion."

Carlot said, "He could get out later than that. Rather, my cousin Grag says they treat you like a copsik in Basic, but after that you're supposed to think you're better than the citizens. They do think they're better than us, and they don't take just anyone. When you're ready to leave, just do something wrong. Or get sick and stay sick. Tree dwellers do get sick in the Clump. They'll bounce you out."

"You think I should do this?"

She shrugged unhappily. "Whatever you want."

Jeffer said, "I'd really like to get him into the Library."

Booce shook his head. "No dwarf gets beyond Guardian unless he was born an officer, and even then . . . well, Wayne Mickl is officer and dwarf. They need him as a Guardian, so he'll never *use* his higher rank. Guardian is the lowest rank that can reach the Library, but they can't use it because they aren't taught to read. And you wouldn't be a Guardian for years, Rather."

Jeffer jumped on it. "But he *could* reach the Library. And Rather *can* read, and I can teach him how to use a carm keyboard!"

Rather was feeling trapped. He knew how to talk to Jeffer the Scientist, but how could you argue with a door?

"I hate to pass up the chance," Clave said. "Rather, you're reluctant. How do the rest of you feel? Debby?"

"It feels like we're selling him as a copsik. I'm against it."

Thank you, Debby!

Clave stared at her. Then: "Rather, does it feel like that? I wouldn't *do* that. We're just talking now—"

"They want his loyalty, stet, Booce? They've been doing this for going on four hundred years," Debby said. "Maybe they can *get* his loyalty—"

Clave snapped, "Treefodder, Debby. London Tree was keeping copsiks for about that long. When the chance came to bust loose, they did it!"

"Not all of them, Clave!"

". . . Uh-huh. Booce?"

Booce said, "We're talking about power, Navy power, and it cuts two ways. If Rather was Navy, the Serjents would see a certain friendliness emerge. I'd love to put a son in the Navy."

"Carlot?"

She spoke to Rather, not Clave. "If you can stand it. Remember what I said about Basic. They worked Grag's tail off . . . hey. You're stronger than Grag. You lived in a tree. You just might give them a shock."

"We know you can fit a silver suit," Booce added. "Even Bosun Murphy doesn't know that."

"I'm scared."

Clave just nodded, but Jeffer snarled like static. "Oh, Rather! We're *here* already! Back in Citizens Tree, that was the time to be scared." Pause. "What are you scared of?"

"It's all too strange." Rather was suddenly, unbearably homesick. This wooden house, all angles—

"It'll keep being strange. Nobody fooled you on that."

"Scientist, I came here *looking* for strange. I wouldn't *be* here if it was going to be just like Citizens Tree—"

"Then—"

But Rather had the words straight in his mind now. "I followed you here, but the idea was to face the Admiralty in the company of my friends and my elders! And my father. Are we all going to join the Navy now? Is that what we're talking about?"

Clave said, "Jeffer?"

The door said, "I'm for it, of course, but the boy's got a point. It's his risk, not ours."

Rather wasn't finished. "You're asking me to swear to something that isn't true. I am *not* loyal to the Navy. If you thought I was, you wouldn't like it."

Nobody wanted to answer.

"You can feed your secrets to the tree. I will not join the Navy. But I can go talk to Wheeler, if you think it'll help. I'll do that."

"I go with him," Debby said firmly.

"And Booce, you tell me how to look unsuitable." A black depression was settling over him. He felt rejected by all of his companions save Debby; but Carlot wanted him out of the way. For Raff Belmy.

Chapter Eighteen

Headquarters

from the Citizens Tree cassettes, year 384, day 2050:

JEFFER THE SCIENTIST SPEAKING. CANDIDATES ARE
CONSIDERED UNSUITABLE FOR THE NAVY IF THEY ARE
SICKLY, OR UNDEPENDABLE, OR EASILY LOST OR DIS-
TRACTED, OR LOYAL TO SOME ENTITY OTHER THAN THE
NAVY. THEY MAY HAVE UNACCEPTABLE MOTIVES FOR
JOINING. IF A FAMILY MEMBER ACCOMPANIES, CANDI-
DATE MAY BE RELUCTANT OR MAY NEED SUPERVISION.

ACCEPTABLE CANDIDATES WOULD PRESUMABLY
HAVE OPPOSITE TRAITS. DATA ARE AS ACQUIRED FROM
BOOCE AND CARLOT SERJENT.

HEADQUARTERS WAS A PILLBOX: A SHORT, WIDE CYLINDER,
blurred to Rather's weeping eyes. The rim was dark
wood. The nearer flat face was concrete covered with a
variety of doors, platforms, winches, coils of line . . .

and a broad strip of glittering stuff very like the hull of
the carm. Two rockets were moored near the hub. A
third, larger, was being winched in nozzle-foremost.

Debby looked back. Rather was far behind. When she
stopped flapping, a gust of wind caught her wings and
turned her on a random axis. She sighed and flapped
back to rejoin him. "I wish I could help," she said.

Rather made himself laugh. "I did it to myself. Debby,
you fly better than me."

"I watched the crew when we went to Market. Keep
up a steady kick. Don't try too hard. If you kick with
all your might the wings just bend and don't take you
anywhere."

"What I need is longer legs."

"Longer *wings* might do it. Try the Navy wings too.
Now, what door did Carlot say?"

"I can't tell. Pick one."

"No, I—"

"Debby, *pick one at random.* I don't *mind* if Wheeler
thinks I got lost."

"Oh. The one in the middle, with the guards. We'll
ask them."

It was big and round and rimmed in scarlet paint. The
four guards wore helmets and torso and leg armor and
carried harpoons. Debby backpedaled to stop within a
meter of the harpoon points. She said, "Looking to join
up."

One smiled and said, "I hope they take you, beautiful." His harpoon pointed. "That one, just next to the
rim."

"Thanks." She rejoined Rather. Half blind, he'd been
afraid to fly close to sharp spears. "It's over there. —

Lovely beard on that one. Like goldenwire plant, and
clean. The crew keep themselves cleaner than Carther
States people ever did. Maybe I'll see him again."

"Jeffer'd like that."

"He would, wouldn't he. He probably likes my seeing
Grag too. I wonder what they're guarding?"

The door they sought was a rectangle with curved
sides, marked in print along one edge: RECRUITMENT.

The room within was sizable, but of the same odd
shape. A man made marks on thin white sheets fixed to
a slab of sanded wood. His pants and tunic were blue
with Navy markings. No armor. He ignored them for
a bit, then looked around. "Yes?"

Rather pointed to the wooden rectangle. There were
clips along the edge, and stacks of paper leaves in the
clips. "What would you call that?"

The man frowned. "You never saw a desk before?
What do you want?"

"Petty Mart Wheeler wants to interview me for recruitment. I'm Rather Citizen."

"I'll see if he's available." The man kicked against the
table and disappeared down a corridor. Lack of wings
didn't hamper him: he touched the wall and disappeared
into a doorway in one smooth flow.

Debby smiled at Rather. "Easily distracted?"

"That's why I did it, but look at how the grain of the
wood curls around! I think it must be burl. How did
they get it?"

"There had to be burl somewhere or Booce wouldn't
know it was possible."

When the desk man reappeared, Rather was mopping
at his eyes with his tunic. The man said, "Come with
me."

Debby said, "May I come too?"

"I'm afraid not. Would you be his mother?"

"Stepmother. I really think I ought to be with him."

"That's not permitted."

The office was small, a cube with two curved walls. Petty Wheeler was at a desk, lightly gripping the rim while he talked to another man . . . and that one was Rather's height.

Their talk stopped. Wheeler said, "Rather, good to see you. This is Captain-Guardian Wayne Mickl."

Mickl nodded but said nothing. He seemed relaxed and disinterested. Wheeler said, "We want to ask you a few questions. You probably have questions too—"

"A hundred. Um, whereabouts is Bosun Murphy?"

"Mpf? Last I saw of her she was on her way to the Purser's office. After that she'll be on leave. . . . Why?"

"I thought I might see her before I go."

(Booce had told him, "Try to talk to Bosun Murphy. Your interest in the Navy comes straight from your seeds. If you see her, make a pass."

("What's a pass? Do you mean propose marriage?"

("No . . . yes. That's got just the right touch. All seeds and no judgment.")

Wheeler asked, "Rather, is there something wrong with your eyes?"

"They get this way sometimes."

"When?"

"Lack of sleep. Dry air." His eyes were clearing up now, but they still hurt. To Wheeler they must appear pink and weeping. He was sniffling too.

Wheeler took writing implement in hand. "Where were you born?"

"Citizens Tree, year 370. It's a tree sixty klomters long, six or seven hundred klomters west of the Clump."

"What's your height and mass?"

"One point nine meters. I don't know my mass."

"We'll weigh you on the centrifuge. How did you know the year?"

"The Scientist keeps track. Was I off? This is 384, isn't it?"

"That's right. Put your arms straight forward, finger-tips touching. Now your legs, big toes touching." Wheeler made a note. "Symmetrical. How much do you know about the Admiralty?"

"Not much. We tasted some of the food you grow and had a wild dinner at Half Hand's Steak House." Wheeler laughed at that. Rather went on, "The Serjents told us a lot. I've seen houses and the Market. The ride on the steam rocket was—well, I've never been through anything like it."

"Scary?"

"No, not that." He knew instantly that he should have said *yes*.

"Why do you want to join the Navy?"

"I came to find out if that was true, Petty. And you asked if I had questions."

Petty Wheeler stiffened a little. "Well?"

"I've seen the ships. They're all over the sky. I think I ought to ask, if I become a Navy man, will I in fact be riding one of those ships?"

"More than one, I expect. Over the years you'll fly every style."

"Will I be flying them, or just riding them?"

"You've given this a lot of thought."

"Yes sir. Once I thought I'd be a hunter for Citizens Tree." No need to mention the silver suit. "When I joined Booce and went logging, that was a big jump. I didn't know what I'd find here. The Market, it's frightening to think such a thing could be *built*. So many people!"

Wheeler was smiling, nodding. (In the corner of Rather's eye, Wayne Mickl was clinging to a wall tether, merely observing.) "Daunting, is it?"

Rather nodded.

"The ships, the Market, Headquarters, we built them all. And more. We built a civilization," Wheeler said gently. "Now that you've seen it, how can you not be a part of it? Yes, you'll fly a ship before you're much older."

"I want to know whether I'll be able to visit Citizens Tree."

"Mph. The answer's yes, but I don't know how often. We'll want to contact Citizens Tree at once. Set up some form of trade. There'll be visits, and you'll be useful as an intermediate."

It was the right answer, Rather thought, except for two things. The tree was in the wrong place; and if the Navy did find it, the citizens would have to hide the carm every time the Navy came visiting.

So Rather only said, "That's good. I'd hate to be cut off from my family." (Booce had said, "They want your loyalty. They won't like it if you're loyal to your family, your tribe, *me*—")

"How often do you get these allergy attacks?"

"Usually just when the air's too thin. I had them while we were moving the log; we were too far in. It's like knives in my eyes. I haven't been getting enough sleep lately. It happens then too."

"Would you describe yourself as sickly?"

Rather told himself that nobody would come to a recruitment office if he considered himself sickly, and said,

"No. It's just something that happens. A day later I'm fine. It's almost over now."

"I see. All right, Rather. Go ask Able Jacks to put you on the centrifuge. We'll get in touch with you through Booce Serjent."

Debby and the desk man were ignoring each other. Debby seemed nervous.

"Rather! How'd it go?"

"Fine. Are you Able Jacks?"

"That's right."

"You're to take me to the centrifuge. What's a centrifuge?"

"I'll show you."

The wicker structure resembled the treadmill that ran the elevator in Citizens Tree. It was wider: twenty meters across. Rather was instructed to cling to the rim and wait. Two ratings spun it up, timing it with a hand-held device. The wheel rolled eccentrically with his mass to throw it off. A rating measured the divergence of the hub. "Your mass is eighty-one kilgrams," he said.

They locked the centrifuge in place and made him run.

Pushing himself round the rim gave him the sensation of tide. They had him run as fast as he could. It made him dizzy; the tide became fiercely strong. Then they made him slow down and run at a measured rate, until his legs burned and his eyes blurred. He would have stopped then if he had not noticed Bosun Murphy watching him.

He waved. The motion almost sent him tumbling. She didn't respond. But she watched, and he ran.

. . . It came to him that he was *rolling* around the centrifuge. He'd blacked out.

A rating snatched at his ankle and pulled him out. "Take a rest. Here." He handed Rather a towel, and Rather, gasping for air, mopped a sheath of water from his body.

Murphy said, "That was quite a performance. I could win bets on you."

"I grew up in a tree."

"I know."

There was no animation in her voice, her face, her body language. *Navy thinks they're superior,* Carlot had said; but that wasn't it. "Bosun, are you all right?"

"I'm a little down," she said. "Call me Sectry, Rather. I'm not on duty."

"Does *down* mean something like *miserable?*"

"Yeah. Guys, are you finished with him?"

"He's all yours, Bosun. No need to be careful, he ain't fragile."

Sectry Murphy flashed them a fleeting smile. To Rather she said, "I can't picture the Petty rejecting you after he hears about that performance."

Treefodder. Booce hadn't thought to tell him to hold back on a stamina test. "What's got you down?"

"Not here, stet? I need someone to talk to, not Navy. I just came from the Purser's and I'm ready to tie one on. Want to join me?"

"I'm with Debby. My stepmother."

"Stet. Let's go get her. How does Half Hand's sound?"

Rather was coming down the corridor. There was a woman with him.

Once upon a time Debby had seen Rather and Mark talking in the Citizens Tree commons. Both dwarves, but they hadn't looked at all alike: Mark's face nearly square, Rather's nearly triangular . . . She remembered it now, because Rather and the dwarf woman looked *right* together, though they were clearly from different branches of humankind.

And both, in different fashions, looked worn out. Debby asked, "What happened to you?"

Rather said, "Centrifuge. They ran me to death. I could have lifted an elevator all the way to *Discipline.* Debby, you remember Sectry Murphy—"

Clasping toes felt odd: Sectry's reach was so short, her toes so stubby and *strong.* "Hello, Sectry. I take it you're off duty."

"Right. On our way to Half Hand's. Join us?"

"Sure."

Sectry led them in. "The place is nearly empty," she said.

It wasn't. There were a good dozen people scattered around Half Hand's. But windows were clear, and Sectry led them to one. "It's nice to have a view," she said over her shoulder.

Rather flinched. Debby grinned; she'd seen Rather watching Sectry's kicking legs.

"Grab a pole, someone will come. You hungry?" When one of the women from the kitchen appeared, Sectry said, "Fringe tea and sausages for three, Belind. You two should try the sausage."

"Stet," Rather said. "What's got you down?"

The false gaiety ran out of her, and Debby saw pain. "I've been trying on pressure suits. I don't fit."

Debby said nothing. Rather said nothing.

"They don't let you try the suit till you qualify for Guardian in all other respects. So they got me into the small one and I couldn't breathe." Murphy wasn't wearing armor now. Her breasts stretched her tunic tight. Debby had never had trouble feeding her children, but her own breasts didn't have that *vulnerable* look. "I could have faked it, but the suits aren't all quite the same size. So I tried the bigger suit. My feet wouldn't reach the toes. There are controls in the boots. My fingers don't quite reach either."

"That leaves one," Debby said.

"The large? It's in use. It won't fit. If my damn toes were longer! I'm out. I can't be a Guardian."

Belind was back.

Sausage was a tube seared around the outside, delicious inside: ground meat with bits of plants added. Fringe tea Debby knew from last night. She still had a trace of the morning headache.

The situation felt uncomfortable, and Debby was rehearsing excuses to leave. She asked, "Are you going to stay in the Navy?"

"I think so. I'll never get further than Bosun, though."

"You'll be flying. More exciting than guarding the Library."

"As a Guardian I could spend some time making a home! Get married, carry some guests!"

"Don't they mind Navy people making babies?"

"You go to half pay when you're showing, but you've got a mate working . . . and even if you don't, Navy pay is good." Sectry drank deep. She hadn't touched her sausage.

Rather asked, "Sectry? Why would someone like the Captain-Guardian be interested in a recruit?"

"Wayne? That's easy. If he can get enough dwarves at Guardian rank, he can move up to Captain. He's got the rank but not the duties. Him, he'd be better off if he *couldn't* fit a pressure suit."

Debby took the rest of her tea in two gulps. "I've got to be going. Thanks, Sectry. I shouldn't have come in. I'm supposed to be buying stuff at the Vivarium, now that we've got money."

"Well, remember you're on fringe," the redhead said. "Watch the prices."

"I'll be careful."

Outside, Debby let herself smile.

How would Rather handle it? Let Sectry believe that he'd come to the Navy only to get close to a lovely dwarf woman?

It might even be true.

A sheet of rainwater clung to the window. A blurred puff jungle drifted past.

Rather had finished his sausage. Sectry passed him half of hers. When Belind came past she ordered more fringe tea. She asked, "How do you like the Clump?"

"It's mostly strange. Too wet, for one thing. I think I could get tired of boxes. Huts in a tree aren't like that. Sectry, why did they build Headquarters round?"

"It was built to spin."

"Spin?"

"The early officers, they thought we'd need tide to stay healthy. They gave that up early. They couldn't dock a ship while Headquarters was spinning, and it tended to wobble. So they stopped the spin and they built the exercise room, centrifuge included. Those early Navy men must have been *monstrously* strong. But it turns out we don't get sick. We still use the exercise room, though."

The fringe tea was fizzing in his blood. Sectry Murphy

seemed to glow. His mind was trying to follow a dozen paths at once. It suddenly seemed very natural that the early men would move a tree into the Clump, spin it, try to settle the tufts, get the benefit of tide *and* the clustered resources of the Clump . . . and produce the burl that later generations hadn't been able to duplicate.

At the same time there was a strangeness in what Sectry had said . . . and then he had it. "How do you know all that? Booce told us about the Library. He said only officers' children are taught there."

"Wayne told me."

"Oh."

"We were together for a while. I never thought he'd marry me, I'm not an officer, but when he . . . What I was saying, he told me a lot of history. The Library used to be part of a starstuff rocket. We've never built anything like it."

"What does it look like? Where—"

She shook her head; her hair spread around her like a flaming halo. "I never saw it myself. I'd like to. I wonder if I could talk my way past the guards . . ."

Guards. *That* door.

Voices and vision were turning strange. Sectry glowed; she was the Smoke Ring's most beautiful living thing. Rather took a firm grip on his equilibrium. Offering to make babies with a high-ranking Navy officer now seemed presumptuous beyond insanity. Carlot had warned him: she might be badly offended. Yet he'd never seen a woman like her.

"Then he married a woman three meters tall and thin as a feathersnake. She's got a face that would scare away a drillbit, and when she carries a guest she looks like a line with a knot in it. But she's an officer."

"Money."

"Mmm? No. Rank."

"Money," Rather said distinctly, "is why Carlot is going to marry Raff Belmy." He was losing control of his mouth.

"Oh. The dark girl, Serjent's daughter?" A smile flickered and vanished, but Rather caught it. "That's rank too."

"You saw us."

"Yeah." The smile was back.

"Do you have rank?"

"I'm a Bosun. Crew."

"Do I have rank?"

"No. What's this all about? If you want rank you join the Navy. Then you're crew."

"Would you marry me then?" His mouth was running away with him. Fringe.

She laughed. She was trying to stop, and ultimately she succeeded. "We just met. How old are you?"

"Fifteen."

"I'm twenty-eight. Where do you want to live?"

"Citizens Tree. Any tree."

"Carlot probably wants to live in the Admiralty."

"To the treemouth with Carlot."

"I do too."

"Make babies with me," his mouth said.

She thought it over, while Rather tried to think himself invisible. She said, "Right."

A score or so of puff jungles were in view. Some bore logos. They chose one that didn't, and circled it to be sure. "Quietly now," Sectry said.

"Nobody here but us flashers."

"If we scare flashers out, some meat eater might come after them."

He wiggled through the foliage in her wake. Nice to have a view. The puff jungle was hollow in the middle. A thousand flashers edged warily away, flashing blue and yellow wings at them.

They balled their clothes and threw them at the flashers, causing great excitement.

The birds perched in a shell around the hollow, watching them. She was just his size. She knew more than Carlot: delightful things. There were moments in which Rather resented that knowledge. Others in which he was shocked. His body knew things his mind hadn't dreamed.

They rested . . . running hands and toes across the sweat-slick contours of stranger's flesh, learning each other. *Smooth muscle. Hair red everywhere. Fingers and toes stubby like his own. Either of Sectry's breasts fit nicely into his two hands.*

"We could go back and forth," she said. "Live some in the Clump, some in your tree."

"Do you mean that?" As the fringe died out of his brain he began to wonder what he had committed himself to.

"Who knows? Don't ever make decisions when you're on fringe." Suddenly Sectry wriggled out of his arms. She snatched up her wings and eeled through the foliage and out. Rather followed, curious and horny.

Only her head poked into the sky. Flashers wheeled there, and something much larger circled thirty meters away. Sectry asked, "Want to see something funny?"

A wedge with teeth. "Get back." He pulled at her ankle. She had donned her wings. "That's a Dark shark. Carlot showed me."

"We try to keep them out of the Market region." She thrust herself into the sky, naked; waved her arms and yelled. The Dark shark froze. A window came open in a nearby cluster of cubes. The beast charged.

Rather didn't have his wings. He called, "Sectry! Dark sharks aren't funny!"

The long limber torso whipped back and forth too fast to see. The narrow triangular wing was a rippling blur. Sectry turned and kicked hard. She dived into the foliage, whooping, pulling Rather after her.

They were in the hollow center.

"Are you nuts?" he bellowed, and she laughed. Then the Dark shark burst through in a shower of leaves and splintered wood.

All Rather could see was teeth. His own wings were out of reach. He set his feet against a branch and watched the predator. Which way to jump? Flattened head and the forepart of a thrashing torso, three big crescent eyes, a thousand pointed teeth . . . the eyes beginning to show panic. Sectry couldn't stop laughing.

The beast was stuck.

Rather asked, "You do this a lot?"

"Sure. We don't like Dark sharks." She wrapped her arms and legs around him and laughed into his face.

The predator snapped its teeth at them, raging and impotent. Sectry murmured in his ear. "Gives it a kick, doesn't it?"

Debby was tired. She was flying blind, pushing bags of about her own mass, with no more than the strength of her legs. From time to time she stopped to look past her burden. The Serjent log grew larger.

Logbearer had dropped Debby and Rather near Navy Headquarters on its way to the Serjent log. Now Debby found the rocket moored near what had been the out tuft.

Two days' time had wrought wonderful changes.

A skeletal cylinder perched atop the fuel pod. Men were all over it, placing planks, driving pegs into wood. Booce floated nearby, watching contentedly. When he saw Debby coming he donned wings and kicked to join her.

"No problems?"

"No problems," she said. "Zakry wanted money. I just went down the list and paid him what I had. Here, there's some left. I don't think I got cheated. I've only got half the seeds here. We're supposed to get the rest within five days. Where do we store all this?"

"Not in *Logbearer*. There'll be paint fumes."

They lined the seed bags along a crack in the bark and ran tethers across them.

More men approached, pushing a cylinder of wooden beams. Debby watched as they maneuvered the lumber toward *Logbearer*. She called, "Ho, Clave! Learning a new trade?"

Clave joined them. He smelled of hard work. "I'm learning it, but I don't like it. Too nitpicking. Every board has to be just the right size, just the same thickness."

"I got the seeds."

"Good. Booce, isn't this a bit of a luxury? Don't we have other concerns?"

"Like selling my wood? This'll show off its quality! I'll paint my logo, but I'll leave most of the wood bare. I'll cruise past the Market and anyone can see I've got a good tree."

The hired crew were fixing panels on the long cylinder. Clave, rested, resumed work. Some of the panels were on swivels: windows. The sun swung behind the Dark; the day turned gloomy. When the sun reappeared, passing within a degree of Voy, one whole flank of *Log-bearer* was finished.

A shadow flapped out of the sun and became Carlot with her arms full of gear. Debby flew to help her. Carlot was pushing cooking utensils and a slab of smoke-blackened moby meat. She asked, "Where's Rather?"

"I left him in Half Hand's with Sectry Murphy."

"Mmm."

They stored the gear near the bags of seeds. "We'd better do our cooking here tonight," Carlot told her father. "That paint's awful stuff." Booce agreed.

Carlot asked, "How did Rather do? I keep forgetting we want him to *fail*."

"Yeah. The way Sectry Murphy was acting, he made some kind of endurance record on a big wheel. *Somebody* should have thought of that."

"Me," Booce muttered.

"Might not matter. They seem to want him bad."

The cabin formed with remarkable speed. Now men were pegging crossbars across the bow . . . for pushing against a log? Two men produced gourds; wind brought a noxious chemical reek. Booce excused himself and went to supervise while they painted the finished flank of *Logbearer*.

Carlot asked, "What was he doing with Murphy?"

"You remember your father said—"

"Yes, and I said she might be seriously offended. He didn't actually make a pass, did he?"

"Not while I was there. She's in a rotten mood. They put her in a pressure suit and she didn't fit."

"That's bad."

"She wanted to blow her mind out on fringe tea, and she wanted company. I left them alone. Treefodder,

Carlot, if he does get Murphy mad at him, what'll she do? Keep him out of the Navy!"

". . . Yeah." Carlot began setting her gear up for cooking. She worked with furious energy.

Debby watched. Presently she asked, "Carlot, are you going to marry Raff Belmy?"

"I don't know. I just spent a couple of days with Raff aboard *Woodsman*. He seems—he takes it for granted we'll be married. He's so sure, he hardly mentioned it."

"So? It's what you told Rather."

"I know. Where *is* he?"

There were beams left over from the making of *Logbearer*. Clave brought them an armload. Carlot arrayed them and started a fire.

Booce paid off the hired crew and they departed. His own crew went to inspect the altered rocket. Booce was exuberant. Clave was proud. Debby made appropriate noises. *Logbearer* had been repaired in just four days.

The paint was well done, she thought. She wasn't qualified to judge woodwork. The cabin was as big as the pod, roomy for half a dozen. Booce and Clave began the finishing touches: setting knobs and moorings into the hull, outside and in. Booce wanted particular patterns . . .

The fire was going well: a dim globe of heat, nearly invisible while both Voy and the sun bathed this side of the log. Carlot sliced the moby meat into two slabs. She set sliced vegetables between the slabs, locked them together with wooden pegs, and tethered it all within the fringe of the flame.

A distorted blue-fringed black man-shape swam across Voy.

"Rather! Where have you *been*?" Carlot shouted.

He reached the bark. "I'm in deep trouble," he said. "Where's the Chairman?"

"Working on the rocket. What kind of trouble?"

"Carlot, maybe you can tell me." Rather looked bewildered, a little frightened. "I'm afraid I've gotten myself in deeper than I wanted."

Section Four

THE DARK AND THE LIGHT

Chapter Nineteen

The Dark

from the Citizens Tree cassettes, year 54 SM:

WE'VE HAD SERIOUS ARGUMENTS ABOUT WHY
KENDY CUT CONTACT. MAYBE SOMETHING JUST
BURNED OUT SOME CIRCUITS. MASS DOES CONSTANTLY
RAIN OUT OF ORBIT ONTO VOY—MAKE THAT LEVOY'S
STAR, MY APOLOGIES TO SHARON. A BIG INFALL
WOULD CAUSE BIG MAGNETIC STORMS, MAYBE BIG
ENOUGH TO BURN OUT *DISCIPLINE*'S COMPUTER, AND
THE THICK SMOKE RING ATMOSPHERE WOULD STILL
SHIELD *US*. I HATE TO THINK SO. I LIKED KENDY.

THAT SOUNDS CRAZY. A COMPUTER PROGRAM . . .
I CAN'T HELP IT. KENDY HAD LESS IMAGINATION THAN
THE TURKEYS. I TRIED TELLING HIM A JOKE, ONCE AND
NEVERMORE. BUT I ADMIRE DEDICATION, AND KENDY
HAD AS MUCH DEDICATION AS A MAN CAN STAND. I'M
GOING TO LEAVE THIS IN.

—DENNIS QUINN, CAPTAIN

273

BOOCE HAD BOUGHT A SMALL PUMP. RATHER WAS WORKING it to fill *Logbearer*'s fuel tank. A Navy ship was doing much the same on the other side of the pond. Water had to be shared, this close to the Market. Greetings had been exchanged, and now the two crews were ignoring each other.

Carlot said, "Raym's been running messages for Dave Kon and Mand Curts. They'll know where he is. You'll have to track him down, though."

"No problem," Booce said. "How did he lose his rocket?"

"I didn't want to ask. He's far gone on fringe spores, Dad. We want him, but I don't want him in charge of anything."

"Fine. Rather, stop, it's full."

Rather began packing up the pump and hose. "That was quick," he said, remembering how long it took to fill the carm.

"A pretty good pump for something that's all hardwood. Let's get going. Carlot, you drop me and Clave at the Market and then go on to the house. Clave, you get the rest of the seeds. I want to buy us some clothes. You're all still wearing tree-dweller pajamas."

"You'll bring Raym?"

"I'll send him to the house. If he's too fringey to find it, I don't want him aboard any ship of mine."

Rather had not found the chance to confide in anyone but Debby and Carlot. Maybe that was good. Booce seemed to take it for granted that he would stay where the Navy could find him. Rather's plans were quite different.

Would Carlot help him? He wasn't sure. The way she was acting—

The Market swarmed like a hive. When the rocket came near, a dozen citizens separated from the pattern and flew to look. Booce delayed his exit for dramatic reasons. When he emerged he was surrounded. He stayed to talk, and Carlot joined him. Clave grew bored and flapped off toward the Vivarium at the far rim. Booce took an order for a thousand square meters of wooden planks . . . and the sun crossed half the sky and was behind the Dark before *Logbearer* moved on.

Serjent House continued to drift. It was now radially out from the Market. The Dark eclipsed the sun; Voy shone from the side. Half violet, half black, the cluster of cubes made an eerie sight.

"We'll have to tell Clave," Debby said. "First chance we get."

Carlot said, "I'm still not sure about this."

Rather said, "Booce was right, wasn't he? I want to look undependable. So—"

"They'll think you had Dad's permission!"

"The Navy doesn't own me. Booce doesn't own me. Even you don't own me, Carlot, and if you're holding me as a copsik I want to know it so I can think about escaping!"

"No, I don't own you." The ship was turning, decelerating. Carlot was very busy tending the rocket, too busy to look him in the face. Her voice was almost inaudible. "But it was a fool stunt, running off to make babies with that Navy woman."

"You're going to marry Raff Belmy."

"I said *probably*. Skip it. It was a fool stunt. So tell me this. Does Clave own you? Your Chairman?"

". . . Maybe."

"So ask *him* whether you're going."

"I want to talk to Jeffer too. And one other."

"You keep hinting—"

"You'll see for yourself. You too, Debby. I am tree-feeding tired of keeping secrets."

A random comet had impacted Levoy's Star. It had reached the surface as a stream of gas moving at thousands of miles per second. The neutron star had rung like a bell. There were two hot spots on the rapidly spinning body, at the impact point and the point opposite, where the shock waves had converged. The violet ion streams that normally rose from the magnetic poles of Voy, which natives called the Blue Ghost and Ghost Child, were brighter than Kendy had ever seen them. Radiation was beginning to sleet against *Discipline*'s hull.

But Kendy spared instruments for the CARM.

He ran the record as it came in. Jeffer had been idle: not much there. The house had been empty most of the time. Ah, here was something—

The motley collection of metal and plant tissue the savages called *Logbearer* bumped the wall nozzle-first. Rather, Debby, and Carlot emerged. They tethered the steam rocket to the door, close enough to block the sky. Rather said, "Jeffer. Come in, Jeffer."

Jeffer had been reviewing records from the cassettes. He set up the link. "I'm here. Hello, Debby, Carlot, Rather."

"I'm in trouble," Rather said.

"Tell me."

"Petty Wheeler interviewed me for the Navy."

"How did it go?"

The depth of Smoke Ring atmosphere was blocking most of the radiation and X-rays, and Kendy's instruments too. He could still watch events on the star itself via neudar. A plasma cloud hovered over the impact site, several centimeters high and spreading at terrific speed along lines of magnetic force—

Rather said, "Scientist, I did everything right except only two things. I did what Booce told me. I slept in the silver suit with the humidity turned low, and got there sniffling and crying. Debby came with me, and I really did need supervision. I could hardly see where I was flying. I asked for Sectry Murphy: all seeds and no brain, stet? But Booce didn't tell me not to show off my muscles, so I did."

"You're strong but sickly."

"And I'm a dwarf. If enough dwarves get into the Navy, a certain Captain-Guardian Mickl gets to act like an officer. I'm quoting Sectry. Mickl was there to watch the interview."

"Two mistakes. Did you suggest marriage to Bosun Murphy?"

Laughter, chopped off. "We got high on fringe tea. Then we dived into a puff jungle and—" Quick sidewise glance at Carlot, whose face was like stone. "Jeffer, none of us ever thought she might take me up on it. Now she thinks I'm joining the Navy and making plans to marry her. Maybe she can hold me to it!"

"This is not to your taste?"

"Sectry . . . I don't know. I don't want to join the treefeeding Navy and I don't know how to tell her that!"

"Okay, I'm thinking. . . . Rather, they already know you're allergic. Let them train you. Carlot said they don't give you much sleep in training. Stay awake even when you don't have to. Get sick a lot. They'll give up."

"I thought of something better."

"Listen—"

"No, *you* listen. I went running to Carlot and Debby.

Help, I said. I'm in trouble, I said. The Navy wants me. What do I do? And we talked it over, and what I want to do now is talk to Kendy."

Jeffer's medical readings showed his shock. Kendy stopped paying attention to the impact on Levoy's Star. *Paydirt!*

"Rather? You told them?"

"I'm letting you tell them. You and Kendy."

"Kendy isn't in range yet. When he gets the record—"

Carlot said, "Kendy the *Checker?*"

"The same," Jeffer said. "Kendy made contact with us fourteen years ago . . . fifteen now. I made a mistake with the carm. Kendy told us how to get home. We didn't hear from him again till . . . well, it was just before you showed up, Carlot. He wanted this expedition."

Debby was seething. "Jeffer, you treefeeding mutineer! What game did you think you were you playing, hiding a thing like this?"

Carlot exclaimed, "You can't deal with the Checker! We know all about—"

The record was finished. He'd reached present time. Kendy printed I'LL HANDLE IT across the bow window in front of Jeffer. He sent, "We told Clave. Rather was there, so we told him too. Hello again, Debby. Carlot, it's a pleasure to meet you at last. Rather, you did the right thing."

"And I suppose you'll try to talk me into joining the treefeeding Navy! But I won't do that, Kendy. I want *out* of this."

Rather wasn't aboard the CARM. Kendy couldn't get medical readings; but he sensed truth here. Never give an order that won't be obeyed! Try something else . . .

while *Discipline* moves steadily out of range. Wrap it up fast, but wrap it tight—

Kendy asked, "Rather, what are you planning?"

"Remember Booce telling me to look undependable? The Navy expects me to stay in touch. I'm going Dark diving. Carlot and Debby and Clave are taking *Logbearer* to get mud for Belmy's burl tree. I'm going with them."

"Just to look undependable?"

"It's not a crime. Sectry'll hate me, and I don't like that, but it'll get me off the harpoon."

Kendy finished putting details on his own plans. The speed of his thoughts was one powerful advantage to being a computer. It helped win arguments too. He said, "That's good, but it's not enough. Not if this Wayne Mickl wants you so badly. We need to get you out of the Clump entirely. Mmm . . . Rather, I think I may have something. Booce was planning to take the helmet with him so that Jeffer and I can see the Dark. Still true? Carlot?"

"Stet. Dad wants it out of the house."

"Good. Take the whole suit. Take Rather too. Go into the Dark. Rather, the suit's fully fueled. When you're out of sight of the Market . . ."

They heard him out, looking at each other. The silence that followed lasted only five or six seconds, but Kendy found it excruciating. Then Jeffer asked, "How long have you been planning this?"

"About thirty seconds . . . twelve to fifteen breaths. I think faster than you do, Jeffer."

Carlot's voice held doubt, not anger. "It's mutiny—"

"We steal *nothing*," Kendy said. "We won't harm the Admiralty at all. The information doesn't disappear, but

I can read it, and then it becomes available to Jeffer the Scientist. Rather, Debby, don't you see? We came to learn. Clave and Jeffer won't leave until they know what to tell Citizens Tree about the Admiralty. This way we'll learn everything we want in half a day."

Rather said slowly, "You say you can tell me how to do this."

"I've taken neudar readings. I can see the gross structure of Headquarters. It's most of a CARM surrounded by a concrete shell." The neudar shadow of the CARM was splayed around its aft end, and the back third was missing. The explosion must have pulped any passengers. It had ripped away the outer door of the airlock too. "The Library must be the control room. I'll guide you. We'll time it so I'm in contact the whole time. Even if someone sees something funny, it'll be *too* funny. He won't believe it. Afterward you take *Logbearer* home."

Carlot looked at Rather. "I don't owe you this."

"Losing contact," Kendy said. There might have been time for three words more, but what would they have been? He'd simply have to wait.

The redhead found Booce as he was returning from Market. She looked funny, flying. Her legs chugged faster than a normal woman's and made shorter strokes. She wouldn't have caught up if Booce hadn't been pushing baggage.

She wasn't breathing hard, though. She had a charming smile. "Booce Serjent, do you remember me?"

"Bosun Sectry Murphy. We met when *Gyrfalcon* came to collect customs. How do you do, Bosun?"

"I do okay. Rather's been accepted for training. I'd like to tell him."

Rather wouldn't like that. "He'll be at the house."

"I'll come. Shall I help with those?"

They kicked slowly along. Behind them the Dark moved in uneasy turgid patterns, out and east; the sun crept toward Voy; western rain clouds crawled in long curves. To fill the silence Booce said, "We've finished repairing *Logbearer*. After breakfast we cruised past the Market—"

"Moving slow. I saw it."

"Clave went for the rest of his seeds, and I picked up some clothing and toothbrushes. Can't have my crew looking like savages."

"My superiors may be wondering where you found the money."

"It's not easy. The Navy's taking its own sweet time to bid a decent price for our metal. But I've got some orders for wood, and my crew is going Dark diving."

"Did Rather say anything about . . . yesterday?"

"Not to me. He didn't seem to want to talk. It must have been a strange experience."

She laughed, then grew pensive. Presently she said, "Isn't that Serjent House?"

"Yes, but . . ." *Logbearer* wasn't there.

Booce invited her in. The Navy woman waited while he made the circuit of the rooms. He found nobody. There were no seeds: Clave hadn't arrived yet.

"They must have left already," he told her. "I stayed to bargain for wood. Clave should have come back well ahead of me." It was puzzling.

"Was Rather going with them?"

"No. He should be back soon, wherever he is."

She accompanied him to the kitchen and watched while he made tea. They returned to the common room and passed the pot between them, all in near-silence. Booce wondered if Jeffer had noticed the Navy woman.

What they really needed right now was a metallic voice bellowing out of the door.

"You'd think he'd leave a message," she said.

Booce nodded. *But they'd have left it with Jeffer!*

Murphy was frowning. "Is it normal for Rather to do . . . something like this?"

Booce was quick on the uptake. "He's never done *this* before. Well, he's been worried about whether the Navy'll take him. Maybe he got terminally antsy. A trip to the Dark—" And Booce knew he was right. *If they think you're undependable*— Rather had gone into the Dark.

"—could be just what he needs," he finished.

"It's not what *we* need." Murphy rejected the offered teapot. "How long do you expect them to be gone?"

They weren't seriously hunting treasures such as fringe or blackbrain. All they wanted this trip was mud, so— "Thirty, forty days." But they wouldn't have left without Clave, so they must have taken the seeds he was carrying too. Why?

"Tell Rather we're unhappy. Booce, I've got to be leaving."

Booce hovered at the door to watch Murphy depart. He whispered, "Jeffer?"

Nothing.

Of course, they took the helmet too. He waited until Sectry was no more than a speck before he opened the compartment in the door.

The whole damn illegal pressure suit was gone.

For one magical moment he was nothing but relieved. But something was going on here, and Booce didn't like it at all.

Carlot made her burn with the bow pointed straight

into the Dark. East takes you out, out takes you west.
That a rocket might go where it was pointed was con-
trary to Rather's experience; but he didn't want to argue
with Carlot.

The Market passed them at impressive speed. A few
citizens turned to watch, and were gone.

Raym Wilby had never kept silence in his life. "This
first part of a trip is fun, but you can still get hurt. Carlot,
the tank's near dry, stet? Turn us. Cut the water flow.
Go in facing sideways."

Carlot looked at him.

"See, if something comes at us, you run the last of
the water in. Doesn't matter what way you're facing,
long as it isn't forward. Something's ready to hit us, you
change course. If it's gonna miss, you don't."

"Oh." She and Clave tilted the nozzle. *Logbearer*
started its turn as she cut off the water flow. The slow
turn continued as the sky began to darken.

"Birds are the worst. A pond, a glob of mud, a jungle,
they don't follow you if you dodge. Everybody got harpoons? Stet. Hey, *smell* that. First whiff of the Dark.
State, it's good to be back!"

Logbearer fell straight in. It was like entering a huge
storm cloud . . . a granular-looking storm cloud. The air
smelled of wet and rot and mustiness.

They strung line, using beams on the nose as mooring
points. Raym watched and frowned and told them to
put the lines closer together. "It's got to hold the mud
while you make the burn." When they finished, *Logbearer*'s nose was the center of a great web. "I always
string my extra clothes across the middle of the web.
That way you *know* the mud won't go through and all
over the cabin. You bring any extra clothes, Carlot?"

She spoke through gritted teeth. "You didn't tell me

to. But *yes*, I brought extra clothes, and I don't much
like getting them covered with mud."

"So wash them after. You do it when you're ready to
leave. Then you use what's dirty. Look there, aft of center. Kerchiefs!"

Kerchiefs looked like a score of scraps of pink and
green cloth afloat on the wind. "Those're flowers,"
Raym said. "Not fungus. They'll—"

"Could you spread those to hold the mud?"

"Carlot, they're not strong enough. Touch them and
they shred. Hey, you don't mind dirty clothes when
you're Dark diving!"

They took turns sleeping. The sky thickened and
darkened over five or six days. Then Voy and the sun
were hidden and it was impossible to know *day*. Rather's
eyes adjusted. He saw colors emerging from the dark:
blue tinges, green, orange. Behind them the murky sky
was a blaze of light, suddenly bluer as Voy passed, too
bright to look at.

Raym was forward, inspecting the web again. Or
maybe he only liked the view.

Clave said, "It isn't the risk that bothers me. It's the
fact that I'm not taking it. Feels like this should be my
job."

Rather didn't answer, but Carlot did. "Oh, you're taking a risk. If Rather gets caught, the Navy'll want us all.
Clave, it's not too late to change our minds!"

"Yeah. I know how persuasive Kendy is. And I think
I should have been consulted." Rather started to speak.
Clave snapped, "Yes, Rather, it couldn't be done. Be-
sides, Kendy's right. It gets us everything we came for.
Rather, if you don't come back in a decent time, we're

leaving. I've got the seeds. We'll just burn straight out
and let Jeffer find us in the sky."

"Stet," said Rather.

"And what about Dad?" Carlot demanded. "Why
should the Navy believe him when he tells them he
didn't know?"

"I won't get caught. One big risk and we go home."

"I don't owe you this," Carlot said, as she had said
before. This time nobody answered. (But Jeffer had
said, "You owe Citizens Tree for your life," and it was
true.)

"I think we've gone far enough," Clave said. "Nobody's going to see us from the Market."

Rather nodded. "But there's still Raym."

"He's easily distracted."

The rocket had slowed considerably. They were drifting, not flying. The murky sky was busy with soft, shadowy shapes. Once there was a jagged rock the size of
Logbearer, half covered by . . . Rather stared. That had
to be a fungus. But it was convoluted like the moby's
brain Half Hand had tried to serve them.

Raym pointed through the net of lines. "You can eat
that."

Clave said, "Treefodder! I mean literally. That's a tuft
off an integral tree!"

It could have been, Rather thought. There was the
curved blade of the branch. But where foliage should
have been, now there was a great misshapen lump of
soft gray curves. "I pushed one of those home once,"
Raym said. "Had to. My nets were torn up. It was all
the food I had left, and I barely made a dent in it getting
home. Half Hand served slices of it for the next twenty
days, but he didn't pay much . . ."

Rather tuned him out.

The orange tinge ahead grew gradually stronger. Orange light shining through shadows. Rather had grown used to the wet, musty smell, but something else was in it now. "Raym, what's that?"

"I've been living with Exec ever since the accident. My son, Exec Wilby. He only went into the Dark but once— What?"

"That."

"That's the fire. Carlot, we have to turn."

Carlot jerked around. "Fire?"

Now Rather knew that smell. Fire burning in something wet and rotten.

"It's been burning down here since . . . I don't know when. All my life, anyway. Never gets much bigger, never gets much smaller. Now, don't hurry. Look around and find a pond and steer for that. We need more water anyway."

They looked. There was no mistaking the shape of a pond, of course, even in darkness. Rather found no spheroids in evidence. Carlot said, "I don't see anything!"

"There."

"But that's . . . oh." Raym was pointing to a fungus jungle, a maze of thick white threads . . . and the orange light glinted off something reflective inside. The mass, in fact, was mostly pond, but it was laced with fungus.

Clave used the bellows. The pipefire that had been estivating in the windless murk now blazed up. Carlot blew the last of their water into the pipe while Rather and Clave tilted the rocket.

The fungus jungle drifted across the orange light. *Logbearer* impacted softly against resilient fungus fingers, and recoiled.

"What kind of pump you got? Good. Boy . . . Rather, you want to pump?"

"You pump, Raym," Carlot said. "Debby, you go with him. Keep your harpoon handy."

"Stet, that's good thinking, Carlot. No guessing what's lurking in there." The imaginary horrors didn't diminish Raym's enthusiasm as he flapped away with the pump. The hose slowed him. Debby kissed Rather's cheek before she picked up a loop of hose and flew after him.

Raym disappeared among interlocked white strands that broke where he touched them.

Clave said, "Now, Rather."

They entered the cabin together. The bags of seeds nearly filled one compartment. Rather pulled them out, reached further, and had the silver suit.

Debby saw only kicking wings among finger-thick white pillars of fungus. "Nothing dangerous yet," Raym called cheerfully. "Watch for stinkbirds. Great State! Girl, get me a bag, a big one!"

Debby dropped the hose and worked her way in. "What—"

"Fringe!"

"Oh. Here." She'd taken to carrying the big bags they'd used to collect honey while logging. She passed one in. She couldn't see what Raym was doing in there, but the air had turned dusty. She sneezed.

Raym wriggled out in a cloud of dust motes. There was something shapeless in the bag. "Sixty, seventy chits worth," he said. "I'll just take this back—"

"I've linked up the hose. What have you got?" Carlot had come at his shout.

Raym showed her the bag.

"Dammit, Raym, that's sporing fringe! Debby, get away from it."

"Yeah." Debby kicked out into the air. She was feeling dreamy . . . light-headed . . . happy. But if she'd breathed spores, Raym must have breathed more.

Keep him away from the ship! Debby pulled on the hose until she had the pump. "Raym, take this around to someplace else and start pumping."

"I'll take this back," Carlot said. "Raym, you shouldn't get near sporing fringe! Sure it's worth money—" She gave up. Raym was laughing.

Clave had stuck the helmet to a wall with a dab of glue. It watched him in stoic calm. "Try to do the circle in one sweep," it said.

"Is that how the original was done?"

"First painting was probably a template, but templates wear out. The suits must be painted over and over. Every so often the junior Guardian has to paint it. I'm guessing, of course, but the original looks a little sloppy in Kendy's pictures."

Clave pointed the brush like a pencil and moved in a single graceful sweep. The resulting greenish-white circle wasn't half bad. "Bring it close," said the helmet. "Too narrow and also a little small. Go around again and add some bulk to the outer rim. Rather, when you leave, drape a cloth over yourself. We don't want to get it dirty while it's wet . . . Stet, Clave. Now the dot in the middle. Stet, leave it tiny. Give me another look at the shoulder—"

"Raym found you something, Silver Man."

Clave jumped. "What? Carlot, don't do that."

"Rather, take it. It's sporing fringe. Bring it back if you can. It's worth money."

Rather took the bag. "What's it for?"

"If you're in trouble, throw it. Everyone around you will have a wonderful time while you get away. Make sure *you* don't breathe it."

"Oh. Thanks."

"Sure."

"I'm ready to go."

There was something more that he ought to say, something she expected, but he couldn't for the life of him think what it was.

"You get tired, I'll take over," Debby said.

"No, no, the tank must be nearly full by now." Sweat slicked Raym wherever his skin showed. He was grinning and panting and pumping his legs with the vigor of a much younger man.

The tank must be full already, Debby thought. They wouldn't let Raym stop until—

Raym stopped. "What was *that?*"

Debby turned to where he was looking. "I don't see anything."

Tiny twin flames burned in the Dark, receding.

"Huh." Raym resumed pedaling. "Hope that isn't the fire getting closer. You never know where it's gonna be. It doesn't just drift like everything else, it spreads in spots and goes out in spots—"

Carlot called from the rocket. "Raym! Enough. Let's go find our mudball."

Chapter Twenty

The Library

from Discipline's *records, year 926 State:*

YOUR ORDERS ARE AS FOLLOWS.

1) . . . YOU WILL VISIT EACH OF THESE STARS IN TURN. OTHER TARGETS MAY BE ADDED. WHERE APPROPRIATE YOU WILL SEED THE ATMOSPHERES OF PROTO-EARTH WORLDS WITH TAILORED ALGAE USING THE CANNISTERS YOU CARRY. THE STATE EXPECTS TO SETTLE THESE WORLDS, SPREADING HUMANITY AMONG VARIABLE ENVIRONMENTS, AGAINST DANGERS THAT MIGHT AFFECT ONLY SOL SYSTEM.

2) THE STATE IS AWARE THAT YOU DO NOT REQUIRE A CREW TO OPERATE.

THE HUMAN SPECIES IS NOT INVULNERABLE. THERE IS FINITE RISK THAT THE CREW OF ANY INTERSTELLAR SPACECRAFT MAY FIND, ON ITS RETURN, THAT IT HAS BECOME THE ENTIRE HUMAN RACE. YOUR CREW AND

THEIR   GENES   ARE   YOUR   PRIMARY   CARGO.
CLASSIFIED.

3) YOUR TERTIARY MISSION IS TO EXPLORE. IN PAR-
TICULAR, ANY EARTHLIKE WORLD WITH POSSIBILITIES
FOR COLONIZATION MUST BE INVESTIGATED AND RE-
PORTED IMMEDIATELY.

—LING CARTHER, FOR THE STATE

MATTER WAS TOO THICK IN HERE TO USE BOOT JETS. RATHER
used them to get clear of Raym's sight, then donned his
wings. He wanted to fly straight north, along the axis
of Clump and Smoke Ring both. Matter should thin out
rapidly in that direction.

There were no ponds; but sometimes you could catch
a glint of light from one of the fuzzy-edged fungus jungles. There were white pillow shapes, and flat white
lenses streaked with yellow and crimson, and networks
of interwoven pale stalks. He took care to avoid touching anything; he flew around clouds of dust or spores.
The paint on him would still be wet.

Rather began to understand the beauty Raym found
in the Dark.

Straight lines, rare in a tree, were unheard of here,
save (rarely) for long beams of blue-white or yellow-
white sunlight breaking through the murk. Where he
saw these, he corrected his course to cross them. This
close to crossyear, north would be at right angles to Voy
and the sun. After what felt like a couple of days he was
seeing many more. The Dark had grown rarified. Now
there was room for jets.

He fired a burst of five breaths' duration.

Mist flowed past him as he coasted out of the Dark.
The day brightened. Too bright. His eyes were slow to
adjust.

"Jeffer the Scientist calling Rather. Can you hear me yet?"

Jeffer's voice was scratchy. Rather turned up the volume. "Reception isn't good, but I'm hearing you. I'm nearly out, moving north, coasting. The rest of us are in good shape. How long till we get Kendy?"

"A quarter day to spare. Rather, did you bring wings?"

"Yes."

"Good. You can't approach Headquarters on jets. I didn't think of it."

"I did."

"I have you located. Make your burn now. You're well north of the Smoke Ring. The air's thin, it won't slow you much, but in less than a half day you'll be back in the plane."

"I know, north and south bring you back. So. How long a burn? What direction? I'm well and truly lost."

"I'll time you. Three minutes, about sixty breaths. Can you see Voy? The Market is ten degrees west of out from you, and you have to cross four hundred klomters. You didn't actually get very far into the Dark."

By now he'd fallen into clear air, with the Dark spread out below. Rather wriggled to point his feet ten degrees east of Voy. He would move nearly at a tangent to the flow patterns in the Dark.

He lit the jets. His body tried to sag into his boots. The Dark skimmed below him, a storm with granulations in it, and sudden red and golden and purple glows where the sun shifted just right. Jeffer counted aloud and told him when to fall free.

Flying. The Dark was thinning out, but coming closer too. He skimmed through the fringes of a raincloud—

"Kendy for the State," said the familiar deep voice. "Rather, are you on schedule?"

"No problems. Expedition's in good shape. Raym will probably swear I was there the whole time."

"Repeat after me. 'There's a respectable store of metal here.'"

"There's a respectable—"

"Try to say it like I did. Listen a few times. 'There's a respectable store of metal here.'"

Rather deepened his voice and tried to spit the syllables. "There's a respectable store of metal here."

They rehearsed "You wouldn't want to have to sell your new house," and "I need to consult the Library," and "I relieve you." Rather was lethally sick of it when Kendy quit. "It'll have to do. Try to be in a cloud when you sight Headquarters. Don't make your approach without me."

"Right."

"I've displayed a neudar map of Headquarters for Jeffer. He can guide you if I'm out of range. Back in two days. Kendy out."

"Jeffer?"

"Here. Rather, you should try to sleep."

"*Sleep?*"

"Nothing natural can hurt you in the silver suit. Sure, sleep. You'll be less hungry. You've got no food."

"I'll give it a try."

He slept not a wink. The turning of the Clump spiral caught him up and he had to make a correcting burn. Houses and decorated puff jungles passed, none close enough to see more than a passing pressure suit. Citizens would wonder what the Navy was doing out here.

Within a layer of haze he found the unmistakable shape of the Market. Headquarters to spinward . . . "Jeffer? I have it."

"How close?"

"Forty klomters."

"Get a lot closer. Approach from the Market side if you can. Rather, it just struck me: there are two ways into the Library, and they have to guard both."

"So?"

"I don't think it was ever meant to be guarded. The Library was supposed to be free to all. Just a guess."

"What's the word from Kendy?"

"Any breath now."

"I'll come in through that cloud bank. You see it? I think there's a pond in there. I'll come around that."

"Kendy for the State. Rather, are you in place?"

The boy sounded edgy. "Ready. You missed some interesting stuff."

Headquarters was four hundred meters distant. They'd lose a few minutes crossing that. Kendy sent, "Something I should know?"

"No, just interesting. I watched two triune families arrange a marriage."

"If your helmet faced it I didn't miss it. Time to move. Just wings."

Kendy watched the guards as Rather approached. Would they expect him to have an escort? They spread arms and legs as he came near, with a hand and foot to hold the harpoon. That position had been *Attention!* for any military man in free-fall since long before Kendy's birth. The door behind them was large and massive, and closed.

"Just go in unless they do something," Kendy said. "I've watched them every orbit. You won't need a password because your helmet's closed. Don't hurry. Let them open the door for you."

Checklist: Communications systems nominal. Drive

warming. Course correction ready. Kendy didn't intend to burn fuel until everything else had gone right.

The guards waited until they could read Rather's insignia. One rapped the door with his spear butt. It slid open in time to let Rather pass.

"Left. There's a hall, then another door." Kendy noticed pads of cottony-looking vegetation on the far wall. "Pause. Wings off, then clean your suit. You'll be expected to. Pat, don't rub. Remember the paint."

Rather patted muddy rainwater off his suit. Kendy wished he could see the result. There were paint smears on the pad. The boy moved down the corridor.

The inner door had one guard. He starfished the way the others had. "Captain-Guardian? You're early, sir."

"I want to consult the Library."

"But that's . . . yessir." The man didn't move.

Kendy sent, "You're still carrying your wings. Tether them to your chest plate." The guard must expect that, and it would give Kendy time to think. "No hurry. Aristocrats don't hurry. Shin sticks toward your chin."

To door: no hinges visible. It would swing in. What was protocol here? Have to guess. "Open it yourself, Rather."

"How?"

"Paired handles on door and wall. Grip both. Push the door inward. No, pause—"

As Rather finished tethering his wings, the guard finished pushing the door open and moved aside. "In," said Kendy.

Rather entered. He turned at the sound of the door closing. There was no handle on the inside, though a scar showed that one had been removed.

The light source was electric. Would that bother Rather? No, he was used to electric lights in the CARM.

A man in a pressure suit waited. He held a crossbow. The bow and quarrel were both hullmetal: lengths of stiff CARM wiring, with superconducting cores. So this was how they used their heritage.

The Guardian's voice had to echo through helmet and faceplate. He sounded tinny (as Rather would; Kendy had counted on that) and surprised. "Captain-Guardian?"

"'I know I'm early. I relieve you. I need to use the Library.'"

Rather was slow. "I know I'm early—"

"That's all right, Captain-Guardian."

"I need to use the Library. I relieve you."

"Yes, sir. For what purpose, sir? I'm required to ask."

While Kendy mulled possible answers, Rather had started to speak. Kendy listened. Rather said, "We want to locate an integral tree west of here. I want its probable orbit."

No way to read the silver man's face. The Guardian said, "Yes, sir," and rapped on the door. It opened for him and closed after him.

"Alone at last," Rather said.

The room was much bigger than the machinery it housed. The CARM control system had been re-mounted in a wooden cradle. There were wooden handles on its four sides. Hadn't Booce Serjent said that it was sometimes displayed to the citizens?

Cradled against an adjacent wall was a small portable fusion generator. The Library's light source was a panel running around its rim. The power cable was coiled against its side. "Rather, do you see a coil of line, thick as your wrist, black—"

"Got it." Rather moved toward the generator.

"The free end has to go into a hole in the CARM controls. At the near end, near the wall."

"There are a lot of holes."

"I'll guide you."

They played "cold" and "warm" with the end of the plug. It was taking too long. The power plant might be dead. The computer might be dead. The programs might be scrambled. There would be no second chance: Rather Citizen was probably trapped behind locked doors, with Wayne Mickl already on his way. Once Kendy had established contact with the Admiralty, he might be able to buy Rather loose. The boy was doing his best, after all, fumbling, but doing his best—

"Just push it in hard and turn it counterclockwise. Stet. Face the controls. Tap the white key." A white cursor appeared. "Say 'Prikazyvat Voice.'"

"Prikazyvat Voice."

"State your authority," said a voice so like Kendy's that Rather squeaked in surprise.

"Say 'Rather Citizen for *Discipline*. Open contact.' Watch your accent." With another part of his attention he began beaming his signal to the old CARM computer. Voice was activated; the computer would hear. *Kendy for the State. Discipline to all CARMs. Kendy for the State.*

The computer must be trying to answer. It wouldn't be able to find *Discipline* with its navigational instruments severed. He sent, *Beam to pressure suit 26.*

"Something just started humming in my head."

"Everything's fine, Rather." The signal was being relayed. He sent, *Status?*

CARM #2 sent its tale of woe. Massive malfunctions. Internal sensors out, external sensors out, motors not responding, life support systems not responding, navigational systems not responding, power low. Records intact. Presiding officer: Admiral Robar Henling . . .

Kendy sent, *Copy*.

All?

Y.

The Admiralty Library accepted the Copy program, hummed thoughtfully, and began beaming its records.

That would take twenty-six minutes. Kendy activated the course change he'd worked out hours ago. *Discipline* was about to use a good deal of fuel. It would hold him over the Lagrange point for long enough.

The records arrived in reverse order. Common practice. Recent records were likely to be more urgent. Kendy dipped into the flow. The control board had seen little while housed in the Library room. There were glimpses of the sky during ceremonies. Records of births, deaths, marriages. It had been dismounted in year 130 SM. The CARM hadn't crashed; it had deteriorated over the years, helped by deteriorating maintenance . . .

He couldn't spare attention with so much else going on. The drive ran smoothly. Tank less than a fifth full. *Discipline* accelerated, drive swinging out to point at the stars, to hold the ship close above the L4 point against its own spin. Rather was exploring the room; his pulse and breath rate were rapid. He was bored and anxious. Jeffer, crouched above CARM #6's control board, was in similar shape. The neudar view of Admiralty Headquarters showed fog-spots clumping, then moving in two streams toward the Library.

Something was happening. Little lights brightened and dimmed on the carm control panel. His helmet hummed. It wasn't particularly entertaining. Rather said, "Kendy?"

"It's working, Rather. Don't bother me."

"Jeffer?"

"Here."

"Kendy's busy and happy."

"You've got more than two hours—about half a day before Mickl's on duty. Nobody should bother you."

"I'm hungry enough to eat a swordbird, and may the best entity win."

"Did everything go all right?"

"I'm *scared*, Jeffer. I may never get over being scared. Why on Earth are we *doing*—"

The door opened.

Rather saw a silver suit pointing a crossbow a few degrees wide of his naval. The insignia was familiar. He and Booce had spent half a day painting it on the silver suit, from pictures taken by the silver suit's camera.

The door—

Rather's radio spoke in his helmet. "I know who you are," said the voice he'd been trying to imitate. "What I want to know is why. Let's—"

Rather leapt straight at Wayne Mickl, and fired a burst from his jets for extra force. He couldn't let the door close.

The silver man swung his crossbow aside and braced to kick, too slowly. He'd expected the jump but not the jets. Rather slammed into him. Mickl bounced away. Rather struck the jamb and, spinning, was through the door and out into a horde of Navy crew.

"I know who you are—" Wayne Mickl's voice, pressure suit #5, radio frequency badly distorted by time, and Kendy locked on it. He beamed instructions to the

Library: *Record the view through pressure suit #5 cameras, one snap per ten minutes, henceforth.*

It was a nice bonus. He welcomed it, because he was about to lose Rather Citizen. A dozen Navy crew in the fisheye view, unknown numbers out of camera range—

Jeffer bellowed, "Rather! What's going on?"

"Wayne Mickl came back. Can't talk."

Kendy sent, "Get outside if you can, Rather. Mickl's jets aren't fueled."

"I've got the whole treefeeding Navy here!" They were hesitating, but they wouldn't for long. "They'll swarm all over me like honey hornets— Hey!" Rather's hands came in view holding a bag; ripped it open and flung it. The corridor became vague and golden.

Wayne Mickl could pull the cable! Was he still in the Library? CARM #2 had a hundred years of records to go . . . a solid block of data was running now, data that must have been beamed long ago by *Discipline* itself. Kendy knew he wouldn't want to read that in full, not if it was records of the mutiny. He'd spot-check.

The other pressure suit emerged from the Library and jumped to join the fight. *Good!*

Rather's camera view shot down the corridor, through dust and bodies. Navy crew grabbed at him, clung . . . and let go. It began to look as if he might make it.

What was running through *Discipline*'s receivers was a message from the State, from Earth.

Nothing in his own memory matched. Kendy pulled it and ran it. It was brief.

Rather jumped down the corridor, arms raised to block the men who blocked his path. Impacts slowed him. A burst from the jets compensated. Somebody was riding him, legs around his hips . . . a man impacted heavily against his helmet, slid across his chest, and was gone.

The silver man jumped him. The man who clung to Rather took the force of impact. They tumbled. Rather reached the door, kicked, swung himself around the jamb and was out in the sky. A burst of jets took him clear.

He paused then.

The silver man emerged and, twenty meters away and receding, stopped to put on his wings. Navy crew emerged behind him. Two flailed; they had no wings at all. The third couldn't get his on. Fringe spores must have reached their brains.

That left only the silver man.

Rather grinned. He put on his own wings and kicked away strongly. "Kendy? Jeffer? Are you watching?"

"Jeffer here. I can't get Kendy. He may be out of range."

"Well, watch. This is going to be good."

Mickl was catching up.

Rather's radio sounded calm and a bit supercilious. "Rather Citizen, you can't escape. Your wings are the right color, but they're not Navy wings. You know I don't want to hurt you. I had the chance to kill you and I didn't. But the crossbow is all I have, and it will penetrate—make holes in a Navy pressure suit. There's a hole in one of our suits because one of our Guardians turned mutineer once."

"Don't answer," Jeffer said. "He's guessing. Don't give him a chance to test it."

Mickl was meters behind him, but the drugged Navy crew were nearly out of sight. Rather pulled his wings loose, pointed his feet at the silver man, and fired his jets.

He was head-down to the Dark. Mickl was kicking hard, falling rapidly behind. A scream of shock or frustration burst in Rather's ears; he found the volume control and turned it down fast.

The Dark was around him. He couldn't see the other silver man, he couldn't see the Market.

Jeffer spoke in his helmet: a tiny squeak until Rather turned the volume back up. ". . . due to rendezvous. I've got a ship moving north out of the Dark. Stand by . . . There's a dark blob bigger than the cabin—"

"That's *Logbearer*. They've got their mud."

"Turn seventy degrees clockwise from where you were pointed and, oh, ten degrees north. Make your burn."

Rather obeyed. Jeffer counted off twenty seconds: seven breaths. The Dark thinned.

"We've got to get rid of the silver suit," Jeffer said.

"No." I'm the Silver Man!

"I don't mean feed it to the tree! I mean don't have it when *Logbearer* gets home."

"How?"

"I don't know, and Kendy isn't answering. I don't even know what course he's on now."

"What if I don't go back? You can pick me up with the carm."

"Sure, and what does Wayne Mickl say to the Serjents? You've got to face him and lie."

Rather could see the Market far behind him. Was he in view of Navy instruments? But they'd have to find him, and he'd changed direction.

The deep voice of Wayne Mickl was small and full of the chattering sound of distance. "Rather Citizen, I will wait for you at Serjent House."

"I heard that," Jeffer said. "I've spotted you. Can you see Voy? Sixty-five degrees east, burn for five seconds. Zero north, there's no point in getting higher. You'll both be back in the Dark before you meet."

"Jeffer? Why don't you come get the silver suit?"

". . . Stet. Here I come."

Rather himself had spotted *Logbearer* now, above the plane of the Dark, foreshortened and trailing steam.

Jeffer said, "I'm on my way, but it'll take me nearly a day. If you just ditch the suit it'll fall back into the Dark."

"It's doing that now. You'll have to find it somehow. I've got an idea."

Rather flew through the Dark. He was using wings. There couldn't be much left of his fuel.

He glimpsed a man-shape through the murk.

Carlot. When he opened his helmet she kissed him breathlessly. "I thought I'd never see you again! Did you do it?"

"Yeah. All of it, but the Captain-Guardian knows, or thinks he does."

She talked while she helped him out of the suit. "Raym got too much of the fringe. He's in the cabin getting through the hangover. Debby's with him. She'll keep him quiet. We've got our mud and four tons of walnut-cushion. Two Dark sharks tried to open us up. Debby took them. Rather, I'd hate to have her mad at *me*. We've got the meat, and I'll show you tooth scars on the wood—"

"I hope they were big. I'm *hungry*." He was out. He closed up the suit, leaving the helmet open. "Jeffer?"

"Here. I'm above your position."

"I'm doing it." He closed the helmet. He turned the

pressure dial high and the temperature low. The suit grew rigid. "Now I want to start a fire."

"In the Dark that won't be easy."

"Help me. That . . . fisher jungle, I guess it was." He indicated a mass of dry brush with white things taking root in it. "Help me push the legs in."

They pushed the suit into the decaying fisher jungle. The branches still had some strength. Rather got a good grip, then closed a jet key with his toe. Flame blasted through the rotting fisher jungle; the suit tried to escape. He let the jet run for several breaths before he turned it off.

"Jeffer should find that okay," he said. He was guessing and he knew it.

"Then *tell* me! What happened?"

He told her some of it while they searched out *Logbearer*. The rest would wait. Clave and Debby would have to wait to hear the tale, since Raym could not be allowed to. And Rather would have his chance to eat and sleep. He was exhausted.

Chapter Twenty-One

The Silver Suit

from the Library cassettes, year 200 SM:

CITIZENS MAY NEVER ENTER THE LIBRARY ROOM.
CITIZENS WILL BE GIVEN ACCESS TO THE LIBRARY ONLY
THROUGH OFFICERS, AND THEN ONLY ON CERTAIN
DATES. . . . ON THESE DAYS THE LIBRARY WILL REMAIN
AVAILABLE, WITH A PROGRAMMER ON DUTY, UNTIL ALL
CITIZENS HAVE HAD OPPORTUNITY TO ASK THEIR QUES-
TIONS; THOUGH SOME QUESTIONS WILL CERTAINLY BE
UNANSWERABLE . . .

THEY STOPPED TWICE: ONCE AT THE MARKET, TO LET RAYM
off with half his pay in hand, and once at a pond, to
refuel.

Belmy's log was very slowly turning end-for-end. A
thread of steam poured from above the tuft. As Carlot

made her final burn to bring *Logbearer* to rest near the
midpoint, *Woodsman* cast loose and moved toward them.

Serjent House was just visible to antispinward: west.
Rather tried not to think about the dot visible alongside
it. He welcomed the delay.

Debby said, "I'd like to get this over with—"

Clave shook her by the ankle. "Wrong! We went into
the Dark for mud, and we're back to get rid of it. We
don't know of anything urgent. We're in no hurry at
all."

Carlot shouted from where she and Rather worked
the rocket. "Stet! Treefodder, they always make *us*
wait!"

They had it all figured out. But copter plants were
launching their seeds in Rather's belly.

Woodsman eased alongside. Hilar and Raff Belmy flew
toward *Logbearer*. "You'll like Raff," Carlot whispered.
"*Act* like you like Raff."

"It's all right. I'd make babies with him if it'd make
you happy . . . or get me away from the Navy."

Hilar introduced his son. (Treefodder, but they were
big!) Raff smiled much and said little. He was shy for
an adult, Rather thought. He stared at the tree dwellers,
but his eyes seemed to slide aside from Rather's.

The teapot passed. Carlot asked, "How are you doing
with the log?"

Hilar shrugged. "No burl yet." The others laughed.
"Give it time. We have some spin. I don't think we want
to overdo it. We've splashed a pond against the trunk;
that gives us a water flow. How are you planning to
deliver the mud?"

"I . . . hadn't thought past just bringing it here."

"Raff and I talked it over—"

Raff spoke. "Dad always says keep it simple. We'll

just impact it against the tree, lee side, two, three klomters above the tuft. There's already water running down
to the treemouth. Let it carry the mud too. Easy, steady
delivery system."

He can talk when it's about something real, Rather
thought. "Have you done a lot of logging?"

Raff's head bobbed. "I spend more than half my life
in the outer sky. Sometimes I wondered what living in
a tree would be like."

They were getting used to that question. Clave said,
"I miss it myself. Well, you grow up shorter and
stronger. Cooking's easier. Hunting's different: the
wind *throws* the prey at you . . ."

Rather tuned it out. The dot next to Serjent House
must be a Navy ship. He felt their long-sight devices
on him. What the Navy saw must look puzzling. Let
them wonder: he had an explanation both interesting
and innocent.

His attention snapped back when Hilar said, "Booce
has been making deals. I expect he'll pay back the loan
well before crossyear."

Carlot asked, "Has the Navy bought the metal yet?"

"No. In fact, something's upsetting the Navy. I
haven't heard a rumor I can believe, but . . . stay alert,
Carlot. You know you've got visitors?"

"We can see them. Hilar, Raff, it's time to deliver our
cargo."

It took a day and a fraction and was entirely straightforward. *Logbearer* burned toward the turning tree. Her
crew dismounted the spokes that braced the web that
supported the mud. Mud and lines and wooden spokes
smacked the trunk hard enough to stick. Water flow was
already carving a runnel in the mud as *Logbearer* accel-

erated away. They'd be back to collect the beams and
lines after they were washed clean.

Gyrfalcon was not moored; it floated free a hundred
meters from Serjent House. Two men working on the
hull did not return Clave's cheerful wave. Rather recognized one as Petty Wheeler. They watched fixedly
while *Logbearer*'s crew swarmed out and set about the
business of mooring their ship.

Rather looked around the common room while they
tethered their wings. One fast look and then he'd have
to react:

No teapot. Not a social occasion. Booce Serjent
looked angry and unhappy. Bosun Sectry Murphy
started to jump toward Rather, then pulled herself back.
Three long-limbed Navy men were stationed around the
walls, and a fourth: silver suit, helmet thrown back,
bearded dwarf-face within. Wayne Mickl.

Rather let himself break into a delighted grin. It was
surprisingly easy. He wanted to reassure Sectry; he was
glad to see her. He let his eyes flick from Sectry to
Wayne Mickl to Sectry again. He blurted, "Am I in?"

Sectry flashed from unhappy to angry. Wayne Mickl
broke into delighted laughter. "Very *good!* But, Rather,
there just aren't enough dwarves to make it work. Take
him."

Two of the Navy crew were on him. They pulled him
loose from his handhold, set him spinning in the air. He
caught glimpses of them rebounding from walls. Then
one had wrapped his arms and legs around Rather's
lower ribs from behind, and the other had a foot in
Rather's crotch and Rather's two ankles in his hands,
stretching his legs straight.

There was a wrestling trick. Jill had shown him, in the brief period when she was stronger than he was. You wrapped your arms or legs around your opponent's short ribs and tightened them. Your opponent couldn't inhale. Presently he would faint.

Rather had used it on others afterward, and been punished for it. Most of the children were smaller than he was. Jilly wasn't, but she didn't have the strength of a dwarf after they both got older. Rather had been taught not to fight. He still got angry sometimes, but he learned to control it. Sometimes he wrestled with adults. He generally lost.

The man behind him (call him Navy #1) was letting him breathe, but shallowly. The other (Navy #2) wasn't kicking Rather's seeds into his belly; but he could. Rather held the red rage in check. "Booce?"

Booce answered the implied question. "You tell me. Where have you *been?*"

"The Dark. We've delivered Hilar's mud. We've got some walnut-cushion and—"

"The Navy went through this house like a whirlwind. I told them about the sporing fringe in the concrete. I was about to show them a hiding place I made in the door. I think they'd *rather* chop my house apart, and I get the distinct impression that it's all your fault—"

"Shut it, Booce," Mickl said. "Rather, what did you think you were coming home to?"

Anger made his thoughts murky, but he'd rehearsed this part in his mind. "I thought . . . I saw Sectry and I saw you. I thought the Captain-Guardian had come personally to tell me I was in. The Navy. You know. But—"

"You must know that an officer wouldn't care that much about a new inductee."

"Well, you're *here* and . . . someone told me you're

very eager to put another dwarf in the Guardian slot. What *are* you doing here, Captain-Guardian?"

"It's a mistake!" Sectry burst out.

Mickl didn't shout; he projected his voice over hers. The walls shivered to it. "Let me tell you something about mistakes. There's—"

"No, allow me." Rather reached for the foot in his crotch with both hands. He had it before the leg could snap straight, and he twisted. His rib cage closed. He stopped breathing and kept twisting. The leg buckled; Navy #2 was pulled close; he loosed Rather's ankle and Rather kicked him twice under the jaw. Now his hands were free to pull the constricting arms apart and over his head and down. Torsion pulled the legs free too, and he could breathe.

Navy #2 kicked at Rather with his good leg. Rather caught it on his foot. Reaction separated them: Navy #2 was headed toward a wall. There was blood on his mouth. Rather pulled the other's arms around behind him. They came, not easily, and Rather kept pulling until he had pulled Navy #1's shoulder from its socket.

Clave had a rib lock on the third man.

Rather pushed Navy #1 away. The man turned in the air, moaning, his arm at a crooked angle.

Navy #2 had reached the wall. He jumped. They traded blows: Rather put his heel in the other's midsection, but a fist smacked solidly into the side of Rather's neck. Short arms and legs had cost Rather more than one match.

Again the blows had thrown them apart. Rather's ears buzzed; lights flared in his eyes. He was too far from the walls. He waited . . . but Navy #2 was curled in a tight ball. When a wall touched him he stayed there, winded, resting.

Wayne Mickl was pointing a crossbow at Rather. "Cut it. I'll shoot you someplace nonlethal. You too, Jonthan. Stay there. You, the tree man, let go of Doheen!"

Clave released Navy #3. Doheen was unconscious.

Panting, elated, Rather said, "Stet. But mistakes are something . . . *somebody* pays for, and that's what . . . the word is for. Or am I going too fast for you?"

"Yes. Pause a minute. J— What is it *now?*"

The men in the doorway both looked surprised. One was a Navy crewman. He had Raym Wilby in a rib lock. "Captain-Guardian, this one flew up like he was coming to the house. Then he saw the ship and turned around and flew away. The Petty and me chased him down."

"Who are you?" Mickl demanded.

Raym only gaped. Carlot said, "It's Raym Wilby. He guided us into the Dark."

"Wilby, what were you flying from?"

"I . . . I just don't like N-Navy."

"Stet. Jonthan, wipe your face, then take Wilby into the storage room. Ask him about the trip. Be polite."

Doheen blinked; his eyes opened. The man from the ship took charge of Navy #1, the man with the dislocated arm. Rather heard him yell as his shoulder popped into place. Jonthan (Navy #2) wiped blood from his mouth with a cloth, then took Wayne Mickl by the elbow and towed him away. Rather noticed for the first time that Sectry had a crossbow too. It was pointed at Clave.

Mickl ignored it all. "Now, Rather, tell me about a pressure suit that looks like mine. Don't forget the crossbow."

Rather was still panting a little. He took a moment more than he needed. "Pressure suit? Booce told me. You've got three. Nine crew to use them, but you're short of dwarves." *Which ought to be a pun,* he thought; but he'd irritated Mickl enough without that.

"A fourth pressure suit invaded Headquarters fifteen days ago. You were in it."

Rather stared. "No, I wasn't. Fifteen days? I was in the Dark getting mud. Is that what this is about?"

"Rather, it's your bad luck that I'm interested in dwarves. I know where every dwarf in the Admiralty is right now. There are twelve. Ten are in the Navy. One is eighteen years old. He'll be a Petty soon. Sectry already is. The rest are Guardians. There's a Dark diver's boy, but his brain was thick with spores before he could grow a beard. And there's you."

"And another pressure suit."

"Yes. I want it."

Rather wiped sweat from his face. He was thinking as carefully as if he were innocent. The trick was not to know anything he shouldn't. This seemed safe: "Captain-Guardian, if a pressure suit got into the Admiralty without you knowing it, maybe there was a dwarf in it."

Mickl didn't answer. Rather said, "S— the Bosun and I are about the same size, but I think you're bigger. How big was that fourth suit? Would I even fit?" He was stuttering a little; he had to think every word through first. How clearly had Mickl seen the silver suit? It always looked bigger than the occupant. "Maybe it's smaller yet. Maybe it's so small that it'll fit in places you wouldn't look, a closet in a happyfeet ship—"

"Why that?"

"Happyfeet tried to rob us before we got here. They don't care much about laws. Isn't there a Lupoff ship in dock?"

"True enough, but a closet is silly. He'd suffocate."

"Somewhere else, then." *There's air in the silver suit.*

Am I supposed to know that? What else am I not supposed to know? "What really happened? What is it you think I did?"

"You entered Headquarters in an unregistered pressure suit painted like mine. You got into the Library. You got rid of the Guardian. We haven't been able to find out what you did there, or whether you got what you wanted, but Voice was running when you left. When I came in you scattered sporing fringe throughout Headquarters and got away." Mickl's throat worked, and Rather saw how close he was to uncontrolled rage. "I went after you. I couldn't catch you."

"Um . . . that doesn't make sense. Booce told me never to try to outfly Navy. The wings are different—"

Mickl slashed the air with his arm. "The suit outflew me! This isn't just another pressure suit. You'd be in enough trouble if it was only that. We've *got* to have this suit. It's special."

"How?"

"Classified, you little fungus!" Wayne Mickl closed his eyes. He pulled air in through his nose until his lungs were full, then let it all out. Calmly he said, "Booce, show me this hiding place."

Booce showed him. *We wouldn't have been told this either,* Rather thought. *Secrets!*

Mickl closed his helmet. When he peered into the compartment, light blazed from the forehead. He studied the interior at length. "Ingenious."

"Maybe not. It weakened the door." Booce pointed out the hole. Mickl nodded.

Jonthan was back. A long bruise was forming on his jaw. His glance at Rather seemed disinterested. He and the dwarf officer conferred in low voices. They disappeared toward the storage room.

That left only Navy #3, Doheen. He and Clave were holding a staring contest, Clave smiling, the other poker-faced.

Booce said carefully, "Rather, there's something you should know. You're trying to tell the Captain-Guardian that you're probably innocent. It's not enough."

Rather had thought things were going well. "Raym was with us. He'd have to believe Raym was lying too. Raym doesn't have the brains."

"No, of course not. Mickl believes you now." A quick glance at Doheen, who reacted with something like a shrug. "But just in case he's wrong, he'll stop *Logbearer* from ever leaving the Admiralty, because we might be smuggling that fourth suit. He'll ruin me financially, in case I might say something to save myself. He'll hound you. It'll never be over."

"Then . . ." *What'll I do? There can't be a way to convince Mickl I'm innocent. I'm guilty!*

Admiralty pressure suits don't have working jets. No fuel. There's a suit with jets, somewhere, and Mickl wants it. He'll never settle for less.

Give him the silver suit? He'd know we're guilty then.

If I could— Ah. He had something.

I can't ask Booce. Doheen's listening, and Booce doesn't know what happened anyway. The others—

Fate and air currents had put Rather near Sectry. He moved closer. She moved the crossbow aside for him. Her face was hard to read.

"I shouldn't have left," he said.

"Why didn't you wait?"

"They tell me the Navy takes forever to do anything.

I couldn't just hang around twitching, and we needed the mud."

Their voices had dropped. She said, "I was here. I turned down a flight, but I can't do that twice running. You left me for *mud?*"

It was a miserable thing to have to admit, but it was better than the truth. He nodded.

"Rather, nobody makes decisions when he's on fringe. So tell me, am I too strange? Am I too old?"

"My mother's older than my father. I like strange. I'm in the Clump because I like strange. Sectry, I don't regret anything I said or did." Which was not quite the truth. *Secrets*— "Hilar Belmy is trying to grow a burl tree."

She said, "That never works."

"Well, he's trying something new. Booce bought a piece of the tree. And he owes us."

"So it's not just mud, it's money. All right, Rather. I can understand money."

"That's more than I do. It's power, but it doesn't make you an officer. Are there un-rich officers?"

Her lips twitched. "They marry rich citizens. Their children are officers. The number of officers goes up. One day we'll all be officers."

"Why does Wayne Mickl want that suit so much? I'd think it would be the other way around—"

"It's bad for the Admiralty if happyfeet hold old science. I think Wayne's almost given up on taking his Captain's seat. The pressure suit is as much power as he'll ever have, and he takes his responsibilities—"

They were back: Wayne Mickl and Raym Wilby and Jonthan. Raym was unwontedly quiet. Mickl said, "And what were you discussing with the Bosun?"

Sectry was flustered; Rather answered first. "I was

suggesting that if you did have a fourth pressure suit, you'd need twelve dwarves to man them."

Sectry tried to cover her laugh with her hands. Booce laughed outright. Doheen's mouth was rigidly straight. Mickl was about to explode.

And Rather had learned little from Sectry, but it might be enough. *Go for Gold.* Before Mickl could speak, he asked, "Does it fly better than your suits?"

Mickl's face didn't change. "Yes. How did you know that?"

"You said it outflew you. Besides, I heard something once."

"You'll tell me."

"Privately, if you don't mind, Captain-Guardian."

They took the kitchen. Mickl said, "That fringe-addled Dark diver makes you a poor witness."

"I don't know anything about your Chairman's Court."

"You'll see a court soon enough. Talk to me, boy."

"I don't know anything about your mutineer pressure suit either—"

"Then—"

"I once heard that there's a way to make little holes on a pressure suit spray fire. Then it can fly without wings."

"Go on."

"Maybe I can find a man who can do it. He doesn't have a pressure suit, so he's never tried it."

"Take me to him."

"They don't deal with Navy. They don't even come into the Admiralty." Rather visualized a mysterious happyfeet tribe, isolated and distrustful. "They sent copsiks once. The Scientists don't come themselves."

"Give me a name."

He picked one he could remember. "Seekers."

"There's no such tribe."

Rather shrugged.

"Well, what *are* we doing here, Rather?"

"What happens is, you give me your pressure suit—"

Mickl laughed.

"I take it somewhere." Payment? Not money; the Seekers might not use money. "I take fringe too, maybe twenty kilos. I take tools. I bring the suit back. They keep the fringe and the tools. Maybe the jets work and maybe they don't."

"Let me tell you why I can't give you my pressure suit," Mickl said gently. "First, it belongs to the Admiralty. Second, it alternates among three Guardians. My triad would notice. Third, turning a pressure suit over to savages would certainly be judged as mutiny, especially since—fourth—you might not bring it back. Stet?"

"Not stet. Let me think."

"While you're thinking . . . This mysterious tribe, did they ever have a pressure suit to practice on?"

"They say they did—"

"Could they have got it working again?"

This was taking Rather into empty sky. Treefodder! Maybe it was lost, or stolen, or—

"*Talk* to me!"

"I was trying to remember. They threw it away."

"*What?*"

"It killed three citizens."

"How?"

"The . . . silver was only for one who was worthy.

One day the old dwarf died while he was using it. Three dwarves wrestled for it—"

"That sounds like too many dwarves, Rather."

It did. "I saw two myself, and I never got inside the jungle. I guess Seekers get more dwarves."

". . . Go on."

"The winner put the suit on and died. The one who lost to him put it on and died. The last one was a woman. She started to get into it, but while the—" Rather patted his skull "—this part was still open she said she heard the voice of Kendy the Checker. Nobody else could hear it. They got scared and dumped it and moved to another part of the sky."

"Sounds like the air feed went bad. What then?"

"That's when they found the Admiralty. They say one of your ships tried to rob them—"

"Nonsense."

"We say treefodder. They say you did." It *might* have happened in the past: Navy robbing savages—

Wayne Mickl was looking disgusted. He said, "It's possible. A ship low on provisions . . . this isn't helping."

"Wait. You three who trade your suit off. Are you always on duty at Headquarters?"

"No, of course not. Why?"

Rather took a deep breath. "Your fourth point: of course we'll bring the suit back. Not all of us will go. You'll keep friends of mine to answer for it if the suit doesn't come back.

"Your third point: maybe it's mutiny if you lose your chance at a pressure suit that can fly without wings, especially if it belongs to the Admiralty, which was my first point, and especially if you could get *three*! So let's work on your second point. Can you get the Admiralty's permission?"

"Admiral Robar Henling would rather give up his seeds. At his age it wouldn't— No. Just no."

He *was* getting somewhere. He had Mickl's attention. Think! "Will your, uh, triad try to track down that flying pressure suit?"

"We will. We are!"

"You can go anywhere if you think it's the right direction, stet? You're Guardians. One of you is an officer. Nobody'll ask. Am I completely off the track?"

". . . Not yet."

"So off you go, tracking rumors of a fourth pressure suit. Maybe you find it. You close in. But there's a dwarf in it, and he sees you coming and flies away laughing. What he doesn't know is that your triad was working without a pressure suit for a while. Then it came back. Now off goes the bandit dwarf, but he's doomed, because your suit flies too and he doesn't know it!"

Mickl's grin was not quite a pleasant sight. "Were you a Teller, where you came from?"

Rather knew exactly what he meant. "Our Teller was Merril till she died. These days everyone does some telling. Captain-Guardian, I'm trying to help. I'll bring the suit back whether it works or not."

"But would your Seekers give it back?" Mickl sighed. "I don't blame you for attacking my men, and I won't charge you. We'll leave it at that for the moment. This isn't finished, Rather."

The civilians watched the Navy people fly toward their rocket. Sectry was trailing; and when he saw her look back, Rather snatched his wings from the door and jumped after her.

She stayed in the air while he strapped his wings on. A voice spoke from the Navy ship's cabin; she answered.

Then she kicked away to avoid the rocket's exhaust. She did not fly back toward Serjent House.

The Navy rocket departed.

Rather reached her. He didn't have breath to speak. She said, "You're involved in something."

He shrugged helplessly.

"I don't know what's going on, but I don't want any part of it. I've decided I don't want to live in a tree either."

Rather had his breath back. He said, "We're the right size."

She shook her head violently. Teardrops flew. "Didn't Wayne tell you how many dwarves there are in the Admiralty? Rather, it was a good offer. Nobody makes real decisions when she's on fringe. I'm sorry."

"So am I." His tongue was in knots and his thoughts were scrambled. *The Scientist and the Checker, they caused this, they sent me into Headquarters! Would it be different if they hadn't? Did I mean it, that offer? How will Carlot feel about this? Or Jill?*

"I do want to see you again. After this is over, if it's ever over. You'll be going back to the tree, won't you? You won't like it here, not with the Captain-Guardian on your tail!" She didn't wait for his answer. "Well, sooner or later there'll be a mission to Citizens Tree, and I'll be on it. I hope this is all cleared up by then."

She flapped spinward, toward Headquarters or the Market. He called after her. "We have a rocket—"

"No. Thanks. I'll go on foot." She kept kicking. Rather turned back to Serjent House. He was going to have to do some fast talking . . . again.

Chapter Twenty-Two

Loop

WHERE HAD IT ALL GONE WRONG? A MESSAGE MAY BECOME garbled across fifty-two light-years of distance and interstellar dust. But this was simple, unambiguous, and *repeated*—

from the CARM #2 cassettes, recorded year 76 SM, day 1412:

TO *DISCIPLINE*, YEAR 1435 STATE. RETRIEVE YOUR CREW AND CONTINUE YOUR MISSION.
—FANK SHIBANO, FOR THE STATE

—as if he were a wayward computer in need of reprogramming. Arrival date: Feb 26, 1487 State. Recorded by CARM #2 sixty-one Earth days later.

He'd accomplished his mission! Why this?

He had attempted to follow his new orders. Of eight CARMs he had sent into the Smoke Ring, he located three. The rest must have been destroyed, or worn out, or their sending systems turned off.

From CARM #2 he had learned of the death of Claire Dalton. Claire had died at one hundred and thirty-eight, less than two months before the message arrived. No other survivors were known to the CARMs. Many deathdates had been recorded.

Amazing that Claire had lived so long.

There had been a mutiny. Kendy had stored it in CARM #2's computer before he erased it from his own memory. Sharls Davis Kendy had mutinied against his crew. Fool, not to have seen that! Their descendants used *mutineer* as an insult!

He'd made an irretrievable mistake. But how? His reasoning was straight. His orders were unambiguous . . . weren't they?

1) . . . YOU WILL VISIT EACH OF THESE STARS IN TURN. OTHER TARGETS MAY BE ADDED . . . THE STATE EXPECTS TO SETTLE THESE WORLDS, SPREADING HU- MANITY AMONG VARIABLE ENVIRONMENTS, AGAINST DANGERS THAT MIGHT AFFECT ONLY SOL SYSTEM.

2) . . . THE HUMAN SPECIES IS NOT INVULNERA- BLE. THERE IS FINITE RISK THAT THE CREW OF ANY IN- TERSTELLAR SPACECRAFT MAY FIND, ON ITS RETURN, THAT IT HAS BECOME THE ENTIRE HUMAN RACE. YOUR CREW AND THEIR GENES ARE YOUR PRIMARY CARGO. CLASSIFIED.

3) YOUR TERTIARY MISSION IS TO EXPLORE . . .
                                    —LING CARTHER, FOR THE STATE

How could it be clearer?

Kendy knew how the dinosaurs had died. The State had explored the ringed black giant planet that periodically hurled flurries of comets into the solar system. The State could stop comets now. The solar system was tamed. Ten planets were better than one; cities and industrial sites on thirty moons and hundreds of asteroids were better than none; but the lesson of the dinosaurs remained. Planets are fragile.

Earthlike worlds had been found in the habitable zones of nearby stars. Green life had emerged on two. At *Discipline*'s departure they were in the process of final terraforming. On twenty-six worlds, poisonous air resembling Earth's primordial reducing atmosphere had been seeded with tailored algae. In a thousand years some would be ready for further attention. The seeder ramship program had been running since seven hundred years before Kendy's birth.

And *Discipline* had found a habitable nonplanet!

Humanity was to be spread as widely as possible.

The dangers here were not a planet's dangers. The Smoke Ring and its enveloping gas torus were dense enough to protect Earthly life from radiation from the old neutron star, and from other radiation too. Radiation sources were normal throughout the universe. A supernova explosion near Sol . . . a passage of Sol and its companion stars through a region of star-creation . . . a catastrophe in the galactic core . . . events known and unknown could cause havoc through Sol system *and* all nearby systems. But none could harm the Smoke Ring!

His own message to Earth, sent in year 1382 State, was long and detailed. CARM #2 had the record:

Sharls Davis Kendy had abandoned his crew as they explored the Smoke Ring. Three who remained aboard had been invited to take what they needed from *Discipline* and join the others. He had never given reasons; his secondary mission was CLASSIFIED. He had shut down systems aboard *Discipline* in a pattern that forced them to the CARMs.

Ah, that explained something: those three had not loved cats. Pure coincidence.

Then, the message from Earth. *Put it back the way it was.*

How? His crew was dead!

Faced with conflicting orders, he could not function at all. He would be locked in a loop of reinforcing guilt. Kendy had sequestered all data relating to the mutiny and beamed it to CARMs #2, #6, and #7, then erased it all from memory.

How had he gone wrong? Could the message itself have been garbled? Through 200 repititions?

> TO *DISCIPLINE*, YEAR 1435 STATE. RETRIEVE YOUR
> CREW AND CONTINUE YOUR MISSION.
> —FANK SHIBANO, FOR THE STATE

No explanations, no elaborations. He'd been reprogrammed like a wayward computer. *Why?* He'd accomplished his mission!

Was the message genuine? Check the dates:

Kendy's own mission report, sent 1382 State.

Message from the State dated fifty-two point two Earth years later. He was fifty-two point one light-years from Earth. This Shibano had not lingered over his decision, but . . . it checked.

—Arrived fifty-two point one years after *that*. Check.

. . . Odd. Why would the State expect *any* crew to remain alive? That Claire had survived was partly due to low gravity, good conservative health habits (her mind was that of an elderly corpsicle), youth (via the body of some bright, healthy criminal), and luck. The rest must have been dead decades earlier (and their descendants called him murderer and mutineer and damaged machine).

Shibano for the State. Kendy found it difficult to consider Shibano as separate from the state, but . . . what could Shibano have been thinking? Rescue after one hundred and four years: it was insane.

Perhaps the State's medical resources had improved? Times change. Every generation of mankind has sought longer lives. Thousand-year lifespans might have become common . . .

Speculative.

But times change. Goals change. Kendy's route here had been circuitous. The state that had given Kendy his orders was four hundred and fifty-five years old when he reached the Smoke Ring. Five hundred and seven when Shibano spoke. Five hundred and fifty-nine when his message arrived.

Kendy did not normally question orders. Conflicting orders could throw him into a loop. But he had been round and round this loop, while some voiceless subsystem sought desperately for a way out.

Somewhere in a pattern of magnetic fields there was a change of state . . . and Kendy the man would have laughed. A change of State, yes. Sharls Davis Kendy's State was a thousand years in the past. Dead. Somehow he must serve anyway. His own goals had been spelled out in detail; he would serve those.

Humankind was to settle varied environments. So be it. What was his present situation?

The receding Smoke Ring covered forty degrees of sky. His mind had been following a loop for just under two months! He'd missed the final stages of the explo-

sion of Levoy's Star, the foray into the Admiralty might
have disintegrated by now . . .

To work. *Discipline*'s drive had shut down without his
attention. Good! He still had fuel.

He started the drive warming. His orbit was a comet's,
highly eccentric. Equations ran through his mind . . .
fire a short burst at aphelion. Shed some velocity by
aerobraking, by dipping into the gas torus around the
Smoke Ring, twice. Use Goldblatt's World as a gravity
sling, save a few cupfuls of deuterium that way . . .

Glowing in direct sunlight, the Clump was green-and-
white chaos in *Logbearer*'s steam trail. Clave felt good:
loose and free, cruising through an uncluttered sky.

Rather crawled out of the angular cabin. His head was
metal and glass. "The suit's too big, but I can wear the
helmet."

Clave smiled at the sight. "Getting anything?"

"Getting . . . ? No, Jeffer hasn't called. Maybe he
can't call this suit. I tried Kendy too."

"Too bad." Clave had been watching a distant brown-
ish smudge of vegetation. Now he shouted aft. "Carlot?
Could that be a fisher jungle?"

"Be with you in twelve breaths." Carlot finished what
she was doing to the motor and crawled to them over
the cabin. "Where?"

Clave's toes jabbed east and out.

"I don't see the root . . . right, that's what it is. I'd
better turn off the motor or we'll go past. Rather?"

Rather followed her aft. Clave stayed at the bow while
they worked the motor. Presently the tide behind him
went away.

Closer now, the fisher jungle looked dead enough.
Brown foliage and bare branchlets. Tufts and patches of

vivid green: parasitical growths. The fisher root was half extended, like a dead man's hand with three scarlet fingernails. He looked for the carm . . . and found a man flapping toward him.

Jeffer pulled himself aboard, panting. "Moor to the root. Treefodder, I'm glad to see you, but what are you *doing* here? Is everyone here?" He looked over the edge of cabin and shouted, "Hello, Carlot! Rather, what . . . is that a pressure suit helmet?"

"Yes. The rest of it's inside."

They told it in tandem while they moored *Logbearer*.

"I never did quite know if the Captain-Guardian believed me," Rather said, "but he left Serjent House without taking any copsiks—"

"The Navy watched us for the next forty, fifty days," Clave said. "We weren't doing anything peculiar. Booce sold wood and hired people to cut it. We bought more seeds and some tools and stuff. We're carrying all that. Mickl kept coming around, interrupting us, trying to get Rather to tell him more about Seekers—"

"I tried not to talk too much. I built up a picture of these Seekers in my mind, and maybe I got it across. Secretive. Not very many of 'em. Too many Scientists, maybe half a dozen. They've got a cassette and reader but they don't show it to outsiders. They threw away their silver suit, but they've got records on how to maintain it. And they swear to kill anyone who tells their secrets. The citizen who told me disappeared. He was high on fringe and I was just a kid, but I had a better memory than most kids . . . That part's true anyway," Rather said. "I haven't told Mickl all of this."

"Dangerous," Jeffer said. "You'll have Mickl desperate to meet them."

"Not if I read him right. Scientist, you know the story now, and you can back me up. Give him details I didn't."

Clave asked, "Jeffer, did Kendy get the records he wanted?"

"I haven't heard from him."

"If we're lucky the treefeeder never will call back. Anyway, we must have looked innocent enough. We never did anything odd because we didn't know anything. So. Twenty days ago three dwarves pulled up to *Logbearer* in a Navy rocket. Mickl and another man and a woman, all the same size. Weird. They gave us the pressure suit and went away. We're supposed to get the jets going and pay off the Seekers. Would you like ten years' supply of fringe?"

"No. You'd better leave it here if you're supposed to."

They carried the suit and helmet into the dead foliage. Rather and Carlot set to moving their cargo while they looked about.

Entropy and parasites had eaten a deep cavity into the fisher jungle's dead trunk. The carm was there, and Jeffer's camp: rocks for a fireplace, a rack of poles for smoking meat, a midden a decent distance away. Jeffer had made a third wing for himself, a prudent move for a man alone. From the blackened look of it he'd been using it to fan his fire.

Jeffer had the pressure suit splayed like a bird's flayed skin. "Rather, did you try it?"

"It's too big for me. —And the air feed doesn't work. I got the panel open. A little wheel isn't connecting to anything, and there's a spoke with nothing on it."

Jeffer grinned. "I see."

Rather laughed. "Mickl doesn't want the Seekers

stealing his silver suit! If they try it they'll find out nobody's worthy!"

"I'll refuel it. No guarantee the jets still work."

"Well, if they do work, I get the impression that
Booce will get a decent offer for the Wart. Mickl never
actually said so."

"Three pressure suits?"

Clave said, "Stet. We may have to do this twice more.
And they're searching Dark and sky for a fourth pressure suit. They must be looking hard at where *Logbearer*
went. You may want to move the carm."

Carlot arrived pushing the last of the cargo: not seeds,
but tools. "You're going to love this, Scientist." She separated something out.

Jeffer took it with glad cries. "A pump! Wonderful!
The carm's low on water, and I *hate* the way I filled it
last time. Can I keep it?"

"Stet. We're supposed to bribe the Seekers with it.
Here, this is a bellows from the Market. You anchor
one end. It's easier."

"Nice. Can you stay for a couple of sleeps? I've got
food and—"

"Lonely?"

It showed in his face. "You know it."

"We've got food you never tasted. Dark fungus and
earthlife. You'll love it."

Their exotic dinner was nothing unusual for Rather,
not any longer. What made it fun was watching Jeffer
react.

Jeffer talked while he ate. "I had some trouble getting
the silver suit. I found it okay, but it was right in the
fire. I had to get the bow up against it and push it out

along with a kilton of burning goo. I just wonder how many Admiralty citizens saw me."

"The stories won't match," Clave said. "In sixty days it won't matter at all. I've been thinking. We'll burn the fringe here. If a Navy ship comes they'll find that the Seekers had a hell of a party and then went away."

"Good. I'll have to take the carm someplace you can find it—"

"No. You find us. *Logbearer* will be returning to Citizens Tree in due course, maybe another thirty days. Keep watch. Pick us up well outside the Clump."

"Another fifty days of this? Treefodder. And I never even saw the treefeeding Clump."

"We'll leave you most of our food," Clave said.

Carlot carefully wasn't looking at Rather. "I'll be bringing a guest. Raff Belmy and I'll be married as soon as we get back to the Admiralty. I want to bring him back to the tree. What he tells his father is up to him, but he'll have at least a quarter year to think about it."

"So you decided," Rather said. He felt he had almost gotten used to the loss.

"I'm like you. I'm tired of secrets."

"There's a plant here that grows good foliage," Jeffer offered. "Dessert."

Carlot tossed an orange sphere at him.

Jeffer's acting like a happy eight-year-old, Rather thought as he tethered himself into a foliage patch for sleep. *Being alone out here must be rough on him. Maybe all adults stay children someplace in their heads . . .*

"Rather?"

"Yuh. Carlot?"

She wriggled under the lines and was alongside him.

Rather opened his mouth and closed it again. Then he said, "I don't like lying to you."

"What *now?*"

"I was going to not say, 'What would Raff think?'"

She didn't move away. Presently she said, "You don't understand us."

"Nope."

"We like to spread the genes around. Nobody talks about it in public, but you hear. A man and a woman get engaged. They make babies together. Sixty, seventy days later, they get married. Maybe the first kid looks like the rest and maybe he doesn't."

"But *why?*"

"It's the last chance. See, I'm going to marry Raff, but there are men I turned down. They're not going to just vanish. I wasn't with Raff *all* those sleeps I was away. Raff's been seeing friends too, I don't know who. Rather, it's just different. The officers say it's good. They talk about gene drift."

"Okay."

"What Raff thinks about it is, he'd rather not know. I never did wonder what Jill would think."

Jill. "We never made promises."

"Sure. But who else is there? There's nobody anywhere near her age in the tuft. Just you."

"I suppose. I wish I could have told her I was leaving."

She said nothing. Rather couldn't drop it. "I wish I could tell her it was worth it. You never wanted that raid on the Library. You were right. If Kendy's really gone, then why did it happen? The Navy'll never stop being suspicious of us, and we didn't learn anything, and I can't even tell Jill about the raid because I can't tell her about Kendy."

She stirred. "You don't want me?"

"Sure I want you. Every sleep we're here, I want you. I wanted you for keeps."

"You can't have that. When we marry, that's the end of that. Understand?"

"Stet."

Kendy had run the records from CARMs #2 and #6 over and over. He'd built up a sublibrary of sorts under RESOURCES, LOCAL USAGE.

Here: Citizens Tree was firing mud to make a cookpot. Here: firing the laundry vat. Both had been recorded by the silver suit as it moved unharmed through the fire. One clip every ten minutes.

Here: curing the lines from the spaghetti jungle. Mark the Silver Man unharmed in the smoke.

Here: the elevator in Citizens Tree. Here, recorded years earlier by Klance the Scientist: the London Tree elevator, run with stationary bicycles.

Here: CARM #6 changing the integral tree's orbit. Here: *Logbearer* moving another tree.

Here: Rather collecting honey. Booce's voice explaining that it was usually done with handmade armor. Here: a set of hornet armor made to show the Navy customs collectors, lest they seek for such and find the silver suit instead.

The natives used materials from *Discipline* when they had it. When they didn't, they made do. They were doing very well without Kendy.

Discipline was making its second aerobraking pass, ass-backward through the gas torus. The cone of the fusion drive approached fusion temperatures. That was hardly a danger, but the plasma streaming back along the hull had to be watched.

Velocity, Smoke Ring median: 11 kps. Velocity at

Kendy's distance: 3 kps. *Discipline*'s relative velocity: 20 kps and falling. *Discipline* reached perihelion and began to rise, embedded in hot plasma. The animals were frantic. Kendy couldn't spare attention for them. Nothing had melted on his first pass . . . but the gas ahead of him thickened as he rose, because Goldblatt's World was ahead.

Visual: a raging, endless storm the size of Neptune. Neudar: a core the size of two and a half Earths spun once every seven hours, carrying the storm around with it, until the atmospheric envelope trailed off into the Smoke Ring. Instruments: impacting plasma increased in temperature and density; velocity decreased. The ship was surviving. There'd been the risk that he would have to blow hydrogen ahead of him for cooling.

Goldblatt's World passed below, warping the ship's path into something nearer a circle. Now the plasma density dropped fast.

Fifteen minutes of that was enough excitement for any computer program. In an hour he'd be over the Admiralty and out of the gas torus. He'd make his last short burn then. It would hold him near the Admiralty for a good half hour.

Discipline would be glowing bright enough to see, if anyone looked in just the right direction. That might or might not be good. Kendy had taken his time returning. His long-range plans were in tatters and he didn't know what to do about it.

Chapter Twenty-Three

Beginnings

from the Citizens Tree cassettes:

YEAR 384, DAY 2250. BOOCE RECORDED OUR HOLDINGS BEFORE WE LEFT. HE'S APPALLED THAT WE NEVER ASKED. BAD BUSINESSPERSONS, HE CALLS US. WE DON'T USUALLY BOTHER TO SPELL OUT WHO OWNS WHAT IN CITIZENS TREE. IT DRIVES BOOCE CRAZY.

WE SPENT A LOT ON SEEDS AND FOOD AND WIDGETS, BUT WE STILL HAVE CREDIT—IMAGINARY MONEY—IN SOME VAGUE AMOUNT THAT DEPENDS ON WHAT BOOCE ACTUALLY GETS FOR THE WOOD AND THE METAL. WE'LL LEARN THAT WHEN, AND IF, WE RETURN TO THE ADMIRALTY.

—JEFFER THE SCIENTIST

THE LIFT CAGE DROPPED. IT WAS CROWDED WITH EIGHT PEOPLE and several bags from the carm. Lawri and Gavving,

Scientist and Chairman Pro Tem, seemed distinctly uncomfortable. It wasn't hard to guess why. Raff Belmy
was uncomfortable too. Carlot clung tight to his arm,
possessively, protectively.

"I had some trouble finding the tree," Jeffer said.

"Your problem," Gavving answered. "After all, you
took the silver suit. How were we supposed to tell you
where we were?"

"Yeah, but you moved the tree, didn't you? That
thing next to the lift, is that what I think it is?"

"Yes. Lawri's doing, mostly."

"Hah. Scientist, I thought you'd be twiddling your
toes waiting for me to come home."

"We found ways to occupy ourselves, Scientist." Lawri's pregnancy was growing conspicuous. The formality
between her and her husband did not seen unfriendly.

Gavving said, "I hope you brought something to make
us look good."

The rest of them laughed; but Clave said, "Trouble?"

"Treefodder, yes, trouble! I'd have flown to a new
tree if I'd been *sure* they'd let me have wings. One thing,
the children are on our side. They've been crazy with
waiting to see what you bring back. And Minya stuck
with me."

"She did? Good," said Clave.

"She did, in public."

Clave reached into a bag. He sliced an apple in half
and passed it to Gavving and Lawri. They bit, distrust-
fully, and continued eating. "That'll do it," Gavving said.

"Fine. Here. Don't eat the hull." He'd cut an orange
into quarters.

They gnawed the insides out of the oranges. Lawri
chewed and swallowed a bit from the peel, but did not
take another. Gavving said, "Yeah!"

"We've got seeds," Clave said. "This and a lot of other earthlife. We'll plant them in the out tuft."

Faces like a field of flowers below the falling cage. Two meteor-trails of golden blond hair: Jill next to Anthon, she a meter shorter than her father, both scanning the faces in the lift cage. Rather knew when Jill's eyes met his, but her face didn't change.

The cage thumped into its housing. Children piled out of the treadmill, and Mark with them. Everyone in Citizens Tree was here.

They looked short: a field of dwarves in which Anthon and the Serjent women stood out as normal. Rather had become used to giants. Children and some adults crowded around the cage. Jill and Anthon hung back, not quite hostile, but suspending judgment. Mark had that look too.

For all these hundreds of days Rather had wondered what the tribe would think of his mutiny. He'd almost managed to forget that he had never told Jill, *could not* have told her that he was going to leave the tree.

His mothers were crowding close around the lift, and Karilly and Ryllin with them. The Serjent women hugged Carlot, then Carlot's new husband. Karilly hung back a little. She was conspicuously carrying a guest. Raff beamed like sunlight at seeing someone he knew. They fell into rapid conversation, moving away, taking Karilly with them. "Damn, but I missed oranges . . . Booce had to stay? I'm not surprised, but . . ."

Karilly was silent.

Clave folded his wives into his arms and forced apples on them.

Anthon slapped an orange from Debby's hand. Rather heard: "You took this Admiralty man aboard the *carm?*" before his First Mother picked him up to hug him.

"You treefeeding fool," Minya whispered. "You fool mutineer, you. Drillbits in your brains, both of you, you and your father. He never stopped wishing he'd gone too. Are you all right?"

"I'm in good shape. Mostly." She pulled back to look into his face. He tried to look earnest. "First Mother, I'm allergic to dry, thin air. Not enough sleep does it too. It's like knives in the eyes. I go blind. It lasts for hours."

She started laughing. She said, "I'm sorry, I'm sorry," and hugged him hard, still laughing. There were tears in her eyes. She put him down and saw him smiling slyly. She said, "It'll never happen again. We'll keep the tree where the air's thick. You'd better go talk to Jill."

"Why? What's wrong?"

"Talk to her first. Then I think—"

Jeffer shouted for attention. "I here present Raff Belmy. Raff and Carlot are married by Admiralty law. The record is in the cassettes."

Over the heads of his brothers and sisters, Rather saw the judging-look fade from Jill's face. She moved forward at last. Rather said, "Harry, can you give me some privacy? Take them along?"

Harry said, "Oh. Sure." Somehow he got his siblings moving away before Jill reached him.

The judging-look was back. She said, "Rather. How are you?"

"Fine. Nobody made me a copsik. I didn't get killed. Jill, I wanted to tell you."

"Were you afraid I'd run tell my father?"

"If I wasn't, the rest of us would have been. I couldn't, Jill."

He saw her reject that. She asked, "What was it like?"

"I'll be a lot of days telling you that!" And suddenly it was a pain in him, that he couldn't tell her about the raid, ever.

"What's wrong now?"

"Nothing," he lied. "I was remembering how close I came to joining the Admiralty Navy. I got out of it though. Jill, dinner has to be something special. Is there time to cook some of this earthlife?"

"Couple of days yet."

"I'll show you what to do." Take the kids too? He'd thought he wanted to be alone with Jill, but now he knew he didn't. "Harry! Gorey! Bring those bags to the cookpot."

The Admiralty slid west below him. Kendy began his burn, then turned to his instruments.

Neudar and the telescope array caught Admiralty Headquarters as it emerged from behind the Dark. The Library didn't respond. It must be turned off. CARM #6 was nowhere in evidence. No pressure suit responded to his query.

Sharls Davis Kendy had made more than one mistake. For half a thousand years he had been frantic to begin guiding his citizens in the Smoke Ring. Now he could begin, and now he almost knew how. Opportunities would come.

A part of his attention scanned his growing file on RESOURCES, LOCAL USAGE:

Debby described Half Hand's kitchen for Jeffer's benefit.

Clave carried the helmet on a slow trip through Serjent House.

The camera viewpoint spun erratically through a

cloud of children. Children had knocked the helmet off
its usual perch at the lift, then played with it like a bas-
ketball. Kendy viewed the commons as a series of stills.
Corridor openings, the water trap, the communal cooking area, children laughing as they bounded in slow arcs.

A series of angular Clump houses, wildly various.

Mark's hut in various stages of construction. The silver suit had been housed there for a time.

Abruptly the CARM #2 control board came to life.
Kendy sent his signal. Records came back: stills of various bored Guardians in their shared pressure suits, cul-
minating in (present time) six jungle-giant men in a half
circle around the control board, wearing anxious faces
and spotless new uniforms. These must be officers; and
now Kendy had their insignia.

The signal disintegrated with distance.

He rounded forty degrees of Smoke Ring before he
made contact with CARM #6.

The vehicle was in its wooden dock at the midpoint
of Citizens Tree. It was empty of citizens and cargo. That
was *Logbearer* next to the left cage, and some smaller
structure next to that. Kendy "stared": he enlarged the
image and examined it in detail.

They'd built a steam rocket.

They didn't have a metal pipe or sikenwire, so they'd
used ceramics. Fired mud! The laundry vat was part of
it!

Records: the CARM on its way home. *Logbearer* was
strapped along the hull. Booce was missing. Rather was
present(!). The jungle-giant stranger matched the still
of Hilar Belmy's son.

Raff Belmy's medical readings, originally ominous,
settled down over passing days. Carlot must have helped

to calm him down. Rather was being abnormally polite to both, and keeping his distance. The two spent considerable time out of sight aboard *Logbearer*.

Records: moving toward the Citizens Tree midpoint. The ceramic rocket returned ahead of the CARM. It puffed toward the in tuft, pushing a huge glob of black mud, and passed out of range.

Records: "Year 384, day 2400, Jeffer speaking as Scientist. Carm and *Logbearer* are both docked at Citizens Tree. This will be my last log entry until Kendy calls.

"Kendy, for your information, Rather got out of Headquarters safely. We refueled the jets on an Admiralty pressure suit and returned it. Captain-Guardian Mickl could have had the other suits refueled too, but he never brought them. Now he's got a pressure suit with jets. We gave him some time to play, and then we told him what to do when they run out of fuel.

"We've had no further trouble. Booce got a good offer on the metal. The Navy was carving it up when we left.

"Rather suggests that Mickl wants the flying suit for himself. It's something even the Admiral doesn't have. He's got a secret now, and we know it, and he'll need us to keep it flying. That gives us a certain edge with the Captain-Guardian if we ever want to exploit it.

"We have some wealth and some influence in the Admiralty. We got it without your help. We do not appreciate your abandoning Rather in the middle of the raid.

"I've spent as much time waiting for your call as I care to. I'll be back from time to time. If you haven't called by the crossyear, which is three hundred and ninety-one days from now, I will turn Voice off."

Nobody was near the CARM. The lift wasn't running.

The CARM drifted out of range. Kendy scanned the far arc of the Smoke Ring out of habit; he had never seen signs of industrial activity there.

The Admiralty flowed below him. The Library had been turned off again.

Their ancestors hadn't listened to him either. They'd turned off the Voice subsystems; they'd cut the fibers that allowed Kendy to fly a CARM by remote. He'd been completely cut off for half a thousand years. As he was now.

Rather was scrubbing his teeth and thinking about breakfast when the Silver Man came into the bach hut. He spit and said, "Mark?"

"Who else?" Mark threw back his helmet. The silver suit was filthy and stank of smoke. "I tried that. I felt silly."

"Sure, silly. Mark, I saw their teeth. The older Admiralty citizens still have half their teeth! I bet Ryllin and Mishael have been scrubbing their teeth all along." Rather remembered that this man wasn't his father . . . and didn't know it, and had a legitimate grievance. All in a rush he said, "I stole it. We thought we needed it and we did. It was *right* to go. Treefodder, Mark, you're from a bigger tree! Don't you feel cramped here?"

"Fifteen years I've felt cramped. Relax. You brought back some wonderful things. You brought back the carm and the suit and you didn't ruin the suit."

"You looked mad enough to kill when we came down."

"That was three good dinners ago. I never thought I'd taste potatoes again. I know a better way to cook them."

"You forgive me? Mark, I'm really glad."

"What are my choices? Sure I forgive you. We're firing the new laundry pot."

"Is it that late? I slept like a rock. Needed it too. These first few sleeps I just lay there wondering why one of the walls was pushing against me."

"I've spent some sleepless nights here myself," Mark said. "It's lonely in the bach hut. We built it too big. Big enough for the next crop of men."

"Maybe that's it."

"Have you talked to Jill?"

"Minya asked me that. We've talked. Why?"

"Yeah. Well." Mark sometimes had trouble finding words. "Citizens Tree is strange. None of us grew up the way you did. There are adults and children and a big gap in between, so you couldn't tell much from just watching older children grow up. Maybe there are things we should have said—"

"I know about sex, if that's what you mean . . . Maybe I need to know more. Two women have told me to feed the tree. It hurts. What could you have told me about that?"

Mark whistled. "You started young. Well, someone could have said, 'There's only one suitable mate for you and there's only one for Jill in this whole tuft, and she thinks she owns you, and maybe she's right.'"

Rather let that percolate through his head. "Jill wants to make babies with me? Did she tell you that, or are you guessing?"

"I'm guessing. All I *know* is, when Instant Chairman Gavving told us you'd gone off with all the wealth of Citizens Tree, Jill was madder than I was, and that took some doing. She wanted you thrown into the sky with no wings. A hundred sleeps later she was sure you'd all be killed and she couldn't see for crying."

"I'll go see her. Where is she?"

"Go easy, stet? *You* know you can find other mates. Jill doesn't."

"I don't either. Sectry wants no part of me—" He couldn't say why. Secrets. "And Carlot married someone else. You can't imagine how bad that was. All the way home, Carlot and Raff. They spent most of their time in *Logbearer*. It wasn't any better when I couldn't see them."

Mark said, "When nobody wants you in the first place, that's worse. Trust me."

"Mark, I've gotten very good at lying. I'm trying to stop."

"Good. Go talk to Jill."

"Where is she?"

"Everybody's watching us fire the laundry vat except Jill. I've got to go back and see if anything needs doing. Try the miz hut. Then the commons."

The deep voice hailed him as he entered. "Hello, Jeffer the Scientist. This is Kendy."

Shouldn't that have been *Kendy for the State*? Jeffer said, "Uh-huh. You missed all the excitement."

"Not all. A large Navy ship is moving toward your position. They'll reach you in eighty standard days."

Jeffer took a moment to absorb the shock. He should have known. It wasn't over; it never would be. There was no going back from the Clump expedition. No going back from *knowing* about the Admiralty.

He pulled himself forward to the control board. "That gives us some time to talk."

The square, hard face in the bow window had always lacked expression. It said; "A bad thing happened to me, Jeffer. I learned too much about myself. There was no way I could communicate until now."

"Lie to me, Kendy. Say there was something wrong with Voice."

Kendy said, "The glitch was in myself. I think I have it fixed. Machines go bad, Jeffer. I left you a file under HISTORY. It's selected records from the settling of the Smoke Ring. It explains some of what went wrong. Play it after I'm out of range."

"Can you tell me about it?"

"No."

"Your timing was lousy. We thought you'd left Rather for treefodder. If you ever—"

"I can't talk about it. It hurts my mind. Damage might be permanent. Do you seek vengeance against me?"

The trouble was that Kendy looked and sounded as calm as death. Kendy never showed anger, nor relief, love, pain. It was hard to believe he was hurting . . . yet he was *not* a man. Maybe. Maybe.

Jeffer said, "Well, we got home. I assume you got most of it from the log. The earthlife food stopped most of the arguments. Now all the reunited couples are busy making babies. The arguments haven't gone away, though. They're just simmering. It won't help if there's a Navy ship coming."

"It's coming. I couldn't resolve details of design. There's alcohol in the exhaust, and it's coming from the Clump. Definitely Navy. What have you done with the seeds?"

"Seeds? We'll plant them in the out tuft. Mark's talking about building an extension to the lift before anything gets ripe enough to pick."

"Cut some foliage so the sunlight can reach the plants. I can show you how to use water flow to move the lifts

with less effort. You haven't mentioned the fired mud
rocket."

"That's nice, isn't it? We don't need the Admiralty's
treefeeding pipes."

"You don't need me," Kendy said. He knew the risk
he was taking. It was acceptable. "I've been looking at
records. Most of what can be done with materials from
Discipline can also be done with Smoke Ring resources.
Lifts, housing, clothing, food, domestic animals. Now
rockets. The Admiralty even has a heliograph."

"No, we don't need you," Jeffer said, "but I never
thought you'd know it."

"A bad thing happened to me. I don't trust my judgment any more. My intention has always been to make
a civilization in the Smoke Ring, modeled on the State
that shaped your ancestors. The Smoke Ring will never
be that. How can I make a State in a place where I can't
even make maps?"

"Would we even like your State? Skip it. What do we
do about that ship? I hope Sectry Murphy's aboard.
We'll get some notion of what they want if Rather talks
to her—"

"Hide the carm in another tree. Tear out the dock
too, or put the ceramic rocket there. Show them that.
It's not advanced, but it doesn't need starstuff resources.
It may impress them. Keep the carm manned. There are
two ways you might need it—"

"I won't burn them!"

"One way, then. You can't ignore the Admiralty.
You'd really like to join as officers. You may have to
show them the carm before they'll listen to *that*. De-
mand officer status, but they may settle for giving it to
just the Chairman and Scientist—"

Jeffer laughed. "For a man who doesn't trust his own judgment, you certainly—"

"I think fast. I plan fast. I make mistakes."

"Anything else?"

"Mark might want to join the Navy. Sound him out. See if the Navy personnel might want him. I gather they don't like older recruits, but Mark was trained in London Tree. Karilly may benefit from going back. Is she still mute?"

"Yes, but she's also pregnant and happy. I'm not sure I want to fiddle."

"I'm almost out of range. Back in two days. The code is HISTORY. Tell nobody of what you are about to learn."

"K—"

"Unless in your judgment it would be beneficial."

Kendy had *never* talked like this. "Stet."

The face faded. Jeffer didn't move for some time. Finally he tapped the white button. "Prikazyvat Voice."

"Hello, Jeffer the Scientist."

"Link to the pressure suit."

"Done."

"This is Jeffer calling anyone. Anyone home?"

"Hello? Scientist?" It was Jill's voice.

"I want to talk to my wife."

"I'll get her. She's on the branch."

That would take most of a day. Jeffer started the HISTORY file and listened to it all the way through. Then he started it again.

Lawri climbed in through the airlock. "I didn't have anyone but Rather and Jill for a treadmill team. Everybody else is on the branch. Now, what's all the excitement, Scientist?"

"Prikazyvat Voice. Run HISTORY."

Dead voices spoke. *Discipline*'s crew reported the discovery of a weird cosmological anomoly. Some of what followed was familiar from the cassettes. Some was entirely cryptic.

"How long have you had this?" Lawri demanded.

"Kendy only just filed it. I . . . I've been in contact with him since before we left for the Clump."

Lawri was coldly angry. "That was mutiny! How could you not trust *me*?"

"I'm trusting you now. Listen."

They heard a highly formalized quarrel. Some of the participants argued for settling the Smoke Ring; some were for moving on to an unnamed destination. Kendy spoke in favor of staying, then tried to terminate the argument. It continued.

There were parts of a broadcast from *Discipline* to Earth: it had been decided that they would settle the Smoke Ring environment.

There was a message from Earth: *Retrieve your crew.*

"And that's it. Kendy got conflicting orders," Jeffer said. "It tangles his mind. He can't go for new orders because Earth is too far away, and he can't make up his own mind because he's a machine, and he can't talk about it because it drives him nuts. If that's all true, he must be close to crazy all the time. The question is, what do we do now?"

Lawri said, "We can play it through the silver suit. Play it for the whole tribe. Tell everyone."

"It'll start some fights."

"Feed the—"

He rode her down. "There's a Navy ship coming. The fights'll have to be over when it gets here. A hundred days."

"Stet. Play it at dinner."

". . . Stet."

The situation was ideal in its way. They were together, but they couldn't talk. There were only the two of them to run the lift. It took all their breath. Jill scrambled over the rungs, keeping up with him. Her tuftberry-red tunic was dark with sweat at chest and armpits. Her hair was a golden halo, as interesting and as beautiful as Sectry's scarlet.

After the cages passed each other, they let the treadmill carry them round and round. Then it was time to throw their weight on the brake. The lower cage settled. Rather and Jill dropped into soft foliage and panted.

Rather found his breath . . . and found Jill watching him solemnly.

He said briskly (he hoped), "Mark says you own me. This is a thought that never crossed my mind."

"He says that?"

"Yes. He says I own you too. What do you think?"

"I think Mark doesn't have the right to say it."

He was an arm's length away. He couldn't read her expression. He said, "It's not just Mark. My parents— all four, or all three and a half, and everyone else too, including you, Jill. You all seem to know just where I fit and what I'm supposed to do for the rest of my life."

"Well, you don't take orders worth treefodder." He was not sure that was a smile. "What's bothering you, Rather? You came home on purpose. You're on the cookpot because you volunteered to cook the earthlife. You're the Teller because you've got stories and you like telling them. It gets you off treemouth duty."

"I like all of that. But I'm told where to sleep and I'm told who to marry, and everyone looked at me funny till I changed back into tuftberry red, and the whole damn tribe sent me to talk to you."

"Okay. Talk."

"Rather doesn't take orders worth treefodder. You talk. Are you unsatisfied with me?"

"You went into the sky and left me behind."

"I did."

"Is that over now? Are you back for keeps?"

"No."

"Why not?"

Rather sighed. "I like coming home. I like seeing new things too. Some of us will have to go back to the Admiralty anyway, Jill. Ryllin wants to join Booce. Then there's a whole *sky* out there! Lawri says our gene pool is too little. Fine. We'll go find some other trees and get mates there."

"Should I do that?"

Running endlessly up the treadmill, he'd had some time to think. "Maybe. Or you could marry me, but I'll take trips, and you'd have to put up with that—"

She flared. "You'd be making babies with every woman who talks funny!"

That was manifestly unfair. Rather let it pass. "Or you could come with me."

"Stet."

"That quick? Are you sure?"

"Sure."

This was working out better than he'd hoped. "Did you work on that new rocket?"

"No. Why?"

He hadn't thought it all the way through after all. "We've got time. In a couple of years a dozen kids will be ready to find mates. That's when we'll start visiting other trees—"

"I see it. I'd have to know the rocket inside out, how to steer it, how to fix anything that goes wrong, because I'm the oldest."

"You and the rest of the crew too. Can you fly?"

"Sure. Oh, all right, I don't do much flying. Rather?"

"Here."

"You seem to have a very good idea of where I fit and what I'm supposed to do."

It *was* a smile. "Sorry."

"Maybe this is what being married is like. Anyway . . . I'll go on the next trip. That'll tell us everything we need to know. Whether I can stand it. Whether citizens can stand my company aboard a rocket. Whether I'm any good. Whether I want a mate from somewhere else. Whether you do."

"Next trip will be the Admiralty."

"Stet," said Jill. She stood up. "Let's go flying."

"There's nobody to run the lift for us."

"Off the branch," said Jill. "Fly to the midpoint. Surprise Lawri."

It would do that! Rather began to understand that Jill would go where he would, and try to beat him there too. "We'll have to fly more than thirty klomters out. Can you handle it?"

"Sure. We'll go off the branch and put wings on afterward. Otherwise someone'll stop us. Come on."

Kendy had assembled the HISTORY file with some care. It was unaltered records, but it gave the distinct impression that *Discipline*'s crew had themselves decided to settle the Smoke Ring.

The population of the Smoke Ring was between two and three thousand (Kendy included children). By his original orders, Kendy must consider that they might now be the entire human race. The temptation to meddle was very strong.

He would not shape them. They were shaping themselves, and they were doing it well. For agonizing moments he had even considered severing communications entirely.

But he had things to teach them!

The Library was off when he passed the Admiralty. It wouldn't stay that way, though. Day 2791 was the midpoint of the crossyear, three hundred and fifty-odd days away. If Kendy knew his citizens, they would celebrate, and the Library would be involved. Perhaps he could reach Wayne Mickl. Kendy had a handle of sorts on the Captain-Guardian.

Meanwhile a Navy ship was moving on Citizens Tree. He'd see what terms he could arrange.

Plenty of time. Kendy waited.

Dramatis Personae

The Crew of Discipline

SHARLS DAVIS KENDY   Once a Checker for the State, now deceased. Also, the evolving personality in the master computer of the seeder ramship *Discipline* and its service spacecraft.

SHARON LEVOY   Astrogation
SAM GOLDBLATT   Planetologist
CLAIRE DALTON   Sociology/Medicine
DENNIS QUINN   Captain
CAPABILITY JASPER GRAY   Cyberneticist
CAROL BURNES   Life Support
MICHELLE MICHAELS   Communications

Citizens Tree

Population: 14 adults

GAVVING   Hunter; Treemouth Tender.

MINYA   Gavving's elder wife.

CLAVE   Chairman.

JAYAN and JINNY   Twin sisters, Clave's wives.

DEBBY   A former jungle giant warrior, Anthon's wife.

ANTHON   A former jungle giant warrior.

JEFFER THE SCIENTIST   Co-Custodian of Citizens Tree's knowledge and of the carm. Married to Lawri the Scientist.

LAWRI THE SCIENTIST   Formerly the Scientist's Apprentice of London Tree, now co-Custodian of Citizens Tree's knowledge and of the carm.

MARK   A dwarf; custodian of the ancient armored pressure suit.

RATHER   A dwarf, Minya's firstborn. Young adult.

JILL   Daughter of Alfin and Ilsa. Young adult.

HARRY, QWEN, GOREY   Children of Gavving and Minya.

ARTH   Son of Clave and Jayan

The Refugees

RYLLIN and BOOCE   Loggers. Citizens of the Admiralty.

MISHAEL   Oldest daughter.

KARILLY   Second daughter; mute.

WEND   Third daughter, deceased.

CARLOT   Youngest daughter.

Admiralty

HILAR BELMY   Logger.

JONVEEV BELMY   Runs the business end.

RAFF BELMY   Their eldest son.

RADYO MATTSON   Officer.

DAVE KON   Owns and runs the Vivarium.

MAND CURTS   Broker for goods from the Dark.

RAYM WILBY   A Dark diver far gone on fringe.

ZAKRY BOWLES   Runs the Vivarium.

ADJENESS SWART   Works in the Vivarium.

CAPTAIN-GUARDIAN WAYNE MICKL   Officer, Navy.

JOHN LOCKHEED   Teaches flying and other gymnastics to Admiralty citizens' children.

NURSE LOCKHEED   Maintenance, works in the Market.

SECTRY MURPHY   Bosun, Navy.

GRAG MAGLICCO   Spacer First, Navy.

HALF HAND   Runs the restaurant, Half Hand's.

DOHEEN   Spacer First, Navy.

JONTHAN   Spacer First, Navy.

Glossary

BLUE GHOST and GHOST CHILD—Auroralike glow patches above Voy's magnetic poles. Rarely visible.

BRANCH—One at each end of an integral tree, curving to leeward.

BRANCHLETS—Grow from the spine branches and sprout into foliage.

CARM—Cargo and Repair Module. *Discipline* originally carried ten of these.

CHECKER—Officer entrusted with seeing to it that one or a group of citizens remains loyal to the State. Checker's responsibility includes the actions, attitudes, and well-being of his charges.

THE CLUMPS—The L4 and L5 points for Gold. As points of gravitational stability, they tend to collect matter.

COPSIK—Slave. (Derives from *corpsicle*. In the State, corpsicles had no civil rights.)

COPSIK RUNNER—Slavetaker or slavemaster.

DARK SHARK—A predator of the Clump interior.

DAY—One orbit about Levoy's Star, the neutron star. A *standard day* is an orbit of Goldblatt's World.

DUMBO—Inhabits the integral tree trunk.

FAN FUNGUS—An integral tree parasite. Parts are edible.

"FEED THE TREE"—Defecate, or move garbage, or die.

FISHER PLANT—Boll-shaped, reaches toward ponds with a long water-inflated root.

FISHER JUNGLE—A large fisher plant with sting. May attack big birds as well as ponds.

FLASHER—an insectivorous bird.

GHOST CHILD—see BLUE GHOST.

GO FOR GOLD—Rush headlong into danger, or disaster, or battle.

GOLD—See GOLDBLATT'S WORLD. Secondary meaning: something to avoid.

GOLDBLATT'S WORLD—Gas giant planet captured after Voy went supernova/neutron. Named for *Discipline*'s astronomer, Sam Goldblatt.

HAPPYFEET—Mobile tribes. (An Admiralty term.)

HAREBRAIN—Smoke Ring bird, quail-size. Harmless, edible.

HONEY—Sticky red fluid, used as a lure for treebugs.

HONEY HORNETS—Deadly insects. They secrete nerve poison.

HUTS—Dwellings. In the integral trees, huts are usually woven from living spine branches.

INTEGRAL TREE—A crucial plant.

JUNGLE—Describes almost any extensive cluster of plants.

KERCHIEF—A Dark-dwelling fungus.

LEVOY'S STAR—A neutron star, the heart of the Smoke Ring system. Named for its discoverer, Sharon Levoy, Astrogator assigned to *Discipline*.

OLD-MAN'S HAIR—A fungus parasite on integral trees.

POND—Any large globule of water.

PRIKAZYVAT—Originally, Russian for "command." Presently used to activate computer programs.

ROCKET—Refers only to the steam rockets used by the Admiralty and Seekers.

ROSES—Long-stemmed plants averaging four meters. Dark red blossom uses Voy light. Tide stabilized. Not found in the Clump.

SMOKE RING—The thickest region of the gas torus that surrounds Goldblatt's World in its orbit around Levoy's Star.

SPINE BRANCHES—Grow from the branch of an integral tree.

STET—Leave it the way you find it.

STING JUNGLE—Smoke Ring plant, generally houses honey hornets.

SUN—A G0 star, also called *T3*, orbits Levoy's Star at 2.5×10^8 kilometers, supplying the sunlight that feeds the Smoke Ring's water-oxygen-DNA ecology.

TREEFODDER—Anything that might feed the tree: excrement, or garbage, or a corpse.

TRIUNE—A Smoke Ring bird, large and often dangerous.

TUFTBERRIES—Fruiting bodies growing in the tuft of an integral tree.

VOY—See LEVOY'S STAR.

YEAR—One passing of T3 behind Voy. Half of a complete sun circuit, equals 1.384 Earth years.

Directions

OUT—Away from Levoy's Star.

IN—Toward Levoy's Star.

EAST—In the orbital direction of the gas torus.

WEST—Against the orbital direction of the gas torus. The way the sun moves.

SOUTH—To the left if your head is out and you're facing west, or if your head is in and you're facing east, and so forth. Along Levoy's Star's south axis. Direction of the Ghost Child.

NORTH—Opposite South. Along Levoy's Star's north axis. Toward the Blue Ghost.

DOWN and UP—Usually applied only where tides or thrust operate.

SPIN, ANTISPIN, DARK, and SKYWARD—Directions within the Clump. The general rule as known outside the Clump is "East takes you out. Out takes you west. West takes you in. In takes you east. Port and starboard bring you back."

About the Author

Larry Niven was born on April 30, 1938, in Los Angeles, California. In 1956, he entered the California Institute of Technology, only to flunk out a year and a half later after discovering a bookstore jammed with used science-fiction magazines. He graduated with a B.A. in mathematics (minor in psychology) from Washburn University, Kansas, in 1962, and completed one year of graduate work in mathematics at UCLA before dropping out to write. His first published story, "The Coldest Place," appeared in the December 1964 issue of *Worlds of If*.

Larry Niven's interests include backpacking with the Boy Scouts, science-fiction conventions, supporting the conquest of space, and AAAS meetings and other gatherings of people at the cutting edge of the sciences.

He won the Hugo Award for Best Short Story in 1966 for "Neutron Star," and in 1974 for "The Hole Man." The 1975 Hugo Award for Best Novelette was given to "The Borderland of Sol." His novel *Ringworld* won the 1970 Hugo Award for Best Novel, the 1970 Nebula Award for Best Novel, and the 1972 Ditmar, an Australian award for Best International Science Fiction.